THE MENTOR'S GIFT

THE MENTOR'S GIFT

A NOVEL

DAVID DELLMAN

iUniverse, Inc.
New York Lincoln Shanghai

The Mentor's Gift
A Novel

iUniverse books may be ordered through booksellers or by contacting:

iUniverse
2021 Pine Lake Road, Suite 100
Lincoln, NE 68512
www.iuniverse.com
1-800-Authors (1-800-288-4677)

ISBN-13: 978-0-595-40798-9 (pbk)
ISBN-13: 978-0-595-85162-1 (ebk)
ISBN-10: 0-595-40798-6 (pbk)
ISBN-10: 0-595-85162-2 (ebk)

Printed in the United States of America

To my mentors Denny Haney and George Goebel, thank you so much for filling my life with wonder.

ACKNOWLEDGEMENTS

A great many people have contributed thoughts, critiques, encouragement, and love to this novel. Those that immediately come to mind, in no particular order, include Chris Yavelow, Thomas Keeling, Deborah Richa, Rae Beebe, Christy Struber, Sally Kohlenberg, Chris Davis, Linda Hartman, Jim and Celeste Cull, and Jamie Brennan. I'd also like to thank my wife Janis for her love, understanding, and patience during the many nights and weekends I devoted to this novel, my parents for always encouraging me to pursue my own path, and my Lord Jesus Christ.

Chapter 1

"I do it because I have to." Amy Alexander spoke only to her reflection in the dressing room mirror. She was alone applying makeup for a corporate show. The officers of the company loved her. It was her third year as their spokesperson and entertainer. Tonight they wanted to give back. They'd used their corporate clout to attract Vegas scouts. Her manager Rick was ready to make a deal.

As she lifted a small mascara brush, her hand shook.

"The goth girl illusionist, the only one of my kind," she said. "I can give them a thrill, a scare, a wonder with a touch of class, and I can do it with a come hither look and a bit of humor, or so I'm told."

Amy began her career off Broadway. She wanted to be an actress, but an agent looking for an illusionist to meet the demand of one of his loyal customers, groomed her, trained her, blended her personality with his experience, and within months they'd produced a marketable product. She liked it, they liked her, more gigs followed, and she never had to wait tables again.

Her mouth was parched. It usually didn't get like that until just before show time. She needed a drink; enough to wet her mouth, but stood too quickly and stumbled. Her head was spinning. She hadn't eaten.

She extended a hand to the bare wall of her closet-like dressing room to steady herself as she made her way to the even smaller bathroom. The wall was cold. It was so cold it felt damp. And, the painted cinder block was coarse against her palm like cheap sandpaper. She longed for the familiar comforts of her own bathroom at home in her San Francisco apartment. If she closed her eyes, she could be there in her mind.

Before she could reach the bathroom door, her manager, Rick McAlister, entered her dressing room. He approached her with a bounce in his step and a wide grin on his face. It was fun for him. It was supposed to be fun for her but it wasn't. She was usually pleased with herself after the show but the pleasure was more relief than joy. It was easy for him; all he had to do was make the deal. She had to deliver on the promise and the hype he so eloquently planted in the minds of her paying customers. And, she had to do it with every performance. One failure could mean failure for all time.

"Amy, how ya doin'?"

The sight of him made her all the more nervous.

"I shouldn't have told you about the guests in our audience."

"No, Rick, I'm glad you did."

"But you're sick."

"I'm not sick."

"You look sick."

"I don't want you to start concealing information from me, not now, not ever."

"They're not that special," he said.

"Yesterday, they were 'the key to our future.'" Her tongue was sticking to the top of her mouth. It hurt to speak.

"I did say that, didn't I?"

"Yes, you did."

"Well, every gig matters, and every potential client matters. But they're going to love you. They always do."

"They always do because I always deliver. But, it's getting worse. I'm getting worse. I'm eating less. What little I do eat is bland, but it doesn't seem to matter. My nerves are hindering me when I need to be at my best."

She took a breath, marched past him into the bathroom, and filled a small paper cup with water from the dirty sink. It tasted dirty, but it freed her mouth.

When she returned, he was still standing there, arms folded. He had a stupid grin on his face.

"It's like trying to be a drummer with one arm in a sling," she said, "or a singer with a raspy throat. I don't know how much more of this I can take."

"You always have fun. You've been getting standing ovations. And, I've seen the look on your face at the end of the show. You love this stuff, and you know its working. All you have to do is keep it coming."

He was right. Amy remembered the adrenaline rush she invariable felt when the show was over.

"It is a good show ..."

"See," he said. "I knew you'd come around."

"... for the most part. I need a few minutes."

"After the show," he said, "you'll be wondering what all the fuss was about."

"The fuss is about the scouts."

"Don't worry about them. That's my job."

She wrapped her arms around her stomach, some people called the pre-show jitters butterflies, but they felt more like elephants on a stampede.

"And if I don't deliver?"

"You will," Rick said. "You always do. Before this night is over we'll have the Vegas convention contract."

He touched the back of her neck. His fingers were kind and gentle. As he rubbed, a tiny bit of tension leaked from her body. He began to stroke her short black hair. She felt his cheek brush the top of her head, then his arms around her body. She looked up, his lips were close, and then he kissed her, and for a moment she let him. But she turned her head down, pulling her lips from his.

"Rick, I can't ..."

"I'm trying to take your mind off of your fear."

"You're a regular philanthropist," she said.

Rick was a charming person. He was tall and he always wore expensive suits that made his lean, muscular body all the more irresistible. His hair was immaculately groomed; his eyes were the most mysterious shade of green she had ever seen. And, he had the confidence to succeed in a business that destroyed most who ventured into it.

His advances were difficult to resist. She had no exclusive agreement with Brendon. She'd had no exclusive arrangements with any man, ever. But, even if Brendon had not been a part of her life, she would have been hesitant with Rick.

On more than one occasion, a woman answered the phone when she called him. And, one night in the dressing room of a theatre in St. Paul, after she'd agreed to dine with him, she walked in on him and another woman. His nice suit lay on the floor. The other woman's clothes looked like they'd been torn from her body. The two of them were much too busy to notice her. She could have brought a marching band by and they wouldn't have noticed. So, she left.

Rick knocked on her hotel room door later that night. He wanted to know why he'd been stood up.

"I saw you with that girl in my dressing room."

"And?"

"And what?"

"And that's why you stood me up?"

"Yes."

"Amy, we're not married."

She closed the door in his face.

But, his advances never stopped, never slowed. She knew he had a date after the show with someone else, but he wanted her now.

"Rick this isn't helping. I have a show in a few minutes and I don't want to deal with your insatiable id."

"This isn't about that layman you're seeing is it? What's his name? John, George, Ringo …"

"Brendon. His name is Brendon."

"Oh yes, Brendon Gallardo the rich Napa Valley wine, vineyard, grower, maker, whatever."

Rick pushed his hands so far into his pockets that she was sure he would tear his pants. He frowned and shook his head, shuffling his feet like a boy whose dad had taken his favorite toy.

"Maybe it is," she said. "And the vineyard is in Sonoma, not Napa."

"You are kidding, aren't you?"

"No. It is in Sonoma."

Rick laughed. "You almost never see the man."

"I'm with him as much as I can be."

"The relationship has no future, Amy. It barely has a present. Face it. You've been with the guy for more than a year-"

"Two years."

"Okay. Two years, and what have you got to show for it?"

"I'm not looking for measurable results, Rick. Is the bottom line all you care about? I enjoy his company and he enjoys mine. I'm happy with that."

"Is he serious?"

"That's none of your business."

"Isn't it?"

"We're in business together. You manage me, remember?"

"And your point is?"

She growled before she walked past him to her vanity where she continued applying her makeup.

"So let's say for the sake of argument that you don't really want me."

"Is that so unimaginable?" She laughed.

"Yes. But that's beside the point. Let's suppose that I'm not your man. Okay, fine. Even if I'm not the one for you, Brendon can't be."

"And why not?"

"He's not good for you."

"What are you talking about, Rick?"

"Brendon has no idea who you are, what your business is. He couldn't possibly be an asset."

"I don't spend time with him because I think of him as an asset. Is that why you spend time with me?"

"Of course it is! I am your manager."

"You are a charmer." She snapped her makeup case closed and spun in her seat hoping he would see the glimmer of disgust in her eyes.

"Well, it's true. Why have I never met this Romeo of yours? Has he ever seen you perform? Does he even know who you are?"

Amy looked up at the photograph on her vanity. Brendon Gallardo rarely left his winery in Sonoma.

"I don't really enjoy traveling," Brendon once told her. "You've been all over the world, haven't you?"

"Yes, I have," she said.

"Can you honestly tell me that there is a place more beautiful?"

She looked around at the vines that stretched on for eternity, and the lush green hills. "No. I can't. But, I would still prefer your company on my road trips."

"Amy," he took her into his arms and whispered in her ear, "I ache for you when you're not here. But I need to be on this land the way you need to be on the stage."

She kissed him.

"You ache for me?"

On that day, Tino Valazquez, a long time friend and employee of his, agreed to photograph them. They were sitting on the porch swing. When the photo was taken, flowers were in bloom behind them on that bright, sunny, cool California day. She had had the photo framed, and she always carried it with her. Before a show it usually sat on her makeup table next to her mirror.

"You don't build romance on business, Rick," she said looking away from the photograph and back to her manager.

"Who gave you that loser rule?"

"You manage my business affairs, not my life."

"Wrong again, sweetheart. Your business is your life or, at least, it should be. If you expect to make it, you have to live and breathe the show."

"And you think I don't?"

"You do. But Bruce-"

"Brendon."

"Wine dude is making you believe that there might be an alternative for you."

"Yes, and that's bad because?"

"Because if there is or even if there can be then you won't make it, dear, and the sad part is that I know you can. I know you can go all the way. You've got star quality. It's written all over you, and I will fight to see that your star has a chance to shine."

"Dear God," she said as she covered her pounding head in her arms. "I'd rather be anyplace but here, doing anything but this."

"Yeah," Rick said, "that's what they all say before the show. But after, the rush is beyond compare. Isn't it?"

"It's not worth it."

"So you say. But you're going to go out there anyway, aren't you? And, when the shows over, you'll be driving me and your two doting assistants insane with all of your 'minor changes.' Didn't Dante tell you to leave it alone for a while? That's part of your problem; you know it is."

"The show needs improving," she said, remembering Dante, remembering the most perfect show she'd ever seen. Her father had taken her, when she was a child, Dante the Magnificent, and he was, with his goatee and tux, his lovely assistants, a full band, animals, explosions, and awe inspiring illusions. He was and remained magnificent. He was her inspiration on stage, and her friend and mentor off. Rightly or, in Rick's opinion, wrongly, Amy tended to follow Dante's advise, but Rick would use that advise if it worked to his advantage.

"It'll always need improving. But constant changes have a way of unsettling you," Rick said. "And, you need stability more than you need improvements right now."

"Where's my pill box?" She started moving costumes and cases in search of the tiny box. She carried an assortment of sinus, allergy and over-the-counter pain medication with her wherever she went. She knew exactly which pill to take for which pain, but she'd never found a pill that could make her manager disappear.

"No pain meds on an empty stomach," he said. "You know how that can upset you."

"I want to kill the headache."

"It'll pass."

"Dante once told me that if I can see myself doing anything else, then I should," she said.

"Any good mentor is going to tell his student that. But Dante was right to challenge you, and as I recall, you accepted. You thought about it and then you told both of us that there was no other life for you."

"I did?" She tried to recall why she ever made such a foolish commitment.

"Yes, you did."

"It's almost show time," she said. "I've got to get myself together."

"You are together."

"Get out."

He laughed.

"Get out," she said again.

"Okay, okay. I know when I'm not wanted."

"No, you don't."

"I'm going."

"Go. The door's right behind you."

He laughed again, but headed for the door.

"You know you love this game," he said.

She pointed at the door but she stumbled in the effort. He caught her.

"Are you sure you want me to go?"

"I'll be fine."

"If I hadn't caught you you'd be on the floor."

"If you hadn't been here there would have been no need."

"I don't want you fainting on me again," he said. "It makes the customers nervous."

"I'm sleepy."

"That's a good one. I'll write it down."

She took a step and stumbled again.

"Poor baby," he said, "it's tough to be famous."

She was breathing as if she had climbed several flights of stairs. She blindly put a hand out, and he guided her to the chair.

She was trembling.

"You're showing some symptoms I haven't seen before."

"Will you please leave me alone?"

"I don't think so," he said.

She beat her fist on the table.

"Concentrate, Amy. The show works. You've done most of the routines hundreds of times."

Her hands were still shaking. She couldn't stop them and she wondered how she'd get through the night.

"Maybe you should go out there and make an ass of yourself. The crowd would love it, and you'd learn once and for all that the world will not come to an end if Amy Alexander gives a less than perfect performance."

"I need to put my head down for a minute. Go on, I want you to go schmooze. You do it so well."

"Well, at least you're breathing. It's always a plus when my featured entertainers can actually breathe."

With her eyes closed and her head down, her breathing was slower and steadier. Soon her adrenaline would begin to restore what her fear had stolen. And then, she would be ready.

"You're getting too thin," he said.

"I thought you said I could never be thin enough or rich enough."

"Well, I was wrong."

"Ha!" she said, feeling strong enough to lift her head. "I never thought I'd hear those words from your lips."

"What, that you're too thin?"

'No, idiot, that you were wrong."

"Feeling better?" He laughed.

"I'm working on it."

"Yea, well, the next time I proposition you before a show, say yes. I guarantee it'll cure your jitters, and you'll go out on stage more relaxed than you've ever thought possible."

"My hero; so self sacrificing."

"Hey, what's a manager for?"

"Getting me more business," she said. "That's what a managers for. Now get out there and get to work."

The man only heard what he wanted to hear, and only did what he wanted to do. She could scream in his face. It wouldn't matter. He'd stay until he was ready to leave.

"How do you feel about the new routines?"

"They're as good as they are going to get in rehearsal. Like any other routine, they need a live audience to sharpen them up, and that's what they'll get tonight. Why, are you considering one of them for the Vegas show, if we get the show?"

"Vegas is important for us, Amy. It's possibly the most important opportunity we've ever had together. But, we've got some time to think about it and-"

"I like to stick with the tried and true when it really counts."

"I was about to say that. But in this case, most of your audience will be looking for something original, or at least something they haven't seen before, and believe me they've seen a lot. The promoters will be more easily impressed if the crowd around them reacts well. The tried and true is perfect for the corporate crowd. But this-"

"I don't want to think about it now Rick. I've got an audience tonight that's expecting my best. Those are the people I want to concentrate on."

"You're right, Amy. I'll leave you to it."

And then he left.

She checked her reflection once more and retouched her dark and heavy makeup. Rick had asked her to tone down the goth, to make herself a bit more corporate. She did give up some of her piercings but she still preferred dark eyes, black lips, and black nails.

She changed her costume as she often did after a spell. New clothes made her feel fresh and clean. She'd been punished by whatever demon felt the need to constantly torment her for her success, and now she was ready.

When she finally went backstage, she had twenty minutes before curtain. She checked every prop, every placement, and every marker on the stage. Then, she checked again to be sure.

By the time she was done, it was show time. Her assistants, Jason Johns and Freddie Stone, had arrived during her second inspection.

Amy was working for Data Trek, a corporate client in Malibu, when she met her two young sandy blond assistants.

"The goth and the beach boys," Rick said. "Oh yea, that'll sell." But he'd done no better in his own efforts to recruit talent into the show. After the Malibu gig, Amy decided she needed some quite time and headed for the beach. She watched two young surfers hitting ride after ride. She applauded their cuts and moves, and screamed her cheers loud enough to turn heads three blocks away. When the guys came out of the water, they stopped to meet the "gnarly goth babe," as they liked to call her.

"So what's a goth chick doing on a beach?" Jason half teased.

"It's overcast," Amy said. "I don't need to worry about damaging my pasty complexion."

Amy wasn't looking for talent but she had a need and so did they. The boys wanted to be surfers, pro-surfers, but they weren't winning enough competitions and sponsors were scarce. Amy discovered months later that Freddie's dad was a VP at Data Trek. He wanted his son to work for him but, Freddie "wanted to be free."

They needed extra income and time to surf, and Amy needed help with her ever growing show, she thought it was a good match. Aside from their skills as showmen, in evidence on the waves, they also had great abs, and Amy thought they might not be hard on her eyes in the long hours of rehearsal or during slow times on the road.

Jason and Freddie knew not to bother her while she was checking her props, and more importantly, they knew not to touch anything once it had passed her inspection. So, they watched her perform the ritual they had witnessed many times.

The house lights dimmed. A hush fell over the crowd.

She squeezed her small body into a cleverly disguised space that had been built to her precise weight and dimensions.

The music began; the house lights were completely turned off; the stage lights came up. Her name announced sounded muffled from inside her prop. The audience applause nearly obscured the swirl of the curtain as it opened.

She nearly missed her cue. In that moment, her heart skipped a beat. Would she remember her lines and what of the complex sequence of movements in her new routine? Had she really rehearsed enough?

CHAPTER 2

Amy's heart beat so fast, she thought it might pound itself out of her chest.

"What an image, the curtain will open, and there I'll be, dead with a big cavity in my chest where my heart used to be. That will thrill them."

For a moment, she worried that the audience might see the rapid rhythm of her heart through her costume.

When the audience senses fear in you, the show is ruined, she told herself. But, the thought only made the beating louder, faster.

Like her mouth, her eyes began to dry. She'd forgotten to blink.

She was about to make her appearance. Her mind was focused with the clarity that fear often begets.

Inside of the illusion, Amy's body froze, and her audience saw only a steel frame on a chrome platform. The rectangular frame was barely two feet by three feet. Jason placed clear glass panels on the frame as he danced to the music.

"I love my audience. I love my audience," she said. Dante told her Thurston used to say that before he took his curtain.

The thick glass entombed her. She'd performed this illusion many times, and she enjoyed it in rehearsal, but in front of an audience it made her claustrophobic.

Jason installed the glass sides and then positioned the top.

As Jason stepped away from the glass box, a mist began to envelop the contents. The mist began to glow. She forced herself to move rapidly. She was acting on instinct. She forgot about her heart, about her mouth and eyes; she forgot she was afraid. Her body knew what to do.

The lid opened on its own, only slightly at first, allowing the fog to dissipate. Amy could be seen within. She wore a black, French cut, long sleeve teddy with matching heels and a tiny black bow tie. The back of the teddy was fitted with tails so that it resembled a modified tuxedo. On her head was a top hat, all black with a black rose on one side.

She rested on the left side of her body with her arched right leg nearly touching the glass. It was an uncomfortable position but it had a certain audience appeal. She turned on her magical smile and threw her head back a tiny bit as if to say 'hello' to the audience.

Their applause reassured her, renewed and inspired her. Now, her smile was as genuine as her joy. The fear in her gut became energy and excitement, sincere pleasure that she knew how to give back to her audience.

The lid continued to open. She stepped up and over the walls of the case. Jason came to assist her to the floor. All her movements were by rote. She didn't worry about the delicate placement of the pointed high heel of her shoe. It had already been rehearsed to perfection. Every move was as graceful as a finely choreographed dance.

As she stepped to the floor Jason handed her a black cane. It was familiar in her hand, and the lights were warm and soothing. It was home.

She flipped the hat down her right arm, then she gave it a toss back to her head. It landed at the perfect angle. The cane she twirled like a baton between the fingers of her left hand. Then the cane began to dance in the air around her body. She danced with it and the audience cheered as her body swayed.

When her dance reached its climax, she bowed to the loving appreciation of applause. The sweet sound made her feel loved, but it was a love that came with a price. It demanded and she gave. She wanted to empty her soul to the people beyond the footlights, people she could not see but only sense and hear.

Jason came out to remove the cane. Then she addressed her audience and her heart stopped its ferocious pounding. She loved to talk to them, to hear their laughter at her well-rehearsed and well-placed remarks, jokes and anecdotes. It was the magic itself that made her nervous, not the people. She loved people.

Some of her apparent ad-libs were genuine improvisations. And, when those tiny details got real laughs, Ricky would make notes so that, for the next show, those ad-libs could become a permanent part of her performance.

As the show progressed, she never lost her stride, never missed a line, or an opportunity to get a laugh. Neither did her two young assistants. They were on. The tempo of her performance was flawless.

Occasionally, she would look at the cue cards on either side of the stage behind the curtain. But, it was always a natural glance, covered by a larger movement and the audience never noticed.

She was ever mindful of her responsibility, at all times, to direct the attention of her audience, and the value of that responsibility to the final outcome of her performance.

For some routines she would change her costume. Her audiences always responded well to rapid costume changes. But, rapid costume changes were physically demanding and one could not be shy or modest to accomplish them.

She had grown accustomed to costume changes in the wings when she performed in Off-Broadway theatre. In those days, between the other actors in the play and those few involved backstage, she never knew who was touching her body. Nor did she care. What mattered was the show, the suspension of disbelief for the audience. And, a speedy costume change was essential to that theatrical illusion. So, she paid the price and grew accustomed to it.

Most of the male costume designers she'd worked with were either gay or close friends of hers. In any case, they were theatre people and they were as dedicated to the outcome of the performance as she was.

Freddie or Jason helped her when she needed it. They were like brothers to her, and, while they were both young and mischievous, neither had anything but the most professional attitude during the show. She was as perfectly comfortable with Jason, Freddie, and even Rick, as she would be with any other cast member of any other show. They were family. No one else was allowed backstage.

She wanted to protect her dignity as well as her secrets. But, occasionally, Ricky would succumb to some business man's wish and let him back stage where, not only could he gaze at trade secrets he had no business gazing at, but he could also get an eye full of Amy during her rapid wing costume changes. Such was the case that evening.

She wore nothing beneath her scant costumes so it bothered and distracted her when, during one such costume change, she glanced up and into the glaring eyes of the latest horny businessman Rick was trying to sell.

He was grinning, sheepishly smiling at her. She glared at him, but he didn't seem the least bit embarrassed. He didn't look away. Her looks-could-kill glare had been wasted, as his eyes never met hers. They were occupied elsewhere. But, Rick saw and shrugged his shoulders at her as if to argue, 'it's all part of the business, dear.'

"He's a potential client," Rick had assured her earlier.

"But, I don't want him backstage. It's embarrassing for me and it's not good for the show."

"Believe me, Amy, you've got nothing to be embarrassed about." He always said that.

Despite the nuisance this potential customer was making of himself, she was relaxed and her pace was on target, at least to the casual observer. Inside, however, her energy was rapidly draining. It was as if she was on a long journey, miles from a gas station, and her gas gage was slipping dangerously close to empty.

There were some children in the audience, which was unusual but not unheard of at a corporate show. Some of the children volunteered whenever she called for help from the audience. She loved to get a kid up on stage. She enjoyed their sincere enthusiasm and appreciation. Her moments with the children were the happiest of the show for her. And, her audience enjoyed the children as well.

She had been warned that kids and animals would always upstage her. But, she never objected to being upstaged by anyone or anything. The outcome of the show was of supreme importance. The end result was all that mattered. The bottom line was the sense of fun, joy, and pleasure that her audience walked away with. As long as that was achieved, she didn't care who got the credit for it. In fact, making her audience volunteers look like the star and the hero or heroine was a skill that set her apart from many of her peers.

She had strict personal rules about the use of volunteers on stage. She always treated them with respect, as if they were personally paying her fee. She never made fun of them or made jokes at their expense. The routine she involved them in had to make them look good. After all, the audience would be identifying with the volunteer. And, if the volunteer felt good and looked good, it made everybody happy and comfortable.

If a volunteer ever objected to doing anything, she did not force. She would go instead with what they wanted. And, she always presented anyone who helped with a gift.

She treated her audiences well, and they returned her love and respect tenfold.

The show presented that night was scheduled to run a full two hours with a brief intermission. It seemed she'd only begun, but the first half was already drawing to a close.

The first half closed with the substitution trunk. It was often used as a finale, particularly when she was doing shorter shows with fewer props.

Many performers use the trunk. They continue to do so because it never fails to excite the audience when performed with flawless precision and timing. No matter how often she performed the trunk trick or how many audience members have seen it before, it pulls them to their feet every time.

A volunteer was brought to the stage—a man. Jason asked him to examine the chains, the locks, the trunk, and Amy. People always laugh at the man's inevitable blush when he is asked to examine Amy. This particular gentleman didn't blush. He went at Amy like a dog after a slab of beef.

The audience thought that was funny but Amy smelled alcohol on his breath. She gently slipped from his arms, leaving him facing the audience in a near stumble that Jason averted by pulling him back to the trunk. His drunken antics would undoubtedly be the gossip of the office for the next week.

Then, the volunteer placed chains around her arms and body, chains he secured with padlocks. The iron dug into her wrists. It would leave bruises.

She held her arms above her head and snapped the chains. Then, she stepped into the trunk and then into a canvas bag. Jason and Freddie pulled the bag up and over her head and the volunteer tied the opening shut with rope. Breathing was difficult inside the bag.

Jason and the volunteer secured the lid with padlocks. She had grown accustomed to the total darkness of the trunk's interior. But her trunk was smaller than most and when she moved she hit her head on the lid. Then, she hit her knee on the front side and her elbow on the back. The trunk was made of solid pine. Every point of contact stung and throbbed like it had been hit with a baseball bat.

It was difficult to hear from inside the locked trunk, so she had to listen carefully, even as she worked hard to make her escape. Her movements had to be timed to Jason's actions and his speech.

She heard him thank the volunteer. Her body moved more rapidly now, and she began to pant like a long distance runner. She closed her mouth to force her breath through her nose. She often got cramps when she allowed her mouth to fill her lungs with too much oxygen. Then she heard the stomping of Jason's feet on the top of the trunk.

It was time.

"One," he shouted. His voice was muffled like he'd shoved his face into a pillow.

"Two ..."

Freddie would be running from stage left to stage right. In his hands he'd carry a flag bearing the corporate logo of the company for which they were performing. The flag would obscure the trunk from the audience for but the briefest of moments, and Freddie would not slow his rapid run to allow for even the slightest margin of error. Their timing had to be perfect or the illusion would be ruined.

Her body sprang to position.

"Three," she shouted from atop the trunk.

Her rapid appearance and the costume change she'd bruised herself to make inside the trunk thrilled her audience. She had entered the trunk in black and emerged in white, a radiant white that all but glowed. It gave her an angelic appearance. Even her make up had changed. It was softer, designed to create an almost soft focus appearance under the bright overhead lights.

Their screams and cheers were exhilarating. She threw her arms up in triumph, like the statue of Rocky in her hometown. She jumped from the trunk, and unlocked the locks and loosened the chains. The crowd was on its feet.

Jason emerged from the sealed canvas bag in a different costume.

The break gave her audience a chance to stretch, and it gave her crew a chance to strike the sets that had been used in the first act, and prepare the props for the second. They worked frantically but as with any performing routine, the transition had been rehearsed to perfection. As the audience returned to their seats, the second act was ready to go.

By the second half of the show, Amy had made her personal adjustments to her audience and was ready to give them what they wanted. The second half always seemed to flow faster than the first. Perhaps it was that she was more relaxed, perhaps it was that she knew she was almost finished, or perhaps it was that the routines were more exciting.

At the climax of her show, a large target stood between but approximately three feet to the rear of two large columns of wood. Each column had a black ring of steel at the top and bottom.

At center stage, she loaded a crossbow with a small arrow to which she'd attached a long yellow ribbon.

She took aim and fired. The arrow shot across the stage pulling the ribbon taunt until it hit the target and quivered. Then the ribbon fell limp and still.

"Ladies and gentlemen," she said as Jason removed the arrow, "in the spirit of the great masters of my craft I would like to issue a challenge. In a few moments, strong and able volunteers will tie my limbs to these columns. My task; to escape before the rope burns through and sends the arrow into my body."

She placed the bow in a stand, positioned it at her target, attached a rope to the trigger and ran the rope over a candle that had not yet been lit.

She left the stage to select two men from the audience. She wore a long white gown that clung. It had no lace and no zipper. Her feet were bare and the tile of the floor was colder under her feet than the hard wood stage had been.

The men followed her onto the stage and tied her wrists to the upper ring of each column. Her arms were tied so high that she had to stretch on her toes to avoid hanging from them.

She insisted that they should be tied as tightly as possible and with as many knots as desired and the men complied. She clenched her fists. The thick ropes dug into the skin of her wrists.

When her wrists were bound the men proceeded to her bare ankles. Her volunteers treated her with gentlemanly caution. She encouraged them to hurt her, to bind her so that if they themselves were bound they could not hope to escape.

Again, they complied and secured her ankles to the lower rings of the columns.

When they had finished tying her to the columns, her body formed a perfect X in front of the large target. She instructed them to check the bow, to make sure it was pointed directly at her mid section. They did. Then, they lit the candle beneath the rope.

She thanked the men for their assistance as they returned to their seat.

The rope began to unravel as the flame burned beneath it. It would require time to burn through. It was a thick rope, but already a piece of it was gone. It was burning faster than anticipated.

She struggled.

Her right wrist began to bleed. Her hand became numb. Her nails worked vigorously at the knot. It was too tight.

She bent her elbows and pulled her feet off the floor in an effort to break free but the ropes were too tight. They squeezed into her ankles as if they were alive, willfully resisting.

She looked at the burning rope. It was burning too fast.

Jason took a step toward her from behind the crossbow, but she shook her head and he stopped.

The rope lurched but did not break.

An audience member screamed.

She tightened her stomach, pulled up with her knees and down with her arms but the ropes didn't flex. Her feet began to tingle. In a moment they'd be numb.

"Jason, I can't get out!"

He ran to her side with a knife to cut her free.

"Hurry, damn it something's wrong!"

He began to cut her right wrist free. His eyes were wide with fear.

"No, not me, get the arrow! The arrow."

He ran to the bow but it was too late. The hush of the audience amplified the swish of the arrow as it soared through the air.

Amy screamed, a blood curdling 'save me' scream that most people never hear.

She threw her head back so she wouldn't have to watch the flight of the deadly arrow.

Her body stiffened and braced for impact.

Her fingers stretched to heaven as if God himself would save her.

The arrow struck above her navel, stopped only by the target behind her. Again it quivered, this time sending splashes of blood about the stage like a painter tossing red paint carelessly upon a canvas from a too full brush. A trail of dark blood ran down the bull's eye of the target and into the white ring from the head of her arrow.

She gasped for breath, breath that she could no longer hold. Then she slumped in her bonds; her head bowed low, her screaming silenced.

Her body trembled as the last bit of life drained from it. And then she was still.

Blood ran from the hole in her stomach, a hole from which the yellow ribbon still protruded. It dangled loosely in front of her body, but from her back it was stretched taunt to the arrow that led it on its grizzly path. Her blood was dark, almost purple; the kind that comes from deep inside. It completely covered and dripped from the part of the ribbon that protruded from her backside and it ran down the end of the ribbon that dangled loosely from the front like the slow creep of the afternoon shadow.

"Oh my God," someone said, "is she dead?"

"No!" Jason screamed. He ran to her. Tears filled his eyes and slowed his progress as he cut her feet free and then her hands.

She fell limp in his arms. Her blood covered his face and hands and its warm dampness on his white shirt made it cling to his chest.

The lower half of her once white dress was now soaked in blood and a small stream began to flow from her nose and mouth.

As he dragged her body toward center stage the ribbon remained attached to the arrow and the audience gasped as it was pulled free, blood dripping from it to the floor in an almost steady stream.

"Oh dear God, I can't watch this," another person said.

"This is disgusting."

"It'll terrorize the children."

People were murmuring, some were crying. One young man came up on stage to assist.

"Please," Jason said. "Get away from her. Please."

So the man backed down the stairs.

Jason struggled to revive her. He patted her hand; he put his ear to her mouth, and listened for breath that wasn't there.

"Amy, oh God, Amy."

He pulled a large silk, emerald green, cloth with a gold dragon on it from a nearby table and he covered her entire body with it.

He picked her up. Her legs, covered by the dark green shroud hung limp over one arm and her head over the other. From beneath, her hand dangled visibly and blood dripped from her index finger.

"I'm so sorry, ladies and gentleman, I'm afraid …"

As he spoke her dead body began to lift from his arms.

"Amy?"

Her body began to straighten as it rose and drifted away from him.

It rose slowly to a good ten feet or so. And as it did, it became long and rigid, forming a perfect parallel line to the stage floor.

Jason struggled to keep her body closer to the earth as if by letting it go he was releasing her spirit to the afterlife.

He made one final leap and caught the hem of the cloth. As he returned to the stage the shroud slid from her floating body. As the linen came down, her body slowly melted away until all that was left was the blood stained silk covering.

In that moment, when the shroud hit the floor, a loud whistle was heard from the midst of the audience. A spotlight quickly illuminated the area from which the noise came.

Amy was standing on a seat in the midst of the audience. She wore the same white dress she'd had on moments before but no blood stained it and no hole appeared where the arrow had penetrated.

She leaped from the seat and ran down the center aisle to the stage. Some were shouting, some were applauding, most were rising to their feet either from exhilaration, appreciation, or shock.

She and Jason bowed to a standing ovation. She blew a kiss to her audience and followed it up with a wave and a smile as the curtain closed.

Ricky walked to her applauding and smiling. His expression told her he liked her work so she returned his smile. He took her in his arms and they kissed.

"Nice job, Amy," he said, "You're the best."

She smiled at him but his face became fuzzy, and then blackness surrounded her.

CHAPTER 3

Amy lay in Rick's arms limp and lifeless.

"Jason, Freddie," Rick called and they came to assist. Jason and Freddie supported her hips and legs, and Rick carried her upper torso against his body back to the dressing room. Her arms swung freely, and her head shifted to one side against Rick's chest.

"What happens if she faints during the show, man?" Freddie asked.

"She hasn't," Rick replied.

"But what if ..."

"Shut up, Freddie," Rick said. "I don't want to discuss it now. Get me a damp cloth."

"Is she alright?" The business man, the potential client asked.

"She'll be fine, sir."

"Does this happen often?"

"No," Rick replied without a glance in his direction. "No, it doesn't."

"Well, what if she does it during a show, what if she does it for my show? You're asking a hefty fee ..."

"Mr. Long, Amy has never fainted during a show, and she never will. Now, if you don't mind, I'd like to attend to my girl."

The businessman bobbed his head back and forth and frowned. Then he walked slowly away with his hands tucked into his pockets and his head bowed like a kid sent home from school for bad behavior. Rick wasn't sure the man would make a deal, but at the moment, he didn't care.

They had placed her on the floor in her dressing room with a rolled up towel under her head. After the potential customer left, Rick began to tap her hand hoping that the sensation would draw her back to consciousness.

Jason grabbed a wash rag from his bag and ran it under some water. After ringing it out he gave it to Rick who placed it across her forehead.

"Damn it," he said as much to himself as to Freddie and Jason. "She won't eat before a show. I know she'd lose it but she needs energy. We're going to lose her if this keeps up. She's operating on adrenaline and she loses her strength quickly when the adrenaline rush is over. Look at her, damn it."

"She'll be okay," Jason tried to reassure Rick slapping him across the back of his shoulder. "She always comes round."

"Yeah, sure," Rick said as he checked her pulse. "Amy. Amy, c'mon girl, come back to me. Jason."

"Yea 'mon."

"Get the smelling salts from my briefcase."

Jason handed Rick the small potent container, and he waved it beneath her nose. Amy's eyes, though shut, squinted, and she pulled her head back slightly to escape the stench.

"Guys …" Rick said as he looked around at both of them.

"I know," Freddie said. "Time to go."

Both Jason and Freddie left shutting the door behind them.

Amy opened her eyes.

"Hello, angel," Rick greeted her.

She smiled and then turned herself from him to cough and gag.

"Hi, Rick," she said, laying her head back against the towel.

He removed the damp cloth and kissed her forehead where it had been. He pulled her up into his arms and held her tightly with one arm supporting her body and one her head.

"You've got to stop doing that to me, girl."

"I've got an idea for Vegas."

"You've been unconscious. And I should be with those scouts right now rather than nursing you. Why don't you try to relax?"

"No Rick, listen to me. I want to do Pepper's Ghost, my version of Pepper's Ghost I mean. I want to see my father again."

"I think you're delirious."

"I'm serious, Rick. Before you revived me, I saw it."

"You saw what?"

"I saw the act, the whole thing. It was as if I was already performing it, props and all. And my dad was there."

"Your dad's been dead for years, Amy."

"He was there." She started to cry.

"Okay," he said. "I'm sure he was."

"I saw my daddy," she cried. She pouted like a helpless child.

"I know," he said.

"I want to do it."

"Okay," he said. "We'll do it. I need you to rest for now?"

"The show needs passion."

"It's got plenty of passion Amy."

"No it doesn't. The show needs my father. It needs the love I have for him. Don't you see? If my passion, my love, can come across the footlights we'll have something special for the big shot promoters in Vegas. Something they'll never forget."

"We need to get you there first."

"I thought it was a done deal."

"I couldn't close it. I had to be here with you."

"Go, Rick. Don't sit here another minute."

"I'm going, Amy. I'm going."

CHAPTER 4

Far from the stress of the stage and the heat of the lights, there was a place as close to a home as any Amy had ever known. It wasn't the place where she lived. In fact, she didn't spend much time there, relative to the rest of her days. The land and the vineyard belonged to Brendon, but he shared the land and the labor of it with friends that were as close to him as family, and employees as responsible as partners.

When her tour was over and her props packed neatly in their cases, Amy drove from her apartment in San Francisco north to Brendon's vineyard.

The vineyard had been in his family for generations. It provided a good living for him as it had for his father before him. Brendon wanted for nothing, not so much because he had everything, but because he wanted what he had. And, in the moments she shared with him, Amy understood what he often referred to as 'being still.' Her compulsive urge to do something, anything, was quiet, and she enjoyed simply being alive. But, those moments were as fleeting as the time she spent on the farm.

His land gave Brandon so much, but the most important gift it gave him, he often said, was peace. He once told her that he could feel the earth breathe beneath him, and that he could sense when and where the vineyard needed his tender care. He never seemed rushed or anxious about anything; he was steady and progressive, like the earth itself.

Tino Valazquez managed the vineyard. He had managed the vineyard when Brendon's father owned the land. He wished for nothing more than to spend the rest of his days tending to the vines, and in his dreams, his daughter Carmen would someday succeed him as manager. Tino and Carmen lived on the grounds in a home that Tino had built for his wife before her death. He'd raised Carmen alone.

Brendon's home was a Victorian. It sat atop a small hill surrounded on three sides by lush and green trees, trees that stood taller than the house itself. Brendon had painted it in colonial blue with white trim. It had a wraparound porch with a porch swing large enough for two.

A garden, immaculately cared for, stretched from both sides of the front steps that led to the porch. Something was always in bloom or Brandon would plant something new simply to watch it bloom. He loved to put his fingers into the soil of his land. He loved the smell of the earth and its cool soothing texture.

The home itself was as meticulously cared for as the garden and the vineyard. Brendon enjoyed the carpentry and the painting. He said it afforded him a welcome break in his routine.

As Amy brought her car to a stop at the end of the drive, the dust from the dirt road blew past her. The house appeared to be deserted. If Brendon had been within earshot of her arrival he would have come to her. He always did. She assumed that he was checking his crop or sipping some new vintage.

The sun had burned off the morning fog, but the cool of the day lingered. As she stepped from her car, she heard a sound like that of a booster rocket, and then she saw the slow creeping shadow moving steadily toward her on the ground. Tourists in hot air balloons were a common spectacle over Brendon's vineyard. The sight of one always thrilled her. She shielded her eyes from the sun with her hand, as she looked skyward. It was low flying, drifting on the wind, and someone waved from within the basket. She waved back, allowing the broadest sweep of her arm. Another burst of flame and the balloon rose like a bubble from a child's toy.

The drive up the coast wasn't that long, but she was tired. She watched the balloon drift out of sight, and then she settled down on the porch swing, the old chains that suspended it snapped and adjusted under her modest weight, and the wood creaked and bent to receive her. Amid the rustic snap of the swing in motion, she listened for a moment, to the music of nearby birds. Closing her eyes, she rested her weary head against the back of the swing.

She pulled a round pillow out from behind her back and hugged it to her stomach. She pushed with her feet, and the swing creaked as it rocked again with renewed vigor. With its forward momentum, she went up onto the balls of her feet, then she pushed back again. The swing generated a satisfying motion that threatened to lull her into a daze. As she swayed, her mind drifted.

She smiled at the memory of Rick shoving his hands into his pockets in mock jealousy. Rick had other performers in his fold. But, he spent an inordinate amount of time with her, and she thought she knew the reason why.

Carmen had asked her once if there were any other men in her life aside from Brendon. She'd heard Amy speak of Rick, but she'd never expressed an interest in him until that one lazy afternoon while they rocked together on Brendon's porch swing sipping lemonade.

For Amy, that was a delicate moment. Carmen loved Brendon and would be concerned for him if she thought the woman he cared for did not return his affection.

"Ricky wants to get me in the sack," she told Carmen that day. "And, as long as he wants it but doesn't get it, he'll be panting around me like a dog around the dinner table."

"Is that a good thing?"

"Rick's a powerful man in my industry, Carmen. He brought me this far, and he can take me farther still."

"How do you know he wants to sleep with you?"

"Well, I'd like to say its intuition, but Rick's not that subtle. He can't keep his hands to himself. And, when he's not touching and grabbing, he's asking."

"You mean he asked you to sleep with him?"

"Ricky's not the shy type. If he wants something, he'll ask for it. And if he doesn't get it, he'll ask again and again until he finally does."

"But he's your manager."

"I assume by that," Amy said, "you mean to imply that it is somehow inappropriate to mix sex with a business relationship."

"I don't know if inappropriate is the word. Maybe what I'm thinking is that it's not wise."

Amy laughed, "No," she said, "I suppose it's not wise at all."

"If Rick is as persistent as you say, do you think it is possible that he might eventually catch you at a weak moment?"

"You mean: do I have any intention or inclination to sleep with my manager?"

Carmen nodded.

Amy smiled at Carmen, put her arm around the young woman's shoulder, and squeezed.

"I'm sorry, Amy. I know it's none of my business."

"You're worried about Brendon, aren't you?"

"No, Amy," Carmen explained, "I'm worried about you."

Amy laughed. "That's so sweet," she said as she pulled her squeeze into a full hug.

"Aren't there other people that worry about you?" Carmen asked.

Amy stopped smiling and looked away. "I'd rather stick my hand in a brick oven than sleep with Rick, Carmen."

"Why?"

"He doesn't want me," she explained. "He might think he does, but I know that what really interests Rick is the income my audience appeal can generate. Rick thinks that if he can get a handle on my heart, he'll have a handle on my career. He thinks I'm his property. He wants to protect his investment, and, he thinks that a relationship would be a good way to do that. If its one thing I know about Rick, it's that he's a businessman first, foremost, and always."

Carmen nodded as if she understood, but she had a glaze of confusion in her eyes that Amy was not inclined to relieve. And so, the conversation went on to greener pastures that day.

Now, Amy wondered where Carmen might be. Brendon was often busy with his land or with any one of numerous stages along the process of wine making. But Carmen was almost always available and as eager to see Amy as Brendon himself. They'd shared many fine conversations on the porch swing where she rested.

She thought of the tension before every performance. And, even in memory, it made her uneasy. Then, the faces of her audience flashed before her, the nameless faces that smiled and laughed for her, and stood to applaud her final bow.

"That's why I do it," she said aloud.

"Do what?"

CHAPTER 5

Amy looked up, and Brendon was standing before her. He was a tall sandy blond. His manner was as casual as his dress and his voice as quiet, gentle and deliberate as his movements, but he worked as one consumed with passion. Wine was his passion.

"How long have you been there?" she asked surprised to see him.

"Only a moment, you looked upset."

"Oh no," she said as she slid from the porch swing to greet him. "I'm not upset."

He kissed her and the touch of his lips against hers sent a shiver down her spine. He leaned away but she pulled him back for more.

"Amy," he said between kisses.

She didn't stop.

"Sweetheart," he said.

Amy backed her head away from his and smiled coyly. His breath was heavy and rapid. He moaned and looked up as if seeking strength from above. She kissed his cheek and walked back to the porch swing.

"Wow." He puckered and let out a long breath.

"I think about you constantly when I'm on the road," she told him. "I dream of you."

He walked over and sat down next to her on the swing. He took her hand in his, "I love you, Amy."

"I love you too." She smiled back at him

"Do you?'

"Yes." She frowned. "I do."

"What were you thinking about when I interrupted you a moment ago?'

"You?"

"One would think that an actress could do better than that," he said. "It should be said more emphatically, 'You!' Not like a question, 'You?' It's a dead give away."

"So now he gives acting lessons."

"What were you thinking about so intently that you couldn't hear my approach?"

"Magic."

"Now that was believable," he said. "Another grand illusion your obsessive mind can't stop thinking about?"

"No," Amy said, "I was thinking about the performance of magic. About performance art, about how it makes me feel."

She slid onto his lap, and nestled her head under his chin. Her ear was against his chest; the slow and steady beating of his heart filled her ears, her heart and soul. It was one of her favorite positions as it told her so much about him that he never knew she knew. His arm supported her back and she stretched like a kitten preparing for a nap.

"How does it make you feel?" He kissed her head.

"Afraid."

"Why afraid?"

"That one day they won't applaud. That I'll be through before I've even begun."

"Do you enjoy performing?"

"Yes. Well, maybe."

"Well." He laughed. "Which is it?"

His heart was steady; hers was racing.

"It's not so much the performing; it's the struggle of getting to the stage."

"You're still struggling with your nerves."

"Yes," she said. "Everyone told me I'd get used to it. I knew I'd always be nervous, but I expected it to get better, not worse."

"And it's gotten worse?"

"Oh yes, much worse. Some nights I don't know how I can get out there but I do. And then, the audience responds, and we have fun. I start to enjoy performing and then the show ends, we pack, and get on the road for the next show, and the vicious cycle begins again."

"Maybe your body is trying to tell you something."

"What do you mean?"

"Well, when I'm out in my vineyard, I'm not nervous. I look forward to every stage; every step in the process excites me, from the grapes on the vine to the label on the bottle. I love my work and I can't wait until the next harvest begins, and I would never refer to it as a vicious cycle."

"That's beautiful." Amy lifted her head from his chest and smiled at him.

"Well, I believe that life should be joyful, and that if what is in your life is not bringing you joy, then maybe it shouldn't be there in the first place."

Amy stood from his lap and walked to the railing.

"I'm sorry, Amy," Brendon said as he followed her. He put his hands on her shoulders, and whispered to the back of her head. "I know how important magic is to you. And I'm not suggesting that you give it up. All I'm saying is consider the possibility that maybe it is taking you down a path that you do not want to go. And, maybe your body is trying to tell you what your mind is refusing to acknowledge. Life is bliss or, at least it can be if you are willing to let go of what you like, in faith, believing that you'll discover what you love."

"Why can't I hold onto what I like with one hand while I search for what I love with the other?"

"Because," he said, "if you were a scale you'd tip over."

"I'm not a scale." She turned in his arms giggling. "I'm a woman."

She ran her fingers into his hair and kissed him. She kissed him passionately and longingly. She wanted him to take hold of her. And he did embrace her. She pushed herself into him as close as the boundaries of their bodies would allow.

She wrapped a leg around the back of his, and ran a hand to the inside of his shirt. His chest was hard, firm and hot. He tried to step back again but she would not release him. She looked into his eyes for a moment, then closed hers and kissed him again.

"Amy," he said.

"You don't want me." She grabbed his hair with both hands, shook his head and growled, "You're driving me crazy!"

"Amy."

She released him.

"You know I want you." He took a step back. "We've had this discussion before."

"Then what's wrong, Brendon? I'm here; we're alone. Is there a problem? Are you embarrassed?"

"No I'm not embarrassed," he laughed. "I could never be embarrassed at your side."

"Then what is it? Why don't you want to make love to me? We've been dating for two years. I love you. I love the person you are, and I think you feel the same for me. But every time I try to get close to you, you push me away."

"I'm not pushing you away." He took another step back and leaned against the front door of the house.

"It feels like it to me."

"Amy, I've told you before—"

"I know what you said before Brendon, but I didn't think you were serious."

"Well, what did you think?"

"I don't know what I thought. I guess I figured it was the old 'I care more for you than I do for sex' routine. You know the one, if the guy acts like he doesn't want it, it makes the girl crazy. All the guys know that. And, some of them do it very well."

"I'm not playing games with you, Amy. I love you. Why should I ever want to be so dishonest with the person I love? And it's not that I don't want you. I do. Can't you see that?"

"Then what are you waiting for?"

"Haven't you ever met anyone that wanted to wait?"

"Well," she searched her memory, but had to say, "no."

"I want you," he said, "but not this way, not this moment. I want more."

"What more is there?"

"Love."

"I wouldn't be here if I didn't love you."

"Love and commitment are synonymous in my mind, Amy," he said. "Commitment makes the difference."

"You mean I can't love you unless I'm yours and no one else's?"

"No."

"Well, what do you mean?"

"Please, come over here and sit down." He gestured for her to sit on the swing. She did.

"This isn't the way I planned it," he said as he walked to the front door.

"Planned what?"

"Will you wait there a moment?"

"Sure, Brendon," she said as he disappeared into the house.

Brendon's rapid footsteps faded as he advanced deeper inside of the house. He was looking for something and she wondered what it might be, what could he possibly bring her that would explain his bizarre behavior? She considered it for a moment then her attention drifted to the birds once again. In less time than it took her to close her eyes he had returned and Amy sat up to face him.

He came to her and sat on one knee in front of her. He took both of her hands in his and kissed them.

"Amy, I believe there is only one person that I am meant to love in every sense of the word. Years ago, I made the decision that I would give her all that I have to give. I decided I would share that part of myself with no one else until the time of our marriage, of our promise to really love each other."

She smiled, and hoped he didn't see her tremble. She wanted to pull her hand from his but she worried that the gesture might hurt him. So, she left it where it was, in contact, at risk of exposing her fear.

"Are you trying to tell me that you're a virgin?"

CHAPTER 6

"Yes," Brendon confessed. "I am. I've been waiting for you, Amy."

"Brendon," she said as she pulled her hand from his. "I can't return that kind of a gift."

He let go easily.

"I don't expect you to."

"You mean you weren't putting me on? You really have waited?"

"Yes," he said. "That's what I've been trying to tell you."

"I think that's very romantic, I really do. And, it's so sweet; I can't believe there are any men like you left, and at your age. And, well, look at you, Brendon. I mean you must have had plenty of opportunities."

"I haven't been looking for opportunities. I've been looking for you."

He stretched one bare hand toward her until she felt his finger against her ear. When he pulled it back, there was a ring with a large solitary diamond on the top part of his first finger.

"Marry me, Amy."

She tucked her knees up to her chin as if by forcing herself into a ball she could escape the question. She looked at the ring, and then at him, and then at the ring again. It sparkled in the sunlight; begging to be worn. But her thoughts quickly ran to Rick, to Jason and Freddie; her life, her show, her career. She thought of her father. Would he be proud? Would he like Brendon?

"Amy?"

"Are you asking me to marry you?"

"I think that's what I said."

"No one's ever asked me that before."

"Well, their loss is my gain. If you say yes, that is."

She stood and walked past him to the steps. She was supposed to stay the weekend, but she suddenly felt claustrophobic. She had a sudden urge to run, to free herself as she had freed her hand from his. She took a step down the stairs, but couldn't go further. She looked at her car. It was closer to her than he was. Maybe she could leave. Maybe he'd understand she needed more time. She'd come to him for fun, not for more complications. She had enough to worry about without a wedding. Besides, committing to one man was impossible. She wasn't ready for a cage, however attractive the cage might be.

She stepped back onto the porch and hugged the post. It was dry and comforting like the feeling her favorite pillow used to give her when, as a child she hugged it to her in the night. She looked over at Brendon. He had seated himself on the swing and was patiently, lovingly awaiting her answer.

"Brendon, you don't want me. Really, you haven't thought this through."

"But I do, Amy, and I have. In fact, this is all I've been thinking about for quite some time. Surely you knew I was in love with you."

"No. I mean, yes, I knew you were fond of me, and you've often told me that you loved me. But so many men have used the 'love' word on me. What they really mean is that they want sex. I thought you had a unique approach to seduction."

He got up from the swing and took a step toward her. She let go of the post and took a step back, so he stopped.

"You don't really want to marry me, Brendon. You hardly know me."

"We've been together for two years. My parents married after one. You are as much a part of this land now as I am. You are a part of me, and without you, I'll never be complete."

"Listen to me," she said. "I've been to places you've never been. I've done things you've never done. And I've done them with people you wouldn't like. If you knew, you'd hate me. Someday, when I'm at your side, some of those people, some of those memories might catch up with me.

"You're a nice guy, and I've enjoyed these past two years, but I thought the relationship would run its course, like all the others in my life, and then we'd move on. That's what I wanted; that's what I expected. I never wanted to marry you. I never thought your feelings would get this complex, and I certainly don't want to hurt you. But I can't let you do this. It's a mistake. I know you can't see that right now. All you can see is something sweet, something you desperately want. But what you think you see and what really is are two different things, and at the risk of destroying what was good in what we shared, I'm going to try to make it plain for you."

He sat back into the swing with the look of a man who'd gambled his last cent and lost. He clenched the ring in his fist and closed his eyes. She went back to the post; she needed to hug something.

"My life is on the road, not on a farm, however lovely this farm might be. I come here as often as I can, but what you see is what you will get for as long as I can keep my career going. I don't want a man telling me where I belong or how to spend my time. I've made those decisions, and I'm living them."

He nodded and opened his eyes to her. "I've never treated you possessively. I've never wanted for you anything other than your happiness, and I will never insist that you do anything that you do not wish to do. I respect your career choice. I'm glad that you are successful in it, and I know how hard you've worked for that success."

"Thank you," she said. "And I do care for you. If I didn't this would be easy. I'd walk away. But, I can't do that."

"I believe in you Amy."

Amy shook her head. *Could he be so naive? Maybe I'm the one with the wrong impression.*

"Then take a good look," she said. "Watch me close. Listen with your heart and not your ears because I'm going to tell you things I've never told anyone."

"I want you to, Amy. I want to hear about you. I want to learn everything I can about who you are, and how you became the person I love. And, I'm not the least bit afraid of what I might learn."

"To begin with," she said. "I'm not a woman you can have or hold; I'm a commodity. People buy and sell me every day. So, you see I can never belong to only one man because I've already given myself to so many."

"I don't understand."

"It's not my show I sell, and it's not my show the clients buy, it's me they want and it's me they buy. I'm a thing; I'm not a person any more. Maybe I was once, but that person is long dead. All that's left is an illusion. I've been manufactured, painstakingly crafted and shaped for your entertainment pleasure. Do you know how many men want me? Encouraging that desire is part of my job; it is what I've been trained to do. You're supposed to fall in love, you and every other man in my audience. You're supposed to want me, and women are supposed to want to be like me. It's the grand illusion of life, that there really is something better, something more desirable, and something to strive for. It keeps us all occupied so we don't realize we're living and dying with no real purpose.

"People are afraid of the truth. They want beauty, or the illusion of it, but when beauty fades, when age has its way, they replace people like me with younger fresher versions of our shallow selves. Time is my enemy, and I have far less of it than you. That's why I can't afford to let you or anyone else derail me. Not when I'm on the very pinnacle of my success."

"There is nothing more beautiful than growing old," he said, "if you're growing old happy, loving, and being loved. Youth sells tickets, so it's worshiped throughout your industry. But youth isn't what makes you beautiful or desirable to me. I understand what you're telling me, I really do. But you don't have to embrace this life style and make it your own if you don't want it. Beauty and youth are not the same. Beauty is who you are. You are beautiful, and you always will be regardless of your age. Youth is a commodity we'll all eventually lose. And, you're wrong about purpose, Amy. My life is full of purpose and meaning, and I want to share my life with you. I don't want to squander what's yours; I want to give you what's mine."

"Let me ask this a different way. You do find me attractive, don't you?"

"Of course I do," he said.

"I have physical attributes you find appealing?"

"Absolutely."

"But you act as if it doesn't matter. Your words make me think you'll love me when I'm no longer lovable."

"My God, Amy, do you really believe your love-ability is based solely on your physical attributes?"

"I don't want to believe it. But the evidence of my experience is overwhelming."

"Physical attraction is what brought us together, I admit that. I was attracted to your appearance the first time I saw you. Physical charm is like training wheels on a bike, or a handicap in golf, or lighter fluid on charcoal: it's a starting point, a spark. But if physical attraction is all you have going for you, no one would want to remain in your company, and love would never have a chance to grow. I admit you have a lovely spark, but you also have the substance to back it up. Your beauty got my attention, but your grace and gentle heart are holding it."

"But for how long? Will your heart remain when you truly see me for what and who I am?"

"Neither love nor lust has blinded me as you suppose. It has opened my eyes to see what, at this moment, I don't believe you can see."

"And what is that?"

"The essence of the person I love with no illusions or manufactured lust involved. At this moment, I would love you if you took the form of a grumpy old man. It's you that I love. We've grown together like the vines in the fields, separate but intertwined. To separate one from the other could be devastating to either. That's the way it is now, that's the way it will be for evermore"

"How can you be so sure?" Amy turned away from her post, away from him, and walked across the porch with her arms folded over her stomach. "How do you know it's not your hormones talking, convincing you, and me, of something we both want to believe, but that we both know is a lie?"

"Ultimately," he explained, "beauty is who you are. It's not what you look like. Beauty emerges from the choices you make."

"And what choices have I made that so endear me to you?" she asked as she turned to face him again.

"I've been with you in crowded places, and I've seen the way you treat people, people who don't owe you anything, people that can never repay the kindness you show them. You are the most considerate person I've ever met. I once saw you run to help an older woman who was unsteady in her walk. I saw you assist a dirty, smelly and badly limping man who was having difficulty reading labels in a food store. You helped him get his food, and when he discovered he didn't have enough food stamps, you gave him what he needed, even though it meant you wouldn't have enough for whatever it was that brought you to the store."

"So, I used my debit card," she said, "big deal."

"It was a big deal to him. You, my lady, are a cheerful giver, one of the rarest and most precious of all human qualities."

"Not always," she corrected.

"No," he said, "not always. But my point is you are a generous, kind and considerate person. You'd rather suffer yourself than watch someone else suffer. And, despite your beauty and success, there is no sense of superiority about you. You treat everyone you meet with the same kindness, the same generosity of spirit. You treat everyone you come in contact with like they are some kind of royalty. The question isn't why do I love you, it's how can I not love you? How can anyone not fall in love with a person that so freely offers love and respect?

"I know people have disappointed you," he continued. "I know I have disappointed you. But you weren't angry with me. You are patient, aren't you?"

"I like to think I'm understanding," she said. "And, you had to work. Things happen …"

"I stood you up," he said. "You, the most precious and beautiful person I know. And, you forgave me."

"I forgave you because you had a very good excuse."

"You understood when Jason didn't show for rehearsal, or when you lost a gig because Freddie was sick."

"Of course," she said.

"But you work sick."

"I have to."

"And when you mix with the elite," he said. "Do you remember the party?"

"You mean with that bunch of high society blue bloods you sometimes cater for business purposes?"

"That would be the one," he acknowledged. "You listened to a woman boast all evening of her fine jewelry and expensive cars and cats and everything else, and you seemed delighted in her happiness. You never once tried to show her up or put her down, though she continually made denigrating remarks about your profession."

"Not everyone likes what I do," she said. "It's my choice, and if I like it, that's all that really matters."

"I've watched you slow down to let others beat you in line."

"I'm in no hurry."

"I've never heard you brag, and if anyone has a right to, it's you."

"I'm not all that special."

"You are to me."

"That's what you see," she said, "when you look through the eyes of love."

"I can say what I want around you. I never have to worry about offending you because you're not the touchy type. But, that's not to say you're not sensitive. You always seem to know how I'm feeling, and you always ask the right question at the right time. And, if that's not enough, you're optimistic, persistent, hard working, and loyal. If you could only see for one moment what everyone around you sees when they look at you, you'd know how truly deserving you are of the very best life has to offer."

"You mean I deserve a great guy like you to take care of me?"

"You don't need me or anyone else taking care of you," he said. "And, 'great guy' or not, I think you run when you get close to someone because you don't think you deserve to be loved. I'm not entirely sure why that is, but if you'll let me, I'll love you like you've never been loved before. And, the tenderness of our love will still all the fears that intrude on your sleep."

"Did you read that in a fortune cookie?"

"You have every right to be skeptical of any man's motives," he laughed. "But I'm not asking you for a one-night stand. I'm offering you my life. So, now that I have explained my self and my feelings, why not tell me more about yours. Tell me all about this person that if I really knew I wouldn't like. Let me see her, and then judge for yourself if my love is real."

Chapter 7

"Do you really want to wake up with the same person every morning for the rest of your life?" Amy asked.

"It sounds like you don't."

"I …" she hesitated. "I don't know what I want. I really haven't had time to think about it."

"Well, maybe you should take some time to sort it through. Maybe the question I need to ask you first is; do you want to be married at all? If you decide you do, then you can consider if I might be the one for you."

"So what happens?"

"When?"

"In the future," she said, "in the years to come, will you love me always?"

"I can't see into the future and neither can you."

"Will you love me always?" she asked again.

"Right now, I'm looking at the woman, the person I most love in this world, and I can't imagine growing old without her."

"But will your love be as strong twenty-five, thirty-five, or fifty years from now?"

"Can any man answer that question with absolute certainty?"

"I'm asking you," she insisted.

"You're asking for unchanging, forever, and always love."

"Yes," she said, "I am."

"But unchanging, forever and always love can only come from an unchanging, forever, and always source."

"What does that mean?" she asked.

"It means I'm a human being," he said. "I can promise you my undying love, but I'm going to need an unchanging, forever, and always source to help me keep that promise. Human beings change, and human beings die, and human beings fail. Eternal love is not mine to give, but what I have right now, today, and who I am, right now, today, is yours for the asking. I promise you my best. I promise you love."

"And you will love me no matter what I did?" She bit at her lower lip.

"I don't know," he said. "I know how you regret some of the choices you've made. I know—"

"Did you know that I used to perform nude?"

"Magic?"

"No. Not magic."

"Did you enjoy doing that?" he asked.

"I was nervous at first. But after a time, I found it rather exciting, a turn on actually. I liked it. Are you surprised?"

"Are you trying to shock me?"

"Maybe," she said.

"Are you telling me the truth?"

"Do you have to ask?"

He smiled at her and started rocking the swing. It squeaked rhythmically as he swayed.

"It was something I did," she explained. "It's not something I'm ashamed of nor am I proud. Would you like to hear about it?"

"I'm not sure."

"Are you afraid it may change the way you feel about me?"

"No. No I'm not."

"Well, it's a part of who I am," she explained, "and if you want to marry me, then you should know who I am."

"If you'd like to tell me," he said, "then I'd like to listen."

"Good," she said, as she walked to the stairs and leaned against the comforting and familiar post.

"The first time, I was barely nineteen," she said staring down at the hardwood floor. "I'd won what I thought was an exciting role, and I knew I'd have to be naked, it was only for one scene and then only briefly. My character was 'caught in the act' so to speak. I was nervous about it, but I thought I'd cross that bridge when I came to it.

"The director knew I was inhibited and scared, and he didn't want my anxiety to come across in my performance. So, one day, during rehearsal, he dedicated the entire session to me. He asked me to stand, and so I did. Then, he asked the other cast members to gather around me in a circle, and they did. He blind folded me, and instructed the others to push me gently from one person to the next. The circle was tight, but even though they were close, I was still afraid they would drop me.

"'Relax Amy,' he said. I tried to relax. I remember making a conscious effort to trust them, and soon, I did relax. My body became less rigid, and I started to fall loosely and deeply into the arms of the actors around me. Then, when the director saw that I was comfortable, he asked them to expand the circle. With each expansion I stiffened, and fear returned, and then I learned to trust that they would always be there to catch me, that they would not let me fall. And, with each moment of victory, came another expansion of the circle until I was almost hitting the floor, but I was always caught.

"When he finally said I could remove my blindfold, I looked into the faces of those who had caught me. They were all smiling at me, and they applauded, and I felt closer to them in that moment than I had ever felt to anyone.

"Then the director asked me to strip. 'Take your clothes off Amy,' he said. 'You must learn to be comfortable with us naked before you will be comfortable with nudity on stage.' I knew he was right, but the fear was back, and everybody knew it. The tension was all over my body and my face. I started to unbutton my blouse. My hands trembled with each button, and then I dropped it to the floor and stood there in jeans and a bra. I crossed my arms across my middle, but I wasn't cold. I was embarrassed. Then I slipped out of my tennis shoes, and unzipped my jeans. I pulled them down and stepped out of them. I was wearing a little blue bikini panty with a tiny bow in the front. I ran my thumbs into them at my hips, I wanted to drop them but I couldn't. I began to tremble all over. I felt alone.

"I was about to panic. I might have cried. I might have run from the theatre and never looked back. I'm still not sure what I would have done if no one had come to my rescue. But, one of the girls in the cast came over to me. She wrapped her arms around me from behind, and she kissed the back of my neck. 'I love you Amy,' she said. And, as she held me, another cast member came to me and did the same. After each member of that cast, male and female hugged and kissed me, and told me I was loved, they striped, every one. I was the only one that had to be naked on stage. I was the only member of the cast that had to overcome my fear, and at that moment, I was the only one left with a stitch of clothing.

"I looked at the men, and they were flaccid. There wasn't a sexual thought in any of their minds. And, when I looked at their eyes, I saw concern, I saw love, and it was easy, at that moment, to remove the rest of my clothes. We did the rest of the rehearsal naked, the entire cast. And, I never felt ashamed or embarrassed about my body again."

"That's a remarkable story," he said. "I never realized that kind of rehearsing went on behind the scenes of a show."

"It depends on the show," she said. "I only mention it because I want to tell you about one performance in particular."

"Please do," he encouraged her.

"It was some time later, but this one show was special. It was called The Merry-Go-Round. Shelly Young was the star. Everyone knew her in the business, and I knew if I could be seen with her, they would know me too," she said. "This time I was proud. I wanted the world to see.

"My instincts told me that telling my mother was a bad idea. But, I felt successful, and she'd always told me I'd fail. I wanted her to know I'd made it. I was an actress. I had a real part in a real play, and it wasn't a low budget, Off-Broadway production or another independent, go nowhere film from some kid at New York University. It was a big budget deal, and I was being paid well for my services. I was proud of myself, and I wanted my mother to be proud too. But, I knew she wouldn't be proud if she knew the whole truth, so I didn't tell her the whole truth.

"I've come to think of my body as a professional asset. I didn't at first. I mean who does? I always thought I'd get parts based solely on my ability. But, that's not the way the game's played. Everyone has talent. Every contender does anyway. But, when the part calls for something specific, you've either got that something, or you don't get the part.

"Well, in this case, I had the look they wanted, and I could do the job, so I got it, and a hundred other girls didn't. It's a competitive business. You can't be shy. You know what I'm saying, Brendon? I'm not shy."

"You did what you thought you had to do to succeed. I understand that."

"You do, huh? Well, I wasn't ashamed is all I'm saying. But my mom's a little old fashioned in that department. Well, my mother came to see the play. Do you believe it? She has never supported anything I've ever done. She didn't even come to high school plays, and yet she traveled all the way to New York to watch me perform. She was proud, as I had hoped she would be. In fact, she was so proud that she told all of her friends. And many of them came too. They wanted to see the kid that they had all watched grow up become a star.

"Well, they saw more then they expected, let me tell you. It was a good play. But I imagine that if you had seen me in it, you'd have been ashamed of me too."

"Don't imagine that, Amy. If you played your part with integrity, I would have been proud of you. Doing your job to the best of your ability leaves you with nothing to be ashamed of. An actor or actress does what the part calls for. It's that simple; that's the job."

"Well, my mother was embarrassed. She called me that night, and she described her humiliation to me in painful detail. It was late and she'd had a difficult train ride back to Philly with her friends. She told me that she had to love me. She told me that all parents had to love their kids. But, she told me she'd never like me again. And then she told me that I was no longer welcome in her home. I'd left without her consent, and she was angry, but she hadn't shut me out. After that night, I knew I could never go home again.

"I made her ashamed of the family name. I made her ashamed to be an Alexander. I embarrassed her in front of her friends and neighbors. And, if a parent could ever divorce a child, she surely would have done so that night.

"I thought I had given a commendable performance. The part called for nudity, and it made sense to me so I was proud of that too. I told her so, and my mother said that no daughter of hers would ever be proud to be a slut. I asked her what she thought of my performance, of my acting ability that I'd work so hard to develop, and do you know what she said? She told me she never wanted to see or hear from me again and then she hung up on me. My home, the home I'd grown up in, was forever gone.

"I stood there with my roommates all around me waiting to hear what my mom had said. I was listening to a dial tone. I pretended to respond to my mother's voice so my friends wouldn't suspect that she'd hung up on me. I said, 'I love you too, mom.' I was trying so hard not to cry it hurt. And, then I hung up, and I told my friends some watered down variation of what had transpired.

"That was eight years ago. Eight years and I haven't spoken to my mother in all that time. I lost my brother that night too."

"Did he disown you?"

"No. He's my little brother. Nothing can separate us, nothing but my mom that is."

"That's a sad and terrible story, but it doesn't make me love you less. I'm not your mother. I don't share her convictions or her attitudes."

"That's not where the story ends. I couldn't sleep. I needed someone to talk to; my roommates were asleep, and I didn't want to wake them. Then, I remembered something the director had said to me. He told me that if I ever needed anything, I could call on him anytime of the day or night. In the light of day and with a clear mind, I would have known that those were only words, but I was desperate. I went to the director's apartment that night. I knew it was late. In fact, it was nearly dawn, but I was in pain.

"I respected him. He was the first real successful show business person I had ever known. I told him what had happened, and he took me in. We were sitting by his fire talking. I liked him, but I didn't love him. I'd had a few drinks and I was dizzy.

"We made love on his living room floor. And, Brendon, he wasn't my first. We made love, and the next day I left while he was still sleeping.

"Some time later, I started to vomit. Then I went to a doctor and found out I was pregnant with his child. So I went back. He wouldn't let me in because he had someone with him, another girl. So I stood at his door and I told him, and he laughed at me.

"He apologized for the inconvenience, and then he reached into his wallet and pulled out five hundred dollars. He said that he thought five hundred should cover my expense, and then he told me to go take care of it and not to bother him again. Then, he slammed the door in my face.

"I was looking at the brass room number on his door with five hundred dollars mashed up in my fist for what seemed a long time. Then, I did the only thing I could think of to do. And I wasn't pregnant any more."

Brendon looked down at the ring that still shined on the tip of his index finger. He frowned and asked, "And you feel ashamed of yourself for this?"

"Do you?" she asked.

"No," he looked up at her. "I feel no shame for you, and you should feel none for yourself. If anyone should feel ashamed of his behavior, I'd say it should be your director friend."

"I never saw him again. It wasn't long after that that I met Rick and my life began to change."

"It must have been horrible," he said.

"It wasn't the worst. It was simply the first story that popped into my head. The first of many that I thought might give you some clue as to what you're asking for. Don't you get it? I've loved being with you. I've loved every moment I've spent with you, and with this piece of heaven you call a farm. But, what have your friends told you about me?"

Brendon shrugged his shoulders and put up his hands.

"What have they said?'

"I haven't asked their opinion."

"Well, what would they say? 'It's cool to date a show girl.' All the guys at the bar say, 'Way to go, boy, you're doin' a showgirl. That must be great.' don't they?

Well, don't they? But what would they say if you told them that you saved yourself for a showgirl, what then?"

"I don't spend a lot of time in bars or with the guys. I'm frankly too busy for that kind of nonsense. But if anyone ever asked, I'd tell him I love you. You are a person to me, not a thing."

"They'd say, 'Are you crazy? She's not the marrying kind, 'ol boy.' That's what everybody says about me. 'She's good in the sack, but don't marry her. She's not the marrying kind. She's a slut.'

"No one has ever said that to me, Amy," he stood and walked toward her, she backed away again. "I wouldn't tolerate it if they did. But, you're right about one thing; you have been to places I've never been, and I'm glad I've never been there. But, you don't have to stay there if you don't want to. As far as being the 'marrying kind' is concerned, I think I can decide for myself who is and isn't my marrying kind. And, for me you are, and always will be, the only marrying kind I'll ever want or need."

He approached her faster than she could back up and he caught up with her. She tried not to look him in the eye, but he put his hand under her chin and lifted her face to his. He ran his other hand into her short hair, and around to the back of her head. And then he kissed her, first on her tiny nose, then on her lips. Something broke within her when his lips touched hers. She felt vulnerable but safe like she had in the circle of actors when they were catching her.

"Aren't you ashamed of me now," she asked, "now that you know?"

"No," he pulled her into his arms. Her nose pressed against his chest and she could smell him, it was like burying her head in a fresh pillow, it was clean and comforting, and his chest and arms were warm. "I'm not ashamed of you. And if you say yes, you'll make me the happiest man alive."

She closed her eyes and held on. A moan escaped her throat and soon a first tear followed her carefully muffled ache. It ran warm down her nose, and it dropped onto his shirt. Another tear followed the first, and then another.

"I never dreamed you'd be shedding tears of pain at this moment. I imagined that you would cry," he said. "But I hoped the tears would be the happy kind. I've asked you to make a life altering decision. One that I'd hoped you'd been expecting, but I guess you weren't. So take whatever time you need. I am not going anywhere; my love for you will never change. And, my offer stands how ever long you decide to wait, my offer will always stand."

"Don't say you'll wait for me." She pouted and her body began to shake like the earth was moving under her feet. "I couldn't bear it. Sleep with me. Sleep with me now. Let's have today, let's take this moment and make it all you've ever dreamed of. You'll think more clearly, you'll see. Then we can work in the vineyard together before I must go."

"Amy, is that what you really want?"

"I don't know what I want."

"You will."

"What if I never know? What if I'm never really sure? How long can you wait?"

"As long as it takes, Amy."

"You'll find out."

"I'll find out what?" he asked.

"You'll end up disappointed in me."

"I love you, Amy."

"I'll let you down too, and you'll hate me."

"I love you, Amy."

"You think that character makes one beautiful. Well, it does. You're right. But, mine isn't at all as beautiful as you've imagined it to be." She pulled herself from his embrace and ran.

CHAPTER 8

"Where are you going?" Brendon asked when he caught up with her.

The car door was locked but the convertible top was down. Amy could have leaped over the door but her keys were stuck in her back pocket. She'd be sitting in a parked car trying to dislodge her key from her pants, so much for a dramatic exit.

"I've got to go." She walked away from the car and away from him. Running had its appeal but he was faster.

"But you only recently arrived and you're tired. You nearly fell asleep on the swing only a few moments ago."

"Brendon I can't stay the weekend. Not now." She'd finally fished her keys from her pants pocket. It hurt where one stabbed her. She walked back to the car keeping her head low so she wouldn't have to look at his face, and so he wouldn't see hers. When she got to the car she saw only his legs in front of her door.

"Please don't go," he said. "I made a mistake. I should have waited. But, I won't speak of it again. I won't pressure you. I have reservations tomorrow night at a restaurant I know you're going to love. And, Carmen's been asking about you all week. Please." He put his arms around her and held her. "Stay."

She didn't want to leave. She didn't even know why she felt the urge to run. And, in his arms she was comfortable. Her tears had subsided; all that was left were tiny pouts.

"That's better," he said.

She wanted to fall asleep in his arms with her head buried in his chest. She looked down at his worn jeans, pushing her thumb through one of his belt loops. His body was pressed between hers and the car.

"My girl," he whispered as he kissed the top of her head and stroked her back with his hands.

"I don't want to go."

"I'm glad."

"But it won't be the same. I've hurt you. I know I have."

"I'm not hurt. Really, I'm not. And no, things never stay the same, but that doesn't mean they have to get worse. My cards are on the table. You know my heart, and I know yours. How will that hurt us?"

She looked up into his eyes, smiled, and kissed his cheek

"Okay," she said.

* * * *

There were three tower rooms. The middle one was hers. She'd stayed there so often that everyone referred to it as "Amy's room."

As she walked up the old stairs, they creaked and sank under the weight of her foot. The sound made by the wood was familiar, as if the house itself was glad to see her.

The room was wallpapered in a floral design against a deep green background. Her bed was made of iron, a faded dark iron. It had so many curves throughout the design it looked almost musical. A plush green quilt lay smooth on top of the bed, and four of the largest, fattest, frilly pillows were propped against the iron headboard. An antique lamp with long fringe sat over the bed and on her vanity stood a glass vase holding fresh cut pink pastel roses. She loved pink roses. Brendon learned her favorites early, and made sure she was surrounded with them.

The fragrance of roses filled the room and mingled with the fresh country air drifting in through the open windows. White lace curtains that hung on the room's five windows muted the light from the still long and promising day. A gentle breeze pushed the lace curtains toward her as she walked to the side of the bed.

She dropped her overnight bag on the floor. She had enough clothes and necessities in the draws of the dresser that she never needed an overnight bag, but she carried one anyway.

She kicked off her tennis shoes and sat down on the edge of the bed.

Marriage.

This guy wants to marry me.

She laughed and then a sob escaped her. She put a hand to her mouth to suppress the emotion. The intensity of her feeling surprised her. Every time she thought she had a grip on her pain it surfaced again.

What's the matter with me? This is ridiculous. I'm a grown woman.

She slid a soft pillow over her stomach and hugged it like a child.

I'm so close. I can't have this distraction right now. Rick was right. The stage is my husband, the only man I'll ever need. Illusion is my child. The show is my life.

"No," she said aloud, as if resisting a spirit, an intelligent ever-present entity. Her eyes closed as the tears flowed. The pillow was getting wet. She looked at the phone. It was a replica of an antique phone: faded brass with an ivory handle. She picked it up and started to dial.

"Hello," Max Levante answered the phone. Max had been Dante's builder during the years Dante performed. Now he was his driver, butler, cook, best friend; she wasn't sure what he was, but he was always there.

"Max. It's Amy."

"Oh Amy, how delightful. We've been hearing good things about you. When will you be coming to see us again?"

"Max please." She took a slow breath struggling to hold back her tears. "Is Dante home?"

"My dear, you sound distressed."

"It's nothing Max, really. Is Dante home?"

"No, Amy. I'm afraid you missed him. He and the Missus went into town to catch a show, I think. I don't expect him back until late this evening. Shall I have him call you?"

"Yes, um, no, I mean not tonight. I'll be home on Sunday. Would you ask him to call me then?"

"Of course."

"Thank you, Max."

"Always a pleasure, Amy. He misses you, you know. We all miss you. But, such is the price of success. We understand, and we're so proud."

Her hand covered her mouth. Her eyes were shut with force as if to shield from a brilliant light. She covered the receiver with her palm to muffle the moan that would betray her distress.

"Amy? Are you sure you're okay?"

"Thank you so much, Max. I'll be fine. You'll have him call Sunday then?"

"I know he wouldn't miss it for the world."

"Thank you. Bye, Max."

The room seemed silent and empty after she'd hung up. She wiped her face on the pillow then tossed it against the others. When she looked at it, it seemed inviting.

For a moment, I'll lay my head down but only for a moment.

She pulled her feet up onto the bed, put her head against the pillow, closed her eyes, and fell asleep.

Chapter 9

Brendon rested against Amy's car after she walked away from him and into the house. Two days was all she could give him this time, and the better part of the first was nearly gone. He removed the ring from his pocket and held it to the light so that the sun reflected brilliantly in its many cuts.

"I had hoped you would blush, and cry, and hug me, and above all, say yes, Amy Alexander," he said to the ring. "I'm such an idiot. My gut told me you weren't ready."

He clutched the ring in his fist and walked over to the swing on the porch. He sat down with a flop that tested the strength of the chains. As he reflected on Amy's reaction, he heard again her words, words he would never forget.

Someone ran toward the porch, and he knew it had to be Carmen. She leaped up the stairs, he hadn't thought it possible to clear every step, but he didn't hear one creak until she landed on the porch and headed for the door.

"Hold it young lady."

She stopped with the screen door open in her hand and she looked over at him with an impish smile.

"Where do you think you're going?"

"Amy's here."

"She's tired."

"She can rest another time."

"Carmen."

She frowned at him, but released the door, and let it shut on its own.

"Thank you," he said.

"Did you ask her yet?"

"Don't you have anything better to do?"

She walked over and sat down on the swing next to him. They swung together in silence, and then he noticed she was staring at his clenched fist. He looked up into her eyes, and saw that she understood. She frowned.

"She'll come around," she said.

CHAPTER 10

When Amy awoke it was nearly dark. She pulled a lace curtain aside, and looked out at the long shadows on the land.

Oh what have I done? First I turn him down, and then I sleep through the day.

But she felt refreshed, like waking up to a new day. The proposal had some distance for her. It had only been a few hours since that unexpected question, but it felt like weeks. Had it remained fresh in her mind, she might have chosen to stay in her room all night.

She looked at the clock. Brendon had an old ticking thing in the room before she started staying over. But the tick tock, tick tock, all night long kept her awake, and since she rarely slept through the night, she liked to be able to see the time. So, she brought her own clock in, and Brendon took his ticking machine out.

Her stomach growled when she realized that she had missed dinner. Dinners on the farm were events. Everyone came, Cindy, Jared, and Gordy from the office, Tino and Carmen. Ramona, Brendon's housekeeper/cook, prepared meals to rival the finest restaurants in town. They would talk about their business, their success and traumas. But more often than not, they would laugh and love each other like one happy family.

It was nice to be included. As infrequently as she came, everyone seemed to look forward to her visits. She was simply one of their own. She smiled when she thought of them, and then wondered if Ramona would be kind enough to heat some leftovers for her.

She crawled out of bed and stretched her still sleeping muscles into a more workable condition. She grabbed one of the iron bedposts and used it to stretch the muscles on her arms and back. Then she sat down at the vanity.

Oh, no.

Her short hair was sticking out all over. She ran her hands over it to flatten it down, but when she let go, her hair bounced back up. And her eyes looked like a raccoon's. Her mascara had run.

She tore off her clothes, and jumped into the shower. The water was cold. She could have adjusted it, but the cold water gave her an incentive to move as quickly as possible. She didn't want to keep Brendon waiting any longer than was absolutely necessary. Within moments she had touched up her makeup, heavy on the dark eye shadow. She slipped into a black dress with a ribbon-laced corset front and lace sleeves that were long enough to cover her hand but for her black painted and manicured fingernails.

As she laced up her black platform boots, she heard voices in the parlor room so she made her way downstairs toward them.

"Ms. Alexander," Ramona said. She was a hardy woman in her fifties, and she was fiercely demonstrative. When she saw Amy approach she pushed herself out of a white wicker chair, and shuffled over to her with her arms open wide.

Amy was swallowed alive. Her body vanished under the folds of the woman's arms and her face got mashed into the side of Ramona's. Then Ramona took her face into her hands, and kissed her wet and icky right on the lips. The gooey sensations made Amy laugh.

"It's nice to see you, Ramona."

"Oh, darling," and Ramona squeezed her again, and when she thought she might suffocate, Ramona let go.

Ramona put a hand over her mouth and shook her head as if wanting to say something she couldn't find the words to say. Then she walked off in the direction of the kitchen. Amy saw Tino and his daughter Carmen seated together on a white wicker sofa smiling at her but she didn't see Brendon until she walked into the room. He was sitting on the other side of the wall in a dark navy blue pinstripe suit.

The man never wears a suit.

As she entered the room, Carmen got up and gave her a hug, and Tino followed his daughter's example.

"Is good to have you home senorita," he said.

While she was hugging Tino, she was clinging to Carmen's hand. She knew by the squeeze of her hand that Carmen understood, and that they were still the best of friends.

Brendon stood during the greetings, and was now close enough to hug.

"Come along Carmen," Tino said. "It's time we went home."

"Tomorrow, Amy," the young girl said as her father pulled her across the hall and out the front door.

Amy walked the short distance to Brendon, stretched up on her toes, and kissed him as deeply and longingly as he would allow.

"Did you sleep well?" His arms enfolded her and he squeezed until no space remained between their bodies.

"Very," she said. "Why are you all decked out?"

"I thought we'd go out."

"But haven't you already eaten?"

"No."

"You didn't have a dinner tonight."

"Ramona made one of her finest, but I didn't eat … much. I thought you might like to go for a drive, get a change of scenery, and maybe grab a bite."

"So you waited for me?"

"Yes."

"Can you wait a moment longer?"

"I can wait for you for the rest of my life."

She gave him a smile before she broke from his embrace, and ran back up the stairs.

CHAPTER 11

Waiting for Amy at the bottom of the grand staircase, Brendon checked his hair more often than he thought a man should in the mirror that hung within the coat rack in the foyer. When he heard Amy's door shut, he came to the foot of the stairs.

She stood at the top for a moment, and smiled down at him. It always amazed him how her presence could alter the emotional climate of any room she entered. It was like the clean smell that permeates the air after a spring rain. There she stood, at the top of the stairs wearing the shortest and tightest little black dress he'd ever seen. With it she wore patent leather pumps and a small choker like string of pearls with matching pearl earrings.

In her right hand she carried a small black purse that matched her dress, and her left hand slid down the mahogany banister toward him. He watched her perfectly manicured and polished nails as her hand slid along the banister, and he wondered if perhaps she might be the most perfect woman in the history of the world.

When she reached the bottom of the stairs she paused for a moment before him. Her fragrance filled him like the bouquet of a fine wine. Then she moved her lips slowly and gently to his and kissed him. She let her purse drop to the floor as her hands went into the hair he'd so diligently groomed.

"Are you sure you want to go out?" she said.

He enjoyed her teases.

"You would rather stay here and watch TV or play Parcheesi?" he joked.

She kissed him again, this time, with a more lingering passion. He loved it when she kissed him that way. It made him feel like the luckiest man alive. When his lips were on hers, the world stopped its incessant movement, and nothing existed or mattered around him but her.

"Not particularly," she replied.

"No. How about Scrabble then?"

"Okay, Brendon," she frowned as she walked past him to the door. She paused at the front door and gazed demurely over her shoulder at him. Her big dark eyes had a kind of cocker spaniel look about them. She was waiting for him to do something but he wasn't sure what.

"I'm not dressed for board games," she said, and she gave him a clue by looking past him to the coat rack on which her coat hung.

He grabbed it from the hook, hugged her with it, and as he did he caught her scent, not the fragrance of her perfume, but the aroma that was uniquely hers. It was always in her hair, even after a shower. And, while her perfume was sweet, the aroma of the awesome creature that stood before him was the sweetest he'd ever known. He squeezed her tight and closed his eyes to take her in, as much of her as his senses could stand.

When he opened his eyes again, the ocean of her dark eyes met his. His heart ached when he looked into them. Sometimes he imagined their future in them, the children they would have, and the happiness they would always share as long as they were together.

He smiled, and she kissed him again, this time on the cheek. It was an affectionate kiss, not devoid of passion but intended for another purpose. It told him that she more than wanted him, it told him that she enjoyed his company and that she was pleased that she'd decided to stay.

She walked out the door to the car, and he followed, closing the door behind him as he left the house.

For the locals that frequented the quiet and off the beaten path restaurant, there was always a wait, but the owner was a friend of Brendon's, and they served his wine, so they were seated in a quiet little nook that was as elegant as it was private. The table was small with soft white linens and in the middle, a candle provided a soft romantic light that seemed to dance in her dark eyes and shimmer on her moist lips.

After the waiter left with their order she started chatting. She'd only had a half of glass of Chardonnay but that was usually enough to loosen her up.

"So I've got this dream. I've been dreaming about it since I got into magic, or since magic got into me. The audience will see a ghost. Thinking about it gives me goose bumps."

She shivered a bit, and then took another sip of wine.

Brendon didn't comprehend much of what she was saying. He'd never actually seen a live performance of magic, and he'd only seen magic on television once or twice while flipping channels looking for a baseball game. He tried to imagine what she was describing but her words were leaving her mouth at a speed much too fast for his ears. So, he smiled and nodded, and tried to act as if he understood. She was happy, and that was enough for him.

"Wow, Amy that really sounds great."

Her face lit up with a wide grin. "Really? Do you really think it'll work?"

"Well, sure it'll work. I mean if it was done once, it can be done again and there is no one more competent to try than you are."

"Well, thanks, Brendon. That's sweet."

She looked at him more intently and said, "Boring show-business talk eh?"

"No, not at all."

"I was thinking of bringing back my dog too. But, that might be a little too complicated."

"Your dog?"

"Yes. I had a little cocker; well, he was part cocker, part golden retriever. I loved that dog."

"What happened to him?"

"We feed him too many sweets, and too much junk from our dinner table that's what. His teeth rotted, and the poison in his system eventually killed him. I'll never forget the day the vet called.

"We hated to leave him overnight at a vet's. Once when he was young, he had kidney stones or something. He couldn't urinate."

Brandon pursed his lips, and squinted as if he'd tasted something sour.

"Oh, I'm sorry." Amy said.

"No, that's okay. I can handle words like 'urinate' while I'm eating."

"Anyway, the vet said he wanted to keep him for observation after the surgery. But, old Sam kept getting worse."

"Sam?"

"That was his name, Samson. He was the strongest and biggest in his litter with the longest golden hair. So, the vet's got him day after day, and Sam won't eat. The doc figures it's gotta be the surgery and won't release him to us. Then, when Sam is nearly skin-and-bones, we decided that, if he's going to die, we want him home in our arms. That's what we wanted for him, to die in the loving arms of his family.

"But, when we went to get him, and he knew he was coming home, you should have seen him. He wagged his tail and ran around and ate. He ate everything he could find. He would have rather starved himself to death than live out his life in a cage without us."

She took another sip of wine and slowly patted her mouth dry with a napkin. She probably thought she had cleverly disguised her touch of emotion. She'd created a logical diversion that gave her time to regain her composure without seeming obtrusive. She was good at that, and he found her misdirection endearing. At first, it worked, and her emotion went unnoticed. But it was increasingly hard for her to hide even her most intimate thought. She'd become an open book to him. What he found so perplexing was that she felt the need to conceal her emotional reactions. Why did she do this over and over? It was like playing tic-tac-toe with an opponent that knows all the tricks and strategies so no one ever wins. But he loved her tenderness incognito demeanor. In fact, he could think of so very little that he didn't love about her.

"We had him for fourteen, maybe even sixteen years," she continued when she could more easily do so. "He was the best dog. But, as he aged, the tendons in his legs wore thin. He was always jumping off of beds that were too high. That's how he injured his legs. He found it difficult to climb stairs and eventually difficult to walk at all. Then, his teeth started to go. He ended up in so much pain.

"He loved to celebrate his birthday. We'd put a little party hat on him and sing to him, and we even baked him a cake. When we knew we were losing him, we tried to celebrate his birthday, even though it was months away. But, he barely looked up at us. He began to bleed on the carpet, so we took him back to the vet.

"The vet thought he could remove some more teeth, and then old Sammy would be okay. But he died in the night alone in a cage in the vet's office. And, I knew how much he hated to be there, and how he so desperately wanted to be with us in his last hours. But, we thought we could prolong his life if we took him to the one place he hated to be.

"You know I've lost all kinds of people, aunts, uncles, cousins, even my own father. But I'll never forget the way my mother howled in misery and ran to her bed to bury her face when the vet called that day. I picked up the phone she'd dropped and the doctor told me how he died. She said he was in no pain and went peacefully. But, all I wanted at that moment was to put my arms around his neck and hold him and I couldn't because he was dead.

"When we finally got him back, I did hold him. And, when my parents left that night to do some grocery shopping, I screamed at God to give me one more moment to say goodbye. But, no life came back to him. My chance was lost. In trying to save him, I lost my chance to say goodbye, my one last chance to tell him I loved him.

"We bought a little plot of ground in a pet cemetery, and, with the gravedigger standing a few yards away with his head slightly bowed to give us some privacy, we lowered his casket into the ground. Mom had told me not to cry. She thought it would embarrass her in front of the gravedigger, but I couldn't help it. I wasn't making any noise. I'd learned to suffer in silence by this time, but one of my tears landed on the brown plastic casket. It formed a beautiful starburst when it hit. I looked at that tearstain and knew that a part of me was being buried that day too.

"I promised myself that I would never neglect the opportunities God gives us to tell the people I love how much they mean to me. But like a lot of my promises that one has been tough to keep. I think I've got time. I always think there is more time than there actually is. And then all of the sudden, I wake up and my opportunities have passed me by. It wasn't long after that my dad died. I never told him either. I wonder if he really knew."

Brendon slid his hand across the table to hers, and he squeezed it gently in his own. It was tiny and it almost disappeared in his fist.

"For weeks I dreamed he was alive; my dog, I mean. Well, actually I had the same kind of dream in both instances. I still do. Once, I even heard his chain rattle up the stairs the way it did whenever he'd climbed them to my room. I got out of bed, and I ran to the stairs. I knew he'd be there. I knew God was going to answer my prayer. But, when I looked down, the stairs were empty, and the house was still."

She took another sip of her wine. She sat the glass down slowly and ran a finger around its brim. Watching her finger, she smiled. Then, she locked her damp dark eyes on his. The flame of the candle glistened on moisture in them. She wasn't smiling anymore. She leaned across the table to kiss him. Brendon brought his body forward to meet hers. Her lips and her tongue were moist, and her breath carried the fragrance of wine.

"I need to tell you something," she said, as she settled beck into her chair. "I want you to understand what I'm feeling; why I can't … I want you to understand that …"

He lifted her hand to his lips and kissed it.

"People say life is a gift," she began. "Some say it is a gift from God and that what we do with it is our gift to Him. Have you ever heard that?"

"Sure," he said. "I suppose my Sunday school teacher told me that a time or two."

"Yes, well I've never really found comfort in those words. Do you know what I mean?"

"Not really."

"It's like there's this really powerful man in my life with all these expectations that I'll never be able to live up to no matter how hard I try. I don't want to disappoint Him, but I never seem to feel His pleasure in anything that I do. The fact is that most of the time I'm ashamed of myself. I always feel not good enough, not perfect enough, kind of sinful almost, like I don't measure up."

"You are a wonder to me," he told her trying to offer comfort but not for the sake of comfort. He really couldn't understand how she could feel for herself anything different that the perfect love he felt for her, a love that covered every blemish past and present.

"I think He wants me to do something," she said. "But I don't know what it is, and I'm afraid. I'm afraid to make a decision that might lead me farther from the path He wants me to walk. I'm afraid of missing the purpose I was destined for. I'm afraid of getting to the end of my life, and only then realizing it was all a mistake. That where I turned left, I should have turned right. If life is a gift, a present all wrapped up under a Christmas tree, then mine has never been opened. It's still sitting beneath the tree, the ribbons and pretty paper are undisturbed, and I have no idea what's inside. Maybe it's you, maybe it's magic, maybe it's both. I have no idea, and I don't know how to open it to find out. All I know right now is what I feel, and what I feel is fear. I can't understand how I could ever love more than one thing with all my heart, mind and soul. Ultimately one thing will win, and I'll love it completely, and the other I'll resent for distracting me from the one thing I was meant for.

"I know you didn't mean to, Brendon, but you've given me a choice, a choice that is going to tear at my gut until it's made. And, when it's made it will determine the joy or despair of the rest of my days. You've asked me to open the box and look inside and that prospect terrifies me. If I choose wisely, I will find joy and happiness. If I do not, I will live with regret and despair. If I didn't love you the choice would be easy. If I didn't believe in my work, the choice would also be easy. But I believe in both but both cannot be."

"I don't understand why?" he said. "Why can't you have both? I've never asked you to give up your career for me."

"There is not room in my heart for both."

"But there can be."

She sat back in her seat. He waited for a rebuttal but at that moment the waitress came with their entrees.

"Oh look our food is here" were not the words he'd wanted to hear.

They feasted on Italian dishes preceded by tossed salads of fresh greens topped with an olive oil dressing with a hint of vinegar and wine. Garlic bread was served, and the dishes were laced with garlic but the garlic was a mere suggestion, not an exclamation as many lesser restaurants would have made it.

Throughout the meal, she talked and occasionally touched him. Perhaps the touch was to ensure that she had his attention. But he thought it was to reassure her self that he was still with her, still in front of her, and still loving her. He would occasionally glance from his food to her eyes, and she would pause and smile at him every time.

She would say yes, eventually. He had hoped it would be during this visit, but if it wasn't, he would wait. He'd made up his mind to be patient, and to gently woe her for as long as she needed him to. She would say yes because he would prove his love to her with patience and kindness. She would say yes. His happiness depended on it.

At times her words disappeared, those around him disappeared, and he sat alone with her on a cloud, looking at the most radiant creature in God's good creation. The muffled conversations around him at other tables were as silent as new fallen snow. He wasn't aware of the waiters and waitresses moving to-and-fro around him.

He wanted to nestle and protect her. He wanted to be her world, her joy. He wanted to hold her until she knew she was truly loved for once in her life. But for now, he was content to sit before her and listen and watch.

"Sir?"

"Brendon?" she said.

"Sir?"

"Huh, uh, what?"

"More wine sir?"

"No. No thank you. Could we see a desert menu?"

"I will return with our cart."

"Thank you," he said as the waiter vanished once again.

"What's with you, Brendon, too much wine?"

"I'm sorry. I was thinking of the first time we met."

"You mean at the vineyard?"

"Yes. Do you remember?"

"Of course, I remember. It isn't every day I get a private tour by the owner of a vineyard."

CHAPTER 12

It had been a particularly warm day. The sky was cloudless. Open house was from noon until five, with tours running every hour. Brendon liked to mingle in the crowd while Tino and company poured the wine. He would often pretend to be a spectator: sampling wines and listening to the reactions of others.

He felt her before he saw her—someone was in the crowd, someone special. Did he know her? Had they met before? He looked at faces in the crowd, but the pull he was feeling wasn't satisfied. Then, from across the field of sampling booths and artisans' displays, his eyes locked on Amy for the first time. She was hard to miss in a black, short dress that laced with ribbon up the front. The arms of the dress billowed out in lace like a medieval gown. There was a black chocker around her neck. Her lips and nails were black. Her platform boots added at least three inches to her petite stature, and the boots buckled at the sides from her ankle to her knee.

He began to move toward her through the crowd. He panicked when a group of people passed between them obstructing his view. But when the group passed, he saw her again. *Was she with someone?* The closer he came to her, the less he felt of the world around him. People no longer stood in his way, nor existed at all. It was the first time his entire world disappeared, but for one person, the first of many times. It would happen again and again, whenever she was near.

She drank a sample of wine like it was the last swig of tequila. He laughed at the unpretentious spectacle as he began to close the distance between them. He looked at her long fingers for a sign of commitment. She had many rings, all silver. But, she had no diamonds or solid gold bands, at least none on the one finger that mattered.

"That was good," she said to a young man behind a tented counter. "Let me try one of those."

Brendon's employee behind the counter looked at him as if for permission. She glanced over her shoulder at him.

"Hi," she said, and when her dark eyes met his and she smiled at him, his knees buckled. Imperceptibly, he hoped.

This is stupid. What am I, in high school?

Her attention drifted back to his man behind the counter.

"Well, how 'bout it senor?" She said.

"Perhaps senorita would like to clean her glass first ..."

"What, I've got to do dishes now?"

Brendon laughed out loud, and in so doing regained her attention.

"He's not asking you to do the dishes. He is suggesting that you rinse your glass with water so your next sample will not be contaminated by the previous one."

"Oh, that's what those jugs are for?"

"Yes," he said, "what did you think?"

"I thought they were there for people, or kids that didn't want to be tasting wine on such a hot day."

"Here," he had said, "allow me."

* * * *

"Oh, that's how you remember it, do you?" she protested. "I knew what the water was for."

"You did not."

"Did so. I was teasing you."

"And I suppose next you'll try to tell me that you knew who I was."

"Well, I knew you had to be somebody important the way your employee looked up at you."

"As I was saying ..."

* * * *

After rinsing her glass, Brendon filled it with a taste of his finest Cabernet.

"First you look at it," he said, as he held the glass inches from her face. She was busy watching the wine, so he was free to stare at and enjoy the full richness of the biggest and darkest eyes he'd ever seen. Even in the bright sunlight, they seemed as deep and mystifying as the night.

Her hair was short, sassy, and even blacker than her eyes. It shimmered in the sunshine like the feathers of a raven. He so very much wanted to touch it.

Everything about her was delicate and feminine. Her fingers were long and slender, her nails polished black to perfection. She had a tiny faded scar so close to her nose it looked a part of it. But, even her flaws were perfect, like they were meant to be. The scar drew his eye to her sleek nose, a perfect nose, thin and finely shaped like something fashioned by a sculptor. He imagined running the tip of his finger down to her moist lips, lips that he wanted to taste.

He followed his imaginary caress to her ears. They too were tiny and flat against her head. She wore earrings, three on each side but not the dangling kind. Each was silver, each small, running in line from her lobe to nearly halfway up her ear.

"See the beauty in its coloration," he said, lingering on her and not the wine, "the brilliance of its reflection in the sunlight. Notice that there is no sedimentation. It is clear and tempting to the eye."

"Are you still talking about the wine?" she said flirtatiously.

"Yes," he said. He swirled the wine around and forced himself to shift his gaze from her elegance to the elegance in the glass. Her eyes were on him now, and she might think him rude if he continued to stare. "Now, when your eye is inspired, swirl the glass in your hand."

"I've seen others do that," she said. "Why?"

"To release its bouquet."

"Like a bunch of flowers."

"Well, what's the first thing you do when someone hands you a bouquet of flowers?"

"I smell them."

"Exactly. You want to fill your head with the scent of the wine before you taste it. So you swirl, and then smell. Here." He held the glass to her nose. As she closed her eyes and inhaled, he leaned toward her and enjoyed the fragrance of her hair. Her scent filled his mind and imagination. It made him burn inside, and yearn all the more for a taste of her lips.

"Umm, the wine smells wonderful," she said.

"Yes, it does. Now, when you drink it in, let it surround your tongue and seep into every corner of your mouth. Make sure that you engage every nerve with its flavor."

She let him gently tip the glass to her lips and fill her mouth with its wine. She tilted her head, and once again closed her eyes.

Brendon tried to imagine what her neck would taste like as she let the wine fill every crevice of her mouth.

When her head came forward, her eyes opened to his and she smiled.

"That was wonderful," she said.

* * * *

"Oh, you sad man," Amy said.

"I was smitten," Brendon confessed, "from the first moment."

"Smitten?"

"The first time I saw you, your beauty inspired in me the deepest longing that I have ever known. But, seeing you now, this moment with the candlelight dancing on your face, knowing you as I do, your hopes, your dreams, your fears; it's as if I've never loved before. It's a tender ache that hurts so sweetly; it's a dream from which I wish never to be awakened."

"You've been the perfect gentleman all this time." She ran a finger along his hand, "and the perfect man, and the perfect friend. My life hasn't been the same since I first laid eyes on you either, Mr. Gallardo."

The waiter arrived with desert. They split a piece of cheesecake that had a thin layer of Chambord. She slid her chair toward his until they were touching, so they didn't have to push the plate they were sharing back and forth on the table. As they ate, she ran her free hand along the inside of his thigh.

When the last crumb of the cheesecake was gone, she rubbed her tiny nose against his. Then her lips gently grazed his. She kissed his cheek and then nibbled on his ear, and down to his neck. When she rose again, their lips met in full. They tasted as full and rich as he'd first imagined they might, and every bit as satisfying. Both of her hands came to his face and she backed off enough to look him in the eye.

"I do love you, Brendon."

CHAPTER 13

The next morning, the sun was poring through Brendon's open bedroom window along with a fresh but chilly early summer breeze. Outside, the laughter of his darling Amy echoed among the vines.

He got out of his bed and went to the window. She was running through the vineyard in her bare feet, picking grapes with Carmen. She wore bib overalls with a short sleeve blue cut-off shirt beneath, and behind her ear, she'd strategically placed some tiny flowers.

He smiled as he watched her laughing and running like a little child. Carmen was having a hard time keeping pace with her.

Tino appeared beneath the window. Both Amy and Carmen ducked behind a large vine. Tino didn't allow play in the vineyard. He didn't object to the occasional tour, but if a branch got damaged, he could get pretty hot.

"Carmen," he called and there was no answer only the faintest giggle from Amy. Tino muttered some words in Spanish and started into the vineyard.

Amy emerged from her hiding place.

"Senorita Alexander, I beg your pardon. Have you seen my daughter, Carmen?"

"Carmen? Why no …"

"Amy," Brendon shouted from the window.

"Busted," she said and Carmen emerged from hiding.

Tino began to shake his finger at Carmen as he lectured her in Spanish. Carmine's head was bowed in respect of her father.

"I'm sorry, Mr. Tino," Amy intervened. "It was my fault."

"Is fine, Ms. Amy," Tino said, keeping his eyes on his daughter. "Is fine but Carmen, she knows I don't like her running through the vineyard."

As Tino spoke Amy slithered from his sight to the water barrel beneath the house. She'd filled a wooden bucket full, and was on her way back to Tino.

"Tino heads up!" he shouted from the window.

Tino turned as Amy was about to dump the bucket of water over his head. He assumed a ready stance that made him resemble a mountain lion after prey.

"Come on now, Tino," Amy said. "Take it like a man. You know you need a good chilling off."

"Now, Ms. Amy, put the bucket down."

At that, Brendon was fast on his way to rescue his best friend from the wrath of his most loved.

"Stand still," she insisted.

"Ms. Amy …"

They were dancing around each other like two timid boxers in the first round of a slugfest. She lunged forward; he darted to one side. A small amount of water spilled out as she withdrew. She repositioned. He repositioned.

"Now, Ms. Amy, I don't want my branches broken."

"Do you see any broken branches, Senor Tino?"

"Well, no."

Brendon came at Amy from behind. Tino lurched forward at her. Sensing her impending capture, she launched her arsenal, but Brendon took most of the damage. He stood in front of her sopping wet in boxers and an old torn flannel shirt. The water was cold and, in the crisp morning air, a shock ran through his body that cleared his mind and called him to attention.

She giggled at him.

He swatted some excess water from his arm, and it hit her. Though it was only a few drops, her jaw dropped and her eyes widened, so he followed up with a shake of his head like a dog after a bath. She screamed, held up her hands in a futile effort to defend against the water, and started to back away.

"That's cold," she protested.

"No kidding," he replied, as he started after her.

She gave a catch-you-later smile to Carmen as she started in a run through the vineyard.

"Run quickly, senorita," Carmen yelled.

"Not in the vineyard," Tino admonished as they ran.

"Why, senor Gallardo, you are looking a bit damp this morning," she taunted him over her shoulder as she ran. He was gaining on her, so she made a quick turn to her left around a vine then she ran back down the way she'd come. She cleared the vineyard and headed for the front of the house. She leaped the four front stairs but the door was locked.

She tried to go left, but he captured her from behind. He got her in his best vise grip—the one he used in high school to take down wrestling opponents—but he didn't squeeze quite as hard. Maximum effort or not, she was going nowhere. She shifted in his arms until she was facing him; he let her slip that much. Then, she looked him square in the eye, and turned her expression, no doubt strategically, from playful to seductive.

He lightened his grip for what he thought would be a kiss when she broke free, and leaped by him and down the stairs to the dirt pavement below.

When she'd reached what she must have thought was a safe distance, she turned around and said, "A little misdirection Mr. Gallardo, magicians are a slippery lot."

* * * *

They went to dinner again on Saturday night. Her mind was already drifting back to her show and her business. She spoke of Rick and of the news she hoped he would bring her on Sunday of some show she wanted to do in Vegas. He knew Dante was in, or somewhere around Vegas, and that she would have the perfect excuse to see him if she got the show. But nothing was certain, nothing was ever certain with her.

And then it was Sunday morning. He was an early riser but she was a notorious sleeper, he knew at least that she liked to linger in bed. But on this particular Sunday morning, she was up and ready to go early. Carmen had already said goodbye. Amy hugged her with a warm lingering hug, and then she ran off to church with her father.

"What's the rush, Amy? You don't have another show for a month."

After throwing her bag into the trunk and slamming down the lid, she hugged and kissed him lightly on the lips.

"Rehearsal, darling," she said, "rehearsal, rehearsal, rehearsal. That's what keeps the show clean and your little woman employed."

Brendon ran his fingers into his hair. He thought if he pulled it hard enough, his physical pain might soften the ache in his heart.

She closed her eyes, put her head against his chest, and purred.

"Don't stay away so long this time," he said.

"I'll miss you too." She slid her arms around him and squeezed so tightly he found it difficult to breathe.

Then, she got in her car and drove away.

Brendon stood in the dirt, in the spot where he'd last embraced her, and wondered what he might have done differently when he'd proposed. Was there anything he could have said or done that would've made the outcome an affirmation instead of a kind rejection? He'd planned to give her the ring on Saturday night at the restaurant, but the timing seemed right when she first arrived. Or was it that he didn't want to wait? Tino told him he was too impulsive.

"Timing is everything and you need to think more, need less, and wait for time to ripen like we wait on the crop," he told him.

"What an idiot I am," he said, as he kicked some dirt and walked to the porch. "She was exhausted. She'd completed a long grueling work schedule, and I didn't even give her a chance to sit before I started asking for the commitment of her lifetime." Brendon tucked the ring in his pants and slapped himself on the forehead. "I wish I had that to do over again."

"What's that, Senor Gallardo?"

"Olla, Tino," he called as his friend made his way onto the porch. "I thought you and Carmen went to church."

"We can still make the later mass. When Carmen told me the senorita was leaving, I thought perhaps I'd linger."

Brendon smiled and sat back on the swing, "Amy, Tino, I was thinking about Amy."

"Ah, see. Senor Gallardo is disappointed that senorita has not responded as planned, yes?"

"Disappointed? Yes, you could say I'm disappointed. But somehow that word doesn't seem adequate. How did she seem to you?"

Tino sat in a white whicker chair and said, "As impish as ever."

Brendon laughed, "No, I mean did she seem more distant, less attached than usual."

"Amy has never struck me as one that is as you say, attached. In fact I know of few that are less attached. Attaching is the natural inclination of most of the people in the world. But, from time to time; I meet one for whom this is not so. One thing is certain: when she is with you she is happy. When she leaves you, her sadness returns."

"Do you think she was happy I asked her to marry me or was it too soon?"

"Se, se, I think she was happy; not too soon, never too soon, only too late."

"Then why didn't she say yes?"

"Senorita's soul is at war within her."

"Tino, there you go again. Amy's a happy girl. She's in demand, you know. That's why her schedule is so full all the time. Success in her business is not easy to come by."

"Oh, you know this much about her business?"

"Now you know I know nothing of her business, other than the fact that it's a competitive field. Everybody knows that."

"And for this she should be thankful?"

"I imagine she is."

"Perhaps your imagination misleads you."

"What are you saying, Tino?"

"Why would a woman so happy in her field fall in love with a man with no interest in sharing in it?"

Chapter 14

No haze or low-lying cloud obscured the view of Alcatraz Island from Amy's bedroom window on that Sunday afternoon. Her eyelids grew heavy while she read the morning paper in her king-size bed. It was scattered in sections over every part of her bed and floor. Between reading and the steady, mesmerizing sound of the baseball game on television, she offered little resistance to the slumber that overcame her.

There was no engagement ring on her finger, but she hadn't stopped thinking about it either.

She loved Brendon, and wanted to marry him, but, she also wanted to be sure.

She had known and loved men that thought they wanted her. They would tell her that they loved her, even as Brendon had. But in time, they came to understand that what they really loved was the pursuit of what they did not already have. Once attained, their interest faded and eventually disappeared. She was thankful that she'd never married.

She wanted a man with staying power, a man for whom the words love and commitment were synonymous. She wanted a man with the ability to look past the packaging to the woman that so yearned to be known and loved. She knew that, if Brendon loved her image, his love would quickly fade.

She had to know the depth and intention of his love before she could give herself fully. And, she had to know that he understood who she really was: her past, her career, and her future.

As she watched the game, she thought of him. As she read the paper, she thought of him. As she drifted to sleep, she thought of him.

She loved Sunday afternoon naps. When she had been a little girl, in church with her parents, her eyelids would become heavy as she sat on the hard wood pews listening to the man in a white rob speak of God and destiny. She understood the minister's stories, but rarely his messages. It would have been easy to drift off under the steady hum of his voice, but she would force herself to stay awake. Her head would nod a time or two on the way home in the backseat of her parent's car. Then, once they arrived home, her dad would kick off his shoes, pull out his shirt and put on a ball game—baseball in the summer, football in the winter—and she would drift into the soundest of sleeps on the floor in front of the TV, or, on special occasions, resting on her daddy's lap.

She remembered how he used to stoke her long hair. His occasional outbursts of cheer at the game would wake her for a moment, long enough to remind her that he was near, and that she was safe.

His funeral was the darkest day of her life. When she received word of his death, she ran to a rope swing that hung from her favorite tree in the backyard. She beat that tree with her fists as if it were responsible for his death. Then collapsed on its long full roots and hugging the base of its trunk, she wept.

After her father's death, her mother was never the same. She'd barely shed a tear at the viewing and the funeral. But, in the darkness of night, in the wee hours of the morning, she often heard her mother sobbing. It sounded smothered, as if she were crying into her pillow. She would weep for her mother, wishing she weren't too proud to show her pain to her friends and family, friends that might have helped, family that would have cared, had she asked.

But, her mother bottled up her grief and pain like the homemade preserves she sealed in jars. Her frustration came out in other ways. She was given to fits of rage. Eventually, her screaming turned to hitting.

Once, when Amy was fourteen and her brother Chris was ten, Amy came home from school and discovered her mother screaming at and hitting him. Chris was curled up in a corner. His arms were covering his head to shield it from the blows. He was crying, but Mother's rage blinded her.

"Stop it." Amy grabbed her mother's arm in motion and the velocity sent her to the ground. Her mother took hold of her long hair and pulled her across the floor and away from her brother. Amy's eyes watered with the pain. Hair was torn from her head like the brittle fabric of a wash worn pillowcase.

Her mother kicked her in the stomach, and Amy lost her breath.

She started back after Chris, but Amy reached up and grabbed her mother by the backside of her belt.

This time her mother's knee connected with Amy's jaw, and Amy's teeth rattled as her head snapped back. Her legs tingled and she rolled onto her back to relieve the pressure on her lower back. Her mother stepped on her face as if she was trying to crush a large bug, and she began to beat her fists into Amy's chest, and then again into her head.

During the hitting, Amy's mind was oddly disconnected from her body. It was as if she were looking down on the scene from high above. She expected to feel pain, but didn't. She expected to die, but didn't. Her brother sat curled up in the corner of the room with his arms still covering his head, sobbing.

Her mother shouted at her. Her blood was on her mother's hands, and fury was on her mother's face, but she couldn't distinguish the words. Her vision blurred, and then everything went black.

When she awoke, she was still on the floor. Her brother was gone, and her mother was dabbing a moist cloth that stung as it touched the cuts on Amy's checks.

"You gave us quite a scare, dear," her mother said. "Come on now. Sit up. Let's get you into your bedroom."

With her mom's help, Amy walked up the stairs and into her bedroom. She sat down in front of her vanity, and looked into the mirror. Dried blood was on her face and matted in her long black hair. Her nose was swollen and her right eye was bruised and cut. It would not open, even when she tried to force it. It hurt to cry, so she moaned at her reflection.

She didn't think about the scars that could leave a permanent record. She thought only of her friends at school, and how she would try to explain once again how she happened to look this way.

She thought mostly of a boy whose attentions she'd been trying to catch, and how he might not be inclined to look her way for a while.

It's okay. He need not look at me. Tomorrow I'll wear black, black to disguise the pain and the bruises, black to express the sorrow, black to create distance and protection.

She would wear black from that day on *until they bury me*, she thought. *And then they'll all wear black for me.*

Her mom began to brush out her hair, even hair that was tangled and matted with dried blood. The brush would catch and her head would be pulled with the brush until her mother let go.

"Such beautiful hair you have," her mother said. "You know, most girls would love to have such long thick hair, a gift from your father, I suppose. So black and shimmering, it reminds me of the wings of a crow. And your skin ..."

She closed her eyes as her mother stroked her cheek with the backside of the same fist that a moment before had beaten her to unconsciousness.

"… So clean and smooth and dark. You'll be a heartthrob some day, sweetie, like your father before you. He was a handsome man."

A tear ran down her cheek and she struggled to contain the rest. She dare not expose a weakness to her mother; she dare not weep. Her mother had told her once already how disgusting the sight of tears were to her.

With every stroke of the brush, her mom would run her other hand over her head and Amy's body would ache under the gentle touch of her mother's violent hand. She promised herself in that moment, that someday she would run, and from that day on her mother would never touch her again, not in love, not in anger, not at all, ever.

"You rest now, dear. I'll go and get dinner."

When her mom left the room Amy tried to take a deep breath. She wheezed and struggled for the air. She lifted her shirt. Black surrounded her right ribs, blood beneath the skin. She ran both hands into her long hair, the hair her mother so admired. Then she reached for the scissors on her dresser and began to cut.

Long locks of black hair drifted to the floor around her like the falling leaves of autumn. She cut, and cut, and with each cut cried the more, until all that was left was short boyish strands sticking straight out all over. Her body shook, and she dropped the scissors into the pile of hair on the floor.

She knew that when her mother discovered what she had done, she was going to be beaten once again. But she hoped, at least, she would not have to face another gentle touch.

CHAPTER 15

Next to Amy's mirror was a small box. It was round and made of brass. Her father had purchased it for her after the Dante show he'd taken her to see when she was only nine.

She remembered the love she'd shared with her father that night, and how he'd praised the wonderful Dante. She knew that only that kind of praise would satisfy her longing. She wanted to hear the applause of people like her father the way that Dante had so many nights before. And, she wanted to get away, far away from her mother.

Amy continued to love her mother; her mind could not easily close the floodgates of her heart. But her love was inseparably mingled with fear as her hair had been inseparable mingled with blood. She wanted and needed to please her mother. But, pleasing her became more difficult with each passing year. During her high school years, her mother would sometimes scream at her the moment she returned home.

She wanted to know where Amy had been after school, and whom she'd been with. No matter what she said, it was the wrong answer. As far as her mother was concerned, all of her friends were a bad influence; all of her dreams were foolish.

Amy developed skill with makeup. She loved to dabble and experiment, but her skill was more the child of necessity than fascination. While many girls her age sorrowed over blemishes, Amy had to conceal the beatings, bruises, and swells left as gifts from her mother. Before long, the questions stopped, and few people ever knew what really went on behind the closed doors of the Alexander household. But, as her graduation from high school approached her dreams of escape grew until it was nearly all she could think of.

She would become an actress. She would be famous. Then her mother would want so desperately to be with her, she would admire and not hate her. But she would ignore her mother's phone calls and visits. Her mother would know at least some portion of what it was to want what could have been so freely given but what was always out of reach.

She wanted to run to LA, but she didn't have the courage or the funds to make the journey across the country on her own. So after graduating from high school, she withdrew her savings and moved to New York. She waited tables and shared a room with some other girls, most of whom had no interest in trying out for the chorus lines, bit parts, or TV commercials that Amy was always going to between her work shift or her acting classes at NYU.

Every day was a struggle, every audition seemed more difficult than the one before, and she'd come to expect rejection. Her mother told her relentlessly that she'd made a mistake, that she'd never amount to anything, that she had her father's stubborn streak and his talent for wasting time pursuing pointless goals.

"Why can't you come home and earn a real degree in computer science or accounting like Shelly's daughter? You know she's making one hundred and fifty thousand dollars a year right now. And, her company has a pension plan and profit sharing. She's dating an attorney, you know. I tell you, she's set for life.

"And look at you? What are you doing with your life? What have you always done with your life? Exactly as you please, that's what. No matter how it hurts me. No matter how it hurts anybody else. You don't care. You're selfish that's what you are.

"Do you hear me? Are you listening to me? You are selfish to the core like your father was, God rest his soul.

"Your choices do hurt me you know? I'm your mother you know?

"You should listen to me. I know what's best for you. Get a real job and find a man with some earning potential instead of hanging out with those fly-by-night flaky theatre people."

Her mother would often finish her speech with a complaint about the long distance rate that she was paying.

Amy twisted in her sleep to expel the demon of her mother's memory from her head. Parts of the paper fell to the floor. Then the phone rang.

CHAPTER 16

"Hello," Amy answered. The shrill ring of her phone cleared the cobwebs from her mind and brought her back to the serenity of her room. The sunlight still promised a long and peaceful day away from the spotlight, away from clients, excessive makeup, and costumes that fit too tightly.

"Amy?"

"Hello."

"Hello, Amy. You sound weary. I hope I haven't awakened you. If I did, I'm sorry. I'll call back."

"Dante?"

"Yes."

"Dante don't be silly I've been trying to reach you."

"I had hoped to catch you in," he said. "Max told me you'd be home on Sunday."

"Dante, I have some news."

"Good news, I hope."

"I hope so too. Brendon has asked me to marry him."

"Well, congratulations. I know you love him."

"Thanks, Dante."

"So, when's the wedding?"

"Oh … um, we uh … haven't set a date … exactly."

"What's wrong, Amy?"

"Well … that's why I called."

"Amy, romance isn't really my department."

"Romance isn't your department! Dante, You've been married to the same woman for forty, fifty—"

"Forty-eight years," he said.

"Thank you. Forty-eight years, you've performed together, worked together, loved together. I'd say you know quite a lot about romance."

"You flatter me, as always. But that's not what I mean. It's not that I don't know what love is, or that I haven't been lucky enough to have found a woman willing, not only to put up with my insanity all these years, but to actually help me at it as well. What I'm saying is that I can't help you make this decision. I don't think anybody can.

"I'm a magician, a retired magician at that. I can tell you how to have poise on stage. I can show you how to palm a billiard ball. I can give you the history of the latest illusion you are working on so that you will understand its original purpose and function. But, in matters of love, dear …"

"You're more than a mentor to me, Dante, and more than a friend."

"And I love you like my own daughter, but I don't know Brendon. I've never met the man. I've only heard you speak of him."

"I don't have anybody else, Dante."

He was silent. Then he finally said, "If you need to ask, maybe you're not ready. Maybe you should wait."

"He said he'd wait."

"He sounds like a good man."

"Oh, Dante, he is a good man. He's the sweetest, most tender man I've ever known. And I do love him."

"So what's the problem?"

"I'm not sure."

"Is it Rick?"

"No, it's not Rick. Rick is my manager."

"So?" Dante asked in surprise. "Did I ever tell you how Liz and I met?"

"No. Please do."

"She was an agent, someone I'd called on and mailed to as often as I could. I knew she could get me the big money gigs, so I was relentless with her. Well, as it happened, she passed a couple of gigs my way. I did a good job with them, and then she decided we could both make a bit more cash if she took to managing me. She managed me, Amy. Exactly the way Rick manages you. She was a talented business manager. We took to spending a good deal of our free time together and love blossomed. We were married. She later became my stage manager, and then my chief assistant on stage. She had terrible stage fright. She used to swear I'd never get her near the footlights. But, once she tried it, she loved it and never looked back."

"I never knew."

"It's not that uncommon in this business. And, I know that in his own eccentric way, Rick loves you too and I think you know that."

"I know he wants me."

"It's more than want, Amy. He cares for you. Look, I know he plays the field, so to speak. And, I know why you've always been a little, shall we say, apprehensive about his affection toward you. But I've known Ricky since he was a little boy and I know you smite him. What's more, I think you love him too."

"I never said I didn't. But, it's a different kind of love. I mean I can't really imagine life without Rick. He manages my career. His enthusiasm and excitement over my successes is greater than my own. And, his suffering over my pain is also greater than my own. I don't think it's a good idea to mix a professional relationship with love and sex."

"Well, I did, and I loved every blessed minute of it. I guess I assumed you and Rick would end up together. I mean Rick is theatre people, he's family. I know he'll support your career. And, no, Amy, I'm not only concerned with your career. If leaving the stage could make you happy, I'd be the first in line to welcome you to retirement. But, if the theatre is your life, then Rick can support that, and I'm not sure Brendon can. He may be able to tolerate it. He may even be able to appreciate it, though I rather doubt that. But, he will never be an asset, not that you marry for assets. I didn't. I married for love. As I said, I was lucky to get a good business partner as well as a great wife."

"You never told me how you felt about Rick. You never told me you thought I'd love him."

"I told you, Amy, romance is not my department. It's really none of my business who you love, marry, or sleep with. I care about you, I really do. In fact I care so much that I really don't want to influence you. It's my life I'm babbling about, not yours. I don't want to plant ideas in your head. I only want you to be happy."

"Don't you worry about planting ideas in my head, that's why I love to bounce major decisions off of you in the first place. Besides, I'm a big girl, you know. Perhaps, it's possible that I do have feelings for Rick. Maybe I should explore them before making a final decision."

"Couldn't hurt."

"No, it couldn't."

Dante usually responded quicker, finished his conversations faster, but he seemed to be waiting for something. She apparently hadn't reached the conclusion or discovered the truth or the idea he wanted her too, so she went fishing, "Dante, I'm hearing a thought in your silence and I'd like you to tell me what it is."

"Well, let's look at Brendon's proposal from another perspective. Imagine that you and Brendon alone, as they say, on a deserted island. He's the only man, and you're the only woman, no complications, no career, and no other men to choose from. It's only you and Brendon. What do you feel now?"

"Afraid."

"Indeed, afraid! Now how did I know you would say that?"

"You're psychic maybe."

"Not likely, and you know that all to well. I adore you, you know that."

"Uh oh, this sounds bad."

"No, it's not bad. But if your friends see something that is standing in the way of your happiness, wouldn't you want them to tell you about it?"

"Yes."

"Okay then. And know this: The only reason I see it in you is that I've seen it in me. We've had similar discussions about your performance anxiety, remember?"

"Yes, I do but what does my performance anxiety have to do with my love life?"

"Maybe nothing, maybe everything. You're still struggling backstage before performances, aren't you?"

"Yes."

"Are you sure you want to be an illusionist?"

"Not always, especially not before a show, but after, I'm always glad I did."

"Anxiety can have many meanings and many origins. Only you know for sure what it means for you. It may mean there is something out of sync with the show. It may mean that there is someone in the audience that you don't want to be there. It may mean that you haven't rehearsed enough. Or, it may mean that you are following a path that isn't right for you. I don't know the source of your pain, tension, or anxiety, whatever you want to call it. But, I do know it's pervasive. It's not only showing its ugly head before a show. It's creeping into all of your decisions. It's crept into Brendon's proposal hasn't it?"

"Yes, it has."

"You've got to discover the truth. Without it, you might never feel truly free to marry, or to pursue your career, or do anything else you choose to do. Without knowing, it is impossible to live with confidence that you are indeed living your life. If you don't find the answer, you may never be at rest. Facing the truth is never easy. But once you've looked it in the eye, it has the power to cleanse, to purge, and to put everything into perspective. Are you still with me, Amy?"

"Yes."

"So which is it? I know you're good. I know your show is good. I know you are well rehearsed. Is it the path of magic, is it the way you feel about yourself, or is it something else entirely? To bring the conversation back to romance, which by the way, I have little inclination to do, is it Brendon's love you are concerned about or your own love-ability?"

"Dante I …"

"What did you say to him when he asked you? Were you happy, or did your heart immediately fear? Could you have been happy had it not been for the fear, the same fear that plagues you on stage? Did you tell him in some way shape or form that you don't feel lovable, that you aren't worthy of his love? Is that what you said, Amy?"

"I don't know," she said. But she thought about it. She tried to replay the images in her mind. She tried to remember his exact words and hers, and how she felt at the time.

"It drives all of us. We want to feel significant, we want to believe we matter to someone, anyone, even though deep down inside, no matter the applause, no matter the audience response, we never feel worthy, or satisfied, or that we even deserve to be standing on that stage. That's what keeps us going out there night after night. That's what drives us to swallow our fear, and run for the lights like moths to an evening street lamp. We think we'll find love in that lamp. Don't we?"

"Yes."

"But do we?"

"Sometimes."

"Ah. Now that's an illusion if ever there was one. Let me ask you a question. Do you love yourself? When you look at yourself in the mirror, do you love the person looking back? Or are you sitting on the other end of this phone feeling guilty for even entertaining such a self absorbed thought?"

"I do a good show and …"

"I didn't ask you how good your show was, dear. I know how good your show is. I asked you if you loved yourself. Could you love yourself if you had no show, no claim to fame?"

She wanted so badly to run, but the phone cord would only reach so far and hanging up would be rude. But, she couldn't answer him. She didn't know the answer, and she didn't want to struggle with herself to find one. Dante always did this to her. He always challenged her in ways that seemed so uncomfortable at first, but left her deeply satisfied over time.

Dante had been a great illusionist, one of the nations great performers from the 1950's through the 70's and early 80's. He was dominant in the theatre before the great television-based revival of grand illusion. He was retired now, living with his wife in Nevada, and enjoying his reputation as one of magic's foremost historians.

Ricky had introduced Amy to Dante, but she'd worshiped him long before their formal meeting. Her dad had loved and admired him, which was all the endorsement she needed. When she saw him, when she was with him, she remembered her dad's happiness on the night of the show.

Amy loved Dante from the moment she first saw him. And, he loved her. He saw the potential in her, and it was his delight to nurture it as a farmer tills the soil and plants the seed. Every magician needs a mentor, a model, and Dante had become hers, but he was so much more. Since she had no father, and her mother's love was beyond her reach, he'd also become as a father.

Amy always imagined that Dante would give her hand in marriage when and if she ever did marry. She had visualized the scene many times, how she would smile at him and kiss him before taking the hand of her lover.

Now she looked at herself in the mirror. She had no make up on her face and only a torn gray sweatshirt covering her body. It hung over one shoulder and the long frayed sleeves almost completely covered her hands.

She sniffled, pretending to have some congestion that she hoped Dante would take for a seasonal allergy or a sinus infection. She ran her fingers through her short hair. It stood straight up in the absence of styling gel. She grabbed a clump in her fingers and pulled as if pulling up on her hair could pull back the tears in her eyes.

"Amy," Dante finally broke the silence, "I know your dad died when you were too young to understand that his death didn't mean abandonment. And, I know your mom has had standards that you couldn't possibly meet as a condition of her love. But, you don't have to meet those standards to love yourself; there's no criterion you need to meet to love yourself. You are perfectly lovable whether you ever achieve greatness on the stage or not."

She was silent. She looked up at the ceiling and blinked her moist eyes rapidly. If she spoke she would burst, and she had no idea when the flood would stop if she let it go.

"Maybe we should get together. I'd love to be able to put my arms around you right now, but I can't. You see? Do you see why I'd rather stick to the weather, sports, and magic?"

Amy laughed a tearful laugh. She hadn't lost control, and the laughter was all the release she needed.

"Yes," she said, "I know this isn't comfortable for you, and I want you to know I appreciate what you are trying to do for me." She pulled at the right sleeve of her sweatshirt with her fingers and dried her eyes with it. "And I would love to see you again. There is a chance I'll be in your area."

"Corporate gig?"

"No, actually it's a convention?"

"Oh yes, the magician's convention right here in my backyard."

"That's the one."

"Well, they don't pay," Dante observed.

"I know, but Rick thinks of it as a stepping stone. Anyway, the gigs not mine yet, Rick's been working on it. Either way, I'm sure I could get to Vegas for a day or two. I'll call as soon as I know something definite. If I get the gig, I'll come then, if not I'll check the calendar and get back to you."

"It'll be good to see you again. You've been so busy between working and Brendon. It has been much too long."

"Yes, it has been," she said, "much too long."

CHAPTER 17

Amy ended the conversation with a smile on her face and lightness in her heart. Dante made her feel warm and safe. He had that way about him. It didn't matter to him if he was talking with a living legend or a rank amateur; he treated everyone with respect. He listened to every word, and his response was always well thought out.

He loved people. It was a value he'd tried to instill in her. He once told her that Thurston, before every performance, would stand behind the curtain, jump up and down, and say, "I love my audience, I love my audience."

Amy tried Thurston's technique for a couple of shows before she discovered her own method. She could successfully conjure within herself an appreciation for her audience by peeking through the side of the curtain as they took their seats. She would imagine their lives. She would visualize their struggles and hardships and she wanted to offer them joy, if only for an evening. And so, when her curtain opened, she was prepared to give of herself. She was prepared to do whatever it took to make them happy if only for those few moments that she shared with them on stage.

She slid from beneath her covers. More paper fell to the floor and she bundled it up and put it in a stack by her bed. She walked to her window. It was a large bay style window with a built-in seat. She sat upon it for a moment looking out over the bay and then down on the street as people and tourists passed by. She rested her back against the frame of the window and brought her knees to her chest covering them to her ankles with her baggy sweatshirt.

Some of her toenail polish was broken and marred. She curled her fingers over to examine her fingernails. The finger nail polish looked fine, not a scratch.

"Art is in the details," Dante often said.

He encouraged her to keep her nails manicured. He said, "I know you are a stage performer, and your audience may never know what your nails look like. But you will. And, how you feel about yourself inside will reflect through your eyes and through every gesture you make. You must feel beautiful, you must believe that you are the best that you can possibly be at that particular moment. And that confidence, the confidence that will naturally flow from being at your best, will also show. And, your audience will feel at ease, they will trust you because they will instinctively sense your strength and passion.

"Never perform in a costume that needs cleaning or pressing. Make sure that all of your clothes are clean. Check your make up as well as your props before every performance. Then your mind and your body will be at ease on the stage."

Amy picked up the remote and clicked off the game. She wanted to hear the sounds of the city beneath her. But once the TV was off, all she could hear was the destruction of her carpet by her little white rabbit Harvey. She leaped from the window seat and ran to the living room.

Harvey was under her white sofa attempting to loosen carpet fibers. She loved letting Harvey run, but he loved eating carpet.

"Harvey!"

The rabbit looked up at her, his black eyes peering at her inquisitively. His ears were smashed to his head by the underside of the sofa.

"Don't look at me like that. You know what you did."

Harvey ran from the sofa toward the guest bedroom where his cage sat upon the floor. The door was open so he jumped inside. Amy was running fast behind him and got the cage door closed before he could change his mind.

The rabbit spun around in his cage and began to chew on the door, as if by chewing he could reopen it.

She crossed her legs and sat on the floor in front of him.

"Look, Harvey, I've told you a thousand times no chewing the carpet. Now you can stay in there and think it over."

Harvey paused while she spoke and looked at her. He wiggled his little nose, then balanced himself on his hind legs so he could lick his front paws and clean his ears with them.

She laughed at the sight of him and was getting to her feet when her doorbell rang. She wore nothing under her sweatshirt so she ran back to her bedroom to slip on a pair of torn jeans that hung over a chair.

The doorbell rang again.

"Be right there," she yelled as she hopped to zip and fastened her jeans on the way to the door.

She peered through the tiny peephole at the top of her front door.

"Ricky," she said. "What are you doing here?"

CHAPTER 18

Amy opened her front door enough to peek out, but she didn't unlatch the security chain. She hoped the sight of the gold chain and the imposing sound it made as it reached the limits of its short length would send the message to her visitor that she wanted to be left alone.

"What are you doing?" Rick asked as he made a futile effort to push the door open.

"I'm sleeping. Go away."

"Unlatch the door will ya?" He stood back far enough to allow Amy to close the door if she so desired. She didn't so desire. "Come on Amy, stop fooling around. Let me in."

"Go away."

"Will you unchain this door please?"

"Don't you have anything better to do on a picture perfect Sunday afternoon?"

"We've got work to do," he said. "And you've had a full weekend up in Sonoma with lover boy, so you should be feeling pretty well rested."

"I want to sleep now. Call me later."

"Your eyes aren't droopy."

"Are you trying to tell me I'm not tired?"

"Yes." Rick bluntly returned.

"Are you trying to tell me how I feel?"

"Yes."

"Are you ever going to go away?"

"No."

Amy slammed the door as hard as she could given the short distance it was open. It made a disappointing clank as it closed. So she unlatched the chain and opened the door wide. Rick must have thought it was an invitation because he started walking toward her.

"Stop," she demanded and he did with a look of utter bewilderment.

She slammed the door again. This time it provided a much more satisfying and lasting impression. The walls shook with the impact and she grimaced slightly at the sight of a picture that almost came off of its hook. It twisted but didn't fall.

Three gentle taps came from the other side of the door.

"Feel better," his muffled voice said.

"Alright," she grunted, "I'll let you in. But only for a few minutes."

"Amy, wait 'til you see the place," he said with a smug I-won smile on his face as he pranced over to her sofa. "The stage is elegant, Victorian, very feminine, the kind of crap I know you love."

"What place?" she asked, as she closed the door.

"Now remember this'll be a crowd of magicians," he continued as he fell into her sofa. "And magicians, especially the amateurs, which most of them are, aren't like normal people. They'll be bragging on each other about how you did this, and how you did that, and how they'd do this better if only they had your looks and your money, the whole time you're performing. But what an opportunity this is."

"The Vegas gig?"

"Of course, the Vegas gig. What did you think I was talking about?"

"Well the last time we spoke it wasn't in the bag."

"They wouldn't have sent scouts if they weren't really interested. It didn't take much to convince them."

"You stood outside their door until they were forced to either kill you or offer you the contract?"

"Something like that."

"So we're going to Vegas?"

"What did I say?"

"You didn't say."

"Okay," he said, "okay. You got the gig. Are you satisfied?"

"Thank you."

"You're welcome," he smiled.

"I like magicians," she said.

"What?"

"You make it sound like a drag," she said. "But I like magicians. I think they appreciate the best in the art. All laymen want is a good laugh and a sub trunk."

"A good laugh and a sub trunk has put you on top my dear," he frowned and shook his head as if to say will-she-ever-learn. "I've told you many times if you do the standards better than anyone else and make 'em laugh while you're doing it, you'll go as far as you want to go."

"So what's the catch?"

"What do you mean what's the catch?"

"You walk in here all energetic and full of spunk; you're warming up for a sales pitch. I can tell."

"Okay," he put his hands up as if in surrender, "so it's not as much money as we typically get and there are a few stipulations ..."

"Oh God." She fell into a plush wide chair near the sofa in a mock faint.

"Now don't get upset."

"Rick, didn't you tell me we had to hold the line on price even if it meant losing business?"

"Yes."

"Are we going to make any money on this deal?"

"On this deal?"

"Rick." She sat up and Rick sat back.

"No," he said. "In fact we'll probably lose money."

"The stipulations?"

"I was getting to that."

"I can't wait."

"They need something original."

"What do you mean original?"

"You know," he said, looking around the room as if searching for a muse, "new, novel, original."

"I know what the word means, Rick. I can't"

"But what about the dead daddy thing?"

She tried to respond but the words that flashed through her mind were either too vulgar to speak or simply inadequate to express her revulsion at that moment.

"I'm sorry," he said. "Did I offend?"

"The 'dead daddy' thing, as you so bluntly and crudely put it, is a pipe dream."

"You said you wanted to do it."

"It'll take years to develop, not weeks."

"We don't have years."

"It'll need constant rehearsal, precision timing and blocking. We'll need to make alterations to the stage. We'll need advisors and choreographers."

"Then it's settled."

"Nothings settled," she said. "I want to do the bit. I even said it might be a good number for the Vegas crowd. But you've got to remember I was barely conscious when I said that. In fact, I was delirious. That's what I was, delirious. And you can't hold me to anything I said in a delirium."

Rick smiled at her.

"You already told them we would. Didn't you?"

"Yep."

"Oh," she said as she grabbed her stomach with both arms.

"Now don't start that."

"We don't have time, it'll never be ready."

"Now don't start that either. I know you want to do the trick. You know it too. And magicians are the only people that might, and I mean might, tolerate that kind of nonsense. So before you let your anxiety drive you into the bathroom, why don't you slow down and thank me for giving you the chance of a lifetime."

"What chance?" She glared at him in horror. "You're not talking about the chance to perform the Pepper's Ghost are you?"

"No sir-re-bob," he gleamed and slapped his hands together. "Representatives from one of the biggest resorts in town will be in the audience. They are thinking contract. I've got them convinced, I think, that you've got what it takes to meet their specific need."

"No money, new routine, untested routine, in Vegas, in front of the media, my peers, and scouts from one of the largest clubs in town." She slid to her knees and buried her head in her arms on the glass top of the coffee table. "Oh God, oh God, oh God."

CHAPTER 19

"There, there." Rick patted Amy's back. "To catch a big fish, you need a big boat."

"What?" She lifted her head; the room was already twirling.

"Stretch; take a chance; I wouldn't have committed you if I didn't think you were ready. I'm your manager. Remember?"

Her moment of peace was gone. The day no longer felt like a Sunday. She wouldn't be able to fall back into that blissful slumber that Dante's call had interrupted. She might not find that kind of slumber again for some time. Her world never seemed to stabilize. She'd conquer one obstacle, only to be confronted with another even larger and more intimidating than the one before. But she was wearing out; she was tired. As the obstacles got bigger, her resolve got smaller, and the rewards for victory grew less satisfying. She tried to recall her haven of rest, her room in Brendon's home, his arms around her, the smell of the vineyard, Carmen's laugh. But the vibrations of fear in her head held her most cherished memories at bay.

Rick rarely asked permission. He rarely, if ever, told her what was going on behind the scenes, what was approaching. If he did, even once in a while, maybe she could prepare herself. He had control; she had none. But it wasn't only her career, only her business. Her business infected her whole life; it was her life. Apart from Brendon she had no other life. And so it was that her life was spinning out of control.

She hated when he did that—when he made plans without consulting her. But she knew he had to. She knew he didn't have the time to be out with the wolves, making the deals, wondering if his prized talent could or would deliver.

She knew he was doing his job and she knew she had to deliver if she wanted to keep them both employed. She couldn't remember a time when his ideas were not better than hers, when his guidance and judgment hadn't turned out for the best. It wasn't his judgment she distrusted. It was her ability to continue to deliver on his promises that she most doubted. For all his faults and arrogance, Rick knew his business, and she had to trust that he knew her limits.

She buried her head in her arms and moaned.

"As I see it," he said, "the Pepper's Ghost is the perfect routine for this venue and this particular gig. It's an established routine; it's been proven, but it hasn't been seen often, owing to the production costs and complications. If we can pull this off, I know we'll knock the socks off the scouts. You'll be in the front running for the contract."

"Contract," she moaned with her head still buried in her arms, "more about the contract."

"One year is typical. But it could be for longer or shorter. It depends on what they want—how they feel about you. Lots of factors weigh into it. It'll be another negotiation when we get to it, if we get to it."

"Vegas full time?" Her breath was making her face hot but it felt good to her—comforting, like a humidifier in winter.

"For at least the term of the contract."

"But what about my other gigs?" she lifted her head. Her eyes had already adjusted to the darker atmosphere her arms created so she had to squint to look at him. "What about the agents that depend on us? What about Brendon?"

"Who?"

"Rick."

"Our commitments are all negotiable. They'll pay more if you make a name for yourself, in Vegas anyway. As to Bladen …"

"Brendon."

"Right. You may have to cool it for a while. You'll be a busy girl. And if he's really worth your time, he'll understand."

She opened her mouth to object. He took a cell phone from under his jacket and began to dial, holding his first finger up to her mouth. She wanted to bite it. Not in a loving way; she wanted to bite it hard.

"Yea.… Sue.… Yea … listen: can you get Jason and Freddie to give me a call?.… Yea … at Amy's.… Yes, I'll be good. Do it for me, will ya, babe. Bye."

"Ricky, it's Sunday afternoon."

"So what's that supposed to mean? Since when are you off on Sunday?"

"I was sleeping."

"Sleeping?" he got up in a mock angry trot to inspect her bedroom. "With who? Is that no good Branson, Brandau, Bartholomew here."

"Brendon"

"Whatever." He went looking into her bedroom.

"No," she said, "he's not."

"Good." He turned from the bedroom door with a smile. "We can work."

"Ricky, do you have any other speeds other than fast forward and sleep?"

"Who said I sleep." He leaped back to his comfortable spot on her sofa.

"I was watching the game."

"I thought you said you were sleeping."

"Yes," she said, "and watching the game."

"How can you sleep and watch the game?"

"Okay, I was reading the paper."

"How can you read the paper and sleep and watch the game?"

"I was managing fine 'til you showed up."

"Where's Harvey?"

"In his cage."

"Eating carpet again, huh?" Rick sat up on the sofa, spread his legs, and looked between them at the chewed up carpet fibers under her sofa. "Uh huh, what did I tell you about rabbits and carpet?"

"Ricky, we've done a national tour. My bones ache, my body aches, my headaches …"

"And you can't wait to do it all again," he said as he looked up at her. He was close. He could easily touch her at any moment.

"Don't you have other performers to manage?"

"None more important than you, my dear."

"Why am I so lucky?" she asked.

"I've often asked myself that very question," he said as he folded his hands behind his head and leaned back in the sofa.

"Okay, Ricky, if you won't leave, then, by all means, tell me more about the show."

"It's one of those convention things," he explained. "You know, when all the magicians in the country get together to see something new and buy something new, and go without sleep for three days."

"And they really want to see me?"

"They came to see you work didn't they? I have the contract don't I?"

"They must be insane. I never appear in the periodicals. I've got no videos or spiffy new tricks for sale."

"But they know you anyway. You're headlining, honey."

"Well listen I'm gonna take the opportunity to—"

"To see Dante. I know."

"How do you know?"

"I assumed you would. You get to Nevada; you see Dante. Isn't that the way it works?"

"As much as I can. Is he coming to the show?"

"Who can say when it comes to Dante? His only interest, aside from you of course, seems to be his collection and his historical research."

"They'll need to re-build the stage and install the glass."

"As it happens, the stage was built with special effects like the Pepper's Ghost in mind. No one's ever done it. Why, I cannot say."

"Cool." She smiled, and in that one moment like a flash in her head she saw the glory instead of the agony; she saw what could be instead of what it would take to make it so. And she liked it.

"That's my girl."

She stood up, yawned, stretched, and headed for her bedroom.

"Where are you going?"

"To bed, don't wake me unless Jason and Freddie are standing here ready to go. You got that?"

He laughed, got up, and followed.

"And where do you think you're going?" she asked with her arm across the doorway to bar his entrance.

He looked beyond her to the bed and grinned.

Chapter 20

"Oh no you don't," Amy warned, "if you want to stay, then stay, but I'm getting a nap."

She slammed the door behind her, but Ricky caught it before it shut. She tried to argue, but found herself in his arms. Before she could speak, he kissed her. She put her forearms into his chest to force him away, but she didn't push. And the longer his lips stayed on hers, the less resistance she gave.

It felt good to be kissed.

She opened her mouth to him, and he acknowledged her permission by lifting her to the bed. Before she could react to his instincts, she was on her back. He was on top, kissing her neck, and running his hands up her shirt.

"Rick."

His hands found their target and her body began to tingle. She wanted to wrap her legs around him, her body needed it, but she thought of Brendon and Carmen and the vineyard family.

"Rick, please don't."

He stopped and looked into her eyes for the approval that he apparently already thought he had.

"Rick, please. Get up."

"Well, what was the kiss about?" he asked.

"You come on so strong. I don't know. You've got to give me time to think."

"Think? Think about what? You're here. I'm here. Nuf said."

"Ricky, that's not enough. Don't you get it? That's not enough for me anymore, and it hasn't been for a very long time."

"Good kiss though, huh?" he said with a boyish grin as he removed his hands from under her sweatshirt.

"Yea, Rick, it was a good kiss. Now get up."

He laughed, but he didn't seem to want to move as fast as she hoped he would, so she slid from under him to her window seat. She looked around the room awkwardly as she sat on her hands.

"Oh come on, Amy. It's only sex. Either you want it, or you don't."

"No, Rick. It's not 'only sex' for me. I don't want it. I know I was like that once, but I've changed. My feelings have changed. I want something more now."

"Uh oh, the 'I want something more speech.'"

"Ricky, I'm serious."

"What do you want?" He stopped smiling and sat up on the bed.

"I need to make some changes," she said.

"I wish you would. I think your whole pre-show routine is a little strange and unhealthy. You can't go on stressing your body the way you are. Something's gonna break if you're not careful."

"Maybe something already has."

"You need carbs to carry you through your performances. You're not getting them. Then your body collapses from exhaustion when the adrenaline runs dry. It's not healthy."

"I know that, and I've been doing some soul searching lately to get a handle on it. I've been passing out more and more after performing, especially after the long shows. It takes more energy than ever to get myself emotionally ready to go on, and I've begun to wonder if, maybe someday, maybe even today, I don't have it anymore."

"Every performer feels that way from time to time," he said as he laid his head back on her pile of pillows and stared up at the ceiling.

"No, Rick. Can't you see? It's not jitters anymore. I don't know what it is. When I'm on the road, I pull from some energy source that has lately run dry, and when I'm home all I want to do is sleep."

"So, you want something more," he ran his hand across the bed where she'd lay. "Like what? Something more from me, from Bronson—"

"Brendon."

"Right Brendon. Or, something more from your show?"

She looked away form him and ran both hands into her hair.

"Do you want me to go?" Rick rolled his eyes and laughed again.

"I did," she said, "but, now I want to talk."

"Oh God." He put his hands to his face as if he'd seen a ghost.

"You're up for sex, but not for talk is that it?"

"Yep."

"Well, you barged in here unannounced and uninvited. Now that you're here, I've got something I'd like to discuss with you, and it's not about the show or my performance anxiety, it's about us."

"About us?" He sat up and bounced to the edge of the bed to face her. "Do you want to talk about us as a business team or about us as couple? I was under the impression there was no us as a couple as far as you were concerned, so it can't be that. What about us, Amy?"

"Always the business man you are," she said. "Look at you, hunched over, hands folded like you're getting ready to close a big deal, or maybe catch a major league fast ball. Rick, am I more than a product to you?"

"Wow. Where did that come from? Do you think I've been treating you like a product? Of course you mean more to me than a product."

"Okay. How about more than a product with a sexual function."

"So far, you haven't had a sexual function."

"Rick."

"What?"

"Stop playing with me."

"What are you asking me, Amy? Why can't you say what's on your mind?"

"Brendon asked me to marry him."

Rick sat back as if she'd hit him in the face.

"Well, I asked you to be direct, and I got it. So what did you tell him? Are congratulations in order? At least, now I know why you didn't want to have sex with me."

She cupped her hands over her nose and mouth.

"It's never easy for you is it, Amy?" He got off the bed and sat next to her on the window seat. He ran his fingers into her short black hair and kissed her head. He rubbed her back and then he dropped his arm over her shoulder and pulled her closer.

"No. It never is."

"Do you love him?"

"Yes."

"Okay," he said.

"That's it? 'Okay?'"

"What do you want me to say? If you love him marry him." He stood up and headed for the door.

"Rick, please don't go."

He stopped, but his back was to her.

"Rick, are you okay?"

"Sure, Amy. I'm fine," he answered, without turning to face her. "Jim Dandy. Can I go now?"

"Do you really want to?"

"No," he said with a sigh, as he sat down on the end of the bed. "I don't want to leave. You mean too much to me. So, whatever it is you're feeling, I want to hear about it. I don't want to leave this apartment wondering what's to become of the best performer I ever managed. I don't want to lose you."

She smiled. It wasn't often she saw anything that even remotely resembled tenderness in Rick. It was a pleasant thing to see. She got up from the window seat and ran her fingers into his hair. He put his arms around her waist, and sat her down on his knee. She laid her head on his shoulder, and he rested his head on hers.

"You won't lose me," she said.

"Marriage changes everything," he said.

"It doesn't have to."

"That's what they all say. But, it always does."

For a moment, they sat in silence. She didn't want to debate the point. She wanted to enjoy his caress and his nearness. She could hear his heart as she had heard Brendon's days before.

"I'm sorry," he said.

"For what?"

"For you," he explained. "This isn't the best time for such a major decision. I'm moving your career in one direction and your heart is taking you in another."

"It's as good a time as any," she said.

"No it's not. In the next few weeks, if we get the breaks that I think are coming our way, you'll be looking at a Vegas contract, and maybe a good deal more. Your concentration needs to be on your work right now."

"Are you asking me to choose?" She lifted her head from his shoulder and studied his eyes carefully.

"No," he said. "I'm asking you to wait until you have a real choice to make."

"More clients, more deals—it's all the same. It's one continuous never-ending hustle."

"Not this time. This one's a career maker."

"The pot of gold is always around the next corner," she said.

"Some performers think their ship has come in if they earned more than they spent at the end of the year. You, on the other hand, are looking at real success here."

"Why can't Brendon be a part of that?" she asked.

"Does he want to be?"

She slid from his lap and back to the window seat.

"Have you even asked him?"

"He loves me," she said.

"Is that what he said?"

"Yes."

"And you liked hearing him say it?"

"Yes."

"And you're willing to give up everything we've worked for to this point to hear him say it more often."

"I may not have to give up anything."

"Mr. Wine Seller is going to be okay with a wife he sees maybe once a month, maybe once every three months?"

"He said so."

"And you believe him?"

"I want to believe him."

"And I want to be the next king of England."

"What do you want from me?"

"I want your undivided attention. I want you to be devoted to your job. I'm your manager, Amy. What I don't want is to hear about diversions at the most critical juncture of your career."

"Don't get upset."

"I'm not upset," he insisted, though his tone suggested otherwise. "I'm nervous. And, I hate being nervous. I work hard so that I never have to be nervous, and now, I'm nervous."

"You're worried?"

"Yes," he confessed.

"Good," she said. "Now you know how I feel every night at show time."

"Is that how you want me to feel?"

"No," she said. "I don't want to cause you pain. I don't want to cause anybody pain. I only want some fresh air, some space of my own. I'm suffocating. Sometimes, I think I'm dying."

"Do you think I could be to you what your boyfriend in Sonoma is?"

"The whole time you've been managing my career, I've been sending 'come hither—go away' signals." She laughed more from the surprise of his question than from its implausibility. She knew he wanted her, but she didn't think his desire had any serious intentions. "It's little wonder that you're confused. I'm confused, and it's not fair to you. But Brendon does something for me that I really don't think you could do. He's my island, my sanctuary away from all this insanity."

"This insanity is my life. It's your life, or at least I thought it was. If it doesn't make you happy, then why are you doing it?"

"I thought it was what I wanted." She pulled her feet up onto the seat, wrapped her arms around her shins, and rested her chin on her knees.

"And now?" he asked.

She buried her head behind her legs. He sighed heavily.

"You're a great performer, Amy. Of all the performers I manage, you are light years ahead of the rest. And we've both shown a decent profit from your gifts and abilities. But time is something neither one of us can replace. So, if you aren't deriving some sense of satisfaction from what you are doing, if what you are doing isn't making you happy, if you can't wait to get out there and perform again, then maybe the money isn't worth the effort." He got down on one knee so that she had to look into his eyes. To make sure she did, he gently lifted her head with a finger under her chin.

"Listen to me," he said. "That guy of yours, has he ever put smelling salts under your nose to revive you after a show? Has he ever dried your tears when you've lost a deal or had a bad night? Was he there when you were at your lowest point? Did he nurture and protect your development from a want-to-be actress to a theatrical star? You're not simply a performer anymore; you're a star. You're in demand, and I've helped you get there. As far as I'm concerned, he is just a guy, a guy with no name, a fling, a blip on the radar screen that was there for a moment before it quickly faded away.

"I know you want more, and you deserve it. I may not love you the way that he does, but you're not simply 'any woman' to me. Maybe at first, it was all about potential and business. But, it's not now. I've grown accustomed to you—your smell, your smile, and your eyes. My world would be empty without them, without you."

"Are you telling me that you care for me?" She smiled and put a hand to his face.

"Of course I care," he said. "Why do I have to say it? Isn't it obvious from what I do?"

"Yes," she said. "I suppose it is. But I don't know if I can take this business anymore. Every gig is a stepping stone to another gig; every routine is practice for the next. It never ends. I feel like one of those dogs chasing that fake rabbit around the track, while everyone in my life is placing bets on how fast I'll run to catch it, all the while knowing that I never will."

"You finally have a reputation among the people that can keep you employed. Do you understand the value in that? Do you know how long and how hard we've both worked to build it?"

"I understand," she said. "I really do."

"I think you're scared," he said. "And, I think you're using this romance as an escape."

"You think I'm afraid?"

"Yes. Everyone's afraid. It's normal to be afraid but don't give up. Not now."

"Of what am I afraid?"

"Of success," he said. "You know its right around the corner. You can smell it, and so can I, just like you can smell rain before it falls."

"I love him, Rick."

"Is the love of one worth the adoration of millions?"

Chapter 21

Dante built his home within easy reach of Las Vegas. He told Amy that he liked the pace and the seclusion that the desert offered him. But, he was still close enough to the magic capital of the world to enjoy the best in the business.

"No numbers and no names," she mumbled to herself as she drifted along the dark road that she hoped would lead her to Dante's secluded home. She'd been there before, many times, but every time was always like the first, especially at night.

"How am I supposed to find a house that has no number, on a road that has no name?"

There was a dim light in the distance. It could be Dante's porch light. He had said that he would leave the light on for her and in these parts that wasn't simply a pleasant expression. It could also be a street lamp. While there weren't many of those, they did crop up like tumbleweeds from time to time. In any case it was all the direction she had except for the bright shinning stars above.

As she approached the light, she slowed. It was Dante's light. Now all she needed was the entrance to his driveway. It was a small, single lane dirt road that branched sharply from the slightly bigger dusty road that she was on. She nearly missed it. She made a sharp right, as she was about to drift by it. Even at her slow speed the car tilted and the thought crossed her mind that she might flip. How embarrassing that would be. But, she didn't.

As she pulled up to the mansion and stepped from her car, stone gargoyles peered down at her from the roof of the large house. They were each lit from below by a single red light that gave them an ominous glow and the illusion of life. As she stepped from her car under their watchful eyes, she knew that if she looked up she could catch them looking. She might even see one of them move. But she didn't look up.

That's silly. Stone gargoyles don't move.

When she got to the door she turned around, jumped off the small porch and looked up. They didn't move. But they did frighten her enough to run back to the door as fast as she could.

Dante was really good at creating atmosphere, an atmosphere suggestive of magic and everything supernatural. The mysteries of magic were vast, but she wondered if maybe he didn't know something the other magicians didn't, if maybe he was the real thing. Creating that sense of wonder was one of his gifts, and his ability to do it on a grand scale generated a considerable demand for his show during the last half of the twentieth century.

Amy would never admit it in public, but hidden deep in her heart was a private faith that somewhere in the vast universe there is a place where magic is more than tricks and illusions. It's a place where dragons not only exist but telepathically communicate with wizards the likes of which Merlin would be proud, where ghosts lurk and moan in cold corridors of long deserted castles, and where life is always exciting, relationships always inviting, and love always reliable. This was the world that Dante made her believe in. It was the world he created for himself. It was the world of the truest magician she'd ever known.

The front door was as exaggerated as the man himself. It was huge, made from slabs of two-inch thick oak with big round iron knockers on each side. She always felt a bit silly as she banged away on his door with a doorknocker almost too large for her tiny hand.

The door was opened and Dante's curator, cook, butler, builder and longtime friend Max greeted her.

"Good evening, Ms. Alexander," he said as he welcomed her inside. "We've been expecting you."

He walked away from her anticipating that she would follow him and she did.

Dante had hardwood floors throughout the building. He loved the look of natural wood but his idea of wood flooring differed somewhat from the norm, as did his taste in almost everything. The flooring was dark, almost black, but that was the natural color of the imported wood. Each strip was at least twelve inches wide. The pattern of the wood was broken only occasionally by a strategically placed Persian rug.

The house looked like something out of an old thriller, and Dante designed it for chills. He was a fan of classic horror films, and he loved the gothic look. In addition to his collection of magic memorabilia, he had also acquired a substantial collection of vintage horror. He had autographed photos of Vincent Price, Boris Karloff, and Bella Lugosi. He had make-up kits, movie posters, lights, and cameras, all used during the filming of one classic horror film or another.

His house reflected his tastes, his interests, and his history.

"What I like best about it," he once told her of his home, "is that its very architecture creates an air of mystery, and mystery my dear, is what I live for."

Max directed her to a study that she'd been in many times before. Dante referred to it as the Golden Age because it stored the bulk of his magic collection from the era prior to the dominance of the film industry. His collection of Houdini-owned or autographed memorabilia was stored there.

Bookshelves with glass fronts stretched to reach the still higher fifteen-foot ceiling of the room. The shelves were hand-crafted from solid mahogany and were built into the walls. Between the shelves, were posters that Houdini and others of his generation had once used for promotional purposes.

In Houdini's day, the poster was a popular form of advertisement. Artists with the most vivid imaginations created them to attract the passerby, and the posters, like everything else in the life of a true magician, were larger than life.

As she entered the room she was startled by a young Houdini who sat tied to a chair immediately to her right.

"Don't be alarmed, Ms. Alexander," Max reassured her. "It's only wax." Then he left and pulled the twin tall doors closed behind her.

She sat down in front of the wax figure. His eyes seemed to sense her presence and his flesh looked alive. It had pores and seemed almost to be perspiring under the strain of the escape. She reached out to touch it. She expected his skin to be warm; she anticipated the moisture of his perspiration.

It was as if he were frozen in time like in an episode of *Star Trek*. Certain characters in the show moved about in another dimension of time. They could not be seen by anyone other than themselves. Those not of this dimension could perceive nothing but a faint buzz but for those moving quickly, the people and time around them stood still. Maybe this Houdini was alive, only moving slower through time than she, she imagined.

She didn't touch him. Instead she walked to a wall where many autographed photos hung. A single autographed photo of Houdini could be worth thousands, even tens of thousands. Dante had a wall full. He claimed he acquired them through barter and trade. But, she wondered who in their right mind would ever trade an autographed photo of Houdini for anything. Nevertheless, Dante was a dealer in antiquities and if anyone could do it, he could.

In one corner was a photograph of Houdini with his wife, Bess. All of the other photographs of Houdini portrayed him as serious, almost grimacing. But, in this one, his arm hung casually over the shoulders of his wife, his fingers were open and relaxed and he was smiling a wide open 'content with life' kind of smile.

She walked to the photograph. The Houdinis, both of them, laughed. It was a faint laugh as if it were coming from the opposite end of a long corridor, or the opposite end of time. The scent of age was in the air, like a cloud of cigar smoke. As she stared at the photo, the youth and vitality of the great master entered her body like a stream of electricity.

She wondered what Bess must have been thinking with his arm over her shoulder. She closed her eyes and leaned her forehead against the glass that covered the picture. An arm descended upon her shoulder. It was a light touch, barely there but she felt it all the same. And then she heard a whisper, "Amy."

She looked up expecting to see Dante, but no one was there. She looked back at the photograph and Houdini was staring straight at her.

"Did you love her, Harry?"

No answer came. She really didn't expect one. The only response was a frozen smile in an old photograph.

The clear image in the photograph blurred as her eyes drooped under the pressure of sleep. It had been a long day of rehearsals and an even longer journey to Dante's. During the trip, her adrenaline had been rushing, as she feared she might end up lost. But, now that she was safe in Dante's home for the night, the hour was getting the best of her. She lay down on the loveseat in the middle of the room. It was a red plush Victorian chair. She pulled a frayed dark afghan over her body.

As her eyes grew heavy she continued to stare at the picture of Houdini and Bess.

"Amy."

She looked up and saw Houdini standing before her. He wore the same black tuxedo she'd seen him wear in the photo and on the wax figure. She looked over to the wax figure and it was gone, that is, it was no longer struggling in the chair to free itself. Now, it was fully alive and standing before her, speaking to her. She looked around the room for Dante but he was not there.

"Amy," Houdini said again. "It's almost show time. Are you ready?"

She looked down at herself. She was wearing a long Victorian dress with long sleeves that buttoned down on the outside from her elbow to her hand. She had rings on every finger and feathers in her hair.

"Where am I?"

"You must have dozed off. I can understand that. Six shows a day can drive anyone to exhaustion. But, we've got a curtain in five minutes so let's get going."

Amy didn't remember getting up, but she was here anyway, behind the curtain with Harry Houdini. Panic gripped her as if she had been struck by lightning.

She didn't know the act. What was she going to do? Where should she stand? Harry was a perfectionist. He'd know in an instant that she was lost.

"Harry, where's Bess?"

Harry looked over his shoulder and smiled at her. His eyes were like fire, he was charged like a missile on a launch pad ready and eager.

Harry was bold. He loved confrontation, he believed in his own greatness and he knew he would give his audience the show of their lives, a show they'd talk about to their children and their children's children. And, here she was about to embarrass him.

"Harry ..."

"Amy ..."

"Harry, I don't know the act. Please—"

"Places everyone," he yelled.

She looked around frantically like a squirrel in the road. Was there a prop she should be picking up or a mark she should stand on?

He was laughing and rubbing his hands together like he was getting ready for a steak dinner.

"Harry," she screamed panic stricken, "I don't know what my place is. Do I have any lines? What's the first routine? Where's my mark?"

He turned from the curtain to face her head on. He gripped her arms above her elbows. His hands wrapped completely around her upper arms. He squeezed. She looked deep into his energy eyes, eyes that mesmerized. He was still smiling, still confident.

"Relax, child," he said, "stop struggling to find your place and your place will find you."

Over his shoulder the curtain was rising. The footlights were already blinding her.

"No," she said, "I'm not ready."

"Oh, but you are," Harry said. "You've been ready for this your whole life."

CHAPTER 22

"No, no," Amy panicked. She tried to pull free but the grip of Harry Houdini was strong

"Amy," he said, still smiling, still eager like a lion on a hunt, "wake up."

"What?"

"Amy, wake up."

The audience was applauding now. She was terrified.

"Harry!"

"Amy, wake up." It was Dante's voice. Harry's smiling face turned into Dante's look of concern. The gleam and energy and dark kinky hair dissolved into soft eyes, gray hair and a gray, delicately manicured goatee.

She gasped for air as she awoke with Dante's hands gripping her arms above her elbows.

"Amy, dear," Dante said. "Are you alright?"

She looked around the room panting, frantic, and wet with perspiration.

"Dante?"

"Yes, dear." He sat down on the love seat next to her and held her in his arms.

She looked over to the chair where the wax figure sat, and he was there as before. She looked to the photograph on the wall, and he was there as before. She covered her face in her hands and rubbed as if to rub away the memory of the dream.

"You must be very tired, Amy."

"What is it with this house?"

"You're tired. You've had a long drive."

"I saw Houdini. I was about to perform with him."

"You're in a room dedicated to his memory. You've got a lot on your mind, I'm sure, with the convention show, and the new routine. You drifted to sleep, and it all came together in your mind like spin art."

"No, it was more. It was more vivid than a dream. I was there; he was there."

Dante laughed.

She slipped past him and went to the wax figure.

"Excellent, isn't it?"

"It's damn creepy, Dante. It nearly scared me out of my skin when I first entered the room."

"Well, perhaps we'd better leave this room. Max has dinner ready. Are you hungry?"

Amy was still staring at the face of Houdini. She'd never seen a wax figure so real.

"Yes, I am. But I'd like to freshen up a bit first."

"It must have been quite a dream, Amy. I don't think I've ever seen a flop sweat on you until now."

He was right. It was a flop sweat, the physical manifestation of cold terror in the face of certain failure. She'd had bad moments on stage. But she'd always come through them. She couldn't remember ever collapsing in a panic, or breaking out in a soaking sweat.

"Maybe I'd better change my clothes too."

"Max put your bag in your usual bedroom."

"Are your kids home?"

"Home in Ireland, not here. They are visiting my sister."

Dante had two adult children, both living in Nevada, both married, a daughter and a son. But neither inherited their father's passion for the art of magic. He often said that as far as magic was concerned, he had been childless until she had come into his life.

His wife, Elizabeth, joined them for dinner. Max wasn't simply a housekeeper and cook. Over the years he'd become part of the family. So, he would always join them for dinner, and complementing him on a job well done was part of the family ritual. Max was an excellent cook.

They dined on duck, garlic mashed potatoes, and for dessert, Max's own cheesecake; no toppings of any kind were added but every bite was fluffy and light. It sent shivers of delight up and down her arms and legs like goose bumps.

After dinner, the four of them reclined in the den. They spoke of magic, of shows long since performed, of performances that might have been, and of performances that might still be. Max and Beth soon wearied of the single-minded conversation that always enveloped the magically inclined when they got together. They dismissed themselves in that order. Each headed for the comfort of their bed, exhausted by the magic talk that transpired between Amy and her mentor, and sure that the banter would continue well into the wee hours of the morning.

When two magicians' get together; they talk. They talk about old times, and embarrassing moments, and near misses. They talk about ideas, and dreams. They inspire, and thrill one another. With Dante, Amy spoke more freely and more passionately than with anyone. As she spoke, he would nod his head and smile, and his eyes would sparkle when she brought up certain subjects. So she would elaborate on those subjects to watch the sparkle in his eyes still more.

Every time they were together there was a story—a story she had never heard before, and she would sit before him and listen and imagine what it might have been like to have been in the audience those many years ago when the story he was telling actually occurred.

Sometimes he would stand up and pantomime the routine. He would play the part of the audience volunteer as well as his own. He spoke with his hands, and his energy was contagious.

She had two glasses of wine over dinner and had been sipping on a burgundy since dessert. With the depth of conversation, she was beginning to feel the effects.

"Would you like to see my latest acquisition?" His eyes sparkled so much that she'd have said yes if it had cost her her last breath.

"Is it another Thurston artifact?"

"Yes. Actually I've acquired several, but there is one in particular I believe will interest you."

"Lead on." She waved her hand in the air and the room spun a tiny bit as she stood. She looked down at her empty glass and wondered when she'd finished it.

The stairway that led to the room in which Dante stored most of his newest acquisitions was concealed behind a bookcase in the den. There was no reason to conceal it. But, when Dante had the house constructed, he had several hidden passageways and secret rooms included. He told Amy that every magician's home needed them.

The narrow stairway that led into the small storage room was lined with even more authentic promotional posters of the old masters, Houdini, Blackstone, Carter the Great, and at the top of the stairs, Thurston himself. Each poster was behind glass, framed and matted in curator fashion so that nothing actually touched the original work, no acids to fade the exquisite richness of its colors.

The posters were worth hundreds of thousands of dollars. But the true value of the posters was more than money could measure. Each one told a story, and represented a piece of the magical history that brought Amy and Dante to this place and time.

As she walked slowly up the narrow staircase, past each poster, she stopped to admire every one and every one tried to whisper its story, its own piece of history to her when she paused. She would have loved to be standing outside of one of Carter's tents looking at the poster and anticipating the wonders she would see upon entering.

This feeling was magic to her—it was the anticipation—it was the wonder of it all.

Dante waited at the top of the stairs. As eager as he was to show off his new find, he wasn't rushing her and he didn't comment. He seemed to know that her imagination was providing all the comment necessary. And she adored him for his patience and for the free and easy way he shared the treasures of his home.

Half way up the stairs she glanced up at him. His arms were folded like a genie about to grant a wish and a bright childlike smile filled his face.

The room had no windows. The lamps inside were as old as the artifacts it contained. Plush red velvet drapes with gold tassels separated one half of the room from the other. One half contained props: a crystal clock face with a single hand but with no visible mechanism for turning the hand, a set of portable steps that looked thinner than they actually were, and in the middle of the room was a round mahogany table. On it, sat a crystal wineglass that contained cards, old and worn.

The other half of the room contained photographs, albums, letters, and books, all preserved curator fashion.

Amy walked in and drifted from a photo to a prop and back again. But she was particularly curious about the cards in the glass.

"Are they—"

"—the cards that made Thurston famous?" Dante finished, "The cards that rose and danced in air? Yes, they are. They are the very cards his fingers touched."

CHAPTER 23

As Amy walked slowly toward the table her heart began to pound in her chest. Seeing those cards reminded her of a time she went with her class to her astronomy teacher's home. He was single, and her mom thought he had intentions toward her daughter that were not educational. But, as it turned out, she had the time of her life.

She was with friends. It was a dark and cold autumn night. Her teacher had his personal high-powered telescope out on the hill. No streetlights obscured the sky in the remote location of his home. And, for the first time in her life, she looked at the rings of Saturn with her own eyes, not at an artist rendering or some surrealist looking photograph.

The sight had filled her with joy and wonder. She knew that joy the first time she saw Dante perform. And, she knew it again as she looked at the old and badly worn cards on the table.

"I have always read about them, but I never knew they still existed."

"Well, they are real; they do still exist and now they belong to me."

"Did it really happen the way history tells the story?"

"I believe it did," he said.

"Members of the audience would call out the names of cards." She began to recall what she had read as she sat with her face inches from the cards. "The cards, once named, would rise from the pack, leave the pack, then drift through the air to Thurston's waiting hand."

"Exactly," he said, "then Thurston would toss the card, sometimes to the back of those huge old theatres, sometimes to the balcony, directly to the person who called for it. But that's not what I brought you up here for."

"No?" she said. "How much better can it get?"

"It can get as good as your dreams, and as satisfying as your deepest and most secret fantasy. I have a gift for you."

"Dante, please don't," she protested as he started sorting through piles of memorabilia.

He turned around slowly, and in his hands was an aged wooden case. She recognized it at once as the kind of case that would house a special wand, a wand of significance.

He pried the case open. The hinges creaked like an old door. She could see the wand inside and she knew immediately what the wand was and what it represented.

"Dante," she said, "that's not Kellar's wand, is it?"

"Indeed it is."

He removed the wand from its ornate case. He closed the case and sat it on the table by the goblet and cards. Then, he held the wand out to her.

"I want you to have it."

"I can't," she said. "I couldn't."

"This is my most prized possession, and I want it to be yours; it must be yours. Whenever I hold it I think of you. I believe it is destined to rest in your hand."

He stood before her, proudly holding the wand out for her to take. She checked his eyes to make sure it was what he really wanted to do and she saw his love and generosity reflected in them. She reached for it, as if her hand had a mind of its own. But she hesitated; she pulled her hand back. Thoughts of Brendon entered her mind, of the peace she'd found on his vineyard, and of the fear that grew like an untamed beast in her heart for the profession Dante loved.

His smile turned to a frown of concern and confusion.

"There is something I've got to tell you," she said.

He laid the wand gently on the table before her. It rested between her and the goblet containing Thurston's cards. She wanted so much to touch it, to feel its history run through her body and energize her soul. But she wanted him to be sure that she was the one, the one for whom the wand was truly destined. He could never be sure until he knew the whole truth.

He sat down at the small round table with her, and he gestured with his eyebrows and a slight crinkle of his mouth for her to proceed.

"I think I'm going to marry Brendon."

His face lit with approval, and he smiled.

"And I might retire from the stage."

She had never articulated those words, not even to herself, not even in her imagination, and hearing them escape from her own mouth almost shocked and surprised her. But having said them, they felt right, and her mind was at ease, the peace of her mind was guiding her now, leading her to her true destiny, a destiny carved for her and from her, a destiny not of anyone else or for anyone else.

"I see," he said. She studied his face, seeking his true feeling, but he registered no surprise, no shock or disapproval.

"I want you to give me away," she said. "I want you to be at my side. I'm sure my mother won't come; I'm not even sure I want to tell her."

"Oh you must; you must tell your mother. She may have changed. Even the most savage heart can be stilled in time."

"Are you disappointed in me?"

"Disappointed? No I'm not disappointed. I retired from the stage myself you know. But, I am a little puzzled as to why you believe that marrying Brendon means leaving your career?"

"It doesn't," she explained. "I know that Brendon would support me in whatever I choose to do."

"Then why retire?"

"I can't do it anymore." Her head was swimming with fear, and bliss, and regret. She loved the applause. She loved the machine of inventing, rehearsing, and performing. But she didn't love the physical cost, the strain, and the wear and tear on her body. She had tried to deny it, she'd tried to hide it, but her body would not let it go.

He smiled a knowing smile, and nodded in affirmation. In his look, he told her he understood, he understood as only another performer can.

"I loved it once," she explained. "I never thought I'd ever be able to live without it. But, I'm tired. Every show is a strain. There is no flow, no energy like there used to be. And I want quiet, not hustle—peace, not stress. The magic in my life is Brendon, and his farm. It's the harvest and bottling of wine, it's the stillness of dusk, and the promise of dawn on a farm in Sonoma, California."

"We each have a limited number of days," he said. "Mine are drawing to an end, I long to meet this man of yours that has so captured your heart and changed the very course of your life. For my days and my time, that would bring me lasting joy. But for you, I know how you've struggled of late. Rick has told me many times of your illness, vomiting, sweats, dizziness, fainting. Goodness, if I had gone through that every time I performed, I would have left the performance of magic long before I did." He stood and came to her side and kissed the top of her head.

"I don't want to give up. I don't want to prove my mother right. She said I'd fail. She said I'd never amount to anything."

"Failure is not a person. It's not even a trait or a flaw. And you are nothing of the kind. Look at me. Please." He lifted her head with his hand under her chin. With his free arm he pulled a chair to her side, and he sat down to look at her on her eye level.

When her eyes met his, she looked into the eyes of love. Nothing she ever said or did could ever destroy the warmth in those eyes. It wasn't a love she had to earn. It wasn't a response she'd won from a good performance. His was a lasting love that would overcome disappointment and transcend expectation. She could say anything. She could be anybody, even herself, and she would be loved.

He reached across the table and picked up the wand. He held it out and stroked her cheek with one of its cold golden tips. She closed her eyes and absorbed its electric power. A tingling passed into her body, a sensation of being connected with the long past and distant future all at once like passing from the temporal to the eternal.

"Look at the wand," he whispered, and he held it where she could see it when she opened her eyes.

"It's beautiful," she said. "It's so beautiful and it means so much to this art. Shouldn't a real magician have it? Shouldn't someone—"

"—more deserving?" he finished

"Well, yes."

"You never feel worthy do you? You never feel deserving because your mother said so, long ago."

"It's not that," she said.

"Then what is it?"

"The wand was Kellar's, and then he gave it to Thurston."

"Let me tell you something about Kellar," he said. "Where did you say you were born?"

"Well, I was born in Tyrone, Pennsylvania, but my parents moved to Philly before I was one so I really don't remember Tyrone. We did visit from time to time. My mother had family there. She had family all over Pennsylvania."

"That's interesting."

"Why?"

"Kellar had family all over Pennsylvania too. Did you know that he had a speech impediment; he never had the opportunity to go to school, and he was stocky and clumsy with his hands, in an era that demanded dexterity of its magical masters if nothing else? Anyone who knew anything about the art of magic told him to give it up, that he'd never make it. And, I suppose if I'd known him in his early days, I would have told him the same. He didn't feel deserving either."

"Yes, but he wanted it."

"Indeed he did. He wanted it so badly that he was able to endure any mocker, to persevere through any obstacle to get what he wanted. Do you suppose it would have mattered if Kellar had wanted to be a lawyer, or an engineer, or a carpenter?"

"I suppose he'd have been good at whatever he put his hand to do," she said.

"You suppose right," Dante said. "Kellar believed in himself, in the 'beauty of his dreams' as Eleanor Roosevelt once said. And passion motivated him, an undying, unquenchable love and devotion.

"I've always tied to live my life that way—to follow my passion rather than persist at what isn't working, to prove some point I don't understand to some person I don't know.

"Kellar gave this wand to Thurston in Baltimore on May 5, 1908, but it meant more to Kellar than magic, and it was bigger than magic to Thurston. Thurston went on to become the biggest and the best of his time, as Kellar had been in his. But neither man became the best by chasing rainbows they couldn't keep, or wearing suits that didn't fit. They became legends because they followed a dream. They happened to share the same dream. When Kellar knew his time was over, he passed it on to Thurston.

"When you follow your dream, when its bliss that leads you and not fear, your life will be filled, every moment, with joy. You won't be looking back with nostalgia or wishing your life could be different, you won't be contemplating suicide, or vomiting before shows because you'll be too full of happiness, and when you are full of joy there is no room for fear.

"Work that is right for you will never make you sick. It will give you the greatest contentment and satisfaction you have ever known." Again, he held the wand out to her.

"Take the wand, Amy. It doesn't represent the best in magic; it represents the best in us all. It represents the courage to live your life your way. It represented a lifetime of passion to Kellar and to Thurston, and it represents my love for you."

She held out her hands, both of them palm up and he placed the wand into them. It was heavy, heavier than any she'd ever held before. The wood was smooth like a polished rock.

"My gift to you this day," he said, "for this day, and always, my gift is not the wand, but what it represents. May your life be filled with joy, and, in whatever road you choose, may you find passion and love. I no longer perform, and I have no regrets. I love my life. I live my life, each and every moment of it. And, I'm happy." He stood and placed his hands, both of them on the top of her head. She closed her eyes and her grip tightened around the wand until it squeaked.

"A mentor's gift is precious," she said as he parted his hands to kiss the top of her head, "and you, Dante, will always be precious to me. But I'm so frightened. I don't know what to do. Both roads hold promise and regret."

CHAPTER 24

"The lectures and the dealer rooms are for members only, but I can sell you a ticket to the show. It starts in fifteen minutes."

"That'll be fine," Brendon said as he fished through his wallet for the money. He told himself he should've purchased the ticket in advance, he should have told Amy he was coming, he should've made hotel reservations, but he was here now. It had been a last minute decision, so, while his planning could have been better, he was determined to make the best of what was.

He didn't have a reputation for seizing the day so he was giddy and not a little excited at his own spontaneity. Amy told him he should loosen up, take more chances. He hoped that when she saw him the out-of-character element of the visit would thrill her. He hoped his presence would make Amy happy. He couldn't remember a time when she had more enthusiastically described a show. Most of her shows came and went without enough pomp or circumstance to merit a mention. But of this show she had beamed every time she spoke of it. She had said that the illusions she would perform would be one-time-only, and that in itself made the evening a special one.

Beyond that, he had never seen her perform. She had never so much as pulled a quarter from his ear. His interest in magic was minimal, but his interest in Amy was monumental. So, if she thought it important, so would he.

The cashier pulled the ticket from under the table and slid it across the counter to him. Amy's name was printed in the largest lettering. He picked the ticket up, studied her name and the names of the others in smaller print, then he looked around at the massive number of people. The muscles in his stomach tightened. The hum of conversations around him seemed louder and the air warmer, he was nervous for her.

I'm not the one performing. But I love the one who is. So, I guess it's only natural that I should be nervous.

For a moment, he entertained the thought of leaving. *What if she screws up? She said herself that she'd never done the routine before? What if tonight of all nights turns out to be a disaster? Will she be more embarrassed or more comforted by the knowledge that I shared it with her? I should have told her I was coming. What am I saying? Have I no confidence in the woman I love? She'll do fine. Either way, I'll show her the time of her life. However she performs tonight, however it's received by this mob, I'll love her and I'll make her feel my pride in her.*

The crowd was heavy, and grew heavier as he approached the entrance to the main theatre. People were standing shoulder to shoulder, patiently waiting for the usher to tear their ticket stub in half and admit them. Seating was assigned, and Brendon had a balcony seat. Though distant, he hoped it would allow an unobstructed view.

As he approached the doors an usher reached for his ticket and tore it in two. Beyond the ushers shoulder was a large poster advertising the evenings show. Many names appeared on the posters but the biggest was Amy's and her picture was the only one on it as well. She wore a white gown, clingy and revealing. She held a rose to her nose and smiled alluringly.

He trailed behind a small group of men, and he could overhear their conversation about her. One spoke of her sex appeal, another of her talent, and one confessed that he had never had an opportunity to see her perform because she concentrated her efforts on the corporate market.

The stairs that led to the balcony were wide but steep. He could not have turned around if he'd wanted to. The crowd was so heavy it literally pulled him up the stairs.

He found his seat. He checked it twice against the ticket stub to be sure. He was to be seated in the middle of a row, so he had to excuse himself as he slid past those who had already been seated. He tried not to step on any toes, but he did manage to land on a foot or two. His seat was only four rows from the balcony railing.

I like the view. It's not bad for a last minute purchase.

His seat proved to be narrow for a normal sized man. He squeezed himself into it and would have enjoyed resting his arms on the armrests, but his neighbors occupied them both, so he folded his arms. That was uncomfortable, so he put his hands in his lap, and then he pretended to read the program, all the while listening to the conversations swirling around him.

He couldn't remember the last time he'd been to a theatre. He began to wonder if he'd ever seen a live performance of any kind. He did remember seeing the circus with his father once, and another time, a show on ice. And, he remembered a dinner theatre he had gone to on a date with another woman. But he couldn't remember ever being as excited or as filled with anticipation.

Adrenaline was pumping through his veins. Was this sensation, this rush, this burst of lightning that brought clarity to every thought and sense anything like what Amy was feeling at that moment? He tried to picture her backstage running through last minute checks. He tried to feel her tension, and in some telepathic way, relieve her fear.

Could she sense his presence? Did she know that someone who loved her was watching and caring and pulling for her, hoping for her?

As the crowd filled in, he looked over the program that another usher had given him while the first was tearing his ticket. This time he actually wanted to read it. Amy's picture appeared on the first page along with a brief biography and a synopsis of what was called, "Pepper's Ghost Revisited."

As he read, the lights began to dim, and the crowd exploded in applause. A man in a slightly out-of-date tuxedo appeared on stage in a spotlight. He welcomed the crowd, and they responded with another burst of applause. The first performer was introduced; it wasn't Amy but it was obviously an illusion act.

A man dressed like an Arabian jinni made his appearance as the main curtain parted. His arms were spread as if to embrace the audience that was cheering him. He gave them a smile and a nod, and then he pointed to a box. He showed the box empty.

The music was too loud.

When he finished closing the box, it fell apart revealing a tiger large enough to fill the entire interior of the box if not larger than the box itself. Brendon was impressed and he laughed and applauded spontaneously.

Then the tiger was placed in a cage. The cage was hoisted above the stage, far above the stage, and well above the reach of the performer.

The performer clapped his hands; a curtain fell from the top of the cage. It covered the cage for only a moment when it dropped completely to the floor. A woman was inside of the cage where the tiger had been. She had a leopard skin French-cut leotard on with black pumps and tiger ears on her head protruding from her long black hair.

The cage was lowered and the young woman was set free. The performer and his assistant graced forward hand in hand to well-earned applause.

As the performers bowed, other assistants dressed entirely in black moved the cage and replaced it with two large glass tubes, one on either side of the stage.

The girl was helped into one of the tubes. The man went to a control panel. As he moved dials back and forth a light appeared above the girl in the tube. As the light became brighter, the girl became transparent, almost invisible. She threw up her hands as if something had gone wrong.

She looked in pain. Brendon was startled. Tiny gold lights danced all around her body, and she vanished as they increased in intensity. Soon the gold lights faded as did the light from above and the tube was empty.

Then, from the opposite side of the stage, the other tube began to light. The gold tiny lights appeared and began to dance about like lightning bugs. A vague outline of a woman's body materialized and as the glare from all the lights diminished it was plain to see that it was the woman who had moments before vanished from the tube on the other side of the stage.

Once again, both performers walked front and center for applause; once again people in black cleared the stage of props.

This time, from above the heads of the audience on the main floor and slightly higher than Brendon's direct line of vision, a curtain-covered frame was lowered to the stage. As it approached the stage, the curtain was raised. Nothing was inside.

Both performers stepped inside. The frame was hoisted again. As the two performers rose out and above the heads of the audience, they waved and the audience applauded.

As soon as the frame reached its point of origin the curtain was lowered. All was silent now as the audience waited.

A hand stretched from the curtain and waved and before it was fully pulled back inside, the curtain dropped and the frame was empty.

Spotlights raced through the audience until they found their mark. The two performers were standing on chairs in the middle of the audience. Once again, waving and laughing.

Everyone stood and applauded as the two performers made their way back to the stage. They bowed graciously and disappeared behind the closing curtain.

The emcee returned to tell a few jokes and introduce the next performer.

The next performer was a man dressed in a black suit with exaggerated lapels and thick white pinstripes. He looked liked a gangster from the roaring twenties. His banter was fast and furious. Most of the members of the audience were laughing, but the speed at which the performer was speaking and the volume of laughter that followed made it hard for Brendon to follow. He started squinting at his program to see how many performers would be on before Amy. He couldn't see his program in the dark of the balcony, so he returned his attention to the stage.

By this time, the gangster had persuaded a hapless volunteer to join him. The volunteer was a young man, possibly a teen, and he looked out of place and nervous. The young volunteer had his back to the audience for a moment; the gangster quickly remedied that situation by taking him by the shoulders and pushing him around to face the audience. In was an intrusive gesture. Brendon didn't like to be touched and the sight of someone else being handled in that manner helped him recall what bugged him about magicians; they sometimes treated audience members like props.

As he talked to the boy, the boy nodded in agreement to whatever the performer said. The performer touched him and continued to adjust the boy's posture and stance. Every time an adjustment would be made, the performer would hold up an article that apparently belonged to the boy, and the audience would either laugh or applaud. The boy would smile at the audience response, though he apparently didn't know why they were reacting as they did.

Embarrassed for the boy, Brendon looked forward to the next performer.

The next performer was described by the emcee as a "manipulator." Brendon wasn't sure if that meant he'd tell sadistic lies to the audience or make obscene romantic gestures to female volunteers.

As it tuned out, the man was nothing like he'd imagined a "manipulator" would be. The performer wore a black form fitting classic tuxedo with tails and a frilly shirt with lots of feminine fringe. The young man produced doves, candles, balls, and cards literally at his fingertips. Each time an object or bird suddenly appeared; the performer would pause, stare at the audience, smile and nod his head at the obligatory applause that invariably followed his obvious applause cue.

He acted nonchalantly, as if the truly amazing productions-from-nowhere he made were everyday occurrences for him, and that he was merely showing off his talent for an adoring audience. Brendon imagined that if a person could indeed produce objects from air, then the performer of such feats might be as taken with wonder as his audience was. But this man displayed no wonder. Instead his attitude suggested a self-assured arrogance, and his cockiness diminished the wonder of his magic.

Still, the man moved with considerable grace and speed, all timed and choreographed to elegant classical music. So, Brendon decided that he rather enjoyed the elegance and grace of the act, even if the attitude of the performer was bothersome.

The string of performers went on and on, and the audience was, for the most part, pleased with every one. But Brendon's head was beginning to hurt. He wanted to see Amy.

He looked around him. The light from the stage illuminated the faces of rows upon rows of overweight middle-aged men smiling like children in a candy shop.

Once, he spotted a younger man with a woman at his side. The woman seemed bored until the man next to her would look in her direction. Then she would sit up straight, smile, and nod in agreement with whatever he'd said to her. But, when he would turn his attention back to the sparkling stage, she would either drift back to sleep or look around for some other human contact.

Performer after performer graced the stage. Each appeared for an allotted time that varied anywhere from three to twelve minutes. They performed long enough to do a routine or two, and to give the audience some understanding of how they defined themselves as performers. Finally, his beloved's name was announced.

"Ladies and gentlemen: Amy Alexander."

CHAPTER 25

Brendon's mind cleared, and for the first time all night he participated in the applause as enthusiastically as the rest of the crowd.

I wish I could hug her right now. I wonder how she feels. If I'm this nervous watching, she must be a basket case.

As the emcee departed, the lights dimmed. The audience sat hushed, in total darkness.

From the center of the theatre, high in the air, a light appeared. It cast a chilling blue hue over the entire audience, but the light itself was small, perhaps the size of a light bulb but it had no shape. It was simply light.

All eyes were upon it as it crept toward the stage. As it neared, the curtain parted. It drifted to Amy who stood center stage with an unlit candle in her hand. It touched the candle and burst like the igniting of a match. Then the mysterious light was gone and in its place Amy held a single burning candle.

The light from the flame illuminated her face from underneath creating surreal and heavy shadows.

"People, who have died," she said softly, almost in a whisper, "and then returned, have spoken of a light, a light so comforting and medicinal that they want to follow it, to draw near to it. Some have followed. Through darkness, they often say, so thick they could see nothing but the light, they follow until at last they are greeted by friends and family, people they had known and loved, but people for whom they had mourned and grieved.

"A reunion of the sweetest kind, they said, awaited them as they followed the light through the darkness to the other side. And, then they were drawn back, each one, to the operating table, or to the battlefield, where eerily, they saw people beneath their disembodied spirits working on their lifeless bodies. And, like in a dream, they each awakened to the world they had left for but a moment.

"Do you believe in a place beyond? Do you believe in life after death? Do you believe that those you've loved and lost are waiting for you somewhere?

"I wasn't sure I did until one lonely night, many years ago.

"The skeptics among you may say, 'it was a dream.' Or they may say that I only saw what I earnestly wanted to see. But, he was there. I know he was. And I know that you have seen someone you love too. Your heart knows this to be true, even if your mind denies the evidence of its own senses. I saw him once, and I know he waits for me."

The tiny flame in her hand burst into lightning, and when the glare of the flash vanished, a fully lit stage appeared. There was a bed and a kitchen area, like a small efficiency apartment.

She was still standing where she had addressed her audience. She ran her hands into her hair and stretched as if weary from a days work.

She wore a black lace nightgown that had a slit on one side. Her feet were bare. Her presence seemed magical, and Brendon wondered if the people around him felt as he did or if perhaps his feelings were a function of his love.

She had a quiet confidence that filled the air with anticipation.

On the stage, a bed with spun wooden posts but no canopy rested at an angle to her left. There was a dresser and a mirror to the rear of the stage and to Amy's right, a door. The walls were covered with a pastel wall covering and held photographs and paintings, providing an authentic lived-in look.

The set looked so real that it gave Brendon the sense that he shouldn't be looking. He was embarrassed like being caught in a perversely voyeuristic act. The bedroom, the nightgown, and her whisper all worked together to create a sense of intimacy and privacy. No one wanted to speak or breathe for fear of revealing their secret presence to this charming woman who was revealing so much of herself.

As she glided to the bed, her gown fell open at the slit in the side revealing the bare skin of her leg up to her hip.

She pulled back the white satin sheet of the bed and sat looking up at a portrait on the wall.

She stretched her hand to it and touched it.

She picked up a rose that was lying on a side table beneath it and brought it to her nose. The rose was dead: black and wilted.

She fell slowly onto her pillow bringing her legs up into a fetal position.

"Daddy," she said as she dropped the rose to the floor.

The lights dimmed.

The brightness of the room gave way to a warm amber glow like a California sunset.

The rose that Amy had dropped lifted from the floor and slowly continued to rise up and out until it floated over the heads of the audience in the first few rows. The people seated in those rows began to shift uncomfortably in their seats. They searched for some visible means of support but found none.

A dim spotlight followed the steady progression of the rose.

Out of the darkness of the theatre, high above the heads of the audience, an angel appeared. She was dressed in a white robe, gathered at the waist by a golden sash. Her long white wings created a wind in the theatre. Around her head and flowing blond hair, was a wreath of holly. She reached out for the floating rose and merely touched it with the tips of her fingers. It rested there and when the angel blew on it, its life was restored, its petals grew red and blossomed and its dark leaves turned to a vibrant green.

The angel held out her hand and blew across her palm to the rose as if she were blowing a kiss toward it. The force of her breath moved the rose, and it returned to rest on the pillow next to Amy's head. Then, the angel slowly disappeared, and eventually vanished into the darkness from which she had come.

A dog barked in the distance. At first, he thought it was coming from outside of the theatre. But then, in the middle of the stage the dog appeared, slowly and transparently. His tiny form became more substantial and his bark louder.

He was a tiny golden retriever, the size of a cocker spaniel, and stocky.

The dog barked, trying to wake the sleeping Amy. Each time he barked he would wag his tail and dance around in a circle.

Amy rolled over in the bed and moaned. The dog ran from the center of the stage where it had first appeared to the bed and jumped, landing on her. Then, he leaped back to the floor.

He ran in small circles at the foot of the bed beneath her. All the while, he wagged his tail and barked.

She sat up and rubbed her eyes as if to clear the fog of sleep.

"Sam," she said. "Sam, you've come back to me. I knew you weren't really dead."

The dog leaped into her lap waging his tail, trying to lick her face. She wrapped her legs around him and rubbed both sides of his head in her hands.

"Sammy boy! Good boy!"

She rolled and tossed around in the bed with him. He was at times transparent. At times she would touch him and pet him but at other times they would melt through each other as if she were passing through a thick cloud or haze.

The dog would try to lick her face, and then he would pass through her body. But, whenever she could, she would hold him, kiss and stroke him. When he became as mist, when he passed through her body, she giggled and shivered, as if the penetration tickled her.

"For weeks after you died, I would wake up in the morning to the sound of your chain knocking against the stairs. I knew you were trying to come to me, to cross through the veil. I knew you wanted to kiss me again, and I wanted to touch you and smell you the way I've always done.

"But as you reached the top of the stairs, when the sound of your chain against the steps was the loudest, at the very moment I expected to see you emerge, the sound stopped and you were gone.

"I once dreamed that you'd dug your way out of the grave and ran home to me. I held you in my arms and ran my fingers through your fur and smelled your sweet hair. But when I awoke I held only my pillow wet with tears."

The dog barked and jumped from the bed.

"Sam, where are you going?"

The dog sat in the middle of the floor staring at the door and wagging his tail.

"Sam?"

She climbed down from the bed and walked to him.

She knelt beside him and could be seen through him, but she embraced him as if he had substance. The dog stood and walked from her toward the door. He paused and barked again.

A man appeared at the door. He stepped through the closed door and into the room, passing through a solid object the way most people pass through air. He was as vague an aberration as the dog.

The man was dressed in a dark suit and he wore a matching dark tie and shirt. His posture was straight and stiff like a soldier's, and he had the manner of dignity.

As Amy stood to greet her new visitor, her hands covered her mouth. She took a step back but she reached out to him with one hand. As she walked backwards, she stumbled and fell to the floor. She took a shrill breath as if it hurt to breathe.

"Daddy," she said from the floor.

Brendon's throat tightened and he found it difficult to swallow. It wasn't the image that evoked the remembrance of grief in him as much as the pitch of her voice.

She held both of her arms out to him. Her fingers were open wide and this lovely woman became so suddenly childlike in every gesture.

The man at the door didn't walk so much as floated through the air toward her. As he approached her, her short hair was tossed and tasseled as if by wind.

The man knelt to lift her, and she rose, her feet and her legs were no longer touching the floor. Together, in the air, they twisted around each other, spinning slowly clockwise, and they embraced as if in a dance on a ballroom floor.

Their fingers interlocked as they twirled in the air, and from each side of the stage, near the very top, an angel emerged. The angels were both females, both blond like the one before, both dressed in flowing white robes with enormous wings. They flew to the dancing couple and encircled them, flying in a counter-clockwise direction in opposition to the motion of Amy and her dad.

"You have only moments Mr. Alexander," one angel said, "only moments." And then, they both vanished, they melted away in flight and the man that held Amy in his arms returned her to the floor.

The man put his arms on her shoulders. The dog ran in circles around them, waging his tail and nodding in joyous celebration for the reunion of his family.

"Daddy, what did they mean? You can't leave me again."

"But my time on this earth is over."

"I've missed you so much, daddy. I've cried so many tears."

"I know you have, my darling daughter, and I've missed you too. But, you have your whole life ahead of you. I needed to come to you in the night, on this night. I needed to tell you never to look back again. Please don't try to live in what was."

She tried to hug him but she passed through and fell to the bed.

"Daddy I can't ..." she was crying.

"Yes, you can."

"I don't want to forget."

"Cherish your memories but focus on your life, live each day for they are few." His image began to fade. "I cannot remain with you for long," he said, but his voice sounded distant.

"No, please don't leave me," she stood and faced him. "I'm not ready and you've only just arrived."

"I will visit again in your dreams. When you wake and smell me on your pillow, it will be because I have held you through the night. Whenever you need me, close your eyes and I'll be there. And, someday, Amy, when you are ready, we'll be together again. We'll have an eternity to share. And, eternity is everything you've imagined it could be and more. You will never cry again, and you will never hurt. Take comfort in my words, my daughter. They are words that few living souls ever hear from those departed."

He seemed smaller, distant, less well defined.

"Daddy, take me with you. Please …"

"Rare it is that a man can come for even a moment to comfort his own. Know that I am well, that I am happy and that I will always love you. Live your life; live each day; savor each moment. Fondly remember those that you have loved, that have gone on before you. Fondly remember, but mourn and weep no more."

Then he vanished; he dissolved into a single bright light the size of a candle flame, like the one that had first appeared before Amy. Two angels flew to either side of it and together, with the light, they flew out into the audience.

"Daddy no …" she screamed.

"Live, Amy, live each day. Look forward to the morning, to the dawning of each new day, and never look back in the night again." His disembodied voice echoed from every corner of the theatre.

The stage lights went dark as the angels made their way rapidly into the audience. They broke into four, and the four angels separated and flew only inches above the heads of the spectators. Their bodies were translucent. Long flowing robes stretched out in their wake. There was a sound like wind, and screams and gasps erupted as the apparitions passed over various members of the audience. People lifted their hands to touch; the spirits flew so close. Then they disappeared under the balcony and Brendon thought it was over only to find them coming over the railing and straight for him. Their faces were feminine and beautiful, their wingspan enormous, and as they passed over him he sunk in his seat. In their wake, a brush of wind caressed his face.

When the angels touched the back of the theater, they went up the wall, across the ceiling, and back to Amy. They converged into a single tiny light and then came to a stop at her hands. She held a candle, and in a burst of light the angels vanished, all that remained was a small burning candle. As before, the tiny flame illuminated Amy's face.

"I saw him once," she whispered, "on that cold dark night. And, I know he waits for me." Then she cupped a hand over the flame and blew it out.

The curtain closed.

The crowd sat in silence.

And, then they applauded.

He had to see her. He had to tell her how proud he was.

CHAPTER 26

During his search for the backstage area, Brendon came across a vendor in the lobby of the hotel selling flowers. He purchased a half dozen pink pastel roses lightly salted with baby's breath before heading out in search of her dressing room. He hoped he'd be admitted. But if he wasn't he would bribe a hotel employee to deliver the flowers.

Stagehands, performers, and some union people he'd seen during the show watched him as he passed by. They knew that he was not one of their own. More importantly, with flowers in hand, they knew who it was he was looking for. Their whispers and speculations followed him.

One girl, and then another, looked at him with a suggestive smile, knowing that the flowers were destined for Amy, but delighting in the romance of the gesture all the same.

A tall man stepped from a dressing room, he was slender but solidly built. His hair was dark and possibly jelled, a practice Brendon resisted though Carmen forced it on him one evening after dinner. He thought it made him look like a grease stain in a garage so he never tried it again. But on the man that approached him, it looked downright intimidating. His dark tailored suit held to his muscular form without a crease and it smelled of money and success. Brendon had never met Rick, but he'd imagined that Rick might look like this man, so he approached him, hoping that he would direct him to Amy.

"Excuse me," he said. "Can you tell me where I might find Amy Alexander?"

"I'm Ms. Alexander's manager. What can I do for you?"

"Oh yes, you must be Rick."

"And you are ...?"

"I'm Brendon. Brendon Gallardo." He held out his hand to greet Rick, Rick hesitated. He looked at the extended hand and then he looked around him to see who might be watching. Finally, he reached out and clutched Brendon's hand firmly. It was the kind of handshake Brendon expected from a man like Rick, firm and a bit too tight.

"I don't believe we've met," Rick said.

"No," Brendon said. "No we haven't. Amy has told me quite a bit about you. You are Rick McAlister?"

"Guilty as charged," Rick smiled.

Rick looked confused, so Brendon thought some additional details might help.

"Amy and I have been dating, and I—"

"Is that a fact?"

"Yes, for some time now."

"Dating, you call it?"

"Yes. Well, I mean we've been seeing each other."

"When? She is always working."

"Indeed she is."

"Well, Mr. Gallardo, while I am sure that Amy would be delighted to learn that you are here, she has had a full day, and I'm afraid her work is only beginning. When I left her, she was tired. Lately, she's been thoroughly exhausted after performances. She is most likely asleep, and while I don't mean to put you off, she really needs a little down-time right now. Why don't you leave the flowers with me? I'll see that she gets them." Rick held out his hand in an effort to hurry Brendon along.

"Rick, I know you mean well, but I've traveled a long way and while Amy didn't exactly invite me, she's been trying to get me to a show for some time. I'm sure she'd like to know I'm here."

"And I will tell her."

Brendon didn't move. It was becoming an issue of pride. He really didn't expect to see her. He surely didn't want to disturb her rest. But he didn't want to be blown off either.

"There are some business people she needs to deal with right now," Rick lowered his hand and explained. "We've been trying to get their attention for a couple of years, and I think we've finally succeeded. I need her to focus. Do you understand?"

"I know how important this show is to her."

"Good," Rick said. "So please, go back to your hotel. I will have her call you as soon as she is able to."

"Don't you think she might be the slightest bit disappointed when she finds out that her fiancée was here on her big night, and you sent him away?"

"She'll probably be furious," Rick admitted, "and that's okay. I'm used to dealing with Amy's moods, and she is used to my meddling in her affairs. As to being Amy's fiancée," Rick grinned long and wide, "she never told me she was engaged."

"I asked her to marry me recently."

"And did she accept?"

"No," Brendon admitted, "she didn't."

"Then why did you refer to yourself as her fiancée?"

"I like the sound of it," he said. "I say it as often as I can."

"As if saying it can make it so," Rick laughed. It might have been the hesitant tone of the laugh or the way Rick kept his eyes in motion, but it was clear that Amy did in fact, disclose everything to her manager. "Well, Mr. Gallardo, if you really care for Amy, I'd suggest you give her the space she needs to do her job."

People backstage dropped their individual conversations for the one that was becoming much more interesting. What had been clamor and commotion was now silence and intrusion.

"Please." Rick gestured again with his hand for the flowers.

He placed the flowers into Rick's outstretched hand. He didn't want to cause a commotion. He never enjoyed the limelight and he didn't want it now. He was here to make a friendly gesture and he wanted to keep it that way even if it meant going away without seeing her.

"Thank you," Rick said. Then he walked over to the dressing room door he'd come out of and put the flowers down in front of it.

"Will you see that she gets them?" he asked.

"Of course I will," Rick said.

He nodded and shrugged his shoulders and then turned to walk away.

"Mr. Gallardo," Rick called.

"Yes," he turned to face him again.

"Where are you staying?"

"My hotel address and room number are both on the card. I did consider the possibility that I wouldn't get this far. But I hoped to find a willing courier for the flowers. I'm glad I bumped into you."

"I'm a bit amazed that you did," Rick laughed again, this time in delight. "There are security people you must have slipped by like the invisible man."

"Not invisible," Brendon said, "but when you are carrying roses for the star, who's going to stop you?"

"Good point."

"Goodnight, Mr. McAlister," he said. "It was nice meeting you."

"You're going to give up that easily are you?" Rick said as he walked after Brendon.

"Who said anything about giving up? I came here to see Amy and sooner or later I will. I'm sure she is as weary as you say, and I know you have business to attend to. I didn't come here to get in her way or yours. I want to lend my support, and right now I know I can best do that by leaving. I'm sure she'll call me at the hotel when she is ready to see me. I'll wait there until then."

"Brendon," Rick put a hand to Brendon's arm to stopped his forward momentum. He had a look of worry in his eyes that Brendon hadn't noticed before. "Are you aware that she's been getting sick after shows?"

"Somewhat aware," Brendon answered Rick's disconcerting question. "Why do you ask?"

"Well, that's the reason I can't let you, or anyone else see her right now. As disappointed as she might be that she missed you, I couldn't do it."

"I understand," Brendon said. "I'll give her as much time as she wants."

Rick's apparent apprehension intensified. He looked around him at some of the eavesdroppers. "Can we go somewhere and talk please?"

"But I thought you had some places to go, people to see and all that."

"I do. It won't take long. I promise."

CHAPTER 27

Brendon followed Rick through a long corridor to an office. It was a small office, but plush and comfortable. An abstract painting mostly in blue hues hung on a wall over a leather sofa, and next to the sofa was a matching leather chair. Between the two was a glass coffee table with an ashtray and some theatrical trade journals on top. The room smelled like it had been recently cleaned, fresh and sterile.

Rick sat in the chair and gestured for Brendon to take a seat on the sofa, which he did.

"What's on your mind, Rick?"

Rick hesitated, pursed his lips, squinted his eyes, and pushed his fingers together like he was doing some kind of isometric exercise. Then, "I can see that you're genuinely concerned for Amy. If you weren't, I think you would have found a way to get by me like you got by everyone else. But, you waited, and now you're sitting here chatting with me. I appreciate your willingness to hear me out. And, I'll make this offer; if, after you've heard what I have to say, you still want to see her, I'll go and get her. I'll wake her up if I have too."

He sat back in the sofa. It crunched the way good leather does, and settled around him as he relaxed his body for what he expected to be a most unusual discussion. "Sounds fair to me."

"You saw her performance tonight?"

"That's what I came for."

"What did you think?"

"I thought she was amazing."

"A marvel, wouldn't you say?"

"Yes. She has a real gift."

"Indeed she does. It would be a shame if she gave it up. Don't you think?"

"Do you think I'm trying to take her out of this business?"

"Maybe."

"That's not why I came. And that's not my intention. It never was. I want her to do whatever makes her happy. I am committed to her happiness. Married or not, engaged or not, she's free to do as she pleases, and she always will be. I want what's best for her, as I hope you do. If she loves this business, if she wants all it has to offer, I give you my word, I'll support her every step of the way."

"That's nice to hear," he pursed his lips and squinted again. The look reminded Brendon of chess matches he'd seen on television; the kind players make when they are sizing up their next move. "Did she tell you that I have supported her every step of the way? You tell me that you will support her, but I already have. Your promise is for the future, a future that you can't imagine, because you weren't there for the past. I know where she's been, and I know where she's going, and how to get her there safely, intact, and happy."

"You have known her longer than I have, that much is true. And, I know how important you have been to her success; she has talked very fondly of you. I hope you don't see me as a threat to your business interest. As I said, I'm interested only in that which is best for her."

"And, you expect me to believe you would let her struggle and suffer for success in this business," Rick said. "I know she has told you about her recent physical setbacks."

"Nothing comes without a price. I thought the vineyard would be easy to run after my father retired. He'd done all the grunt work building the business. But I found out quickly that if I wanted to hold my ground, not to mention grow, I was going to have to struggle and fight for every inch. Success is always costly. Paying the price makes us what we are."

"So you think the struggle might be good for her."

"If it's what she really wants," Brendon said, "yes."

"Will you concede that I have a different perspective on her than you do?"

"Absolutely, you've had more time with her and you've been able to witness every night what I saw tonight for the first time. I envy you that."

"Envy?" Rick seemed genuinely surprised by the choice of word. "Well, I suppose I can see why. I've been with her while you've been on a farm in California. But I've given this one more than my time and advice. I've been more than her business manager. I've been at her side for the vast majority of her performances; I've negotiated every deal. I was with her when, if you saw her, you might have said she's a no-talent wannabe. I've seen her develop; I've nurtured her career the way you nurture your vineyard. And, now she's ready, like a grape on a vine, she's ready for harvesting, and the time for harvesting is right now. If you missed the ripe moment in your fields, what would happen to the vintage?"

"It might be salvageable. But it would never be as good as it could have been."

"Exactly." Rick sat forward on the chair. For a moment Brendon thought Rick might jump at him so Brendon sat back farther in his. The manager's energy was intense, a palatable substance in the air. Brendon had known a few smooth talkers in his time but none as brash as this one. "Before this night, this moment, she couldn't have handled what she's about to be offered and after this night, she may never find such an opportunity again. This is her moment—the moment she's been waiting for all of her life."

"She's a human being, Rick. She's not a fruit ripening to harvest. My grapes grow for the purpose of being made into wine. But she lives to know the joy of living, and to know that joy she has to be free to make her own decisions. I know she's grateful for everything you've done for her and so am I, but if she's struggling right now it's not because of me."

"She's in crisis, Brendon. She's losing her nerve. She's not sure what it is, but I've seen it before. She's double-minded, and you are the reason."

"Please."

"What other explanation is there?"

"I know she's having doubts." Brendon said. "I've even encouraged her to explore them. We all have doubts from time to time. Doubts will either strengthen our resolve, or drive us into areas more suited to our natural gifts."

"What if I told you she never had doubts before you entered the picture? What if I told you she loved her life and her career until she started kicking back in a vineyard in California?"

"Well, then I'd say that maybe she never knew she had options."

"Options?" Rick said. "Is that what you call it?"

"Yes, that's what I call it. Everyone needs them, even you."

"Have you ever been on a vacation?"

"What does that have to do with Amy's future?"

"How did you feel during the trip?"

"Relaxed and refreshed," Brendon said. "Like everyone else on vacation. Vacations are fun. We all need them."

"And what about after you returned home, returned to work?"

"I love my work."

"Three-hundred-and-sixty-five days a year?"

"Everyone needs a break," Brendon admitted. "Breaks make us more productive in the long run."

"Yes, everyone needs a break, and that's what you've been for Amy. You're a break, a vacation spot. Lately she's been wondering what life would be like if the vacation could go on, if she never actually had to return to work, to the real world, to her real life. If she stays there too long she might lose the one thing she loves the most, and that not because she wants to or because it's what's best for her, but because she's afraid. People only dream about living another life when they're afraid. Do you think she should let fear decide the course of her life?"

"Fear?" Brendon had never considered that it might be liberating for her to face down her fear, go as far as she could go, and then with her success in hand, decide.

"She's terrified," Rick explained. "The realization of a dream is terrifying for most people. They have to adjust to the fact that it isn't everything they hoped it would be. They have to adjust to the fact that life doesn't stop being hard simply because you make more money or have more notoriety. For some people it's easier to live for a dream than to realize one. For some people it's easier to keep dreaming than start living.

"I asked you if you thought I had a different perspective and you were kind enough to concede I did. Even if I didn't care about her on a personal level, I'd still care a great deal about the opportunity that at this moment stands in jeopardy. Do you have any idea how few ever get this close? Most magicians support themselves with nine to five jobs and think they're doing well if their profits from magic can pay for some new props. Amy's one of the lucky ones. She has talent, she has drive, and this night, this one moment, right now, she has opportunity."

"I didn't come here to jeopardize that."

"I believe you, but there's something else."

"Please continue."

"I have a fear too and I think you should share it."

"And it is?"

"If Amy gives up her work, her dream, to go chase a fantasy, sooner or later she's going to regret it. She's going to resent it, and she's going to resent the one that talked her into it."

"But I haven't talked her into it. I haven't tried to persuade her one way or the other."

"Maybe you haven't. If she runs, it may be by no fault of your own. But if you're the one she runs to then you'll be there when the regrets come. Do you think she'll blame herself? Do you think she'll say, 'Brendon loved me. He gave me the space I needed to come to my own conclusions. Like it or not, it was my decision. It's my fault, my life, my responsibility.' Do you think she'll say that, Brendon? My experience is that most people look for someone to blame. It doesn't matter who, as long as they don't have to blame themselves, as long as they don't have to accept the terrible responsibility for their own lives and their own happiness. It's been that way since the first man and woman pointed fingers at each other in the garden of paradise. And, I can promise you that for Amy, there won't be any second chance. She has a moment, and her moment is right now. If she misses it, it will never come again."

Brendon let out a heavy sigh. It was embarrassing. He certainly hadn't intended to sigh.

Rick smiled. It was a tiny smile. It was clear he didn't want Brendon to know he was smiling. Rick had made his point and Brendon could feel it stabbing him in the gut.

"Who do you think she'll resent most in the years to come?" Rick asked. "Will it be me for asking you to leave? Do you think she'll resent me for asking you to give her the chance to find out what she really wants? Or, do you think she'll resent you for giving her an out, for helping and enabling her weakness?"

"I can't make anybody believe anything," Brendon struggled to resist but his efforts were futile. "If she's having doubts …"

"If Amy's having doubts it's because she has options, it's because she didn't burn a bridge like the people who made it in this business did. Don't be that option, at least not now. Wait. That's all I'm asking you to do."

"How long?"

"Until the negotiations are over, a day maybe two."

Brendon rested his head that now felt heavy and weary against the plush leather top of the sofa. Its softness comforted him and eased his tension. For a moment, he closed his eyes. Rick reminded him of his marketing director at the vineyard. He had hired him for his talent at persuasion, and he was beginning to believe that most successful marketing people shared the same gift. It was like hypnosis. It sounded noble. It was the only argument that might persuade him. It could be manipulation plain and simple. But like all great lies, and the manipulators that tell them, it had a kernel of truth. There was merit in what Rick said. Maybe despite himself, Rick had actually said something true and valuable.

Brendon opened his eyes, and stared up at the ceiling.

'The first one who speaks loses,' his marketing director once told him. Rick had made his pitch, and was now trying to close the deal.

But, the decision was his. He could walk out the door and go straight to Amy's dressing room, or he could leave her to make a decision on her own that could impact her life and his life forever. Rick had another agenda, he was certain of that. Rick's interests were his own, and they were clearly self-serving. Rick might believe himself to be concerned for her greater good, but the manager's concern more closely resembled the concern of an investment banker for his stock portfolio than it was anything like love.

He dreamed of their wedding day, of the children they might share, of waking up next to her every morning, and kissing her to sleep every night. They were the dreams he most often had of her but now he could see that day when she might come to resent him. He would ultimately lose her if she ever held in her heart a bitterness and blame for a distraction he caused at a time when she should have been left alone. It was a sure bet that Rick had no intentions of doing the same, but that didn't matter. If she decided in favor of the contract, and if in fact it was even offered to her, they could always negotiate their relationship. If on the other hand, his presence distracted her, and she lost out on the opportunity all together, then she would never really know. That was the scenario that gave him the most cause for concern.

He wanted to see her. But did he want it for selfish reasons? And was he willing to leave her to face the most important decision of her life unencumbered by the complications his very presence might cause her?

"I'm more than a vacation spot to Amy," he finally said, "and she's more than a vacation spot to me. You need to know that. I love her."

"I understand," Rick swallowed hard. Brendon's honest and heart felt confession must have made some kind of impact on this heart-of-iron manager's soul. "And I don't mean to trivialize your relationship or your love, but vacations tend to create a little bit of an illusion and so does love. We all concoct elaborate expectations and images in our minds. In some ways, we all believe that 'the grass is always greener.'

"I think she's under the delusion that her life is going to be so much better than it is now if she can get away from the difficult and challenging, and take life easy on a farm. It's a fantasy. Maybe her love for you isn't, but the lifestyle certainly is. You know it and I know it."

"I know you think so."

"Has she ever been around long enough to see the work, the work that I'm sure you and the others on the vineyard do?"

"No, she hasn't."

"And what if she saw it?"

"Then she'd know how difficult it is to run a successful vineyard."

"Exactly. And have you tried to shield her from the labor, and expose her only to the fruits, if you'll pardon the pun?"

"Perhaps I have. I certainly don't work as hard when she's around. I try to spend most of my time with her. But, I put in long days when she's not there."

He didn't need or want any more of Rick's persuasive tactics. He still struggled, however, with a primal urge to talk the situation over with Amy. He wanted to walk past Rick and see her smiling face when he greeted her. He'd traveled a long way to do that, and in some ways he wanted to complete his mission for its own sake. But he wanted her to be certain, even more than he wanted to see her in that moment. He wanted her to work through all of her choices and arrive at love on her own terms.

Love is born in freedom. The freedom to choose is the womb of love. If his presence even remotely interfered with that freedom, she would, at some point come to resent their love.

"Brendon," Rick interrupted his thoughts. "Amy's personal life is none of my concern, but, I'm her manager. She needs this weekend; she needs to focus, to be as sharp as she can be. Can you give her that, one weekend? Don't call her; don't see her, let her concentrate. If your love is real it'll stand the test of time. Are you confident enough in your love to offer her this one chance?"

She had a turning point in her life to deal with. What was the role he should play in it? He'd already asked her to marry him. She could have said yes then and there, but she hesitated. And now he stood in front of Rick with no real claim to make.

Rick's argument was weighing heavier in his mind as he pondered it. He was beginning to believe that she would regret it if she didn't give herself fully to the challenge before her. Whatever else they did or accomplished together, this one regret could eventually outweigh even their love. He wanted her to have every opportunity to make a decision. Most of all, he wanted her to be happy and maybe if she could overcome her fear and find real success in her chosen field, she would be happy, and not only happy but free, free to leave, free to love.

"Okay," Brendon said. "I'll go."

CHAPTER 28

Amy reclined on the sofa in her dressing room for several minutes after Rick left. Her body wanted sleep but her mind rehearsed with pleasure and affection. She wished Brendon could have seen it. It was the best she'd ever done. She tried to remember a sweeter moment but couldn't. Tonight's performance would be the one by which all others would be measured.

She had hit every cue, her timing had been perfect, and the effect on the audience had been exactly what she had hoped for. If her career ended this night, she would be satisfied. Everything came together and as she performed she felt an energy in her body that carried her through. It was as if an intelligent entity had been working on her behalf. It was an entity that not only inspired and controlled her movements but it also connected her to her audience in a way she'd never known before.

She smiled, and then she stretched and tucked her hands behind her head. Serendipity had worked in her favor tonight and the blissful rewards of its presence were hers to savor.

Unable to "sleep it off" the way Rick asked her to, she slipped from the sofa and exchanged her bathrobe for a form-fitting pair of faded black jeans and a ribbon cross-laced bodice. She sat down at her vanity and began the process of peeling layers of stage makeup from her face.

She glanced up at Rick's reflection in the mirror when he entered. Her eyes grew round and her jaw dropped when she saw the roses in his hands. She spun on her stool and sprang to her feet.

He held them out to her and she reached for them. Then she caught herself in the embarrassing act of grabbing, and waited until the flowers were formally offered. When they were, she buried her nose in them, inhaled deeply, and smiled.

"Be careful," he admonished, "there might be thorns, bees or who knows what else lurking in the midst of those things."

"'These things,' as you call them, are my favorite; what a surprise." She searched for a card but as there was none; she assumed that Rick had made a lucky guess or maybe it was simply her night, serendipity's way of saying she was highly favored at this one moment. "You know, sometimes you amaze me. You've never bought me flowers before, and tonight of all nights. They're beautiful. Thank you so much."

"You deserve them, Amy."

"Now this is something Brendon would do. He loves to shower me with little thoughtful, appropriate for the moment, gifts like this. In fact, I can't remember a time I've come to visit when he didn't have fresh cut pink roses waiting for me in my room. It's so strange that you would choose pink roses. I mean, you've never even bought me flowers before and the one time you do, you manage to choose my favorite. It's a sign that's what it is. Tonight is the perfect night. This is my night. And, you've put the finishing touches on the canvas of the evening. Thank you so much." She walked over to him and kissed him. He looked surprised, a kind of caught-in-the-act expression. But she found the look endearing like the blush of a child.

"Well, Brendon's not here."

"Yes. I know. I really wasn't expecting him. He never said he'd come, and I never formally invited him. But we spoke so much of this show, and he always seems to do the unexpected. I guess I'm a little disappointed that he is not here. And, when I saw the flowers, well, I knew Brendon could never get by you, so I figured he had given these to you to deliver."

"Perhaps you've misjudged both of us."

"Yes," she looked up from the flowers and smiled coyly at Rick biting at her lower lip ever so gently. "Perhaps I have."

"Anyway," he said, "its best he didn't show up tonight. I need you to concentrate on the deal right now and for the rest of the weekend."

"You're right. Besides, this is your gift, and I don't mean to offend you by speaking of Brendon in your moment of triumph."

"My moment of triumph?"

"Have you ever given flowers to anyone?"

"My mother."

"I see."

"Once."

"Oh."

"A long, long time ago."

"No doubt a very long time ago," she laughed.

Rick smiled but looked away from her glance and started fidgeting.

"What's wrong?" she asked as she returned to her makeup and rested the flowers beside her on the vanity.

He came up behind her and began to gently massage her shoulders and neck.

"Absolutely nothing. The show was perfect. Your delivery was over the top. You got a real talent for acting. Maybe I should be trying to expand your options. I've always believed in doing one thing better than anyone else but you might be able to crossover."

"You think so, do you?" she smiled as she continued to work on her face.

"Sometimes I wonder what might have happened if I had left you to struggle in New York."

"I'd have starved," she laughed.

"For a time," he said, "but I think your talent would have brought you to the surface somewhere. And, it might have been in the mainstream, theatre or film or both."

"Or," she pondered, "I might have waited tables the rest of my days, or maybe starred in a commercial for toothpaste or something. Why speculate? What is, is. I have no regrets."

"None?"

She snapped her makeup box closed and pumped some moisturizer into her hand. She started to rub it into her face but paused, bent her head back and looked straight up at him. It was not his most flattering angle but he was cute all the same. She put a gooey hand on his and said emphatically, "None."

"You're a good girl, Amy," he said as he kissed the top of her head. She returned to moisturizing, and Rick rubbed his hands together vigorously until his damp hand was dry.

"Maybe I wasn't acting," she said.

"What do you mean?"

"I mean the best actors never act. I was reliving every genuine emotion I ever felt for my dog and my dad, and even though I couldn't see the images that the audience was seeing, I knew they were there, like I know my daddy's near me, at times. I could feel him, and I could feel Sammy too. I think somewhere they are both proud and warmed because of what we did tonight. It was a remembrance. Not a somber, morbid grief, but a fond, 'I remember you.' That's what they would have wanted. My dad used to tell me that all he needed to be happy was to be sure that I was happy. And, I am happy tonight. I feel more in touch with my dad than I did the last time I saw him alive. And, that makes me happy."

"I'm glad," he yawned as he patted her shoulders and sat on the folding metal chair next to her vanity.

"It's not like I'm still grieving," she continued, watching her own reflection.

He looked at his watch, and yawned again.

"I still miss them, but I have a strange sense of peace about it, like everything's okay, like they really aren't gone, at least not for good." She looked over at him. "Do you believe in an afterlife?"

"I don't know; I guess so." He looked at his watch again.

"Late for a date, Rick?"

"I'm all yours," he smiled up at her.

"Really?"

"Yes."

"Even if I want to talk about something other than business."

He closed his eyes and scratched his head as if weighing the pros and the cons. "I suppose at least in some form we go on, if not in some kind of conscious way then at least as food for worms."

"That's my Rick."

"Worms that feed birds, that feed people, and so on, and so on."

"Is that all you want for yourself, to be worm food?"

"Does it make a difference what I want or what it comforts me to believe? Maybe what will be will be no matter how much I wish otherwise. But one thing I'm sure of …"

"Today, right, Rick?"

"Today is all any one of us can ever really be sure of, and today is a wonderful day for you and for me."

"Well, I'm not talking about worms or the cycle of life, or *carpe diem* or any of that stuff. I'm talking about an eternal consciousness, a knowing, an awareness of love for eternity. I believe in it, Rick. And, tonight I could feel it."

"Well, whatever it is you think you felt, however it is you managed to deliver that performance, it absolutely killed."

"I wish you wouldn't use that word. It's so negative."

"You know what I mean."

"Yes, I do."

"You mastered; you ruled; the stage belonged to you as did every member of that audience; that's what matters, Amy. Victory, success, the thrill of facing a difficult challenge and coming out of the battle unscathed."

"Is it?"

"That's what matters now, and now is all we've got. I know you have a hard time dealing with first time illusions, and this one will probably never see a theatre again, but you, my dear, were magnificent. If there's a contract to be had in this town, you deserve to have it."

She smiled and softly blushed.

"Amy, you're a natural."

"I don't feel like a natural."

"Being good at something," he explained, "doesn't mean you don't have to work hard at it or that it's going to be easy. What you accomplished this evening required long rehearsals. It also required years of experience in lesser illusions, for lesser money, and lesser opportunity. It meant putting your heart and soul into routines that either never get seen or get a dull response when they do. That's the business. But when all is said and done, you are one of the best."

"You're sweet," she put a hand to his face. It was a bit bristly; he probably hadn't shaved since before breakfast. At that moment the energy left her body. She looked up at her reflection and saw her face change. It suddenly became drawn and tired. Dark circles formed under her eyes. She yawned, stretched, then slumped in her seat, and dropped her head on her folded arms.

CHAPTER 29

It was back, Amy's weakness, her exhaustion. The pump was gone and now it was time to pay for the borrowed time. Even with her head buried in the darkness of her arms, she was dizzy.

"Why don't you lie down on the couch a while, take a little nap. Jason and Freddie are packing up the truck. I'll join them and let you sleep it off."

There it was again. Rick's magical elixir, 'Sleep it off.'

"You read my mind lover." She left her chair and weakly limped to the sofa where she stretched out on her back like a kitten preparing for a long rest.

Rick sat down next to her. He stroked her short black hair gently; it was a tentative touch like he wasn't sure he had permission or like he wasn't sure how to be nurturing.

"Thanks for the flowers," she closed her eyes and kissed his palm. "It matters, you know, it means a lot to me. It means you care."

She could sleep with him watching over her. She trusted him and she felt at ease under his watchful eye. She trusted him with her career and with the show and the props and with Jason and Freddie, and she trusted him to see her through the weekend, to keep her safe from the pit bulls around the business table. She was beginning to doze; time and space were blurring in that blissful space between awake and asleep.

"I want to ask you something," he said, but was she dreaming? She opened her eyes and her mind cleared.

"What is it?"

"Will you marry Brendon?"

She smiled, squeezed his hand and kissed it again, but she didn't answer.

"Do you think I'm prying?"

"I don't think you ever understood the concept of a boundary to begin with, so I can't accuse you of prying. But, I'm not ready to talk about it."

"I need to know."

"And, I will tell you when I'm ready."

"If you know now, I want you to tell me now," he said.

"I've given it a lot of thought, but I haven't spoken to Brendon yet. I'd like to talk with him before we discuss it."

"So you've made a decision?"

"I believe I have," she said as she yawned, closed her eyes and stretched.

She squeezed his hand in a way that expressed both appreciation and finality. She was tired and wanted to sleep, if only for a few moments. But she knew him all too well. He had to be in control. He had to know where he stood. He had little tolerance for ambiguity and he certainly wouldn't let the issue rest if he even suspected an answer was to be had. And now, in acknowledging that she had made a decision, he would surely never give up.

"Amy," he said, "I know you're tired but I'd like to tell you something."

She opened her eyes wide again.

"There comes a time, in every career I've managed, when a decision must be made. Sometimes this decision, this crossroad, seems to the performer something small and insignificant. The lucky ones recognize it for what it is, a life altering decision. Regardless of what we may perceive, the fact is every decision we make is life altering. We can never follow two paths at once. We must choose, each moment of each day, we must decide what our destiny will be, what really matters to us, what and whom we love, and what and whom we do not love. And, most of the time once we've decided, the road we left behind simply ceases to exist. Even if we want to return, we never can.

"You'll never be able to return to this moment. Once it has past, it will never come again. Your decision today will determine your success or failure this weekend and not only this weekend but for the rest of your life."

"Rick," she sat up on the sofa, "I can't believe my ears. Aren't you the never-give-up guy? Aren't you the one that's always telling me how much better it's going to get?"

"It's taken me a lot of years to get you here," he said. "If you lose heart on me now do you think we could get it back? Do you honestly believe we'll ever get another shot like this one?"

"I think my decision to marry or not will have little bearing on my performance either on stage or in the negotiations."

"It will. I know. I've been here before. This is your time. I know that you do not believe your choice has anything to do with your career, but it does. In the coming hours, we will be negotiating the toughest deal of our lives. I want to know where I stand, and I need to know where you stand."

"You will stand with me as you always have. And I will stand with you when it comes to negotiating deals. But, when it comes to marriage, you know I love the show. Married or not, I'm here, I'm committed. It'll be the same as it always was."

"You can't believe that."

"I do," she said.

"Then you can't truly love Brendon."

"And why not?" she laughed.

"Because it's impossible to hold two great passions in your heart, together, at the same time. When you are with Brendon, the show diminishes in importance, doesn't it?"

"You said yourself that my performance tonight was over the top."

"And when you're working, where is Brendon?"

"He's on the farm."

"Not physically, Amy. I know where he is. I mean in your heart? How often did you think of him tonight?"

"I love them both," she said. "I think constantly of both, and both are always with me. It's a question of the priority of the moment."

"For now."

"Didn't you say that that's all we have?"

"Yes," he admitted. "I did. But, love grows. And that which does not increase, will almost inevitably decrease. Magic will demand more, and so will Brendon. You will have to choose. No one can keep two great lovers satisfied for very long. And, those who try, often end with both hating them."

"You don't know Brendon," she frowned, shook her head and looked up at him disapprovingly. "He'll never ask me to choose."

"He won't have to," he said. "Your own heart will demand it. Any love worth having is worth giving all you have to give. You can have a show business career that is insanely successful. I know you can. Or, you can have an absolutely wonderful relationship with one very special man. But, you'll never have both, not in this lifetime."

She interlocked her fingers with his and then she bent his wrist back until he grimaced. She wasn't intentionally trying to cause him pain but she didn't want to make a decision between her lover and her career. It wasn't fair. No one else had to. This isn't the nineteenth century. "Are you suggesting that a woman can't have a successful career and a successful marriage at the same time?"

"No," he laughed and seemed genuinely surprised and amused. "Sweetheart, this has nothing at all to do with gender. If you were a man I'd be telling you the same thing. In fact, I've already had this conversation with more than one man in the business. You might be able to be a successful attorney, or an accountant, or a programmer or something. It's not about success versus marriage. It's about passion. This business demands passion, it demands undivided attention and absolute focus. If you're going to make it in this town, divided loyalties simply won't do. I want you married to the show. You need to want it too."

She had never lied to him, and she never would. He didn't always like what she had to say, and he didn't always agree with her decisions, but she had never deceived him. She was tempted now more than ever before. As she sat staring into his eyes, eyes that begged for answer, she wanted to tell him, 'you're right. I'm not marrying him. It was simply a fling.' But it wasn't just a fling. It was love and it was growing inside her like a baby. She wanted to see that baby grow. She wanted Brendon and that was the truth that was too painful to speak. He wouldn't like it, but he deserved to hear it.

"Will you marry him?" he asked again.

She let go of his hand, folded her arms under her chest, and bowed her head.

"Amy."

"I'm in love with him Rick," she felt a hot tear escape her eye and she quickly wiped it away with her hand.

"Give me this weekend," he sighed.

"I will. I need to know as much as you do. I want to know if I can do it, if they want me. I want to know what I'm worth."

"Have you no doubts about this man?"

"Can a person ever be sure?"

"I think so," he said. "And you're not, are you?"

"No," she said. "I'm not sure about anything and I haven't been in some time. But you are. That's one of the things I love about you. You're always sure. You always know what to do what choice to make, which door has the grand prize hiding behind it. You're a rock for me, and I love you for it. I need this weekend as much as you do, but maybe for different reasons."

"These negotiations won't be easy, and when they're over, the results might not live up to your dreams. But if you really want it, it will be the substance from which all your wildest fantasies for this business can be realized. It's opportunity,

Amy; plain and simple, it's opportunity. And opportunity is what you make of it."

"I'm with you, Rick. I'm right here, right now, holding your hand, and I'm telling you I'm in. I can do this. I promise."

"If you want to survive in this business." He brought her hand to his mouth and kissed it. "Then you can't let the ups and downs of a single performance, or single negotiations determine your future."

"You don't think this is going to go well, do you?"

"I know what to expect," he said. "I've been here before. In your state of mind, I fully expect you to turn tail and run."

"I've never let you down. How can you think that I would do such a thing?"

"You've never been in love before."

"Where's the Rick McAlister that fears no man, that never takes no for an answer, and never, never, never says die?"

"He's waiting for his star to do the same."

She closed her eyes and laid her head back until it hit the wall.

"I can't give him up," she said. "I love him too much, and I love you too much, and Jason and Freddie, and the show. You don't understand. How can you? Have you ever been in love, really in love?

"Perhaps someday you'll meet a girl. And, when you look at her, you'll know in your heart that you'd do anything for her, you'd give anything for her. Someday you'll know what love is. But today is not that day.

"You love the dream. At night when the lights are out, and you're supposed to be asleep, you lie in bed staring into the darkness imagining the glorious future that you and I will have together. Me, the star of Las Vegas, and you the feared and respected manager that gave her wings to fly. This vision is where your passion lies. Right now, you think that's all there is to living. But that's not all there is, not by a long shot.

"Someday, maybe someday soon, you are going to look into the eyes of a woman and tell her that you love her, not for what you're afraid to lose, but for what you hope to win, for what you must win. When that day comes, and I know it will, you'll understand.

"Sometimes, when I see your capacity to give, something I don't think you've ever seen in yourself, I know that you're gonna make a great lover. And, I truly do envy the girl that frees that part of you. Life isn't all business, and we don't have to sacrifice our souls to succeed. You'll see."

"I have seen," Rick said. "It's you who has not."

CHAPTER 30

In the afterglow of giving her best, with the echo of applause lingering in her ear, Amy returned to her hotel room unescorted and alone. She didn't feel particularly exhausted but it was late and her bed looked inviting. She wanted to lie down and stretch for a moment before slipping out of her clothes and under the cozy covers. But once her head hit the pillow, she was asleep.

In her dreams she walked the streets of Philadelphia. She was a girl again holding onto her daddy's strong hand as he led her down a busy inner city sidewalk.

"Where are we going, daddy?" she asked.

"To a special place," he told her.

They came to a stop in front of a store room window. Behind the glass, a golden python had wrapped itself around a pole. Tightly wrapped, as it was, it still towered above her. Little birds were feeding on seed that had been scattered about on the floor of the display.

"Why are the birdies in the snake's cage, daddy?"

"Dinner," he said.

The snake seemed to recognize her. It blinked then stretched its diamond shaped head until its nose bounced off of the window. It bobbed its head up and down, and then in a circular motion seeking escape from its glass container, seeking a closer look at her. It didn't seem interested in the birds. Its tongue slithered in and out through its frown of a mouth.

"What is this place, daddy? Why are we here?"

"There is a magic shop upstairs. A beautiful place I want you to see."

"I want to go home."

She tugged on her father's hand. She wanted him to take her away but his grip was tight, it squeezed her tiny hand until it hurt. She tried to dig her feet in to hold her ground but she couldn't slow her father's momentum.

The door they approached was red and weathered. The brilliance of its color had faded long ago and the bare wood bled through in spots. On the top of the door in faded gold lettering were the words, Magic Shop, and beneath them was a tarnished brass knocker that looked liked a lion's head.

"Who wishes entry," the lion spoke.

She tried to hide behind her father but with one eye she peeked around his leg.

"I've brought my daughter," he pulled at her and pushed until she stood in front of him.

"Ah yes," the lion said. "Master will be pleased."

The eyes of the blackened beast glowed like the golden lights of a Christmas tree as it stared down at her. It smiled and flecks of black soot like dry skin descended at her feet. The door opened but beyond its frame was utter darkness.

She pushed herself into her father's leg and wrapped her arms around his enormous thigh. Near his body, she felt safe.

As they started up a narrow set of steps, enclosed and dark, he pulled up on her hand as if pulling it would force her foot up as well.

"You're going to love the dealer. I told him you were coming today?"

"Daddy, please take me home."

"Come along," her father laughed at her timidity. "You'll thank me for this later." He dragged her by the arm the rest of the way up the flight of stairs. The wood yielded under their weight with a crack, she feared the stairs might collapse beneath them.

The walls were covered with damp naked bodies that slithered like slugs up and down, back and forth. Their eyes gleamed and glistened in the darkness. A hand reached out to her. She pushed herself deeper into her father's large thigh and it brushed her hair as she passed by.

"I've touched her," it whispered and the others moaned in envy.

When they finally reached the top stair, her father opened a small, narrow, old wooden door and they walked through into a tiny magic shop. A bell rang when the door opened. Posters of magicians long dead covered the walls of the old shop, much as she'd seen on many occasions in Dante's home.

The smells of books and cigarettes and lacquer were familiar and comforting, as were the display cases and the props within. Like most magic shops, this one was cluttered with piles of magazines and half-opened boxes. A cloud of cigarette smoke filled the air and left its signature on every object in the room. Before she knew what cigarettes were, she believed it was the smell of magic and she loved it. Amidst the clutter a treasure lay hid, another step toward the dream. And the wonder of it began to dominate her mind and obscure her fear. The right book, or the right prop, the promise of it was here in the shop, waiting to be found, waiting to be possessed by she for whom it was intended.

The dealer never revealed more than the student was ready to receive. The rules were simple and she knew them well. If she did not know what it was she sought, the dealer would make small talk to inspire a vision within her and she would leave with something she liked but couldn't grow with. But, if she knew her need, if her destiny was clear, the dealer would guide her, like a game of hot and cold until she discovered as if on her own the treasure she sought, the perfect prop, book or gimmick. It was all there, an endless reservoir, in the magic shop.

The tiny shop before her had all the romance and mystery of the greatest shops she'd ever seen and more. This shop was small and secluded, well off the beaten path. The best shops were all hidden, like the secrets of magic. The treasures she'd find in this place would be rare indeed.

The moment she walked through the door, her father was gone and she was no longer a child. She was a strong, young, beautiful woman, more secure and sure of herself than she'd ever been as a little girl. For a moment she continued to hold her hand out as if held by her father. And for a moment she continued to feel his grip though he was gone. She held her now empty hand up and looked at it. No trace of her father remained.

"Daddy," she called out but there was no answer.

A small man appeared. He couldn't have been any taller than four feet. He had long black hair and a beard. He wore bell-bottom jeans, sandals, and an East Indian beaded shirt. A peace sign dangled from a long gold chain around his neck. In his mouth was a burning cigarette. Limp, flaccid ashes arched from the end of it and looked as though they would fall to the floor if he so much as breathed.

"I've been expecting you," he said in a gritty, old raspy voice. A cloud of smoke escaped as he spoke and covered his head.

He walked past her. He did not look up and though she couldn't get a good look at his face, he seemed familiar.

He stopped at a door. It was a hard wooden door as if from some old castle. It had a small window in the center toward the top that was covered and almost completely obscured by wrought iron bars. A large ring of keys dangled from his belt and he shuffled for one, a long one, worn with age. When he found it, he used it to unlock and open the door. Its rusty and old hinges creaked as if it hadn't been open in many years. Cobwebs attached to the door and the wall stretched until they broke.

"Come child. I have something to show you."

"I don't think I want to go in there." But despite her verbal protests she found herself following this peculiar figure of a man through the door and down a long dark corridor. It was musty, damp and cold inside with the smell of age and decay. As she followed him, the door behind her creaked and then slammed with a shout of finality. She looked back into absolute darkness.

The dealer had advanced rapidly in the brief moment she'd taken her eyes from him. He scurried off in front of her but she saw him more distinctly when he passed a torch that hung from the wall. Under the torch were black iron manacles that held a man captive by his wrists. The dealer hadn't even noticed him. He was naked and skinny, skeletal, on the verge of death. It was as if he'd been hanging there for days, weeks, or months without food or water.

She ran to the man. His wrists were bleeding from an obviously futile attempt to free himself. Her emotions were overcome when his eyes met hers. She couldn't bear to witness such human suffering. She tried to free him but could not.

"Save yourself," he whispered when, as she fought with his manacles, her ear neared his mouth, "while there's still time, run, run from this place."

She backed away for him.

"I can't free you," she said. "Help me," she screamed. "Somebody help me."

"Run, run from this place."

"I want to help you. How can I help you?"

The man began to convulse. He beat himself against the wall and then breathed his last. His eyes continued to stare but they were empty and lifeless.

She backed herself against the opposite wall of the tunnel. A black, nearly invisible arm reached from the wall at her ankle and grabbed a hold of it. Another grabbed her other ankle; another wrapped around her throat and two more took hold of her wrists. She struggled to free herself but their grip only tightened.

The manacles snapped apart and the man's dead body fell to the ground. His bones shattered under the force of the fall. Large black beetles scurried from the walls and descended upon the lifeless body. They began to consume it in a frenzy, what small pieces remained they carried off into the darkness.

"We have another," came a whisper in the dark.

"She's a lovely one," another whispered. "It'll be fun to watch her rot."

She felt her body being moved toward the chains.

"No," she cried. "Let me go."

The chains moved toward her like the hungry tentacles of an octopus.

"We love you, Amy."

"We need you, Amy."

"We'll protect you."

"You'll be safe with us."

"Safe and secure."

"Isn't that what you want?"

Whispers surrounded her, their presence, their voices, their strength was irresistible but they had no faces, no bodies, only shadowy limbs that held her in their grip.

She screamed. She didn't want to share the fate of the man she'd tried to free. She fought and struggled but her efforts were futile. Their force was too great.

"Help me please," she cried but no one came, no one heard but the whispering voices in the wall.

And then she was released. She fell to the ground and when she looked up there were no shadows and no whispers, only the silhouette of the tiny dealer. He stood far enough away from the light to keep his face in darkness.

"Why am I here?" she asked him as she lay on the cold ground weeping.

"Because you want to be," the dealer said.

"No," she protested.

"I told you to follow me. Why did you stop?"

"I'm sorry," she cried as she pushed herself onto her feet. "I won't do it again." When she looked up his stride had already taken him several yards from her. She ran after him.

Under the next torch was another naked skeleton of a man, barely breathing, and barely alive, hanging by his wrists from manacles like the first.

"Water," he pleaded.

There was a dark wooden bucket near his bare and blistered feet. It was filled with water.

She looked down the tunnel. The dealer was moving away from her rapidly.

"Water," he pleaded again.

Crying, she picked up the bucket and poured it toward his mouth.

He gulped and gulped and then began to choke. She removed the bucket that obscured his face. Leaches had attached themselves to his eyes and nose. They were on his lips and cheeks and they were rapidly swelling with the poor mans blood.

The whispers rushed her with laughter, many at once like a great wind. She dropped the bucket and ran.

"Now you're learning," they called after her. "Never stop to care."

"Where are you taking me?" she screamed and ran as fast as her legs would carry her but the dealer was far away and did not answer.

He kept walking and she kept following.

Eventually they came out of the corridor and into a small chamber. The chamber couldn't have been larger than twelve feet square. There was a black hole; a doorway with no door, in the middle of every wall leading to what she presumed was a corridor and on either side of the hole was a torch. The eight torches gave a brilliant luster and warmth to the room. The walls were made of stone, each individual in shape but somehow fitted together perfectly.

In the center of the room was a rectangular stone slab that was large enough for a single person to lay upon. It seemed to have been cut from a single large stone as there were no seams or joinery of any kind. The slab had a set of manacles like those that held the two victims in the corridor from which she'd emerged.

She had entered the room after the dealer but he was gone and she was alone. She walked toward one opening and then another looking into the darkness of each but seeing nothing.

"Where are you," she screamed into darkness but no answer came except the echo of her own voice. Then the dealer emerged from one of the dark holes.

"Take off your clothes and lie down on your back," he gestured toward the slab.

"No," she said. "I will not. Why? What are you doing? Why do you want me? What's this all about?"

"Don't you want to be a star?" he asked. In the light of the flames his face glowed, but he was still at too much of a distance for her to make out any distinctive feature, or to see clearly into his eyes. His skin looked like wax and as he approached a flame it seemed to melt from his bones.

"If you want to be a star," he said, "you must die."

"No."

"I can make you great."

"I don't want to be great. I don't want to be a star."

"They all wanted to be great," he said. "They all thought they could be the greatest of the generation in which they lived. And, I offered each the same choice I now offer you. I ask again, do you want to be great?"

"I don't want to die."

"You fear the death of your body. You should fear the death of your soul."

"Let me go," she moved toward the door she'd come out of. He was half obstructing it and she hoped he would move back as she approached.

"Run if you want. Run back the way you came if you can remember which door you passed through."

The room began to spin; it wasn't simply the dizziness of her mind. The walls were actually moving around her as if each stone had a life of its own. The stones crackled as they pushed against each other. The doors moved like shells in a three-shell-game, and when the movement stopped, she was thoroughly confused. She had no idea which of the four doors would take her back the way she'd come.

"Remove your clothes and lie down on your back," he began to walk toward her. "Don't be modest. I know you like your own father. He brought you here. Don't you remember? I watched you grow. I saw what your mother did to you. Wouldn't you like to prove your worth to her? I can give that to you. All you have to do is trust me. I love you and soon everyone will."

"You're going to hurt me."

"No. I'm going to put an end to that which hinders you. I will dig out your heart with this knife." He held a blade to her face and it reflected the light of the flame in her eye. "But I promise, you will live. You will live for me, for the dealer, and I will make you great, like the others."

"Who were those men on the wall?"

"Men you should have passed by without a thought—men you will pass by when I possess your heart."

He finally stood close enough that every detail of his small face was clear. His skin was as wax, and it was melting, but underneath was another layer of skin. It was leathery and reptilian, dark and red. His eyes were black, empty sockets.

She screamed at the sight of him and ran for the closest way out. She ran down a corridor hoping that it was the way she'd entered. When she passed the man still in agony, still screaming and struggling under the leaches that consumed his face, she knew she was moving in the right direction. She wanted to help him, but he was beyond her help, and she found comfort in the thought that he would soon be dead. She ran until at last she reached the door.

She struggled to open the door. She beat against it and screamed.

The disembodied whispers were distant but advancing.

Again she screamed and beat upon the door.

"Amy, is that you?"

"Dante, Dante, open the door."

His face peered through the iron bars that obstructed the tiny window.

"But, aren't you enjoying the illusion?"

"It's no illusion. Open the door, Dante."

"The dealer said he had a special piece that he knew you'd appreciate."

"Please," she wept and slid down the wooden door to the ground. "Please let me out."

"Alright. If that's what you want."

The door opened and she crawled out. She wrapped herself around his legs.

"Shut the door," she said.

"But Amy—"

"Shut it, Dante"

He did. Then he knelt beside her, and hugged her, and kissed the top of her head.

"The dealer can be frightening when you first encounter him. But in time he'll be your closest ally. He means you no harm. We mean you no harm."

"Please get me out of here. There is this little man. I think he's insane …"

"He's the dealer, my dear. He won't hurt you."

"Tell it to the men on the wall in there."

"They failed him," he laughed. "He hates failure. He can't tolerate mistakes. But you won't, you can't. You are destined for greatness."

"And what if I don't want to be great, Dante? What if I simply want to be happy?"

"But without greatness you can never be happy. You will never find contentment on a porch swing, my dear. Let me take you back to the dealer. He's waiting for you."

"I don't want to go," she tightened her arms around his knees so he couldn't take a step toward the door. "I don't want it; I don't want this. I want to be free."

"You want to be free? But, you will never be free. Once you are in the grip, it never lets go. You know that."

"I want to wake up."

"What makes you think you're dreaming," he laughed.

"Please."

"My dear, you are free to go any time you want. Wake up if you truly want to. Leave this dream and never return. But you won't, will you? You're curious, aren't you?"

She pulled herself up with her hands on his belt. With his hands under her arms he helped her to her feet until they stood so close his breath was on her face. She wiped the tears from her eyes. She wasn't afraid while Dante was near. He cared, and would never hurt her.

"I'm leaving, Dante."

"Then go with my blessing," he kissed her head. "But please take the wand with you. It belongs to you now."

On a plush velvet pillow, atop a glass display case sat the wand he'd given her the night before. She reached out and took it, and when she did, the floor suddenly gave out from beneath her feet. She fell. She looked up. Dante stood looking into the abyss into which she'd fallen. His face was diminishing in size rapidly as she plummeted ever deeper. Within seconds he was gone. Darkness surrounded her. Warm wind blew across her face as the earth pulled her.

Then, her left hand caught a branch that grew from the side of the abyss. Her body snapped to a violent stop. She bounced when she hit the wall. Her knees were cut and bruised by the impact. But she didn't let go. Above the branch was a cave. She tried to pull herself up, but her right hand still clutched the wand and her left arm wasn't strong enough to pull the weight of her body alone.

"What are you doing?" she heard someone ask above her. Her mother emerged from the cave. "I told you you'd amount to nothing."

"Help me, mother, please."

"You made your bed," her mother said, "now lie in it."

"Mom, please help me."

She looked down. She couldn't see the bottom. She had no idea how deep it was. Something struck her head from above. Warm blood ran from behind her ear to the back of her neck and down her spine. She looked back to her mother. She had stepped out and onto the branch, but instead of offering assistance, she held a switch in her hand and was beating her with it. It struck her across the face and stung so bad she wanted to let go but she feared the fall more than the beating.

"Mom, please."

"You evil girl," her mother cried. "Let go of this branch and fall to the abyss you crawled out of." She repositioned her foot to the top of Amy's knuckles and twisted it as though she were crushing an insect or snuffing out a cigarette.

Her hand began to bleed. Another slap of the switch caught her across the eyes and momentarily blinded her.

"You deserve to burn in hell. You've been a torment to me since the day you were born."

"Mommy," she cried as she fell. Her mother's smiling, satisfied face diminished and disappeared in the distance.

Then there was light. It was dim, at first, but it was growing rapidly brighter. And it was getting hotter. The temperature was rising with each passing moment.

It rose to an unbearable degree. Below her and approaching rapidly was a pool of fire like molten lava.

She'd never let go of the wand. It remained in the death grip of her right hand. She clung to it as if it would preserve her life against the fall and the flames.

She closed her eyes and screamed anticipating the flame that would consume her body. But, as she was about to be burned alive, a hand caught her left wrist. He body was jerked violently as if a parachute had suddenly opened.

She looked up and into the gleaming face of a being of pure light, and her eyes, used to darkness, had to squint to look at him. He was an angel, a messenger of God. He looked like every angel she'd ever seen in paintings or in books. He looked like what she'd always imagined an angel would look like if one ever cared for her enough to appear.

Though seconds before she feared for her life, she was now flattered and amused by his presence as though he were some kind of celebrity for whom she had some infatuation. She'd always wanted to see an angel and even in her dreams, until this moment, she never had. In some part of her mind, she knew she was only dreaming. But he was with her in whatever terror she found herself, real or imagined.

The angel was white. Not white like a color but like the sun. His robe shimmered like sunlight on still water. And he had wings, beautiful feathered arches the width of which spread from one side of the abyss to the other. With gallant thrusts, his wings fought against the pull of the abyss. The heat from the flame beneath her brushed against her face with every pull of his mighty wings.

His grip was strong, and for the first time, perhaps for the first time in her entire life, she understood what safety really was. His grip redefined any sense of security she had ever known before. It could not fail. Though the flames beneath her raged and hungered for her, as long as she was in his grip, they could not have her.

"Amy," he called out to her. "Drop the wand and take hold of me with both hands."

She looked down at the wand in her hand. She loved it; she loved it more than life itself. It represented all that Dante had ever been, all she had ever known. If she let go of it her life would forever change, but into what she did not know. She could not let go of what was familiar to cling to a future unknown.

"Why can't I keep it?"

"You must hold to me with both hands."

"But you can hold me," she argued. "I know you can hold me."

"You've got to want saving. You've got to want it more than you want that wand. There is no time for wavering; your moment is now. Reach out to me with all your heart, give me your soul without reservation, and forget the rest."

She looked up to the angel. She expected to see his shining face, his golden hair, his white robe and wings but it was Brendon that held her. It was his hand that griped hers. He was sweating with struggle. With one hand he clung to a vine that grew from the side of the abyss, and with the other he held her. It was a fertile vine. Ripe, round, luscious grapes grew on it, some of which were crushed by Brendon's grip. The purple juice ran down his bare arm.

"You must cling to me with both hands," he told her. "It's the only way I can save you. Please, Amy, let it go." His grip was considerably weaker than the angel's had been. In moments they might both fall to their deaths.

She looked down again at the wand, then back to Brendon.

"I love you, Brendon."

"Amy, please, let go of the wand and hold me. I'm slipping. I'm losing you."

"I can't," she said. "My darling, don't die for me. Let me go."

His hand was perspiring and wet. He struggled to readjust his grip and in the effort, he lost her.

His eyes round with terror; his scream followed her into the liquid fire. Her clothes melted into her skin. Her body began to decompose in the hot darkness that surrounded her. The intensity of the flame that consumed her was unbearable, like no pain she'd ever known before. With her final breath she screamed.

CHAPTER 31

Amy threw her arms out. The bed bounced violently beneath her. She sat up quickly, screaming as hard and as loud as ever she'd screamed. Then she struggled to breathe as if something were caught in her throat. She looked around the room. There were no flames, no Brendon, no Dante, and, to her relief, no tiny dealer. Her clothes were wet with perspiration.

It was hot. She had forgotten to adjust the air conditioner before falling asleep. That was it; that's all it was. It was the unbearable heat of the room that caused her to dream.

She was breathing now without struggle.

The lights were on because she'd fallen asleep before turning them off. Still, she looked carefully for any sign that perhaps she might still be sleeping and perhaps the tiny dealer might be near. But, the room was calm and the air around her had the feel of the material world.

She looked at the clock. It was 5 a.m. The sun would be rising soon but there was no sign of it from her window. Beyond the glass the world lay in darkness and the light in her room, like a single candle in a vast wilderness, stood between her and that darkness.

She laid her head back down on the pillow that was still beneath the bedspread. It too was wet and in the few seconds she lifted her head from it the dampness had grown cold. It soothed her now as she rested in it.

She cried. It was a brief spurt of tears accompanied by an uncommonly audible sob; it brought a convulsion to her body that shook the bed. She rubbed her eyes as they burned with the salt of tears. One tear ran into her mouth. It tasted sweet to her.

She sat up in bed and twisted to the side so her feet would hang over.

"I'm alive," she said. And then she cried some more.

On the nightstand, under the lamp, sat the case that held the wand Dante had given her the night before. She picked it up and opened it. She'd never seen anything so beautiful. She ran her finger over the cold wood. She imagined Kellar offering it to Thurston, a poster in Dante's home he referred to as "The Mantle" depicted the scene. Thurston was receiving a cape from Kellar. It had happened. It had happened in Baltimore. Tangible proof rested in her hand, tangible proof that dreams really do come true, both good and bad.

She closed the case and returned it to the table. Then she picked up the phone and started to dial Brendon's number.

It's five o'clock in the morning. Brendon's whole household is asleep.

She put the receiver down.

It was only a dream. That's what it was. It was a bad dream.

I've had bad dreams before.

Nevertheless, it was nice to be in a bed and not a pool of flames. She was thankful for the walls that surrounded her, walls that could not or would not move like the walls in the dungeon. She was glad that of all the dealers she'd ever known none were anything like the little man of her dream. And, she was glad that for the first few moments of that dream she'd held her father's hand.

She got up out of the bed and walked across the room to the thermostat. It was hot but there was nothing wrong with the air conditioner. She'd simply forgotten to set it the night before so she made some adjustments then she pulled off her clothes. They clung to her, but she fought each piece until she freed herself of it. She left behind a trail of clothes that followed her into the bathroom. The air was cool against her bare moist skin.

She climbed into the shower long enough to wash off the perspiration that covered every inch of her body. As her skin temperature dropped her mind relaxed until she became blissfully drowsy.

She dried herself with white heated towels. With one she wrapped her hair. Then she walked out to the bed and pulled the covers back. The maid had tucked them under the mattress. She slid between the sheets; it was like slipping into an envelope. The bed was still warm in the spot where she had dreamed. She avoided the area.

Within moments she was asleep. After the shower, she hadn't given another thought to the dream. Nightmares were a common occurrence for her. Sometimes they could go on for an entire evening. She'd wake up, think it was over, then sleep again and the dream would continue like a movie interrupted by commercial breaks. But she had a sense that the devil was through with her for the evening. And so she slept without fear.

It wasn't that anything had been resolved. But, there was simply nothing more to be said. Whatever demons her subconscious mind was trying to exorcise had come out. Besides, she was exhausted. Even if she feared encountering the little dealer again, she could not resist the needs of her body. When she opened her eyes to a much brighter room and looked at the clock, it read 10 a.m.

It seemed she'd closed her eyes a moment before but the bright morning sun was streaming through the joints in the closed vertical blinds that covered her window with the promise of a new day. The creatures that tormented her from the shadows of the night had cowered from the sun's revealing light. The events of yesterday evening were at a safe distance. She could admire her accomplishments and forget her tormentor.

The stench of the dream was gone but a vague curiosity remained. It had been five hours, a lifetime for a dream, but its questions lingered and she wondered what her mind had been struggling to tell her.

After another quick shower and a change of clothes, she ran downstairs to the café for breakfast.

She was enjoying a quiet moment with her cereal and fruit when Rick walked up to her table. He stood over her waiting to be invited to sit. She knew he was there of course. She also knew he would sit down when he was ready to sit invited or not. But she truly enjoyed teasing him and she suspected that he enjoyed being teased.

"You look like you have news," she looked up from her cereal into his smiling face.

CHAPTER 32

"May I sit down?" Rick asked.

"Since when do you need permission?" Amy replied.

He sat down in the chair across from her, the only other chair at the table.

She turned her attention back to her cereal. She didn't want the milk to become lukewarm for the sake of casual conversation. She carefully collected a spoonful of flakes then she forced a single piece of fruit on top as she tilted the spoon to drain excess milk. She liked milk well enough, but not when it saturated her cereal.

She kept her concentration on the spoonfuls of cereal she was precisely shoveling into her mouth. She didn't eat much or often, but when she did it was a serious business. She had rituals for every meal and she hated being interrupted during one of them.

"Amy."

The fruit was long gone. That was another Amy thing; she had to finish the fruit first. She pursued the elusive flakes and one by one captured them until all that was left was some slightly discolored milk.

It pleased her that he waited, tolerated her rituals. She might have exaggerated them a bit when he was around.

"Waitress," he called. "Waitress."

"Yes sir," she approached the table graciously.

"I'd like a toasted bagel with cream cheese and some orange juice please."

While he was chatting with the waitress, she pushed the bowl as far from her as the small table would allow. She finally looked at him and let out a heavy sigh as if eating had required the physical exertion of exercise.

"You know," he said, "your stomach problems could be related to your eating habits."

"What's wrong with the way I eat?"

"It reminds me of a pack of wolves competing for a dead carcass. You devour; you don't eat. Why can't you savor, enjoy, relax?"

"I can."

"So why don't you? And, what's with the concentration, and all those rituals?"

"What rituals?"

He laughed.

"There is nothing wrong with the way I eat," she protested.

"Okay, okay. There is nothing wrong with the way you eat," he said it but he didn't sound like he believed it.

"You tell me how to perform on stage and who to perform for," she said, "don't start telling me how to eat."

"Alright," he said and he put his hands into the air in a sign of surrender.

"I eat fine, but not here."

"What do you mean not here? Do you mean in this particular restaurant? Here in Las Vegas?"

"I mean here on the road. It's the business that does this to me. I never seem to have problems when I'm at Brendon's. A hotel is not a home."

"And how would you know what a home is?" he asked. "You've been on the road so long I'd have thought you'd have gotten used to it by now."

"I'll never get used to this."

"Well," he said, "you may not have to." His head moved from side to side like it always does when he's feeling cocky and confident. In this case he was probably referring to the contract. "But, you can't tell me you eat any differently at Brendon's."

"And why not?"

"Because you are who you are. I've been with you long enough to know. It doesn't matter where you go or what you do or who you do it with, the one constant is you. It's inescapable."

"It's different, that's all I'm trying to say."

"What does Brendon feed you for breakfast?"

She shrugged pretending that she didn't know or couldn't remember.

"You eat cereal, don't you?" he wasn't buying.

"Not always."

"You eat cereal," he said smugly. "Only the low fat varieties with no added sugar, preferably something 'natural' with little bits of chopped up fresh fruit."

"So what?"

"So you're making a fantasy out of Brendon and the whole Sonoma vineyard thing. You're running from success because you're afraid of what it might mean to you if you realize a dream."

"Why would I be afraid to realize a dream?"

"Because you're afraid it won't live up to your expectations. You'd rather believe it could have made all your fantasies come true than face the sad truth that nothing can, nothing that is but you. And, you can do it anytime you like. You don't need Vegas contracts or vineyards. All you really need is to decide to stop running."

She looked around the room to see if anyone was watching or listening. The few people that sat at the tables around them were eating and talking in their own worlds. She rested her elbow on the table and pushed her knuckles under her nose with her fingers covering her mouth. Then she looked at him and frowned.

"Analyze, analyze, analyze," she yawned, not that she was tired but she wanted him to think he was boring her so she stretched and yawned. "Stop trying to psychoanalyze me you silly man. I'm a big girl now and I know exactly what to expect from this town, my audience, and you."

"I think you expect too much of me," he didn't seem to be buying her yawn act either. He was going to be a tough customer this morning. "You expect too much of Brendon, not that I give a—"

"Okay, that's enough."

"You expect too much of Jason and Freddie, you expect too much of yourself, and most importantly of this town. I might be able to get you a contract but I can't promise it'll make you happy. I can get you a television special, but it won't make you feel any more loved, or worthy, or whatever it is you don't feel now. The only reason you've been disenchanted by your more than stellar career thus far is that your expectations have been too high.

"So maybe it doesn't satisfy your deepest inner longing, or fulfill your wildest dream. So what? Why does it have to as long as it pays the bills? Do you, of all people, really believe that you'll ever be satisfied? Sweetheart, listen to me."

Here it comes. Whenever he says, 'sweetheart listen to me' he's about to make a point that even he did not know he was going to make. But, she secretly enjoyed his little sermonettes. She found them actually inspiring at times, especially times when she wanted to quit and walk away.

"There is no pot of gold at the end of the rainbow," he said. "The sad truth is, rainbows only appear after storms and no matter how hard you try, no matter how fast you run, you'll never catch up to the end because it has no end. It's a false promise, a myth; it never existed in the first place. Rainbows are for looking at; they'll never belong to you or anyone else. And, so it is with life itself. Work well done is its own reward and you do your work oh so well. Can't you ever take pride in that? Everyone else does.

"It's a job, Amy. It doesn't have the power to make you feel better about yourself, or to make you happy. No job does. It can give you an exceptional income if you dedicate yourself to cultivating it. But if you expect more of your career, your love life, or anything else than it can give, you're only setting yourself up for heartache, disappointment, and disillusionment, the kind of disillusionment that makes people quit when they should be working harder."

"I expect to enjoy my work," she said but she understood the hurt in his voice. He'd given his time and energies to many like her and many quit on him at the moment they were truly ready to produce. Others worked hard but never got the chance. Not everyone in his fold had the same amount of talent, luck, and perseverance. He'd expressed his frustrations to her and she'd listened and now recalled that he had the same look in his eye when he told her of those other performers.

"I thought you did enjoy your work," he said. "Are you telling me now you don't?" he emphasized the word 'now' as if to remind her that it was the worse possible time for cold feet.

She thought a moment, then she said, "No. I mean I do love to perform but I don't like what I've been going through before shows lately."

"No one does," he said. "But, that's as much a part of this business as rehearsal, study, or improvisation. You simply do it. It's your job. It comes with the territory. Everybody knows that. As your manager, I expect your best shot, do you hear me?"

"What was last night?"

"It was great, but I need you as committed in negotiations as you are on stage, and in particular, I need you committed to this deal."

"I told you before, Rick—"

"Tell me again. Come on tell me again. I want you to tell me you want this as much as I do. I want to believe it. Make me believe. Convince me."

She laughed.

"I know you're afraid. Somehow, somewhere in that clouded past of yours, some people told you you'd never amount to anything and you believed them. But, they lied to you. They lied. You can have whatever you want. You deserve it, but the best way to handle fear is to face it head on. The faster you run the faster it runs to catch up. Let it catch you darling. You'll see. It's not all that bad. When you run from fear, it's a giant. When you face it down, look it square in the eye, and don't flinch, it's a mouse, an insignificant little rodent."

"I know that in your own sweet, lovable way, you care for me," she reached across the table and clutched his hand in hers. "You've always looked out for me and without you I might have never known theatrical success. I know you want Brendon out of my life because you think you know what's best for me. But, it's my decision. Please try to understand. I don't want to hurt you. I don't want to hurt or disappoint anyone. But we both know I'll never be able to please everyone. I've got to do what's best for me. So please, stop trying to cheerlead me into proving something to you that I don't want to prove to myself."

"You're right," he said. "It is your decision."

"Brendon always tells me the truth. I may not always like it but I know it's the truth."

"The truth? Do you think I'm lying to you?"

"Not in any malicious way," she said. "You call it marketing. You call it showmanship but it's all lying to me. I know you don't want to hurt anybody. You simply want what you want so bad that you're willing to do or say anything to anybody to get it. You've been doing it for so long that I'm not sure you know the difference between a lie and the truth anymore. That's all show business really is at its core. A big lie, I mean, created to entertain the masses. It's an opiate. The world can fall apart, but the show must go on. People must believe in something, and show people give them that something to believe in. Am I so wrong to want what's real?

"You, me, and everyone else in this business create lies. We live on them; we breathe them. Without them we are nothing. Deep down inside, you know it. We cling to fabrications of reality. Illusions we create, we begin to believe. We confuse the image marketing people like you so carefully craft to sell tickets, with the real thing, and right now, my life is too full of lies. I can't stand it anymore."

"Lies Amy, right. You're full of—"

"Everything is a lie. My life has become a lie to me. It's not fear I'm running from, it's truth I'm running to."

"I've never lied to you."

"You mean I've never caught you."

"Okay, well maybe once," he confessed and almost blushed.

"You're adorable," she laughed as she pulled her hand back and rested it under her chin. "And, I do love this business, lies and all. I'll never forget the feeling of wonder I experienced the first time I saw Dante on stage with his big show. I've been searching for that feeling again all of my adult life. But every time I discover a new wonder, a new joy, I lift up the cover and what lies beneath is another lie.

"I want something that is true, something that is real. I need a place that I can run to where no secrets are kept and no lies told. I need a place where people are who they say they are, guileless and pure."

"Not on this planet."

"Really? If that's true for you then this is all you know and that's sad. I love him. Maybe if he can be real for me, my anchor, I can go and live my life in illusion. Maybe, I don't know. I'm sorry if this hurts you, but it's the truth. It's no lie and it's no illusion. I love Brendon and when this weekend is over, I'm going to him, and if he still wants me, I'll marry him."

"And nothing I can say can change your mind?"

"No. But it won't impede my judgment here or impact my performance in any way."

"Now who's lying?"

"You said you wanted me to convince you. I'm here for you this weekend. I'll do whatever it takes to see this thing through, and Brendon will support whatever decision I make."

The waitress slid his bagel beneath Rick in a way that purposely did not disturb the conversation. She placed his juice on the table inaudibly, and then she was gone.

"What if I told you that a contract is on the drawing board?"

"Long hours for low pay," she said.

He didn't speak. He didn't try to contradict her intentionally sarcastic comment. He simply smiled. If spreading cream cheese on a bagel could be smug he was finding a way to make it so. She knew a contract was in the air. They'd discussed it before this. So why was he acting so sure of himself, so positive that she'd want whatever bait it was he had in his back pocket?

"It's not only a contract," he said. "It's not a part in a show, it's your show, your own stage, every night, long hours, yes, but low pay, absolutely not."

"Is this another one of your schemes?"

"As a matter of fact, it is. Some influential people expressed an interest in you, and I asked them to the show last night. They saw it, and they loved you. They're chomping at the bit."

"Well, wasn't that the idea from the beginning? Isn't that why we came?"

"Yes. But this is even bigger than I had anticipated. I thought I could get you some exposure. I expected some gigs, maybe a revue. They want to give you your own show. Don't you get it? You'll be a headliner, and they are going to back it up with extensive publicity."

"So when is the meeting?"

"I've got a meeting set up for lunch. Then, later this evening, we'll be meeting with the real players, the showroom reps will be there as well as producers, and a sponsor that thinks you are what they need to promote their product on television."

"You are talking about a special?"

"All yours."

"I can't believe what I'm hearing." She rapped her fingers on the table. Maybe the hard work would pay off. Maybe this wasn't going to be simply another gig in another town with another deal to close at the end of the day for more of the same. The daydreams of her childhood were rushing into her mind again and she couldn't slow the floodgates of the vision. She imagined her name on the marquee, her name in the proverbial lights. People would want her. They'd travel to Vegas to see her. Her mother would find out. She'd know she was wrong and she'd be sorry for the way she treated her daughter. Oh yes, this could be big, this could be it, everything she'd been waiting and working for since she'd left home so long ago.

"Why can't you believe it? You worked for it," he said. "Did you think success would never come?"

"I expected to have to grind out a living for the rest of my life. I thought I was as successful as I was going to get. There's got to be a catch."

"There's no catch. You were discouraged. We all get discouraged from time to time. In fact, you were miserable. Now there's a sparkle in your eye. I can feel the energy in your gut. You want this. I know you do. It's what we've both worked so hard for. You're going to make it. This is your chance. This is your opportunity. Life is knocking at your door. All you have to do is let it in."

She closed her eyes. She wanted to see more of her glorious future but from the corner of her mind the tiny dealer crept, knife in hand.

"Little demon," she said.

"What?"

"Nothing. It was only a dream I had last night."

"Well, you're not dreaming anymore. This is the real thing."

She clutched her stomach with both of her arms. The smile on Rick's face quickly faded.

"Are you in pain?" he asked.

She nodded. It was becoming an all too familiar pattern to her. She'd get excited about her work, she'd trill in anticipation, and then she'd get sick.

"It's only fear."

"Only fear," she said. "Isn't that like saying it's all in your head?"

"Well," he said, "it is all in your head."

"Tell it to my stomach."

"You speak of illusions, lies, secrets and truth. Fear is the biggest lie of all. Don't listen to the voices of doom, especially those that emanate from within. Look instead to the evidence of success in the world around you. You can do this. You simply need a little confidence. Once you get your own stage and you're doing basically the same show several times a week, the routine and familiarity will comfort you. Nobody likes change. Anything new, however grand, is anxiety provoking at first. But, you'll grow into it. You've done it before. Every time we went after a new market you did it, and you'll do it again here.

"It's growth pains. That's all it is, growth pains. Once you're settled in you'll be having the time of your life. You'll get used to the new level and you'll come to expect it and then you'll grow some more.

"This is a good thing. Embrace it. It's not the lies you hate. It's not lying at all. It's showmanship and you loved it at one time. You need to rediscover that moment. You need to rediscover the truth that show business lies reveal. All art is fabrication. Art is a lie that uncovers the truth in us all and it gives us a common experience that binds us together and makes us a people, a culture. It may be a lie but there is nothing immoral about it. It's a noble lie and those who tell it are noblest of all."

"Nobility," she laughed. "You are a pitch man and you've outdone yourself this morning. I've never heard you preach so eloquently. It's a grand show you're crafting for me right now. Showmen don't offer hope. At best, we provide a momentary diversion from the pain that surrounds most people's lives."

"A showmen has given you more than a momentary diversion," he reminded her.

"Yes," she remembered Dante, his show, and all he has given her over the years. "He has."

She started to bite at the nail of her left first finger.

"What has Dante told you about that?" He pulled her hand from her mouth. "Do you want to meet these people with one nail chewed to the bone and the rest polished, filed and long?"

She examined her nails. They were perfect, and she wanted to keep them that way, at least for the night.

"What time is the meeting?"

"Seven," he said. "If you get the job, you will need to relocate to Vegas, put together a full-evening show, and work on a television special. You'll be committing to some very long work days."

"No time to be fooling around with my personal life you mean."

"You said you wanted the truth."

"I do."

"I don't know how you think you're going to pull off a wedding and build the biggest show of your life at the same time."

"Vegas is famous for both. I will be too."

"That's my girl," he said. "A little grit, a little determination, a willingness to make it work, that's all I ask."

"I want to see this through. It's an open door and I believe in walking through open doors."

"I know you do."

"You mentioned an afternoon meeting?"

"Lunch."

"What time?" she asked.

"He'll send a car at two."

She looked at her watch. He wasn't leaving her much time to create the face and look that closes deals.

CHAPTER 33

"You have reached the home of Brendon Gallardo. Your call is very important to me, so at the beep please leave a message." The tone of the beep rang in her ear like the wrong answer buzzer on a game show. It mocked her yearning to speak to her lover and it emphasized with cold mechanical finality that her need would not be satisfied.

"Brendon, it's me, Amy. The show went well. I wish you could have been there but I'm sure you were plenty busy with the vineyard. I've got some meetings to attend. I might even have a contract before this is over. That, I suppose, is something we'll need to discuss, but it can wait until I see you. I love you. I miss you ... bye."

She hung up. For a few moments she sat on the edge of her bed looking at the phone, imagining where Brendon might be at that moment, what he might be doing. Thoughts of the rows and rows of growing vines warmed and comforted her. She looked at the clock. She hadn't long to prepare.

She needed another shower, her makeup had to be done, and her hair was a mess. Short hair was at times an advantage. But it still had to look right. She looked in the mirror.

"Great," she said. "Puffy eyes."

Her work was frantic but perfection was the result. Her hair was jelled and tucked back around her tiny ears allowing a clear view of the diamond studs in each lobe. Her eye shadow provided a depth and dimension to her already large dark eyes that she hoped would be intimidating. As she applied the last of her mascara there came a knock on her door.

She assumed it would be her driver. Rick told her that a driver would be sent to escort her. As she walked to the door, she put on her black pumps. She opened the door and smiled but the man who returned her smile looked nothing like a chauffeur.

"Ms. Alexander, Ms. Amy Alexander?" he asked.

"Yes."

He smiled. He was young, maybe thirty, and tall. His skin was naturally dark and his hair was black and pulled back into a tight ponytail that extended down his back to below his shoulders. His eyes were brown, almost black but soft, and inviting. He wore a light gray tailored suit that danced with light, and in his hands he held a bouquet of six white roses with soft, pastel pink tips on the buds.

"Oh my," she said as he held the flowers out to her. "I go for six months, no flowers, and in the last twenty four hours I've received them twice." She took them in her hands and inhaled.

"I'm sorry," the charming gentleman said. "You do not approve?"

"Oh no," she said. "I most certainly do approve. They are lovely. Are you …"

"Please forgive me. My name is Morgan, Morgan Bordeaux."

"Does your boss know you're giving me flowers?"

"No. I generally don't consult her. She trusts my judgment on such matters."

"You aren't the driver, are you?" she said more in observation than inquiry.

"No. I'm your date."

"Date?" she laughed both at his presumption and his charmingly juvenile language.

"Rick did tell you about lunch?"

"He said an exec wanted to meet me and that he would send a car."

"Well, I'm the exec, and my car is in the garage downstairs."

She smiled at him again, scrunching her nose a bit to let him know she was amused. He was nothing of what she'd come to expect. He was polite, considerate, attractive, and generally pleasant. She was beginning to enjoy the prospect of lunch with a businessman. She'd never really enjoyed that prospect before.

"Okay, Mr. Bordeaux …"

"Please call me Morgan."

"I suppose you'll want to call me Amy."

"Whatever your preference, Ms. Alexander."

"Amy will be fine. It's nice to meet you, Morgan."

He bowed nodding his head and closing his eyes as he did.

The gesture surprised her. She'd never been bowed to before. It was a delicious experience.

She put the flowers in the clear plastic water pitcher on her nightstand.

Morgan led her from the room and down the corridor with a gentle hand on the small of her back. He made sure the elevator door didn't shut on her as she stepped inside, and when they reached his car he opened her door for her and shut it after she was comfortably seated.

As they drove to the restaurant, she had the distinct feeling that she might be on the losing end of this transaction. Whatever it was he wanted of her she already felt predisposed to offer him. His like-ability, charm, and gentlemanly grace were most seductive and his small talk was both pleasant and inquisitive.

His line of questioning gave her the sense that he was genuinely interested in her and not simply her product, her show. He asked her about her interests apart from the theatre and magic. He asked where she'd come from. He asked about her parents, and her dreams. While she did enjoy his interest, she also knew his kind. He was not essentially different from Rick. They were in the same business, bread of the same pedigree. Rick would know how to charm and seduce, and she expected no less sophistication from her host. He was proving himself to be an expert in making his prospective business associate feel at ease. She also knew that anything and everything she said would be weighed in his mind against a potential contract. For all his pleasantries, it was her worth to his casino that he was trying so subtly to ascertain.

At the restaurant, the soft-spoken gentleman that led them to their table beat Morgan to her chair and slid it in behind her as she sat down. Morgan had about him a look of disappointment, presumably because he'd missed the opportunity to seat her comfortably himself. Brendon would have had the same look. In any case, it was not the kind of behavior she was accustomed to seeing in gentlemen of Mr. Bordeaux's profession.

The restaurant was dark. Though the sun was blazing and the temperatures scorching outside, like the inside of most casinos, it was perpetually night.

"What's your favorite drink?" he asked as they looked at the menus.

"Before a meal, during, or after?"

"Before," he clarified.

"Chambord and cream," she said.

"Really? I don't believe I've ever tasted that drink. It sounds sweet, more like an after dinner, or a desert drink."

"It's sweet," she said. "But I like it before a meal. You must try it."

With a slight lift of his chin and a motion of his finger, he summoned the waiter and ordered two.

"So you've been performing magic for eight years?"

"Yes, it's been eight years now."

"And with Rick?"

"Well, if it weren't for Rick, I wouldn't be doing it at all."

"Yes, I understand you were an actress."

"I still see myself as an actress. I've enjoyed a long run in a single part, but the plot is not all that well defined."

"Do you see it gaining definition here in Las Vegas?"

"I can't think of any greater challenge than performing here in Las Vegas."

"Vegas showrooms abound with magicians," he said. "Some believe that the magician's time has run its course, that those responsible for booking the talent should look for other kinds of variety acts."

"I think magicians will always be headlining in Vegas," she asserted.

"And why is that?"

"People who come to Vegas want to believe in magic, they want to see the impossible, and believe that what they see on the showroom floor can be replicated at the gaming tables, a fairytale ending to a hard and difficult life. Isn't that what Vegas is all about? I mean, it seems to me that the success of the magician and Vegas itself are inseparably tied. One fosters belief in the other."

"We like to think that we can provide an entertainment experience that will result in a state of euphoria for the majority of those in attendance. We serve them drinks, which reduces their inhibitions. Then, they see a performer, perhaps a beautiful one, with a charming disposition, one such as you. In the joy of the moment, they stumble from the showroom to the gaming tables, and that's when we make our money."

"It's meant good business for this town for decades," she said.

"It has," he admitted, "and business is what brings us to this table, and business is what we shall discuss in more detail later this evening. For now, I'd like to ask you a personal question."

"Please," she said, "don't be shy."

"I'm not." He smiled at her. His eyes gleamed in the soft candlelight. "Do you believe in magic?"

"I believe in love, and love is pretty magical," she laughed. "I believe that dreams have the power to make life magical particularly those that force us to stretch beyond what we thought we were capable of. I believe that the hard work and dedication required to fulfill any dream, is its own reward. At the end of the day, whatever the outcome, if I know I've given my best, the sense of gratification I walk away with is magical. But I don't believe in luck, or that my fate is in the stars. I don't believe that spells, positive thinking or any other kind of mumbo jumbo can satisfy me or determine my future. But I do believe in wonder and the experience of joy that it can provide. The power of wonder is miraculous, and that power is harnessed in a properly executed illusion show. That is magic, Mr. Bordeaux. I can and do create it every time I perform."

"And what about fairytale endings?" he asked with a smile.

"I suppose we'll find out tonight."

"Oh no, I'm not letting you off that easy. Tonight we'll negotiate one contract, probably for one year. Even if you are a mega success in this town, it won't sum up the grand total of your life."

"You want to know if I expect my life to lead to a fairytale happy ending."

"I want to know if you believe it can."

"I'm open to the possibility. But you won't catch me in despair if it never happens."

He smiled and then their drinks arrived and each took a sip from the twin miniature straws in their glasses. The drink was so cold her forehead hurt. She enjoyed the rush so she drank some more.

"Wow," he said, "this is good."

"You've never had Chambord before?"

"Once as a topping on cheesecake," he said. "Never in a drink."

"It's a fabulous flavor."

"Wonderful," he agreed.

"It's perfect," she said. "I'd even call it magical."

"Yes," he laughed. "I suppose it is. So, if you enjoy sweet drinks before dinner, what do you like after diner?"

"A coffee drink," she said, "preferably decaf with a bit of whipped cream on top. What do you enjoy before dinner?"

"It depends on what I'm having," he said. "Sometimes I like a white wine, sometimes something with a bit more kick."

"But always wine with dinner?"

"Usually," he said.

"Do you like wine?" she asked while her mind drifted to the vineyard and to Brendon.

"The right wine can make the meal."

She closed her eyes as she sipped again on her drink. The last time she'd had a Chambord and cream she was with Brendon. They were laughing together in a restaurant with an ambiance similar to the one in which she now sat. The memory was sweet and fresh. The emotions rushed back to her and nearly swelled a giggle but she caught herself when her present moment intruded upon her memory. She suppressed the giggle but a smile escaped her, a happy contented blissful smile.

"What are you thinking?" he asked. His talent for observation was as well disciplined as his ability to ask strategic questions.

"How pleased your guests will be with our new show," she said.

"Perhaps you were." He laughed. "Or perhaps you were thinking of wine, the many flavors and aromas, and the way you can taste the oak when it's been aged in an oak barrel. Perhaps you were thinking of a place where such wine is made, and of a man who makes it."

CHAPTER 34

"Who are you, Kreskin?" Amy tried to redirect the conversation. She wasn't sure how Morgan knew of Brendon or why he would bring Brendon into this conversation.

"Kreskin?"

"He's a mentalist."

"Oh yes, Kreskin. Yes, I know him," he said. "No, I'm not Kreskin. But I am an investor that wants to know the history, the complete history of whatever commodity I decide to invest in."

"Past performance is the best indicator of future performance," she said. She'd heard that once during a job interview.

"And a person's past inextricably leads to his or her future."

"Exactly how much of my past do you already know, Mr. Bordeaux?"

"Most of what you have told me was already known to me. I was pleased that you neither embellished nor distorted any event."

"Why don't you ask me what you feel you need to know?"

"I wanted to hear you speak. I wanted to hear your history the way you tell it."

"How did I do?"

"You freely reveal some intimate details, and carefully conceal others."

"Does that disappoint you?"

"No," he said. "It is to be expected. We all have private places that we would prefer to keep private."

"Indeed we do."

"Is privacy important to you, Amy?"

"I think everyone is entitled to keep private what they wish, and to disclose what they wish as long as that disclosure does not invade the privacy of another."

"And what of celebrities? Your name may become known outside of your profession. It is already spoken of widely in the business."

"Are you asking me how I feel about a potential invasion of my privacy or about my feelings on the subject in general?"

"I'll let you decide how to answer."

"I detest the tabloids, sir. But at least the tabloids are honest. Honest in the sense that everyone knows they exaggerate and distort. They don't really pretend to do anything other than lie and exaggerate. Everyone knows they go for the jugular. It's the so-called respectable journalists that bug me the most. They are supposed to have standards. They are supposed to represent the facts without bias, or at least make an effort to do so.

"It doesn't much matter to me what a person's claim to fame is. Politicians, actors, athletes, they all have private lives and how much or how little of it they disclose should be their choice and that choice should be respected. We all have boundaries and we, as a society, should learn to respect them."

"But people love to hear about the private lives of the people they admire. We don't have an aristocracy in this country, Amy, but people still make of their heroes a kind of royalty. They want so desperately to find something to identify with."

"And that's why you think the gossip stories sell."

"More than sell," he said with a touch of passion. "The best of the best in our business have learned to exploit the need of the people, and ride the wave to greater fame and popularity. The press can be your enemy or your friend …"

"And I can feed it stories to satisfy its hunger and to foster my own image."

"Exactly," he smiled. "Or a shrewd third party can do it for you."

"Have you been spending too much time in Rick's company?"

"Rick is a talented manager. His efforts to market your image have come to our attention, and we are seated here because of it."

"I understand," she reluctantly consented to a truth she could not deny or refute.

"Do you?" he asked, implying that she did not. "The everyday person has for centuries lived vicariously through the lives of the people they perceive to be the privileged few. The tabloids, as you call them, provide for these people a glimpse into the private life of privilege. For a moment they feel they know these larger-than-life people, and for that moment they feel larger than life themselves."

"That's sad," she said.

"Perhaps it is but it is the nature of our business to find ways to keep people like you on the front page. I believe it was your own Houdini that acknowledged the fact that any press is good press. More than anything else, Houdini was a master publicist. We both know that the finest illusions ever created aren't the ones that appear on the stage. The world's greatest illusions are its public personas, its celebrities, the so-called rich and famous. The grass really isn't greener for the people whose names everybody knows, but it helps if everyone thinks so. It's the carrot that keeps them coming to the box office."

"Well, that's a lovely sentiment, Mr. Bordeaux."

"You don't approve?"

"I'm not going to pass judgment on what you, Rick, or anyone else does. I don't think I would be comfortable intentionally feeding a lie to the press. That's all I'm saying."

"Who said anything about lies?"

"Isn't that what you mean?"

"Heavens no," he said. "I don't want my talent to lie. Even the press can see through a lie. I want my people to intentionally make their private lives more interesting. It draws attention and attention sells tickets and ticket sales sell the casino and so on."

"So how does my private life measure up to box office success?"

He shrugged his shoulders and frowned.

"Is there something you'd like to ask me about?"

"Perhaps," he said, "something or someone."

"Brendon," she said.

"Now there is a personal name," he leaned back in his chair and gazed into the air as if contemplating the name or the relationship. "Brendon."

"He knows nothing of this industry, Morgan."

"A pure heart is he?"

"I think so."

"How do you think he might feel about freelance photographers sneaking through his vineyard to get a candid photo of the two of you in a, shall we say, more casual atmosphere?"

"I'd like to leave him out of it," she said.

"You might like to. I'm sure there has been a good many seeking the kind of success you're seeking that wished they could keep those they love out of it as well. Perhaps the best way to keep him out of it is to not get into it in the first place."

She stared down at her empty plate and the menu that rested on it. He had pitched her a ball she wasn't prepared to take a swing at and like a major league hitter stunned by fast ball heat she watched the comment slip by her for a clean strike. How many strikes would she get before she was out, she wondered.

"Brendon Gallardo," his heat kept coming. "It is Gallardo, isn't it?"

"Yes," she said.

"And he is the proud owner of a Sonoma County vineyard, and love interest, I presume, of the young lady my employer has developed an affection for."

"And you think he represents a conflict?" she asked.

"Curious," he said. "I never said anything about a conflict. Why would you say that? Does his presence in your life somehow represent a conflict for you?"

"I don't know why he should," she said. "But Rick has expressed some concern."

"Oh yes," he said. "Naturally your manger would be concerned. Anything that draws attention away from the business might not be desirable. Distractions can be disastrous if not handled properly."

His eyes met hers. For a moment she feared he might see in them more than she wanted to reveal. For a moment she thought he might even have the ability to penetrate her most intimate thoughts so she looked away.

"Or perhaps," he continued, "it's not the business he's concerned about."

He knew too much or she was inadvertently revealing too much. She was no match for him. Rick should have come. Surely he knew this man's ability. Why would he let her go with him?

"And what do you think?" she asked.

"About Brendon?"

"Yes."

"My primary concern is for the contract and for your ability to sustain your end of the contract. We're prepared to make a substantial investment in you. We want assurances that you are prepared to make a substantial investment in us. What you do or do not do with your personal life is your own affair unless it results in a conflict of interest with your professional obligations. It would be nice to know, at this juncture, if, in your mind, there exists any potential conflict of interest. It would not be a deal breaker one way or the other. It would merely be another chip on the table."

"Whatever you've heard about my personal life, about Brendon, it didn't come from me."

"That's why I'm here. I want to hear it from you."

"And I want your confidence."

"I believe I am giving you every opportunity to earn it."

"How am I doing?"

"Splendidly, my dear," he laughed heartily and loudly. "You are delightful company and your stage presence is equally delightful. It is easy to see why Brendon, or Rick, or countless others might fall in love with you and I hope for the sake of the business that many, many do."

"So you think I'll do well in this town?"

"That depends," he said, "upon the disposition of your desire."

"I don't think I follow you, Morgan."

"Do you prefer to spend your time on the stage, or strolling through fields of vines? Are you willing to offer stories about your love life to the press, or would you prefer that they make up their own? If audience attendance begins to waiver, are you willing to play a little rougher to sells tickets?"

She looked into her nearly empty glass and took another sip that finished what remained. It made a horrid sound that her mother always told her not to make as she was growing up, but she loved Chambord and at this moment she needed every drop. When she had finished slurping, she looked up at him and held her eyes to his firmly and without blinking. She smiled ever so slightly, but uttered not a word.

"I see," he said.

"Is anything else on your mind?"

"As a matter of fact, there is."

"Well, don't be shy now."

"You are accustomed," he smiled, "to being on tour, to dealing with clients where and when you find them, to delivering a good show, and then moving on. But imagine what it might be like if, instead of traveling to a client's site, the client had to travel to see you. What if people waited in line to buy tickets and they spent seventy-five or even one hundred and seventy-five dollars they can't really afford on a single ticket to see you? And what if they did it twice a day six days a week? How much would you love the stage then, and would you love those people or would you, in time, resent them? What if you never went home again? What if this place, this city, this casino, became your home? Would it ever feel like home to you? Could it ever feel like home?"

"If we're going to enter into negotiations," she said, "I would prefer to have Rick join us."

"This is not a negotiation. Negotiations will commence later this evening. This is an informal meeting of two parties that may be interested in a long-term arrangement with each other. I think what we are both interested in, at this point, is the kind of bedfellows we will make for each other. Don't you think so?"

"I really wasn't thinking in those terms."

"No. I suppose Rick trained you to go after the gig regardless of whether you wanted it or not and then, after the deal is done, decide how you really feel about it."

"I've never thought about 'how I feel' about a gig."

"Maybe you should, especially this one. If you decide to go through with it, it's going to cost you. It's going to demand from you more than you've ever given to this business before. I think now is the perfect time to ask yourself this question, 'do I really want this?' And if you can answer that question with an honest yes, then ask yourself another, 'what am I willing to do to get it?' So, Amy, how bad do you want it?"

His eyes were dark and unblinking. In negotiations past she'd learned that any movement or gesture, the tone in her voice, the pitch, would all telegraph her ability or inability to deliver what was expected of her. She could have the deal or lose it based on her next move. It was like reaching check in a game of chess. If she were careless the game would end. She wanted to bite at her lower lip but her mind out-raced her body. Such an action would destroy his confidence in her. She stopped. She froze every muscle and she forced every contrary thought from her mind, every doubt, and every fear. With the passion of a person obsessed with a mission, she chased into captivity every contrary notion and she proudly put on her game face.

He was silent. Silence was part of the ritual but she didn't blink.

A waiter approached as the two sat in silence and asked, "Are you ready to order?"

CHAPTER 35

"Close your eyes," Rick took hold of her hand and she complied with his request. He led her from the lobby of their hotel toward the street.

The night air was warm against her face. She was tentative in her movements and held him to a slower pace than he might have wanted. She was delighted when he told her he had a surprise for her but holding her eyes shut while he guided her required a vulnerability that she hadn't anticipated and a trust she was not eager to offer. When wind from a passing bus struck her face she feared he might be walking her into traffic so she stopped. He pulled but she wouldn't budge.

"Where are we going?" she asked.

"Okay," he said. "You can open your eyes now."

When she did she looked into the face of a beautiful chauffeur. She was standing by a black limo holding the rear passenger side door open to her.

"Good evening Ms. Alexander," she said with a nod of her tiny head that was almost a curtsey. Her hair was short and blond; most of it was underneath her black cap. She wore a mini-skirted tux with a black tie and black buttons on a white blouse and her eyes were a blue/green like the waters of the Caribbean.

"You've got to be kidding," she whispered.

"Don't you like it?"

"You rented a limo?"

"For you."

"We can't afford a limo."

"You aren't paying for it," he said. "I am. So don't worry about it. It's a special night for both of us. I wanted to do something special for you. I haven't had too many shots at this town and I'm grateful for the hard work you've put in to give us the chance. Whatever the outcome, I want you to feel like royalty tonight."

"You're sweet," she kissed his cheek.

The driver was waiting patiently at the door, smiling politely, so she made her way into the car. The seat crunched and molded to her the way fine leather does. The car smelled as if it had come from the showroom floor. It had a TV, a bar, and what looked like a small vanity above the bar. The mirror was surrounded by lights like those in a good dressing room only much smaller. The chauffeur was quick to point out these and other amenities.

"I told them that we have a plane to catch after the meeting," he said rather matter-of-factly as he climbed into the backseat from the street side of the car.

She was already buckled in, and when he had his seatbelt fastened the driver slowly edged her way into the heavy evening traffic.

"Do we?" she asked.

"Of course not," he laughed.

"Rick I've asked you not to misrepresent me."

"I'm not misrepresenting you. I'm promoting you, sweetheart."

"But I—"

"Amy, stop right there, I don't want to listen to your delicate conscience. This is the way business is done. I will grant that there is an air of fabrication about it but it's essentially no different than any other illusion. You've created hundreds of illusions, entertained thousands with them, and never felt the slightest bit uneasy about it."

"That's because I know that my audience understands the rules of theatre."

"You think everybody knows that you've created a fantasy world for the purpose of wonder?"

"Absolutely," she said.

"What about the fifty year old executive director that asked you if you had an organ in your body that others did not that enabled you to perform such feats? What about the Bible college students that threw us off campus for being in league with the devil?"

"I tried to explain—"

"You tried, but you did not succeed. They thought you were the real thing. I have to admit it, you were convincing on those occasions."

"I'm not responsible for someone else's gullibility or stupidity. I did my job. When I realized they were getting the wrong idea, I tried to set them straight."

"But they didn't want to be set straight."

"I don't know what they wanted."

"They wanted to be right," Rick said. "They didn't want, nor did they care about the truth. They simply wanted to wallow in the bliss of their own illusion."

"There is a difference between an illusion and a lie, Rick."

"Alright then, think of it as acting. You are going to be playing the part of a successful illusionist tonight. As far as your audience is concerned, you will seem busier than the other guy. You or I will end the conversation first, and, based on how we dressed it definitely looks like we've got someplace more important to go. You need to project an image of success. Image is everything in this business."

"But what if I can't live up to the image? What if they buy and I can't deliver? Why can't I present exactly what and who I am and let the chips fall where they may? The fact is I do have dates. I am booked. I am in demand, but I'm not booked tomorrow. These people aren't stupid. They've seen managers like you before. They've heard all the lies. Why can't we be who we are for once?"

"This is who we are Amy, we're show people and we're going to give them a good show. We did it last night and we'll do it tonight. They want to see chutzpah; they want hunger. They want to see you bend over backwards to impress them and that's exactly what we're going to do. I'm going to give them the image they want. Image is what people pay for and it's what they will pay for. When your image has been properly crafted, refined, and marketed, demand will increase and so will your fee."

"But it isn't real."

"It's as real as this car we're driving in, and much more valuable."

Her stomach tightened. She hugged herself to still the churning.

"Come on, Amy. Get excited. You're in Vegas, the magic capital of the world. You're walking into a negotiation that could leave you sitting pretty after tonight. Win or lose so few people ever get the chance to try. Tonight that chance is yours. Don't worry about your image. Don't worry about what I'm doing to promote you. Don't worry about pleasing everyone. Don't worry about how you'll deliver on the promises we'll make. Enjoy the journey. If you could do that, your life would be so good."

"My life is good."

"I'm glad to hear you say that but it doesn't look like you're having fun. I can't remember the last time I saw you have fun."

"What makes you think I'm not having fun?"

"If you were you wouldn't be clutching your stomach like it'll pop out if you don't. You've made it. You're here. That's image enough. Focus on it, appreciate it, and believe in it. When you think of yourself as successful, others will too. When you behave like a successful person, you will be. Belief always precedes action. The people that get what they want in this world are the people that are willing to do whatever it takes to get it. Success is about doing not desiring."

"Life is so simple for you, isn't it?"

"Life isn't simple for anybody. But, if by that you mean that I operate by a simple set of rules, then the answer is, yes, I do."

"I'm having fun."

"You're uptight."

"Maybe a little tense."

"And the Titanic struck a little iceberg. You're confused and conflicted. You've been in the business awhile. You've seen a measure of success; maybe you're getting bored. You think you're in love. But what you really are is afraid. You love this business. It's in your blood. But you aren't sure you can handle the big time and those doubts are normal. Anybody and everybody that has ever done anything worthwhile with their life has had to deal with doubt. Right now, doubt is making you miserable. I'm sure you'd love to go run and hide on that vineyard in California but I won't let you and when this is over, you'll thank me."

"If we make the deal, will that make you happy?"

"What makes you think I'm not already happy? I'm managing a gorgeous woman that's about to set the world on fire with her grace, beauty, and charm. Everyone's going to say, Rick put that girl on the map."

"And it'll make you happy to hear people say that?"

"It won't hurt," he said. "But this evening isn't about me, it's your night. Imagine no more traveling, no more wondering where the next meal ticket will come from, no more seasons of too many shows or not enough, no more flirting with buyers. Imagine your own stage, your own chorus line. Imagine staying in one place long enough to get familiar with the food at the restaurants or the sheets on the bed."

"Do you want these things?"

"Me?" he laughed, "no, not me. I love the challenge of the road but I've got other talent to manage and they'll keep me busy once you're set."

"Maybe I like being on the road too."

"You did at one time," he said. "But I've seen it in the dark circles under your eyes at night and in your pale complexion during the day. I know you need to settle but I don't want you settling for anything but the best."

She sat in silence as the car slowed to a stop for a traffic signal.

"I'm afraid," she confessed, and the words surprised her as if someone else had said them.

CHAPTER 36

"I know," Rick said. "I'm nervous too."

"No," Amy needed to explain as much for herself as for her manager. "It really hasn't been nerves lately. It's been fear. I'm afraid of something, and the really scary part is, I don't know what."

"It's part of the business. Any normal person experiences fear when they perform, or when they go into a new or challenging situation. You don't need to make a mystery of it; anxiety is a part of living. In some respects, it lets us know we are living, pushing ourselves, I mean. Anybody can rot away in a nine-to-five job, wander aimlessly through the day, and come home at night with no fear, no anxiety, no hope, and no emotion whatsoever. You're afraid because you're living your life instead of wishing it would start the way most of the world does."

"I hope you're right."

"It'll get better, Amy. I know you've been struggling. You've been asked to shoulder more than most in the past few months and everything is coming at you so quickly. Try to get on top of the wave and ride it. Don't get sucked under for a wipe out. Catching a wave is exhilarating. Getting creamed by one is painful. But even getting creamed in the effort is still better than wasting your life away on a park bench."

He wasn't getting it. She wanted him to understand but his words served only to convince her that he didn't. She shifted her body so she could face him head on and then she tried again.

"I used to feel real fear before a show," she said, "and I knew why. It was because I desperately wanted to perform well. And even though I'd rehearsed to death, I knew that something could go wrong, and I didn't want it to. I wanted to give the best performance I was capable of. Now, I'm numb. It's like I'm living in a dream. Nothing seems real to me. There is something, I don't know, inauthentic about my life lately. It's as if the sky is less blue, food less delicious ..."

"And what would you know about food? I never see you eat anything but bland garbage anyway."

"Please listen to what I'm saying. This isn't about food. I'm trying to communicate with you."

"Why do we need to talk about this?" He pulled and twisted his seat belt as if it were too tight. "Why can't you see this opportunity for what it is? On the way to the most important meeting in our lives, you want to tell me about your mystery emotion?"

"Okay, so it's a bad time."

"A very bad time."

"But we're always busy," she said. "We never have time to talk."

"You never said you wanted to sit and talk to me before. I always assumed your boyfriend was filling that void."

"He does," she said. "He does fill that void rather nicely. But, you're my business partner. We've been together for as long as I've been in this field. I need to make a connection with you that will transcend this or any other deal. It matters to me that you understand."

"Later," he sighed.

"The traffic's heavy. It'll take us more time than expected to get there. What do you propose? That we sit here in silence 'til then?"

"I'm a businessman. I'm here for the deal. I'm excited about the deal. I really don't have the desire or the ability to do what you ask."

"All I'm asking is that you listen. I don't want answers. I don't want wisdom. I want to know that you're listening to and really hearing what I'm saying. Talking might be therapeutic. It might help me relax. Wouldn't that be nice?"

"Look around you," he said gesturing at the window. It was really too dark to see anything other that the glitter and flash of neon. "We're in Vegas and we're about to negotiate a contract to keep you here. It's not a fantasy. It is really happening, and you really deserve it. Your life is not a lie; you are not a fraud; you deserve to be here; you deserve success, and you deserve this contract.

"You've worked harder for this than anyone else I've managed. You're afraid, and I understand. This place can be intimidating, but don't sabotage. Be proud, believe in yourself, walk into the room with your chest out and your chin up, and know that you are the center of attention because you deserve to be."

As she looked over the city through the window of the car, trying to imagine success in this town, memories of her mother intruded on her dream. She put a hand to her cheek where it had once been battered and bruised. She listened and the memory of her mother's screaming fits echoed in her ears like words shouted into a canyon. It was as if her mother was screaming them still.

"You're worthless and lazy, and you'll never amount to anything. Now get out of my sight."

Then her mother leaped from her chair like a lion leaps at prey, and she stomped her feet in chase. Lamps rattled and swayed to the point of toppling. Her mother was difficult to escape, and Amy never escaped, not even once, but over time, the beatings stopped hurting. She stopped resisting, stopped running. She would let her body sway like a reed in wind under the punches and kicks of her mother and when her mother was done she would crawl to her room and struggle to breath.

She stared at the lights under the night sky as the car inched toward its destination. As a girl she loved to sit in the backseat of her daddy's car at night and watch the lights go by. Silence between them was never awkward. She never feared her father and the memory of silence shared with him stilled the imposing images of her shouting mother.

"Amy," Rick intruded on her thoughts, "this is your chance. I'm not saying there won't be other opportunities. But you've got to make the most of every chance life offers."

"I'll be alright," she said. "You needn't worry. I told you I'd be in the deal, and I will. I know that my doubts and fears unnerve you—they unnerve me. But I've always come through for you in the past and I will tonight. You've done everything in your power to make this night special. I really do appreciate it and I'm sorry if I haven't embraced the evening with the vigor you expected."

"Don't apologize, not to me or anybody else. If you want something, ask for it. If it's not offered, take it. There is such a thing as too kind and you are that. The people we're seeing tonight will be looking for a lion, not a lamb. I want you to make demands, and don't take no for an answer. You're sweet. You care about me. You care about everyone you meet and I've taken advantage of that and I've allowed others to take advantage of that. Your audiences intuitively respond to your gentility. It's a beautiful thing to watch. But, in business, in this business, you've got to know how to stand up for yourself. Nobody else is going to do it for you.

"You're sitting over there silently sulking in God only knows what memories or imaginations. You think I don't know or don't care how uncertain you are about everything. I know you'd love to tell me. You'd love to put words to all those mixed up feelings inside of your right now. But I want you confident. I want you focused. Stop the introspection for one minute and focus all of your energy out there," he pointed beyond the front window of the car toward the resort at their journey's end. "Maybe you should accept that a little inner conflict is normal for you."

She offered him a smile and he gave a strained tentative smile in return. She neither accepted nor denied his observation, but she would never be content to live with what he called 'a little inner conflict.' It might seem little to him but it didn't seem little to her. It didn't make sense. She should be happy. Why wasn't she? If a night like tonight couldn't thrill her, what would? She wanted to be excited but she wasn't. She wanted to experience the joy of success but her heart wasn't joyful. She was supposed to be happy. She had what everyone else wanted. So why wasn't she happy?

She expected Rick to launch another barrage of affirmations any second. It was a big night for him too, and he liked to get himself ready by talking positive. She was used to the ritual. She'd seen it many times before but it never meant as much before. It might well be his biggest night and she didn't want to damage it for him. If she could make him happy she wanted to. If he needed her she wanted to shine for him. But what did she want? When she asked that question of herself she drew a blank. If anyone else asked her what she wanted she wouldn't know what to say. The easiest answer would be to ask what the asker wanted of her and then try to deliver.

She was happy to have him by her side. She glanced over at him in the dark. He was staring out of the window perhaps at the casinos and clubs as they past by. Or maybe he was trying to imagine the show and what it would do for his own image in this town and among his peers. He had always been her strength in negotiation. She couldn't envision entering into one without him. She didn't know what she was worth. If she had to negotiate alone, she'd think any deal was a generous one. He had the guts to ask for more than she thought she deserved and he had the power to get it. It was his gift.

"Comfort zone," he said. She wondered if he were speaking to her. His voice was barely audible.

"What?"

"Comfort zone," he repeated.

"Are you talking to me?"

"That's why you're not as happy as you think you should be."

"Okay," she said. "Why?"

"Anybody would be nervous in a situation like this."

"Are you trying to tell me you're nervous Rick?"

"Me?" he laughed and gestured to himself the way campy actors did in old silent movies.

"You'll do fine," she said.

"No wait," he said. "This isn't about me."

She reached over, wrapped her fingers into his and squeezed.

"Okay," he admitted. "So maybe I need to talk myself up. You should try it. Come on, let me hear you tell yourself you're going to conquer this town tonight. You're going to be so good. They're going to love you."

She unfastened her seat belt. It snapped away from her like it was being pulled. She slid across the long leather seat until their hips were touching. She turned his head toward hers with a finger under his chin. She positioned her lips close to his and when his eyes shut she tickled him under his ribs.

"Stop it," he giggled as he brought his knees up and pulled her hands away by her wrists.

"You stop it," she said.

"You're going to mess up my suit."

She twisted her hands free and ran her fingers into his hair. He had so much jell in it; it cracked and almost broke as her fingers penetrated to his scalp. Then she got a fiendish idea. She rubbed and pulled and shook his hair until once again he pulled her hands away. This time his grip was considerably tighter.

"What are you doing?" he shouted but the damage was done. His hair was sticking straight up in spikes. He looked like a well dressed punk.

"Now you've got something to worry about," she said, looking up into his eyes in the dark of the backseat. "No one's going to want to sign a deal with a manager who has messy hair."

There was a mirror above a small bar in front of him. He struggled to find his reflection in it but as he refused to release her, he was unable to lean far enough forward for the view.

"Fix me," he demanded.

"You mean like a dog?"

"Well, at least you haven't lost your sense of humor," he said. "No. I mean like my hair."

"Oh you poor thing, you look absolutely ridiculous."

"Come on Amy, we're almost there."

She looked out the window. The casino was within visual range but the traffic was heavy.

"Let me go," she said. His grip on her wrists was making her fingers numb.

"No way."

"Than how do you expect me to fix you?"

"If I let you go you'll do something worse."

"Worse than messing up Rick McAlister's hair? If there is such a thing and I'm lucky enough to think of it, believe me you'll be the first to know."

His pressure on her wrist eased. She twitched and he tightened his grip again.

"This is ridiculous Amy. We're on our way to the biggest night of our lives."

"Your life maybe."

"Oh and you think they get better than this?"

"I'd like to thank the Academy and my director for believing in me. To be nominated with so many fine actresses is an honor and you all deserve to be holding this little golden man but I am! Ha, Ha!"

"So that's what you want. Well, let me tell you something my little angel."

"Why don't you let me go first before you walk in with spiked hair and I walk in with bruises on my wrists?"

"If you get this contract," he released her and she rubbed her wrists and shook her hands until blood flow returned and she could feel her fingers again. Then she made a cat like gesture for his hair.

"Amy!"

"Okay, okay. What were you saying?"

"If you get this contract people will see you, people who haven't seen you before. It'll open up new markets for us, maybe even Hollywood, if that's what you want. I don't have much experience in that town but I know people and they owe me."

"I was only kidding."

"Yea," he smirked, "sure you were."

"Come here," she said. "Let me fix the mess I made."

"It's alright," he released his seat belt and removed a comb from his back pocket as he leaned toward the mirror. A light came on and in seconds his hair was perfect again, as smooth as his temperament.

She at least was more comfortable after their little diversion.

"Was it as good for you as it was for me?" he asked as he sat back and refastened his seat belt. She understood by that that her efforts relaxed him as well.

"Yes," she said. "It was."

"Good," he said, "I'm glad you had fun. Are you ready now?"

"I would've liked that talk."

"It wouldn't have helped. The hair bit was a much better idea."

"Maybe, but when I hold inside what needs to come out, I feel alone and I don't like feeling alone."

"I negotiate deals. I'll negotiate this one. But when you walk out on that stage, as always, you'll be walking out alone to deliver on the promises I've made. It's not easy to hold inside what you want to share. It's not easy to stand alone in the spotlight. But you're ready and I'm proud to be your manager. Whatever the outcome, you are my star, my number one."

"Thank you," she reached her hand to his and squeezed. She had settled back into her side of the long leather seat but she hadn't refastened her seat belt. They had only a short distance to go.

"Did he ask you about Bruce?" he asked.

"Who?"

"Morgan."

"I know Morgan. Who is Bruce?"

"That guy of yours, the one that, if you marry will ruin your life."

"Ruin my life?"

"So maybe ruin is a bit harsh. Let's say divert."

"His name is Brendon. And, no, I mean, yes. I don't know. What does it matter?"

"They want to know where you stand," he said. "What did you tell him?"

"He asked but I didn't go into details. I don't think he was at all discouraged by my relationship with Brendon. He wanted to know if I was willing to go the distance."

"And?"

"I am willing and I think he knows it."

He moaned.

"Stop fussing," she said. "What will be, will be."

"Look who's talking."

She stared at him. Then they both laughed. The car was pulling to a stop in front of the casino. The lights were breathtaking.

"Isn't it beautiful?" she whispered.

"What?"

"The lights."

The leather crunched as he leaned over. His breath was on her neck.

"It looks like hype to me," he said

"Isn't it odd," she said. "We're both looking at the same lights but we each see something different."

CHAPTER 37

The limo turned from the main road onto a driveway, passing beneath a canopy that stretched like welcoming arms from the front entrance of the resort. Small stones in the street crackled and crunched beneath the tires as they drifted to a stop. The chauffeur climbed out from behind her seat and came to Amy's door.

"Ms. Alexander," the gentle and polite woman said in a sweet, hushed almost reverent tone.

"Thank you," Amy replied as she stepped from the car. She had expected to be nervous, or excited, or something. But, she didn't feel any of those things, and she wondered why the moment didn't seem somehow bigger. It was true. A part of her did not want to be in this negotiation or in this town or in this business. That part of her desperately wanted to be with Brendon and could think of nothing else. But she was with Rick. He needed her help and she wanted to give him what he expected.

A friendly, perky young woman in a dark blue, pinstripe pants suit and white blouse walked a plush runway to the car with her hand extended to greet Amy.

"Hi," the young woman said flashing her polished smile. "I'm Mindy. I work in development with Morgan, whom I believe you've already met, and our boss Joan. You will be meeting Joan tonight."

Mindy looked teenage-young. Her blond hair was straight and short. Not as short as her own, Mindy's covered her ears and reached to her neck. It was parted in the middle and it curled up on either side of her face under her jaw providing an attractive frame for the girl's petite features and big blue eyes.

"Hello, Mindy," she said, returning her handshake and smile. "I'm delighted to meet you."

Rick, now at her side with a hand at the small of her back, extended his free hand to Mindy and introduced himself.

She was a gracious young woman, well mannered and professional. She led them both through the grand front entrance. Stepping inside, the magnificence of the place took Amy's breath away, and she stopped to take in the splendor of what could only technically be called a lobby. The ceilings were like the cathedrals of Italy, and equally ornate. In the center, a fountain threw water twenty-five feet into the air. The floor was of marble—at least it gave the appearance of marble.

She expected the rattle of one-arm bandits and the commotion of over eager gamblers to assault her ears, but the noise was subdued, almost silent, like the hush of a library. She expected the smell of nicotine to gag her but she found no heavy haze of smoke. Instead she discovered that smoking was prohibited in the common areas and the air inside smelled clean and fresh, like bed linens hung to dry outside on a cool spring day.

"Ms. Alexander?" Mindy stopped a few feet out in front and turned back when she realized Amy wasn't following.

"Amy," Rick whispered, "what are you doing?"

"It's beautiful," she said.

"Well, shut your awestruck gapping mouth," he said. "You've got the world's worse poker face, do you know that? You should be embarrassed."

"What do you mean? I love it and I'm not afraid to show it," she said.

"Never been out of Kansas, Dorothy?" he teased.

"Ms. Alexander," Mindy asked as she approached, "is everything all right?"

"I guess they don't make casinos like they used to," she said.

"No, they don't," Mindy said. "We like to put the emphasis on resort. It's a family experience here, for the kid in everybody." And then, very diplomatically, she said, "I'm glad you like it, Ms. Alexander. If all goes well tonight, it may be your new home."

Mindy gave her a big smile that she returned and the young woman turned gracefully, almost militarily on one heel and continued to lead them through the resort.

"Well," Rick whispered, "at least you didn't say 'gosh.'"

"I meant to," she said. And then after they walked on a few steps, she paused and waited for him to stop and look at her before tucking her interlaced fingers under her chin and gleefully declaring, "Gosh" while she batted her eyes.

"Try to keep it together," he admonished. "You'd think you've never seen the inside of a casino."

"Not one like this big boy," she said. "This is truly amazing."

Mindy glanced over her shoulder at her and smiled.

"You see," Rick whispered. "Now you've done it."

"Oh, I've gone and let them think I'm impressed. Dear me the sky is falling."

"Amy."

"Okay, okay. I'll behave."

"I'm glad you like it." Rick laughed. "Enjoy it."

Mindy led them into an elevator and during their rapid ascent; she complemented Amy on her performance the evening before. Little Mindy was a ball of enthusiasm and laughter, and Amy found her energy contagious.

Mindy's pace was quicker as she walked the wide, luxurious corridor to the suite. She paused when she reached the door, and resting her hand on the doorknob she waited for Amy and Rick to catch up. When they did she smiled, opened the door and led them inside.

Amy was expecting a penthouse office, in deco with a big and ugly bare glass desk. What she found instead was a hospitality suit, decorated in muted pastel colors with matching modest but comfortable sofas and chairs. The room had a homey feel that put her at ease.

Everyone that was expected to attend the meeting was already inside laughing and drinking. Amy wasn't sure who all the players were, but she decided to wait for introductions instead of taking the initiative. She was on unfamiliar turf and she thought it best to let the evening unfold on its own.

Her eyes met Morgan's and they exchanged smiles. He and another man stood from where they'd been sitting when she entered the room. Morgan excused himself from his companion and crossed the room to her. When he reached her he took both of her hands in his and kissed her on the cheek as if he'd known her all of his life.

"Amy," he whispered, "this is the fun part. All of these people saw you perform last night, and they're eager to meet you."

CHAPTER 38

"Maybe this will be fun," Amy thought.

The man Morgan had been seated with approached slowly. His hesitation gave him the appearance of shyness, but his smile and awkward shifting led her to believe that he was pleased to meet her. When she looked up at him, he looked down at his drink and swished it as if it needed re-mixing. He was, she imagined, in his late forties, perhaps fifty. His hair was thin and turning gray. His nose was long and straight, handsome on his face. His skin had a rather healthy glow, his breathing was slow, and since he had no apparent middle age spread, she assumed he enjoyed some kind of regular exercise beside the usual round of golf. Morgan turned to him and laid a hand to his back to pull him closer.

"Amy," he said, "I'd like you to meet Mr. Henry Collins."

"Mr. Collins," she said with her friendliest smile as she extended her hand to shake his.

"Ms. Alexander," the man said, "you completely beguiled me last night, and you are even more enchanting in person. We've been following your career, and I am so glad my company has chosen me to represent them in this meeting."

"And your company is?" she asked.

"I'm with an east-coast advertising firm," he explained. "We represent a client who has expressed some interest in pursing a magical campaign for their product. They want to launch the campaign with a prime-time special. We showed them a variety of promotional videos, they sent representatives to the shows of a select few, and they want you."

She tried to look flattered. She wanted to present herself as graciously appreciative of the attention his firm had extended to her, but she felt oddly *out-of-body*, as if she were watching the evening's events as a moviegoer might watch a film. She was interested but not engaged. She gave his hand one more squeeze before letting go. It was a gesture he returned with a smile.

"Well," she said, "I'm certainly delighted to hear that. And, I'm glad your company decided to send you, Mr. Collins."

"Please," he said as he ever-so-slightly blushed, "call me Henry."

As he pulled his hand back, the simple gold band on his third finger reflected light to her eye. She wondered how long he'd been married and to whom.

"Okay, Henry," she said, smiling boldly, "thank you." And she let him go.

Henry stepped back and a middle-aged woman in a black suit emerged. Her hair was dark, with a single streak of gray that gave it an almost skunk like appearance. Not that she looked unattractive or eccentric, but Amy wondered if the woman's hair had naturally turned in that one area or if she had purposefully colored and styled it that way. In any case, it was lovely and it gave her a signature appearance, something magicians were always searching for.

Under her suit she wore a white blouse with several strands of pearls, and on her ears, she wore matching pearl earrings. Large diamonds adorned her hands, and on her right wrist, a gold charm bracelet dangled loosely.

In the few seconds that Amy had to take in these details, the small golden profile of a boy and a girl on the bracelet caught her attention. Friends of her mother had worn similar bracelets with similar charms years ago. Those friends typically had a profile for each of their children. She had often wished that her own mother had shown such devotion. Seeing the bracelet, she assumed that each represented the children of the rugged, confident looking businesswoman that now stood before her.

It was difficult for her to imagine this woman as a young mother, cuddling an infant to her breast and kissing his tiny soft head. It was hard to imagine this prim and proper woman smelling of baby powder instead of the expensive perfume she obviously wore. But she tried to conjure that image in her mind. Her children were probably older now, but they must have been infants once, and when they were, what kind of mother had this woman been? Her eyes looked keen and determined; in them there was no sign of tenderness. But somewhere, beneath the mask, there had to be a tender woman. No other would wear such a bracelet.

"Amy," Morgan said, "I'd like you to meet my boss, Joan Applebee."

"Ms. Applebee," Amy said, extending a hand.

"Please," Joan said as she clenched Amy's hand in an iron grip, "let's not do the formal thing."

"As you prefer, Joan," Amy said.

"Can we get you anything before we start," Joan asked, "a Chambord and cream perhaps?"

"I'd love one." Amy smiled at Morgan. He lowered his eyes as if to say guilty as charged. But it was a pleasing guilt and she would get to enjoy her favorite drink as a result.

Joan looked over at Mindy who was already busy behind the bar. Apparently Mindy included tending bar among her many talents.

"So, Amy," Joan said, "tell us, that bit with the disappearing, and then reappearing in the audience, how's that done?"

"I didn't do an effect like that last night."

"We've seen you do it," Joan confessed. "And I've often wondered how that's done."

"Wonder is good," Amy said. "I and others like me work hard to create it."

"Wonder is good for a magic show," Joan explained, "but it doesn't do much for a marriage."

Henry laughed as he was sipping on his cocktail and almost blew it unbecomingly through his nose. Morgan and Mindy, who knew Joan best, didn't laugh, so neither did Amy.

Joan simply nodded at her with the slightest smile on her face.

"The disappearance and reappearance of a human being from the stage," Rick explained, "is an ancient and carefully guarded secret among magicians. If we told you how it was accomplished we'd have to kill you."

Everybody laughed at that tired old line, everyone except Joan. Under her sudden stare Rick shifted his weight and nervously smiled. If she didn't know him better, Amy might have thought him intimidated. Apparently, the others in the room hadn't heard that line before. It always amazed Amy how she could do a routine that so many others had done, or deliver a line that so many others had used, and yet people would respond as if seeing or hearing it for the first time. She even used lines that originated in vaudeville, and they still got laughs.

"Stick with the tried and true," Rick always told her, "but keep it fresh. Deliver the line as if it's yours, as if it spontaneously popped into your head that very moment."

"An ancient and carefully guarded secret, you say," Joan said, "available to the privileged eyes of anyone with a library card and the ability to read two sentences, or if not read then at least comprehend a graphic illustration, such flimflam in this stale profession of yours, Rick. But the customers seem to like it, and we like to give the customer what he or she wants." Joan looked to Amy and continued, "And I think they are going to love you."

CHAPTER 39

Amy took the drink in hand that Mindy offered then she and Rick both sat ready to negotiate.

"The real secrets of magic aren't in books," Joan said. "Isn't that what you'd like to tell me, Rick?"

"We're not here to discuss the secrets of magic real or otherwise," he said.

His abrupt response surprised Amy. She deduced that he must either want too much to get down to business or he must want too much to avenge his ever-so-slightly bruised ego. In either case, small talk could only help their cause and she wanted to get to know these people better before engaging in a business discussion. So she hoped that Joan would not be deterred by Rick's attempt at redirection.

"What do you think Amy?" Joan asked.

"As to the specific illusion that you asked about, I have found that when people do discover the secret or at least a method that satisfies their curiosity, they are disappointed. As I don't like to disappoint people I prefer to maintain a mystery whenever one has been created. As to the real secrets of magic, I think the real secret of good magic is the real secret of great acting or any other performing art."

"You do?" Joan asked, "And what is that?"

"Personality," she said.

"And do you possess this secret ingredient, Amy?" Joan asked.

"I think that is for you to decide."

"Perhaps in this moment it is. But ultimately your audience will decide and we've been watching your audience. I must say, we've enjoyed what we've seen. It's not that what you do is fresh but you are. You've got an edge right now and I might not have noticed had it not been for the efforts of Henry's company and your manager."

"Rick made sure my client got a good look at you, Amy," Henry interjected. "Your manager and I have been kicking it around for a while, but I think at this point, we are ready to sign you and get to work."

"And," Joan said, "when we heard that a prime time special was in the works, you suddenly became much more interesting to us. Not that we weren't looking before, but a national stage will bring our resort the attention it deserves."

"You'll be representing my client," Henry said.

"And our resort," Joan added, "to the world. If you succeed, we'll all benefit."

"It sounds like a win-win proposition," Amy said. Her heart was beginning to pound and her mouth ran dry. The temperature in the room seemed to rise and she hoped that if she began to perspire it wouldn't show.

She sipped on her Chambord. It was cold and it helped to relax her but she wondered why her body was displaying the symptoms of fear. Why would she fear that which she really wanted? Her heart didn't pound, nor did her mouth run dry when she drove along the coast to the vineyard. When she speculated about the home life of the people she was surrounded with she relaxed but when she immersed herself fully in the conversation and in its implications for her future, her stomach churned.

She glanced at Rick. He was smiling. His eyes were like lightning. This was his world. He belonged. She wished she could have put her thoughts together in the car or before perhaps months before so that she could have fully expressed her misgivings to him.

"We think so," Joan continued. "But it will mean you'll need to let go of your stronghold on the corporate market. Rick's done well by you there, and I know your business is good. But, we will need your concentrated effort here. Many talented people think they can do both. They'll put in the shows their employer requires and keep their name in front of their best clients at the same time. What you do with your own time is your business but we won't tolerate any less than your best effort and your complete dedication."

"I understand," she said. "What is the contract duration?"

"We'll need a year," Joan said. "Now that may sound a trifle out of the ordinary, but with all the PR we'll be doing, we'll need at least a year to realize a return on our investment."

"You'll have your own show, Amy," Morgan said. "You call the shots."

"But you'll need to work with my client's people and the television crew," Henry said. "Everyone's gotta be on the same page here."

"And," Joan said, "we're going to want something different. I want an original thinker, not simply original presentations. I want original illusions, an original act, and an original personality. I will expect to see what I've never seen before and I've seen the best of your profession. I've even seen ghosts. Being female doesn't make you stand out anymore. There are plenty of women in the business. I'm looking for one with a fully developed character, one that can interact with a drunken crowd and get the best of them. I want an entertainer. We already have enough acrobats jumping in and out of boxes."

"If you didn't already know that I can deliver," Amy said, "I don't think I'd be sitting here."

"Doing a regular show," Joan said, "day in and day out will be a significant change from what you've been doing. But you are customer driven, and I think that value will serve you well in our organization."

"What did you think of my performance last night?" Amy asked, trying to get a sense for Joan's taste in magic, and for what she considered 'original.'

"I liked it," Joan said, "but I saw you once at a convention. It was a longer show, and you actually had to speak, interact with the audience I mean. I liked what I saw then much more. This town is full of beauty and charm. If that were all we wanted we wouldn't want you. You've got something more, and that something is a real interest in people. It comes across every time you get a spectator on stage. It's lovely. I like it.

"So here's the deal. You start next month, no Jason, no Freddie; you'll use our people. You'll do a family show at 7:00 p.m. on Sunday, Monday, and Friday. On Tuesday, Thursday and Saturday, you'll do two shows, a family show at 7:00 p.m. and something a little racier, but still PG, at 9:30. Wednesday's your day off, and you can determine your own rehearsal schedule. Our staff will be available when you want them within certain constraints that we need not discuss here."

"We'll expect you to begin rehearsal in two weeks," Henry said. "We'll want to start taping in two months if all goes well."

"You'll live here in the hotel for the time being," Joan said. "You can eat at any of our restaurants, they are open and at your disposal twenty-four hours a day. If you can't find anything you like on any of the menus, I'll introduce you to a couple of our chefs. They'll be happy to prepare anything you like."

"Jason and Freddie stay," Amy calmly but matter-of-factly insisted.

Joan threw Rick a cross look. Rick surged his shoulders slightly. Then she addressed Amy with, "It'll affect your bottom line, not mine."

"I'll expect to be pleased with my bottom line regardless," Amy said.

Joan smiled.

Then, they started to talk money. Joan's first offer got a laugh out of Rick.

"Oh no, no, no," he said. "I don't think so, Joan."

And so, he countered, and Joan compromised.

Rick let out a heavy sigh, rubbed his chin with his hand and said, "I think we can live with that. Amy?"

"That'll be fine," she said. She was numb, still in her otherworldly state of mind. The lives of the people around her, images of their private habits distracted and played with her imagination even as the most important elements of her deal were being discussed.

"You understand," Joan said, "that most of the performers in this town started in a revue or in another town entirely. You are an untested commodity in this venue. We're taking a big chance here."

CHAPTER 40

Amy rocked her feet back on the spikes of her heels and twisted her ankles around to loosen the tension that had slowly built in them and throughout her body. She might have drilled a hole in the carpet but Rick put his hand to her knee, and tapped his finger on it once gently. She stopped her rocking immediately and he removed his hand.

Then Henry began to talk about the television special and the needs of his sponsor. He wanted to discuss promotional tie-ins. He wanted to be dazzled with ideas for dramatic product promotion but neither Amy nor Rick yet understood the product being promoted.

"I'm going to need more details, Henry," Amy said. "You haven't told us who our sponsor is or what they have in mind. Perhaps I could meet with the sponsor directly."

"Well, my firm is handling the campaign."

"We could go together," she assured him, "representing as a team, the interests of your employer. You'd be surprised how convincing I can be as an ad exec."

Henry smiled; his wheels were turning as he envisioned the new partnership. "I think I'd like that," he said.

"I think I would too Henry," she said, and from the corner of her eye she caught Joan rolling her eyes.

"Can you fly to New York?" Henry asked.

"Of course she can," Rick said. "Give us a date, time, and location and we'll—"

Henry's smile turned to a frown.

"—she'll be there," Rick concluded and Henry's smile returned.

Business as usual, she thought.

"I'll need more details about the product or products I'll be promoting and I'll need a few days to kick around some ideas," she insisted. "But I won't let you down Henry."

"We've done corporate promotionals," Rick said.

"I know," Henry said. "I saw your work at the car show last year. It was amazing."

"It was supposed to be," Rick said. "The manufacturer was introducing a new line. They had discovered a new niche in the market and they wanted their presentation to be as magical as their discovery."

"It was," Henry said.

As the time passed the factions in the room became increasingly unified in their expectations, and each seemed content with the other. Finally, Joan asked Mindy to 'draw up some papers.' Apparently, among her many skills, Mindy also had legal prowess.

"Of course, the details are subject to further negotiation but we need a firm commitment on your part," Joan said as Mindy left the room.

Rick looked at his watch.

"It won't take long. My assistant knows what she's doing."

Within moments the young lady had returned with a contract in hand. She presented it to her boss. The woman put on reading glasses to look it over. It seemed so odd to Amy that she would do this. Why not wear contacts? But, then she thought, why would this woman care what other people thought? She wasn't a showgirl. She was a businesswoman, an executive. She probably had a nice pension plan, a comfortable salary and actual paid vacation days, not to mention company subsidized medical insurance.

Amy had never known any of those cushy corporate fringe benefits. Her life, until now, was gig to gig. The contract offered her the opportunity to slow down if not settle down, to finally stop worrying about pleasing the next potential customer in an endless chain of potential customers, and simply concentrate on doing the best show she had within her to do.

She'd always dreamed of this moment when all of her concentration, all of her creative energies could go into her show. She'd dreamed of how good the show could be with such an opportunity. And now, it was within her grasp. The pen and the fine print contract were being circulated. Everyone was signing on the bottom line and then the contract came to Rick.

Rick studied it. He put a single line through one sentence, explained his objection and initialed it. Then, he signed it and passed it to Amy.

She looked at it. It was a long sheet of paper with at least four layers of duplicates beneath the white top page. There were pink and yellow copies and more concealed behind the others. Everyone signs, everyone gets a copy and everyone goes home convinced that they made the best choice and struck the best deal.

It intimidated her. The tiny words seemed to have teeth like piranha. She pretended to read, to study. Rick held the pen out to her and she looked at it without removing it from his hand. It was a large, fat, black, ballpoint thing, the fattest pen she'd ever seen. If pens could lose weight, this one needed to.

"It's preliminary, dear," Joan explained. "We can hammer out the fine points later."

Amy went back to her 'reading.' Her head was swirling, as if she'd been sampling wine all day.

Her mind drifted to Brendon even as her eyes ran across the paper. She imagined how difficult it would be for them to make time for each other. She was thinking of the vineyard in Sonoma, and how she wished she were there right now, safe.

And yet, she'd enjoyed the evening. She'd enjoyed imagining the stability the contract offered her and the opportunity to pursue something more than a traveling show. The idea of television excited her too.

She took the pen from Rick and sat the contract down on the coffee table. The weight of the enormous pen cradled between her fingers, its ballpoint resting above the line that awaited her signature; the only signature needed to complete the deal.

It wasn't the money she'd hoped for. In fact, it represented less than she had made the year before, or the year before that. Joan assured her that the money would come with proven success in the venue. But, she doubted it would ever equal the income she enjoyed on the road.

The contract also gave the casino breach options that left her vulnerable. But, living gig to gig had been a vulnerable lifestyle. Vulnerability was something she had grown accustomed to.

There is no gravy train, she told herself. But, despite its shortcomings, the contract held promise. At the very least, it would afford her the opportunity to pursue what every magician hoped for but rarely ever realized, a high profile full-scale illusion show, an evening show, as it was once called. Dante had built his own evening show, on his own terms. But he paid for it, and he never realized a profit from it. He told her that the show had been its own reward. A big show could be satisfying, but satisfaction wouldn't put food on her table.

Maybe Rick was right. Maybe she was insecure, afraid of her own success. Or maybe a part of her actually believed in her mother's prophecy of eternal failure. Or maybe her intuition, that quiet softly spoken voice, was trying to tell her something, a warning perhaps. If so, then signing would be a disaster. Either way, her life would forever change. Sign and she belonged to magic. Refuse to sign and she'd have to figure out now, not later, what she really wanted from her life.

"I need more time," she said.

Rick looked away from her and offered a congenial smile to the people around them. Quick glances were exchanged among the negotiators.

"Well, is there anything in the contract you're not comfortable with?" Morgan asked.

"No," she said. "I think the terms of the contract are fair for all concerned."

"Whatever it is, dear, speak up," Joan encouraged. "We'd all like to put this to bed as soon as possible."

"You're asking for an extensive and exclusive commitment on my part. I'd like to consider all of my options before making such a commitment."

"May I have a moment to confer?" Rick asked with his right index finger up in a 'time out' gesture.

"Nonsense, Rick," Joan corrected.

Amy sensed in Joan a most sympathetic ally not unlike Morgan.

"Let her think it through," Joan said. "I want her to go into this deal confident and sure. More than that, if she can't do it with passion, I don't want her signing at all."

"I'll call you in the morning," she said to Amy. "Will that be enough time? You can have the contract delivered to my attention or you could drop it by, but then," she glanced at Rick and smiled knowingly, "I'm told you have a plane to catch."

Rick didn't flinch. He wouldn't give her the satisfaction of knowing she had caught him in a lie and his poker face was perfect.

"Actually," Amy said, "there is another party that I'd like to consult."

Amy could feel Rick's eyes on her but she wasn't going to cower, not this time. She wanted to consult Brendon, and she wanted his input without pressure or influence from Rick.

"And you don't think a day would give you enough time?" Joan inquired.

"I need two weeks," she said.

"No, dear," Joan countered, "we do have schedules to keep. We can give you a week but no more."

CHAPTER 41

Mindy escorted Amy and Rick to the front entrance. As they walked in silence, Amy ignored the splendor of her surroundings. She didn't want to run the risk of developing a longing for a future that might never be. The messages from her deepest instinct were often clouded by reason. Her mind made so much noise at times that the clarity of her intuitive voice was completely overwhelmed. But this time there was no mistaking that softly spoken whisper.

It pleased her to believe she could be successful in a Vegas resort. The fantasy was fun but the price of turning that fantasy into a working reality could be greater than the return in life satisfaction she expected to yield from it. It was a conviction she wanted to discuss with Rick but he would most likely not understand or misunderstand her compulsion. Her basis of decision was a feeling. Rick would probably want facts and explanations; things that she was unprepared to offer.

In recent days, she'd come to believe that her intuitive voice would never lead her to pain. But the business interests of her clients, the glamour and glitz that appealed to her, and the persuasive tactics of her most trusted ally often did. What she wanted most at the moment was to stop the struggle and relax. She wanted to slow the pace of her life and look around, to stop and smell the roses or the vines as the case may be. She wasn't sure what it might take what it might cost her to leap from the locomotion of her present moment life but when the evening air touched her face as she left the casino, she decided that no price was too high.

"I hope you decide to join us, Ms. Alexander," Mindy said with a broad smile and a firm handshake. "If you need anything, anything at all, please don't hesitate to call me. All you need do is ask."

"Thank you so much, Mindy," Amy said. "You are so kind and delightful, and I have enjoyed meeting you."

Rick hadn't said a word to her since they had left the suite. The fact that he hadn't so much as looked in her direction suggested displeasure no doubt with her decision to wait. She wasn't accustomed to making the people in her life uncomfortable. She didn't want to disappoint Rick or any of the other people involved in the negotiation but she both needed and wanted to make her own decision, one that would satisfy her. If her gut wasn't at ease with the contract, then she wasn't going to sign it.

The driver pulled up to the walkway as they approached. When the car stopped she left her position behind the wheel and walked around the front of the car to the door but Rick beat her to the handle and almost knocked her down in the process. He held it for Amy but didn't look at her as she stepped in. Then, he slammed the door, smiled his goodbye to Mindy, and walked around the back of the car to climb in the other side.

The driver settled into the front seat and Rick told her to drive.

Amy tried to ignore the silence that was screaming at her from Rick's side of the car, but she couldn't.

"I wasn't ready to sign, Rick," she said.

"I kind of figured that out."

"It doesn't mean I won't."

"It's a big decision. It's not all we were hoping for, and I'm glad you negotiated for more time. It sends the message that you're none too eager."

"Thanks, Rick. I know you're disappointed. But, as ever, you look for the silver lining."

He finally met her eyes. He reached across the long back seat, took her hand in his and squeezed. Amy appreciated the gesture. She understood it to mean that they were still friends.

They drove in silence for a few moments. Her mind was a haze of confusion. It would have been easier to reject the deal had Rick been steaming mad. His behavior suggested he would be but his eyes and his touch suggested otherwise. Perhaps he was holding back. Maybe he was really mad but wanted to give her space. Regardless, his generosity was making her ache for him. If she didn't sign the contract she didn't know how long it might take him to position another talent for a similar deal. It wasn't only her life she was toying with. He would suffer if she turned it down and prosper if she signed. He had helped her. The success she'd known was largely due to his management. But, how much did she owe him for that? Did she owe him at all?

"I saw the layout of the stage," she said.

"So what did you think?"

"It's not the only issue but it is a shabby stage for the show they expect to produce on it."

"Why didn't you bring it up?"

"It's small."

"There is nothing small about that hotel," he said. "Even the toilet paper dispensers are huge and luxurious. I saw the stage too. You've worked on smaller. Besides, it has a spacious backstage area, riggings for scenery and it's already preset for Pepper style ghost illusions."

She didn't argue the point. The stage could have been better, it could have been worse. It was an excuse to inch herself into dialogue with Rick, to feel him out.

"It's not about that stage," he said. "But if you do have any legitimate concern, then I think Joan has a right to know about it."

"You're right," she said. She had wanted to discuss her feelings all night but now all she wanted to do was get away from him. The closer she came to confessing her real inhibition the more likely it seemed he would reject her. He'd never understand. How could he? Too much money and prestige was involved for him to respond sensitively to her concerns. Sensitivity was never his strongest virtue in any case.

"I should have mentioned it," she said. "There are extra riggings but none for the sets we need. And I'll have to break in a crew."

"A professional crew," he said, "and we were lucky to get Jason and Freddie in on the deal."

"They want grand but they are only willing to pay for big."

"You know I love Dante as much as you do but he has poisoned you. Those days are gone and they'll never come again. The Thurston show is buried in crates because no one can afford to resurrect it, not you, not Dante, and certainly not Joan. She has a business to run and profits to make.

"I didn't want to have to tell you this because I know how strongly you feel about Dante. He was a great performer, one of the best, but his show lost money. If he hadn't made a killing in antiquities he'd be a poor man today. He had no business sense, at least no show business sense."

"He was committed to the show," she said, "to the spirit and the history of the show. He's an artist. Business sense is why we need people like you. He never had a manger like you."

"Managers were standing in line for him. He didn't want one. He wanted to do his show his way and he didn't want to deal with any deviations. In a profit and loss world it's always about taking detours and compromising. You've got to earn the bucks. You've got to give before you can get. Audience response and how that response equates to box office receipts is all that really matters."

"Not to me."

"And not to Dante," he said, "but it almost cost him everything. Ask him; ask him what he lost and what he sacrificed for the largest show of his time. You've read the biographies. Even in the golden age, most of the showman went down impoverished. Leon and Carter, now those men should be your role models. They knew how to survive in this business. The others could have done well but they had to have the biggest and the best and their lust destroyed them.

"It's a business Amy. That's why they call it show business. At the end of the day, you and your sponsors have got to make a profit. It's icing on the cake if you have a sense of artistic satisfaction but it's not the most important thing."

"Why can't I have both?"

"I think you can. All I'm saying is that if you don't turn a profit, you won't be around long enough to find out if your performance is artistically fulfilling. Profit has got to be your top priority or you won't be able to do anything else, not for long anyway."

Again they were silent. Again she wished she could be anywhere but in the back seat of a limo in heavy slow traffic with him.

"So is it the stage?" he asked. "Is it some vague violation of artistic integrity? Or is all this a smoke screen. What's the bottom line here Amy?"

She looked out the window at the flashing signs and glitzy neon lights and rapped her fingers on the console.

"If not now when?" he asked. "When will you give yourself the chance to make something of your life? What are you waiting for? What's it going to take?"

CHAPTER 42

Amy removed the contract from the brown accordion folder it was stored in. She couldn't see in the dark of the limo's interior so Rick turned an on overhead light. Then he handed her the same fat pen she'd seen earlier. Somehow he'd acquired it. She took it from him, put it in her purse and snapped her purse shut.

"Do you know what most people would give for a contract like that?" he asked as he switched the light off.

"Like this?" She held the contract out to him. "Let's face some facts; it's considerably less money than what we made last year, and I will be too busy to do other gigs to make up the slack."

"But with it comes increased visibility and celebrity," he explained. "It's a trade off I know but it's a decent one. This first year will be slim and we'll lose our grip on our present market. Have you ever had a deal without risk?"

He was waiting on her but she felt the answer was self-evident so she didn't bother to reply.

"The answer is no," he said. "I'll help you with the tough ones, I always do. We both know we'll more than make up for it in years to come. With increased success comes increased negotiating power and more money, a lot more money. Your name will be out there, bigger than ever. Agents and corporate entertainment gurus will want to book the babe from Vegas. It's a good career move. I wouldn't be pushing you into it if it weren't. When all is said and done, we'll be commanding twice what we're getting now, maybe several times what we're getting now, and we'll be attracting new business at the same time."

"You don't know that."

"I do know that. I'm your manager remember?"

"It's still a gamble."

"It's all a gamble. Since when do you believe in guarantees?"

"I'll be out of circulation. The agents will find somebody else for a first call."

"They won't forget you. You'll be more in demand than ever."

"They'd forget me in a month let alone a year."

"Let them."

"They have been the backbone of my business."

"Thirty-five percent of your business has come from client-to-client referral."

"The rest from agents," she emphasized.

"I'm not saying we won't lose some of them. Of course we will. We lose some every time we raise our fee. But, those that stay have always more than made up for those that go. And when you make a real name for yourself, a name that transcends the business, they will all pay top dollar. You'll see."

"The odds suggest otherwise. We both know performers that have come in and out of Las Vegas. Most of them lost business in the end."

"Since when did you ever play the odds, Amy? This isn't a business people go into because they want to play it safe. What do you want a pension plan, profit sharing, company-paid health insurance, a desk or a cubicle? If you were so worried about the odds, why did you run away from home to become a struggling actress in New York? Surely you knew the odds then but you did it anyway, didn't you? And here we are as a result, in the back of a limo discussing a one-year contract with a major entertainment broker in Las Vegas. Those are pretty good odds I'd say."

"I had nothing to lose then. It was easier to take chances. I was younger, I was poor, and I had no one else to think about but myself."

"Why are we arguing about this?" he exploded. "The Amy I knew would have jumped on this contract without a moment's hesitation."

She nodded in agreement. She was not the same person she was when first they met. She was not as hungry as she had been. She looked over at him in the dark of the back seat. He needed something that she was not sure she could give him. He needed her to be someone that she was not sure she wanted to be.

"It's not fun anymore," she said. "And, if I sign then I'll have to make the sacrifices, put in the time, and produce."

"And that worries you?"

"Shouldn't it?"

"No," he said, "it shouldn't. You've been producing all of your life. This is going to be a stroll in the park compared to what you've been doing. You've paid your dues Amy. You've worked harder than anyone ever had a right to expect of you. And now, all you have to do is keep the momentum going."

"It has been a long journey."

"Shorter than some," he said, "longer than others."

"But, I'm not obsessed anymore."

"You can do it," he assured her. "If you couldn't you wouldn't have gotten this far. But think on this …"

"Did you hear what I said, Rick?"

"What?"

"I'm not obsessed anymore."

"Good," he said. "Maybe now you can perform without getting sick."

"No, it's not good for me," she said. "Not in this business."

"And why not?"

"Successful magicians are obsessive ones."

"Not always."

"And I was obsessed once. I was hungry. But I'm not anymore."

"You're tired. I've been working you too hard. Perhaps we should negotiate for some vacation time before you begin at the casino."

"I don't think it's burn-out."

"You don't need to be driven," he said. "Your drive put you here tonight. Your new-found balance can keep you here for the long-term."

"To succeed in this town," she said, "I need more than what I've ever needed before. Charm, a congenial personality, and some of the time-tested classics of magic have put me here, but only novelty will keep me here."

"So," he said, "we'll hire a consultant."

"You can't hire someone to do that."

"Of course, you can," he said. "Most of the performers in this town have done that. We'll talk to a consultant, one that specializes in developing original approaches to grand illusion. They grow on trees in California, you know."

"It's got to come from inside of me," she said. "I need to be the creative force behind this show."

"Why?"

"What do you mean why?"

"You are the talent," he explained. "Other people specialize in creation. When you need a plumber do you fix it yourself?"

"No."

"I should hope not or you'll end up with a big mess," he said. "If you need something new, hire the people that can do that for you and stop worrying about it."

"I think you're missing my point."

"And that is?"

"Even if I choose to work with a creative consultant, I'm still going to have to put in the labor to make it mine. Creating something new is more about hard, disciplined effort than it is about inspiration. And this level of creativity will require more of me than I think I am capable of giving right now. I want to devote my time to something else."

"Someone else?"

"Yes," she said emphatically. Then she said, "Maybe."

"Yes," he said. "Maybe? What does that mean? Are you thinking of giving up the business after all we've been through? That's like getting three steps from the summit of Mount Everest and then deciding you really didn't want to climb that stupid mountain after all. You can't give up now. You have no idea how beautiful the view is going to be until you step out on the cliff and look around. Don't walk back down the mountain, after it's taken so much of you to climb up."

"It has taken too much of me. You're right about that. Can't you see what it's doing? I might be winning battles but I'm losing the war and I'm losing myself in the process. I don't know who I am anymore. I don't know who I'm supposed to be or even who I want to be."

"You're too introspective."

"You're my manager, not my therapist."

"I'm also your friend. Love comes and goes. In the end we're all islands in a vast sea. Some of those islands shine and some sink into oblivion. Yours can shine. Sure, I've seen the toll you've paid. Sign that contract, see it through and you'll know it's worth the price."

"And what if we're not islands? What if we're really connected to and dependent on one another? What if what really matters most is how we've treated the people around us and not how brightly we shine while doing it?"

"It's all about him isn't it?"

"No," she said, "maybe. I don't know. But, I do know that I'm not the biggest and brightest star in the universe. Compared with the real stars in the real universe I'm a glowing candle on a short burning wick. And, I know that I want to be a part of something that is bigger than me. Right now it looks like magic will only be as big as my will to push it. I want something bigger and better; I need something bigger. Something I don't have to push. I want to be carried along in the current. I don't want to keep swimming against it."

"I want to know what you need to succeed here and now." Rick demanded. "What do you want me to do? What do you want Joan to do? What will I have to do to convince you that signing that contract is the single best decision you can make right now? What would make you happy with the deal you've been offered? That's the question Amy. It's the only one that matters. The things you're talking about aren't real. This deal is."

CHAPTER 43

There was a part of Amy that wanted to be persuaded. But there was another part that wanted to breathe. It was a part that she had never listened to before and in some sense, she was beginning to believe that in denying that part of herself she had never really been alive before. If she listened to Rick she feared she might lose that struggling newborn part of herself forever.

"I need a sensation," she said providing him, for the time being, with the kind of discussion he was comfortable with and rescuing her delicate instinct from his grip. "I need an illusion, a bit of business, something that will draw people to the resort. I need something that's never been seen or done before. You heard what Joan said. You know what I need."

"Well, that explains it," he said.

"It explains what?"

"It explains why you're so scared."

"I'm not afraid," she protested.

"I think you are. I think you are desperately afraid of failing at the biggest opportunity you've ever had. So you're setting yourself up for failure but placing demands on yourself that you know you can never achieve. Joan isn't asking you to do what has never been done before. It might have sounded that way but what she really wants is something she's never seen before. There's a big difference. All we have to do is revise and rewrite history in a more contemporary way. As the Proverbial saying goes, 'there is nothing new under the sun.' You need to keep doing what you've been doing."

"Weren't you listening to Joan?"

"I heard her," Rick said. "She wants and deserves originality and that's what we'll give her. If you don't wake up in the middle of the night with one of your brainstorms, I'll hire someone who will. It's that simple. I told you before."

"I'm not sure I can deliver this time," she said.

"If you couldn't," he said, "you wouldn't be holding that contract in your hand. The fact that they want you is proof enough of your ability. You're afraid. This is a big step; it's something new. Fear is only natural. If you'll face it, as I've seen you do so many times, you'll be fine. Your mind is playing games with you. It's the old fight or flight syndrome disguised as an existential dilemma."

"Let me be clear, I want you to understand. I know it looks like jitters but it's not, not this time."

"No, it looks like it's not, but it is."

"Listen to me," Amy said. "My life is so much more complicated, and my values are changing. Please let them. I'm changing. But I don't want to lose you and everything else in the process. I'm looking at everything as if through another person's eyes, and I do not like what I'm seeing."

"Every decision we make," he said, "every day of every week of every year is like that. You can't dwell on it. Grab the chances life gives you, make the most of them, and sort out the problems as they arise. Don't create problems where none exist."

"I need to discuss it with Brendon."

"What has he done to deserve such consideration?"

"I love him."

"Well then, I hope he loves you."

"I believe he does."

"If he does then he won't stand in the way."

"He won't. It'll be my decision, I promise you. I won't make it to please him."

"Good."

"Or you."

"I don't want you to do anything for my sake," he said. "You will sign this contact. And you're right, it won't be for me or for Brendon, it'll be for you. Think about it. Sleep on it. Hash it over with your wine guy. And, when you're through, I'm sure you will realize how special this opportunity is."

"I could listen to you all night, and you could eventually persuade me to do anything you want."

"Not anything."

"You could talk me into this contract."

"I could," he admitted. "But I won't."

"Then you'll be biting your tongue all the way back to the hotel. I know you too well. Not only could you convince me that I should sign, but you'd have me believing I want to."

He laughed. It was a sound that relieved some of her pain. She didn't want to hurt or insult him. She wondered how she could negotiate through the waters she was in without doing either. But his ready laughter suggested that he was amused and not as disappointed in her as he might have been.

"I'm glad you're on my side," she said.

"Well," he admitted, "we didn't get the deal we both wanted."

"No," she said. "The big paydays never seem to materialize for us."

"Sure they do. You simply don't recognize them when they come."

"You know I always thought of myself as an actress. I always thought it would be so much fun to be somebody else, to hide behind a mask. Do you remember when we first met?"

"I remember the first night I saw you in that silly off Broadway play," he said. "But during our first meeting, you told me of your memories of Dante, and I knew you'd take to the art right then and there. Why point out now that 'you're an actress?'"

"What you offered was a steady gig," she explained. "I never had a steady gig, and I wanted to know what it was like."

"And?"

"I never meant for this steady gig to become my life. It was supposed to be a part I would play until my real life began. Now I can't tell the difference between the character I'm playing and the real me. I don't even know who the real me is, or what she wants. The days have past into years but the missing pieces I so wanted to find are every bit as missing today as they were the first day we met."

"What real life?" he asked. "What did you want that you never got?"

"I wanted to be famous," she confessed. She never heard those words leave her mouth before. It was as if someone else was saying them, but suddenly so much made sense.

"Famous?" he laughed loud and hard. "Well, you're a breath away from that."

"I know," she whispered. She was almost famous. The reality of fame was within her reach. It was only a signature away. She was close enough to know that fame wasn't what she wanted or needed after all. Magic had been fun; the theatre was fun, but it could never be simply for fun or even merely a job because it was never about pleasure or accomplishment or money. It had always been about fame or what she thought fame would give her. It drove her, motivated her, and it was gone. It was a tree removed by the roots and only a hole remained. What she really wanted she'd found in Brendon and her silent small voice had been trying to tell her all along. The reality she accidentally discovered along the way to fame made fame look artificial and cheap.

"So," he said, "sign the contract. Achieve your goal. It's that simple."

"Simplicity is an elusive thing, Rick."

"Here we go."

"And what about the others you manage?"

"What do they have to do with this moment?"

"What do they really want?" she asked.

"How should I know? Why should I care? Most are making a good living, and most could care less how famous they are. They were magicians from the start, unlike you. They love the art for the art's sake. As long as they're making money doing what they love, they're happy."

"Most of the best magicians are hobbyists, aren't they?"

"I don't know," he said. "I don't think the best magicians are hobbyists, but I do think that for the very best, magic is as much their avocation as their vocation. But what do I know? I'm a manager, not a historian. What are you driving at?"

"I'm tired of chasing gigs, and clients, and agents around the country. When I left home, I knew I'd have some dues to pay, but I thought I'd arrive someday."

"I think you have arrived and most of those magicians you referred to would think so too."

"Don't you get it?" she asked. "The goal itself was the illusion. This whole town is a façade. It's a metaphor for a life that doesn't work."

"You need a good therapist, or an anti-depressant. I'll call a doctor."

"I don't need a doctor," she said.

"A good night's sleep then."

"I'm fine," she said. 'Really I'm fine. I don't think I've ever been better in my life than I am in this one crystal clear moment. I'd love to bottle it up and never forget the lesson I'm learning right now."

She saw fame for what it was, for what she thought it was. It was like learning the secret of an illusion that had baffled her mind for years. There was a pinch of disappointment but there was also insight. It took root deep within her and blossomed like a flower after a spring rain. She had a new perspective and with the passing of her old one everything became new.

"I let you down," he said. "Didn't I?"

"No you didn't. In fact, you did fine. You did fine. You've done better by me than I ever expected a manager would. This is a competitive town. There's a magician on every corner and six others waiting in the wings willing to work for next to nothing. The contract is a major achievement. Maybe what's wrong is our presence in this town—my presence in this town."

"I know it's a pay cut, but I still think it's a good career move."

"Maybe," she said, "but I think I'd like to slow down. For years I've tried to do what everyone else wanted. Right now, I'd like to try to figure out for myself what I want."

"You need a little time to think it through, to work out some of the rough edges. You always need time. That's your way. I should have eased you into it. I should have prepared you better but I didn't have that luxury. The opportunity presented itself. If I hadn't moved as quickly as I did you wouldn't have a decision to make right now."

"Yes," she said, "I do need time. And I need to feel good about what I'm doing. You've done well by me and I'm grateful. No matter what I decide or how you react, I'll always be grateful to you for what you've already done. But I'm going to make a decision that I'll feel good about long after it's made."

CHAPTER 44

As Amy drove north along the California coast, the mahogany case that housed the rare and precious wand that Dante had given her, sat next to her in the passenger seat. With her free hand, she picked it up and rubbed the wooden casing with her thumb. The box was heavy with the weight of age, history, and tradition and the wood was smooth and hard like stone.

She tried to imagine the night in Baltimore when Kellar presented it to Thurston.

Thurston had labored for years with a show of his own. It had steadily grown and he had developed a noble following. But Kellar was the preeminent illusionist of the time and until Kellar retired, Thurston would always be number two.

Kellar had spared no expense or strategy to amass the world's largest and most grandiose illusion show. He'd hired a mechanic from the Egyptian Hall to discover the secret of levitation, a secret he'd tried to purchase but neither David Devant nor the Maskleynes were willing to sell.

Kellar knew what he wanted and what he wanted was to have the grandest, the best, and so it was that through his determination and will, he became the biggest and the best. When he passed his show on to his chosen successor, Thurston inherited not only the great master's show but his dream and determination as well. He began where Kellar had let off. And, Thurston built the largest and grandest magic show that had ever been seen in the history of magic until that time. He featured illusions from all over the world; he invented new and astounding illusions and he consistently improved upon existing ones.

But, during Thurston's reign, the world changed. Audiences grew accustomed to watching larger than life images on a silver screen that was itself the invention of a magician. On the big screen, magical occurrences were as commonplace and as easily performed as breathing. Thurston's show was shortened to open for a feature film and before he died, he ended up second fiddle to the Hollywood dream machine. Ironically, it had been magicians, eager to offer something new to a thirsty audience, who first used projected images, images that would eventually overshadow magic.

All of that history and tradition, loss and pain, triumph and failure sat in her hand, encapsulated in this tiny case of wood. She loved the history of the wand and the heritage it represented. She loved the father Dante had become to her. She adored her two assistants, Jason and Freddie. And Rick had become as much a part of her life, even of her daily routine, as any friend she had ever known. She was as connected to magic as magic was to her; she was connected emotionally, socially, and financially. A new life was not going to be purchased without pain.

But, performing night in and night out was becoming increasingly difficult and her reasons for dealing with the challenge less clear. Her audiences enjoyed her. They showed their appreciation with applause, ovations, letters and gifts. But she wanted more. When she performed, she wanted every member of her audience to stare with wide eyes and open mouths full of wonder and awe. She wanted them to re-experience the joy they felt the first time they saw a snow covered field or heard a clap of thunder; she wanted the child within to find rebirth, to be born anew in every heart. But that never happened. Her show was enjoyed and then quickly forgotten.

She knew her expectations were high, but that look of wonder on the faces of her audience members was the one thing she always thought magic would do that other performing arts could not. She'd known wonder and she wanted others to know it too. But, after years of effort, her only certainty was that the emotional response of wonder was the most difficult of all illusions to create. Every effort she'd made seemed futile and the road ahead looked bleak.

Money wasn't going to satisfy her longing and neither would a Vegas contract. In fact, the contract and the higher expectations it represented emphasized the point that her real goal would forever and always remain unattainable. The thought of it pained her while the journey to Brendon gave her joy and peace.

When she was with Brendon time and schedules had no meaning. He was a small audience, but when he looked at her, his eyes were always filled with the emotion she longed to see in her audience but never did. He had told her that he loved her often enough, but he never needed to because love was in everything that he did, every gesture and every sound.

Brendon thought she was the wonder, not the finely skilled or beautifully manufactured illusions she presented on the stage. And, what most amazed her was that the wonder and attention of this one man satisfied her like no audience ever had.

She put down the wand and picked up her contract. She had already studied every word, memorized every clause and wherefore and whereas. Glancing at it again as she drove, the tiny print ran together like one massive blob of ink. Contracts like this one were never intended to be understood, at least not by anyone other than a lawyer or an agent. But, they were meant to be binding.

She put the contract down in the seat to devote her full attention to the road ahead. In moments she would turn from the main road, hard, smooth and black, onto a small dirt and gravel road that would take her to Brendon's side. She hadn't told him she was coming. She worried a moment that her visit might be intrusive but the thought was quickly swallowed up in memories of his love and affection.

The beautifully hand crafted sign marking Brendon's vineyard appeared and she turned onto his property. The gravel under her tires made a distinctly different sound than the asphalt road she'd been on. It was music to her ears and it excited her, the way reaching a favorite vacation spot might but Brendon's land was more than a vacation spot to her. It had become home and she was very glad to be home again.

As she drove the dirt road that winded its way across the vineyard she saw no sign of habitation. But for a few birds the lush property seemed deserted. No workers were in the fields despite the beauty of the day, and when her car came to a stop in front of the house, no one came to greet her. She had hoped he might see her approach. His smile was like the wagging tail of a puppy. It delighted her every time she saw it and when he knew she was on her way he often waited for her on or near the porch. He wasn't there. No one was there.

Perhaps everyone was meeting. He held business meetings often though one could hardly refer to them as business meetings. Much eating and laughter normally characterized them.

She removed her sunglasses and closed them in her hands. As she approached the porch dirt crunched beneath her feet. She stood still in front of the door. A gentle breeze tossed her short hair and invited her to sit on the swing and sleep awhile. She reached to knock but lowered her hand. The grip on her glasses tightened until the plastic cracked.

I'm a magician, she told herself. I've got a Vegas contract in the car. All I've got to do is sign it and I'm on my way to becoming a household name. Every one in America will know me before long. I'll have everything I need everything I've ever longed for.

Most magicians spend their whole lives dreaming of this kind of success. So, what am I doing here? Why am I not in Vegas with Rick? Why haven't I signed? Is fame so shallow or is Rick right? Maybe I'm letting fear get the best of me. I hate to be conquered. I'm a conqueror. I decide what I want and then I go out and get it like Kellar and Thurston and all the others that have built a name and a reputation for themselves. But what do I want? I was so certain that I didn't want to sign in the limo the night of the negotiation. Now, I'm not so sure.

She looked around at the land surrounding the house, the rows and rows of endless vines. She tried to imagine life on the vineyard day after day, year after year for the rest of her life. She tried to imagine her future without the stage, without applause. This place was peaceful, the land magical. But could it be enough? Would it be enough if she quit the business and retired the show?

If I could conjure upon the stage half the beauty of this land I'd be a marvel indeed and Joan would have every reason to be pleased.

She walked to the wooden railing where she'd weeks before tried to explain to Brendon why he couldn't, why he shouldn't marry her.

He'll find another girl, she thought. This is ridiculous. I'm not a farmer. I was perfectly happy before he came into the picture. I'll be happy when he's gone. No Brendon to complicate my life, only magic, and the stage, the audience, and their applause. Rick knows what he's talking about. He knows what's best for me. I should have listened to him. But I can't. Look at this place. Now that I'm here I don't ever want to leave again, and Brendon; would my life be the same without him in it?

He had changed her. She knew that now and she realized that she could never go back. The person she had been before they met would never be again and the person she'd become couldn't imagine a life without him in it.

She walked down the porch steps toward her car. Another wind gave her pause as it brought with it a fragrance unique to the farm. She closed her eyes and opened her ears to the song that also seemed carried by the breeze, and the harmony of the birds, a music that was also unique to this place. It was like no other place she'd ever been. It seemed removed from space and time. There was something eternal about it that gave her heart rest. The trees planted in the soil beneath her feet were so fortunate. They alone had the privilege of gazing over the land day and night year after year. If only she had been born a tree instead of tumbleweed how happy indeed she would be.

She had intended to climb back into her car and drive away. Instead, she paused at a tree on the opposite side of the dirt road. She touched it and then hugged it. She remembered again the feel of the tree in her backyard the day her father died, and she began to cry. She'd missed his love so much, and nothing she'd done replaced it.

As she embraced the tree, arms from behind embraced her.

"Amy," Brendon whispered, "welcome home."

CHAPTER 45

Amy didn't want Brendon to see her tears or her conflict. She clung to the tree and he let her. She forced the painful memory from her mind and swallowed her emotions until the wellspring in her eyes dried.

"Are you okay?" Brendon's voice was tender and soothing.

"I'm fine Brendon." Amy put on a smile though she knew he could not see it.

"I wish you had called," He said. "I'd have been better prepared."

"I'm sorry. I know I should've called. I didn't want to take the time. I wanted to be here as quickly as I could."

He kissed the back of her head. His hands rested gently on her shoulders. He might have wanted to turn her to face him but she was confident that he would always protect and guard her dignity.

"I got the contract," she said.

"Congratulations."

"It's in the car."

"You brought it all the way up here to show me?"

"Don't you want to see?"

"Of course I do," Brendon said. "I'm proud of you. You did it. All of your dreams are coming true."

In his arms she was feeling exactly as she wanted. It was a feeling of right. It wasn't something she was waiting for or working for, it was simply there. It was hers for the asking, hers for the keeping. She wanted him to hold her forever. She wanted the calm he gave her to endure.

She turned in his embrace to face him. Her eyes were still moist with the memory of her father and with the agony of something else, something deeper that she could not as yet identify. But her tears didn't embarrass her. The sweet turn of his smile left her believing she would never be embarrassed or ashamed with him.

"What if I were to tell you that I didn't sign the contract? What if I told you that I didn't want to be away from you that much? What if I were to tell you that I'm going to take you up on your proposal and move in here with you for the rest of your life?"

"Is that what you're telling me?"

"Does it scare you?" she asked. "Does the thought of really getting what you asked for scare you?"

"I know what I want," he said. "And, no, it doesn't scare me. But I'll marry you regardless of whether you sign the contract or not. I'll stand by you whatever your decision. If magic is what you want then so be it. I'll do whatever I can to make sure you have every chance at success. If you decide against it, that's fine too. I want to be by your side wherever your choices lead."

"And if I were to never return to the stage?"

"Do you suppose that would disappoint me?"

"Well, it is part of who I am," she said. "If I lose that, I'm not sure I'll be the same person, the person you met and the person you expect to marry."

"When we met, I really wasn't concerned about what you did for a living. It was you I fell in love with, not your image or your mystique. It's your career and it's great but it's not who you are. Change careers as often as you like; you'll always be the woman I fell in love with."

"But if I left I'd be a quitter."

"Mom again?"

"What do you mean?"

"You told me once how your mother never let you quit on anything. 'Once you put your hand to the trowel, you can never look back.' Wasn't that what she used to tell you?"

"Yes, it was. She never let me quit anything regardless of how much I hated it."

"And if you did," he said, "she withdrew her love or worse she beat you until you wished you were dead."

"You remembered all those stories? I didn't think you were listening but it sure felt good to talk about it."

"I'm not going to stop loving you if you quit," he said, "I'm not going to stop loving you if you don't. Unlike your mother, my love for you will never die and it will never waiver and it will never depend on what you do or don't do."

"How can anyone be so sure of love?" she asked.

"I could never love anyone on my strength alone. But I am not alone and neither are you. The source of our love is greater and bigger then either of us. It is not in my self that I place my trust, but in the source of my love, of all love. Love can never fail because He will never fail."

"You're a religious man."

"You know I am," he said.

"I'm Orthodox," she said.

"I'm Catholic, but I can worship in the Orthodox tradition."

"And I as a Catholic."

He smiled at her and she slid from his arms and walked the short distance to her car. She removed the contract and unfolded it as she returned to Brendon who had remained by the tree.

"This is it," she said as she extended it to him.

He took it from her and looked at it.

"Scary isn't it?" he said.

"I've seen contracts before, Brendon. I have to sign one with every gig or Ricky does."

"But this one's different."

"This one will require at least a year of my life."

"But isn't this your dream? It's what you've been wanting for most of your adult life."

"I don't know any more. I used to be passionate about magic. I used to care. Now when I look at a prop, I feel wearied by the sight. I don't want to touch it; I don't want to rehearse with it. I don't want to read the books and the journals and the trades. I don't want to sit in smoke filled rooms and talk routines with the guys. I don't want to get into those skimpy outfits and tell myself it'll all be worth it someday. Someday is today. I'm holding the most important contract of my career in my hands and I find myself asking, was it really all worth it? Is this what I've been working so hard for?"

"Maybe you're nervous. Nerves and fear can distort even the clearest of minds."

"I don't want to throw away the best opportunity of my life for an elaborate form of stage fright."

"Then sign and know that I'll support you—know that I'll be there on opening night to lead the cheering."

"It's possible that fear is playing games with me."

"But you don't really think so?"

"It all feels a bit empty to me," she said. "I expected more money but then I also know the money will come with a proven track record. Rick thinks I'm uncertain about my ability to deliver and I suppose I led him to believe that. The truth is I only led him in that direction because I didn't think he could handle the truth."

"And what is the truth, Amy?"

"The truth is I'm standing at the end of the rainbow and there is no pot of gold, no Oz, only some silly old man behind a curtain with some really cool pyrotechnic tricks but tricks none the less. It's all a fabrication. When I realized how much a fabrication it was I became suddenly fearful that my very existence was a fabrication, an illusion. And now I'm numb, half asleep, but I want to wake up, I want to live again."

"Some say that the striving is the joy, that the journey is the end in itself. It's not easy to achieve your fondest wish, only to discover it wasn't your heart's desire at all. But if you can honestly discern when you have and have not erred, then you are richly blessed indeed. We can know the secrets of the universe, but when our own hearts remain a mystery to us, we're lost at sea, and it is a vast sea."

"So it seems, Brendon, so it seems."

"Is it possible that as long as you were striving, as long as you had obstacles to overcome, you had something to blame for the joy that was missing from your life?"

"Am I so joyless in your eyes?"

"I'm not saying that you are but we both know how restless and uneasy you've become. Perhaps if you stand still, the source of your sorrow will have a chance to find you, and you it."

"And it would be good if that happened?" she asked.

"How else can you make peace with it? Joy never comes from being too busy to notice pain but from reconciliation."

"Reconciliation to what?"

"I don't know. Only you know the answer to that question. But I'll help you find it."

"Why will you help me?" she asked.

"Because I love you."

"Is love a sentimental way of feeling? Or is it an attachment based on compatible personality components or perhaps in biochemistry?"

"None of the above I hope," he laughed as if she'd told a joke. "I believe it is in loving and in being loved that we most closely resemble the one who made us. I believe that He is the source of it, and that it will always transcend our understanding even as He does."

"Religion again," she said. "Why is it so much a part of your life and thinking?"

"Why is magic so much a part of yours?"

"Magic is not my religion."

"No?"

"Well, I never thought about it as a religion."

"Religion is passion; it is the substance that adds meaning and definition to life not to mention wonder and the experience of awe. Isn't that what you strive to inspire?"

"It is but it's not real."

"Does that mean that the experience is any less valid?"

"Perhaps not objectively but intuitively yes. What if those beliefs are the illusion and the secret of life as disappointing as the secrets of the magical arts? What if religion and magic are the same thing?"

"My world would seem awfully unstable if I believed even for a moment that all I held dear was a lie."

"My world is unstable."

"Has your quest for hidden and secret knowledge left you with this one conclusion?"

"No,' she said. "I'm not sure of anything right now."

"Something is knocking on your door, Amy," he said. "Let it in."

"Tell me what you see when you look at me," she whispered to him softly as she locked her arms around his neck.

"Beauty as I've never seen before," he said, "and pain."

"Am I running?"

"Why not stop and listen awhile to find out?"

"I might miss my chance."

"Your chance for what?"

"The big time. Fame."

"What will fame mean to you without joy?" he asked.

"It may bring joy."

"Do you believe you will find joy in what you will have or achieve someday? Didn't you tell me you've achieved what you wanted and found it lacking? Isn't it possible that all the joy you'll ever need is where you are, and in whatever circumstances you find yourself right here and right now? If you don't know that, and if you aren't happy right now, then this contract will never change a thing, neither will I, and neither will this farm. You've got to be happy in your own skin Amy and only you can discover how."

She took the contract out of his hand and crumbled it in her fist. She pouted, a breath tried to escape, and soon she began to cry.

He pulled at her shoulders to bring her into his embrace. She rested her head against his hard chest and listened to the slow and steady rhythm of his heart.

"It's empty, Brendon. All I've ever worked for, all I've ever dreamed of I've finally achieved, and it's empty. I am somebody but nobody cares, and I still hurt so much. What do I do now; where do I go? I'm lost. I'm so lost."

"No," he said as he rubbed her back and kissed her short hair. "You're not lost. You have found the safest place you've ever been and I don't mean with me. Let it sink in. Feel the pain; feel the disappointment and despair and let it sink in. It'll save you years of diversion and agony if you can face the truth right here and right now as you are already so bravely doing."

She continued to crumble the contract until it was the size of a baseball in her clenched hand. She started to laugh, as she tightened her grip on the ball and shrunk it to the size of a golf ball. Something inside of her was free, something that had been a prisoner for many years.

"Oh, that feels good," she laughed.

"Everyone needs a good cry now and then. Especially after the secrets are revealed."

"What have I done? I've given the best part of my life to a fantasy, a dream that was never real. And what do I do now? What do people do when they discover they aren't who they thought they were?"

"What you do now is your call," he said. "I think you see magic for what it is. It's a business; it's not religion. It's not going to fill your emptiness. You want significance, you want security; we all do. But people who look for it out there never find it. They can't find it out there in what they do or have because it's not about what we do or have; it's about who we are. The void is a part of you. It'll follow you wherever you go, it'll be in whatever you do no matter what you achieve or acquire. Once you find real peace, you can do anything, you can embrace anything, and it won't enslave you.

"Wouldn't it be liberating if you could take or leave magic or anything else? Wouldn't it be great if you already had everything you needed and whatever else life offered was simply the icing on the cake? Wouldn't it be great if your sense of worth wasn't tied to how well you perform on stage or the salary in the contract you sign?"

"It would," she said.

"Sign the contract or don't sign but don't do it to satisfy some vague inner longing. You own your life. You thought you belonged to magic and I think, for a time, magic owned you. What do you really want? Look deep, be still, and let your own voice speak."

Her own voice, that was the secret. She'd known it all along. But how did he know it was what she'd been thinking? How could he? She'd never discussed it with him.

"Go on," he said as he held her at arm's length with both hands on her shoulders. "Ask yourself, and listen carefully for the reply. It's quiet here. That's one of the reasons why I love this land so much and unless my instincts are off base, I think it's the reason you love it so much yourself. It's quiet enough to hear that tiny voice that's been drowning in the noise of your life for so long. What do you want, Amy?"

She looked at him and smiled. Then she walked away from him and looked down at the crumpled contract in her hand. After a few paces she turned to face him.

"I want to stay. I don't want to do this anymore. I don't want to look for love from people I don't know; I don't want to run. I'm tired, Brendon, and I need a rest. I don't know what I'm going to do tomorrow. I'm not sure I won't regret it in a year or two. But, right now, all I want is to be still."

"Come here," he beckoned with outstretched and opened arms.

She happily walked into his embrace. When his arms enfolded her she sighed and a tension released her. She laughed. It was a laugh that began deep in her soul and soon filled her whole body.

"I'm free," she said. "I'm free. I don't feel it anymore. It's as if something that had wrapped itself around me and was suffocating me is finally dead. I feel new inside."

Again she walked away from Brendon and she looked up at the trees as if for the first time.

"My head doesn't hurt anymore and I'm not confused."

She closed her eyes and brought the sweet fragrance of the land into her lungs. It filled her and cleansed her.

"No," she said, "I'm not confused about anything anymore. I feel like I'm being born in this very moment and I know what I want."

She turned and looked at Brendon.

"I love you," she said. "I don't need you. But, I want you. I want to love you forever."

She walked back to him and she took his hands into hers. “Brendon Gallardo,” she said, “will you marry me?”

He threw his head back and gave a yelp of glee that echoed throughout the valley.

“Are you sure, Amy?”

“Oh, yes, Brendon, I’ve never been more sure of anything in my life.”

He smiled and his eyes filled with the wonder that pleasured her so.

“I never thought of making a commitment as liberating. Commitments aren’t supposed to bring pleasure are they?” she asked. “But that’s what I feel right now. For the first time in my life, I believe I’ve finally made a commitment to something that I do not immediately regret.”

She kissed him gently on the cheek. Then, she walked over to the tree and sat down beneath it. Sitting there with the dirt of the farm beneath her, she tore the contract into tiny pieces.

CHAPTER 46

Amy expected to regret her decision to destroy the contract. But she didn't. She kept thinking she needed to rehearse, or plan, or study. But she didn't.

Her desire was gone. The voice that for so long relentlessly drove her to the point of collapse was silent. It was as if she'd been struggling with a sickness, struggling for so long that the state of illness had become her norm. And then she awoke to find she was healthy, the memory of the illness only a dim recollection. In the weeks that followed, she changed the sheets on the bed and opened the windows to air out her sickroom, her life. And she recovered. Some of the habits of emotion were still there. But the virus was gone.

She hadn't gone back to her home in San Francisco. She'd stayed with Brendon and they began to plan their wedding. They would be married on the farm. They would walk between vines in the fresh air and under the warm California sun.

She'd asked Rick to come to the farm. She told him she had something important that she wanted to discuss with him and that she wanted to do it in person. He'd pressed on the phone but she insisted they meet and that they meet on the farm.

"After the way I treated Brendon, I don't think he'll let me up the driveway."

She'd learned, of course, of Rick's efforts to send Brendon home form Vegas when he asked her if Rick had given her the flowers. She and Brendon had a good laugh about it.

"Brendon won't be here. What I'd like to discuss is between us, and he will give me the time and the privacy to do it."

"What's to discuss, Amy? You turned down the best contract I've ever been able to secure for any talent, you're living with Brendon, no one has seen or heard from you, and now you want me to drive all the way out there so you can get some closure?"

"I never said I wanted closure."

"Well, what do you want?"

"I want to see you."

"I'm too busy for nonsense."

"I'm sorry you feel that way."

"Now don't go getting your feelings hurt. You were good, Amy, real good. And I like you. When you were devoted to your work, you were fun to be around. But I'm a business man, and if you aren't interested in business then I've got to concentrate my efforts on those who are."

"Do the years we shared mean nothing to you?"

"What we had was good. But times change, people change. Maybe our time is over."

"Maybe it is. I didn't think that our friendship was tied to our business relationship. Why does the end of the one necessitate the end of the other?"

"It doesn't necessitate it. But there are only so many hours in the day. My days are filled with the promotion of magic and magicians. If you are a part of that, we spend time together and time is the mortar of all relationships. But when the focus of our time pulls us in different directions, it's not that I don't care, it's that I simply don't have the time."

"I see."

She sensed that he wanted the conversation to end, and she wondered if he could really be content to let this casual phone call be their final goodbye. But he mattered to her, the years mattered to her, and she didn't want to see them disappear as if they'd never happened. Despite what he had done in recent months, he had been a good friend to her and she very much wanted to affirm that friendship without caving into his business demands.

She waited. If the relationship ended there and then, she would require that he have the courage to say the last word.

"If you want to see me," he said, "I'll be at the club in 'Frisco on Tuesday night. You know the one. I started you there. I booked a new girl in at ten. She'll be rehearsing in the afternoon at two. I'll be watching the rehearsal and I should be more or less available."

"Alright, Rick. I'll see you then."

He wasn't going to come to the farm but she could live with that.

She was sitting on the porch swing. She turned the power off on the phone and tossed it to a pillow on the porch. She was looking at bridal gowns in a catalogue. She liked the shoulders of one and the neckline of another and the veil of still another. But no one gown seemed to have it all.

On a small table in front of her were catalogues of invitations, some of them were so gaudy she couldn't imagine anyone purchasing them. Then there were caterers, bands, and florists. They wanted to be married in the spring but as she looked at the details before her, she imagined it would take some real magic to make that happen.

Magic. She thought on the word. She closed her eyes with a gentle breeze blowing in her face, and she tried to remember. The sound and smell of a theatre, the hum of the many conversations in an audience before the lights go out, the splintered wood of an old substitution trunk.

A sick room is a comfort when one is sick. But, once one has recovered, one wishes never to see it again.

Her friends she would always want to see, but her props were in crates, in storage as were her books and notes and anything else remotely related to the business of magic.

She closed the book of gowns on her lap.

On Tuesday, she drove to San Francisco. She'd been to the old bar many times. It was a small club with a small stage. The manager was a friend of Rick's and he often let him try out new talent on his stage. There was no money involved for the performer. Only the terrifying opportunity of trying one's stuff in front of a genuinely inhospitable crowd. Rick thought it an important first step in the development of the talent he chose to manage. If they ran out screaming, neither he nor his manager friend lost a cent. If they endured they might perform again. And, if they conquered, they might perform again and get paid for it. Amy had conquered.

As she approached the club, the demons she was so glad to be delivered from swirled around her and whispered taunts in her ears.

"You were never good enough," they said. "Come back to us and prove us wrong."

The club reminded her of what was now another life, a more difficult life. The tension she'd felt the first time that she'd passed through those doors many years before, returned to her afresh, as if time had not elapsed. She remembered well the frail terrified girl she had been.

She stood for a moment and looked at the outside of the club. The neon lights were on but dim in the bright afternoon sun. It was like returning to elementary school and thinking how much larger the chairs looked when she had been a student there. She could remember the fear, she could taste it, but her perspective had changed. Time had at least given her a better vantage point.

She hesitated at the door and hoped that the relationship she had forged with Rick was stronger than the business that brought them together. How would he receive her? Would he smile and hug? Would he stand? Or, would he ignore her?

She walked inside. It was dark and it required a few moments for her eyes to adjust. The only light was from the stage. Everything else was in shadows. The tables were empty.

On the stage a young girl was performing with large silver rings. Her hair was long, black and straight, and she was in jeans and a tie-dyed shirt. Amy had always preferred dress rehearsals. She'd wanted to replicate in rehearsal every possible circumstance of the actual performance and thereby anticipate and conquer obstacles to flawless entertaining. She hoped that what this girl was wearing was not her costume. But then, she thought, the causal look had worked for some.

Rick was at a table to the rear, not far from where she'd entered. He was seated with the manager and when she came into the room, the manager looked up at her, said something to Rick, and then got up from the table.

"Good to see you again, Amy," he said as he paused at her side on his way to the bar.

She smiled at him, kissed him on the cheek, and wrapped her arms around his neck for a hug.

"Ricky's been waiting' on ya," he said as he patted her back. "Don't take him too serious, okay?"

"Thanks," she said with a squeeze of his hand. "I won't."

CHAPTER 47

Amy waited behind her former manger. Rick hadn't turned to her but she knew her presence might be awkward for him. The young girl on the stage was still performing to her audience of one, though she could not see even him beyond the bright footlights. Amy walked to Rick's table and stood beside him waiting to be asked to sit. He finally took his eyes from the girl on the stage and glanced in her direction.

"Amy," he said.

She sat down. An unfinished beer was directly in front of her and it smelled flat.

"Who is she?" Amy asked, looking at the girl on the stage.

"She's pretty," Rick said.

"Yes," Amy said. "I can see that."

"And young."

"I can see that too."

"But she thinks the linking rings will kill here."

"They can if she works the crowd with them," she said.

"But she thinks she's a vision of poetry, dancing with them. She thinks audiences will respond to her emotion in the piece. Why do they all start out believing that people want to see that stuff?"

"You haven't told her that the audience needs to touch them?"

"I haven't told this one anything," Rick said. "The lessons she'll learn from a live audience will be infinitely more valuable and enduring than any I might have to share with her."

"Yes but what a difficult way to learn."

"Do you know a better way?" he asked.

"Will she conquer?"

"Not tonight."

"Does she know that?"

"In the pit of her stomach," he said with a glance and a smile in her direction. Then he continued to watch his new talent and for a moment they sat in silence. "I hope she's a performer that will appreciate a good deal when she gets one."

"I didn't want to hurt you, Rick."

"I'm not hurt. It's your life. It's your career."

"But you lost out on the deal too."

"I'll survive," he said.

"And what about us?"

"Us? What us?"

"Rick, you're my best friend."

"I hope not."

"You've been my closest companion for many years. We've been through so much together. Doesn't that time, our friendship, mean anything to you? It does to me."

"I was your manager, Amy, and I think 'was' is the operative word."

"Yes," she said, "and you were a great manager, the best. But, I thought you felt something more for me."

He ran his hand through his hair and made kind of a grunt as he released a breath from his mouth. He always did that when he was caught in a lie or in a jam that made him uncomfortable.

"Did you come all the way down here to see if I still like you?" he laughed a little bit as he asked the question, as if to suggest that such a motive would be beneath those truly worthy of his respect and friendship.

"No."

"Well, what did you come for?"

"You've been a good friend," she explained. "At times, you were the only person I had to count on. You were there for me before Brendon was. And whatever I decided to do with my life and with my career, I had hoped that you would continue to be a part of it."

"You see that girl on the stage?"

"Yes," she said as she looked at her again.

"She is as you were when we first met. She's young and terrified and hoping that this one gig, this gig that will leave her as poor when it's over as before, will be the break she's been looking for. She's hungry, like you were once. That's what

I live for. When you were hungry, I lived for you. Now, I live for her, and for the seven others that I manage."

"And what if I had said yes?"

"To the contract?"

"To the contract, to the business, to more of the same."

"Then," he said, "I'd be watching you rehearse in Vegas right now."

"You're not used to disappointment are you?"

"I'm used to being beaten," he said. "But I'm not used to giving up or being given up on."

"Rick," she said. "I didn't give up on you. It's you that is giving up on me now."

"You quit," he said. "What was I to do?"

"There are many destinies that we will never fulfill, many dreams we will never realize, and many paths that we will never explore. That is the nature of our existence."

"Did idiot wine boy feed you that nonsense?"

"It's not nonsense it's commonsense. We are all finite, with limited resources and time. We must choose, and when we do, we necessarily close some doors so that we can walk through others. But I've never understood why we can't hold on to the people we pass along the way."

"So you want to hold onto something?"

"To you," she said, "to Freddie and Jason. You're my family. I came back here for you. I didn't come to apologize. I have nothing to apologize for. I don't regret turning the Vegas deal down. The years to come will decide if my decision was wise or unwise. But whatever the outcome, I'll always continue to believe that I made the best decision I could at the moment I had to decide. I love Brendon; I love working on the vineyard with him. But I love you too, and I don't want to lose what we had because the magic's over."

"You were hoping I'd be crying in my beer?"

"I was hoping that, however I found you to be, we could be reconciled and carry on."

"Carry on? With what?"

"I guess I misjudged our relationship."

"I told you, Amy, it's a business."

"I should go," she said as she stood to leave. "I'm sorry I disturbed you."

"Don't you want to see how it ends?"

"How what ends?" she asked.

"The act," he said as he looked back to his new girl.

"I guess I haven't been paying attention."

"No," he said, "you haven't."

She walked behind him to the door and as she passed, he asked, "So, when is the wedding?"

"In May, we hope," she stopped abruptly behind him when he'd asked her and answered to the back of his head. He nodded but didn't turn around.

"Congratulations," he said as if he were trying to clear his throat. "She's good. And, she'll learn."

"Yes," she said as she looked at the girl up on the stage. "She does have a certain grace and charm."

"Isn't that a bit soon? I've heard people say they had trouble planning a wedding in a year's time. You are leaving yourself with considerably less time that that."

"We think we can manage."

"You're a show girl, Amy," Rick said.

She came back to the vacant chair and sat down. She put her hand on his to secure his full attention and it worked. His eyes were on her.

"What does that mean?" she asked.

"It's cool to date out of the business. It can make you think you're a normal person, but most of us come to our senses and realize who we are. I don't mean to suggest that show people are any better than anybody else but we each have our own part to play in this grand production we call life. It seems to me that if you were born with a talent and we all are, then you have a moral obligation to use it.

"Sure, it may not be heart surgery, but the service we, that is you and those like you, provide has its place. And, maybe, if it weren't for the service you render, the heart surgeons of the world would have more difficulty rendering theirs. We're all in this thing together. You can't simply cut and run. Try as you may, it's in your blood and by the time you wake up and realize that you cannot escape your destiny, your grandest destiny will have passed you by."

"I'm not running from anything," Amy said. "I've faced my fears in this business; I've given all I know how to give. Now I'm running to happiness. Isn't personal peace the final arbiter of one's true vocation and one's destiny?"

"Maybe, but your sense of personal peace offers the world nothing of what it most desires from its show people."

"And what would that be?"

"Diversion," he said. "Diversion from the daily grind, diversion, and maybe a little laughter, and maybe a little wonder. The show gives people an opportunity to experience a safe emotional catharsis so they can go about doing what they must do to see us all through. Now that may not seem like much to you, but from time and eternity there has always been a stage and there has always been a performer and there has always been an audience needing to see them both."

"Well, someone else will have to do it. I'm not a show girl any more."

"You'll always have the need in you—that gnawing sense of inadequacy that thrives on applause like junkies thrive on a fix. You need to hear applause to validate your very existence. Without someone's praise, you'll begin to doubt yourself. You'll begin to wonder if your life has any meaning at all. You're sick, Amy. That's what made you good, and that's what'll bring you back. You need to hear the applause."

"I have no one to applaud me now."

"You have the adoring Brendon. I've met him. He's a lovesick little puppy, and that's exactly what your soul needs, isn't it? You feel all warm and cuddly with him now, but what if you wake up one day and it's all over? Who will you run to then? Whose applause will you pursue? And, even if he doesn't disappoint you, don't you think you'll get a little bit bored over time? The traditional marriage thing isn't you."

"Please don't presume to tell me what is and is not me. I've had enough people in my life trying to do that and it never helps. I love him and he loves me. Maybe that's not enough, but that's all most of us get, and some aren't even lucky enough to get that. I for one am glad I've been given the chance, the opportunity to love and be loved in every sense of the word, not simply for what I can do with smoke and mirrors."

"You really are in love, aren't you? Blind as a bat."

"Bats have excellent radar and I am in love. If you weren't so busy sulking you might have seen that before now and actually been happy for me." She looked at the girl performing on the stage. She was going through lines and imagining reactions as if a full crowd was at her feet. When she looked back at Rick, he was smiling at her. The girl was squinting hard in an obvious effort to see her manager and the person she, by this time no doubt heard him talking to.

"When you found me I admit I was as you describe. I was needy and lost and you and the business you offered became my savior. But I've grown up. It's true. I once believed that the adoration and attention that fame can bring would satisfy me. I thought I needed to be recognized and honored, and maybe I do, but not by a bunch of people I don't know. It doesn't matter to me now how many nameless faces adore me. All I want is the love of one man and I know how to get it, and I know how to keep it."

"Have you ever wondered how I pick my talent?" he asked as he looked back to his new girl.

"I assumed you auditioned them, or saw them perform."

"That's part of it, but it's not the decisive factor."

"Well, what is?"

"I look for a certain ache in the eye. It's as if they are saying, 'please love me.' I don't know how it got there most of the time and I don't care. What matters to me is the motivational energy that particular inadequacy can generate. The more unloved or abused they believe themselves to be, the harder they work and, in some cases, the higher they fly. You, my dear, flew oh so high. What do you suppose gave you your wings? Was it love or was it the absence of love?"

"Whatever was missing from my life then is no longer missing now. Look at my eyes, Rick."

He did, carefully and closely.

"Is that ache still there?"

He looked away, "No Amy," he said, "I suppose it's not."

"And that disappoints you?"

"It disappoints me that you lost your drive not that you feel better about your life. I'm not a monster. I can appreciate what you think you've found. I'm simply not sure that what you believe this wine guy will do for you he actually will."

"I know you're not a monster, Rick. I never thought you were, not even once. You're a passionate business man and one I've always and will always respect but this business of ours …"

"What do you mean 'ours?'?"

"Okay, yours. This business of yours is horrible. We really never give the audience what it most needs. And by that I don't mean diversion. I mean satisfaction, a deep down sense that everything's okay."

"That sense that you describe as satisfaction is not ours to give," he said. "That's not what performers do. And if that's what you've been trying to do, it's no wonder you've become frustrated and disillusioned. Your expectations are too high. But there's no sense debating the issue now. It's a moot point. You've made your decision. Anyway, I'm happy for you. Really, I am. I'd have been happier if you had chosen to sign the contract. Maybe I'm a bit miffed that you didn't but I'll get over it. I'm glad you've found some happiness. You deserve it."

"Thank you, Rick. I didn't come here to debate or fight. I came to tell you that my career is over. And I came to express my hope that our relationship will not end with it."

"How was that?" a young and timid voice called from the stage. She was holding a hand up over her eyes vainly attempting to shield them from the glare of the brilliant stage lights, but she was still looking in a different spot than where Rick was actually sitting.

"It was fine, Celine. Please come here for a moment. There is someone I'd like you to meet."

CHAPTER 48

Amy watched as the girl on the stage looked out into the darkness in the direction of the voice and then she left the stage. She bumped into a table or two on the way over. Once, Amy thought she must've bruised from the impact, but the young girl kept walking though limping slightly as she approached the table.

"Rick," Amy whispered in protest.

"Be still, Amy, she's a big fan."

When Amy looked up the girl was standing before the table with a smile on her face big enough to drive a truck through. She was squinting probably because her eyes still hadn't adjusted to the dark.

"Amy Alexander?" she said in a breathy 'oh-my-gosh' kind of way, "This is an.... I mean it ... I'm so glad you ... did you come to see me?"

"Well," she said, "Celine, is it?'

"Forgive me," he interrupted. "Celine I'd like you to meet Amy Alexander. Amy, Celine."

Celine reached out her hand and Amy stood as she took it and smiled.

"Ms. Alexander, I'm so happy to meet you."

"Thank you, Celine. I'm delighted to meet you as well."

"What did you think?"

"Well, I uh ... I really didn't get a good ..."

"Tell her what you thought, Amy," he insisted.

"Well ..."

As Amy began the young girl's face filled with anticipation. Her eyes grew large, perhaps in adjustment to the dark but more likely in anticipation of either praise or wisdom.

"I came in during your ring routine."

"I love that routine," the girl gushed. "Oh please, Ms. Alexander, tell me what you thought and don't hold back. I admire you so; I know you can point me in the right direction."

Rick laughed. In another time, she might have swatted the backside of his head for that snide snicker.

"Yes," she said. "Well, thank you, Celine. You flatter me, you really do. Your ring routine is lovely, and you have every right to be proud but ..."

Celine was already bouncing and looking at Rick for his nod of approval. When he gave it, she considered her performance validated but Amy didn't let it stand there.

"But," she continued, "if an audience member never touches the rings, how do they know they are solid?"

"What do you mean?" the girl looked bewildered or confused.

"I mean that, if even for a moment, you hand one audience member one ring, it adds credibility to the whole routine. Magic isn't like the movies, Celine. Despite the success of so many television performers, magic was never intended for the eyes-only. Magic, real magic must be experienced with every sense; it must be touched and felt and heard, as well as seen. Do you know who David Devant was?"

The look of confusion on the girl's face was turning to one of fear or intimidation. For a moment she appeared to struggle with her thoughts, her memory, but then she admitted that she'd never heard of David Devant.

"He was a talented English performer, a golden age magician of the highest caliber. You should read the biographies. Get to know your history. It'll be worth more to you as a developing performer than all of the how-to, latest-trick books combined."

"Amy," Rick said, "what are you doing?"

"Making a point."

"Well then make it, will you?"

"Please, Rick," Celine protested, "Amy has been my role model for some time. She could be a mentor to me. I mean, that is, if you decide to take me on, and since you manage Amy. I only thought ..."

"It's alright, Celine," he said. "I'm sure Amy is enjoying this as much as you. Amy, please continue."

"As I was saying," she glanced at Rick. It felt good to banter with him again. She so enjoyed their teasing and arguing. "David Devant used to click his billiard balls together during his routine. The audience was barely conscious of it, but the sound those balls made when they touched was the sound of solid balls. His audience thought it, if they thought about it at all, an accidental, inconsequential movement. But, because of that sound, something impossible took place—magic was created in their minds. It is the senses that create the magic, and it is all of the senses that we must deceive if we are to be successful."

"So if I hand a spectator a ring, he'll know it's solid?"

"One spectator will know that one ring is solid," she said explained. "But the audience will believe they all are. They will accept the unspoken endorsement of their representative."

"Celine," Rick said, "Amy and I have some important business to discuss. Could you perhaps continue this discussion at another time?"

"Certainly, Rick," she said. "Ms. Alexander, I'm so glad you came. I've been an admirer of yours since I was a little girl."

Rick laughed again. He seemed amused either by Celine's naiveté or by the contrast of his new girl's youth to Amy's still young but decidedly experienced age.

"Can I call you sometime?"

"Certainly," Amy said as she reached for a napkin. Rick handed her a pen and she wrote down her number and gave it to the girl who thanked her then quickly exited. "And I'm not that old."

"She was 'a little girl' only yesterday, Amy. And, by this time tomorrow she will realize that she still is. You seemed terribly passionate about making your point."

"I did?"

"Indeed so for someone who claims liberation from this 'horrible business.'"

"It's served its purpose in my life and now its over. But I won't forget the lessons it taught me and like Dante, I think its fun to pass some of those lessons on when the situation affords me the opportunity to do so."

"That's the mentor's gift."

"What is?"

"The ability to both instruct and inspire the way Dante has for you, the way you this moment did for Celine. In this art there are so many tiny lessons that only get passed on verbally one performer to another. But it's these tiny lessons that make such a monumental difference in the long run. It's truly sad that you never recognized the natural gifts that you had; you never simply enjoyed the success that came so easily to you while others in my fold had to wonder if they were going to eat from day to day.

"Celine might make it, she might not. Right now, she can't afford the apartment she's sharing with two other girls. She's waitressing and auditioning and hoping to get a start somewhere and if she has any talent at all it will probably take her five to ten to reap any benefit from it, and even then she won't be rich or secure."

"Now that's a terribly pessimistic attitude for one contemplating managing this girl."

"It's a numbers game. If I run enough numbers, I do all right. But not every individual I manage does. You did. I wish you knew how rare that was. You were in demand, and if you came back now, you'd still be. You are a known commodity. People have seen you and they trust you to deliver the goods. You can ask for and get a decent fee. That is security."

"There's no security in show business."

"Security is relative. To me it's knowing I can get the fee I'm asking if not from one client then from another. That's what I had with you. That's what I've lost now that you're gone."

"You've got performers in demand."

"Not for the fees you were commanding. No, you were as secure as anyone can get."

"Please don't wish for what was," she said. "I no longer do. I'm happy. I'd like you to be happy with me and for me. You're my friend. It was hard for me to come here. I didn't want to awaken the sleeping giant."

"Sleeping giant?"

"Magic," she said. "It's a living thing and it eats those who search out its hidden secrets and court its attentions."

"A living thing," he laughed. "Oh please. You are more disturbed than I thought you were."

"What I mean is, I didn't want to face that obsessive-compulsive side of my personality again. But I came here for you."

"So what's your bottom line?"

"Come to my wedding. Please."

CHAPTER 49

During the winter months, Amy booked and lost two caterers. Alterations had already begun on her first dress when the tailor disappeared along with a substantial down payment. She never saw the dress again or the tailor. She and Brendon spent more than one evening trying to remember every name that should be included on their guest list. She intentionally left her mother's name off. When Brendon asked, Amy told him that her mother was in good health and living in Philadelphia.

"So what's your mother's address?" he asked.

Amy pretended not to hear.

Ramona was cooking again. The aroma of cinnamon buns was unmistakable. Ramona never made cinnamon buns without glaze and she always served them hot from the oven. They smelled ready and despite the fact that she'd recently finished a healthy dinner, Amy started craving the moist sweet buns.

"Ramona," Amy called to the kitchen, "you're going to be the death of me."

A hearty laugh came from the kitchen. The oven door opened, tin slid across iron. Amy couldn't see what was going on but she knew it was good. When Ramona was in the kitchen it was always good.

"Have you told her we are getting married?"

"Ramona knows we're getting married."

"I mean your mother."

"No," she said. "I haven't."

He nodded his head but the frown on his face suggested that he did not agree with her decision.

"Pardon the interruption," Ramona said as she came out of the kitchen with a plate full of glazed cinnamon buns in one hand and napkins in the other. She sat the plate in the middle of the table with the napkins next to them. "I thought you might enjoy a break."

"We just ate," Brendon said.

"Two hours ago," Ramona countered.

"You know we don't get along," she tried to explain.

"You seem to be getting along fine," Ramona said.

"I mean my mother and I," she said.

"Do you think she'll be hurt if she doesn't get an invitation?" he asked.

"Brendon," Ramona put her hands up as if to quiet him and then she leaned over and put her arm around Amy. With a little squeeze she said, "I'd love to meet your family. We all would but it's your decision, dear. Have a bun, it'll clear your head and don't let him bully you into doing something you don't want to do."

"Bully," he echoed.

"I'm going to my room to read," the great chef glanced at him. "Don't stay up too late now."

"Why don't you join us?" Amy asked.

"I hear the beginning of the conversation from the kitchen senorita," she said. "I think perhaps I leave the two of you alone tonight, no?"

"Whatever the topic of discussion you're always welcome to stay," Brendon said. "There are no secrets in this house and no opinion should go unheard. Bully, you say?"

"Thank you senor Brendon," she said faking a yawn. "But I think I'll turn in."

"Well," he said, "good night Ramona. Thanks for the buns."

"You're welcome dear," she said to him but she kissed the top of Amy's head and then disappeared down the hall. The stairs creaked and snapped under her feet as she made her way up to her room.

"I haven't spoken to my mother in eight years. She doesn't know me anymore nor I her. I'd like to see my brother again but the only way I can do that is through my mother and that's not an option."

"Why not?" he asked.

"She doesn't want to see me."

"That was a long time ago," he said. "People change. She could be worried about you, thinking of you."

"She never called."

"Did you give her your new number? Does she know where you've been? How was she supposed to call? You moved to San Francisco four years ago."

"I lived in the same apartment in New York for four years after the incident."

"Why didn't you call her?"

"At first, I thought she was mad. I thought I'd give her the chance to cool off. Then, as time went by, I started thinking that she should be the one to call me. I had done nothing wrong, and she was my mother. If she wanted to know how I was, I figured she'd call. But she didn't, and then I started to believe that she didn't call because she really meant what she said. And, then I met Rick; I started to get regular gigs, I got busy, and forgot all about it until this moment."

"You haven't thought of your mother until this moment?" he asked.

"No, I've thought of her. I'd rather not contact her."

"The issue is unresolved," he said as he dropped the pen he'd been holding onto the list of names in front of him on the table and sat back in his chair folding his hands behind his head. They'd been at it a while. He might have needed to stretch, more likely he wanted to concentrate his full attention on her. The seat beneath him, an antique that came with the table and twelve other matching chairs snapped like it would break under his weight. It often made such noises but somehow never broke.

"Many issues are unresolved. Sometimes we don't get the answers we seek and sometimes we don't get answers at all. I've learned to live with the uncertainties in my life."

"I couldn't agree with you more. There are many problems we may never resolve. There will always be regrets to live with or people we love that for whatever reason we must learn to live without. But in this instance, your mother is a phone call away."

"And why should I make that call?"

"Do you really want my opinion or do you honestly see no reason to call?'

"Both."

"It doesn't matter who is right or who is wrong. When a relationship is damaged someone has to take the first step or it will never heal. More often than not, the initiative needs to come from the one who is hurt."

"Who said I was hurt?"

"Well, you don't have to say it."

"Do you think I'm hurt?"

"Okay," he said. "Maybe you aren't hurt, but if my mother told me I embarrassed her so much that she never wanted to see my face again then I suppose I might be hurt."

"That's you not me."

"Perhaps, but the point is the person who did the damage usually either doesn't realize they did wrong or they know they did but personal pride keeps them from admitting the mistake. In any case, it's the injured person who goes on hurting the most."

"I'm not hurting. I'm over it."

"Then why don't you laugh more?"

"I do laugh," she said as she laughed to demonstrate. "What could you possibly mean by that?"

"There are many types of laughter. That particular laugh sounded more like you were trying to clear your throat. I'm talking about the kind that comes from inside. When was the last time you experienced a laughter that welled up from deep down inside, from the place that children access so readily?

"The kind of laughter I'm talking about will cleanse your soul as cleanly as a good cry but it'll be more fun. You need harmony for laughter like that. You need to know in your heart of hearts that you've done all you can to bring peace to everyone that matters in your life.

"I've never heard you laugh like that and I'd really like to. In fact, I'd be willing to do almost anything to hear that sound come from your mouth. Speak to your mom. Tell her the past is past and start again. Tell her you love her and then give her a big old sloppy hug and you'll laugh again. I'm sure of it."

"It won't help," she let out a breath of exasperation and grunted like she was lifting heavy weights.

"Maybe you're right. Maybe it won't. But, you'll never know until you try."

"You don't understand. You don't know what my mother is like."

"No, I don't. I don't understand. And if I ever heard the words come from my mother that you heard from yours, I don't know how I'd deal with it. But, from my vantage point, you need to do this for you not for your mother. And I need it too."

"It has nothing to do with you."

"Oh, but it does. This is a relationship issue and she is your mother."

"Why does it matter?"

"Because we're starting a life together. Our separate paths are about to converge, and when we promise our love to each other, I want us both to be as free and unencumbered as possible."

"We will be. In fact, the more out of my life my mother is the less encumbered you are going to be. What's the matter with you, most men loath the prospect of a mother-in-law."

"It's baggage, Amy."

"Si senor," she said. "Now that's more like it."

"What?"

"Baggage," she said. "A mother-in-law is extra baggage we don't need."

"No," he said. "I meant the unresolved issue."

"I know what you meant, silly. I don't want to discuss it."

"Because it's a painful subject?"

"Yes, it's a painful subject. Can we leave it alone please?"

"The relationships we share with the people around us are our most valuable treasure and our most demanding labor. When there is a rift in one, it affects all others because it diminishes us inch by inch, hour by hour. Hurt hinders love, and forgiveness is the only balm for hurt. You're fortunate that you mother is still alive to receive your forgiveness. When we know there is pain, we need to do all we can to heal it."

"You do realize this is your future mother-in-law you're talking about?"

"Of course I do," he looked confused.

"Most men would be glad to get a wife without a mother-in-law attached at the hip. If I were you I'd stop this senseless campaigning right now before you get what you're asking for."

"I don't want her to be attached at your hip."

"No. I didn't think you did. So why encourage a reconciliation?"

"Because I want the best marriage and because I want a happy wife."

"Now I'm not happy?"

"You're happy with certain things and certain decisions. You have joyful moments but is joy your norm?"

"It'll be okay. Stop fussing. It's not that big of a deal."

"We don't always know what we need. That's why we have each other. The people we love help us meet the needs we never knew we had."

"It's not a rift or a problem, and it won't interfere with our marriage, not now, not ever."

"Are you sure?"

CHAPTER 50

"My mother hasn't been a problem until this minute, has she?" Amy insisted.

"Really?" Brendon prodded.

"Well …" Amy leaned back in silence and thought for a moment. "She hasn't been a problem that I thought you were aware of."

"That's my girl," he smiled. "If we don't deal with this now, if we choose to ignore it even though we both acknowledge the problem exists, then there may come other problems. You might be angered by something I do but decide, 'I won't make an issue of it. I'll wait and see if it goes away.' If I encourage you to decide now to withhold instead of share, to acquiesce instead of fight, the next time will be easier and the next easier still until at last we have grown apart. Let's decide right now to always be honest, to always trust, to always disclose. I know there is pain between you and your mom. I want to help you deal with it. I don't want it hidden or buried or ignored, hoping that it will go away. Problems never simply go away. They linger like unwanted guests until we confront them."

"Do you want me to call my mother right now?"

"That would be nice. But if not, then consider sending her an invitation."

She got off her creaking chair, slid onto his lap and wrapped both of her hands around his neck. His eyes widened with surprise as she pushed his head back and forth in a mock effort to strangle him.

"Uncle, uncle," he said. "I give up, I'll let it drop."

She kissed him, straightened out his shirt and returned to her seat. For a moment they went back to scrutinizing the papers that held the names of their friends and family littering every inch of the excessively large table before them. It seemed the subject might wither on the vine. He appeared willing enough to let it drop. Then she slammed an invitation down hard on the table and sat back in her seat with her eyes fixed on him.

"I didn't say anything,' he said.

"You want to."

"I didn't even fidget."

"It's in your mind."

"No," he protested. "I've been deliberately thinking about baseball so I wouldn't think about your mother."

"Baseball?" she said. "You think about baseball when you want to occupy your mind?"

"If you don't invite her, you may regret it," he said.

"There see," she said. "You are thinking about it—baseball indeed."

"Maybe not immediately but over time, you may wish she had come or at least that you had asked."

"Alright," she said. "I'll tell you what I'll do, I'll think about it, and then I'll let you know what I decide, okay?"

"Okay," he said and then he returned to the names on the table as if the whole issue had been resolved. She watched him and when he finally noticed that she wasn't working he stopped, sat back in his chair and folded his arms.

"My mother hates me," she said.

"Do you believe that?"

"Yes."

"Why? Because she said she never wanted to speak to you again? Because she hit you?"

"I have scars where she hit me."

"Is that it?"

"Isn't that enough?"

He nodded.

She got up from the table abruptly and walked to a mahogany sideboard. It was a large Victorian piece, old like everything else in the house and too large for any modern dining room but quit at home in Brendon's. The marble tabletop was chest high and it had heavy doors and draws. Inside the cabinet were various wines but the top held a carafe of Chardonnay, a few wineglasses, and some left-over brownies Ramona had made earlier in the day. She really didn't want the wine but she didn't want him to see her eyes either so she used the ruse of pouring herself a glass to keep her back to him.

"I can't resist these things anymore," he said as he shook the table reaching for a bun. "Do you want one?"

"No," she struggled to say with a clear, normal, unemotional voice. "I think I'll pour myself a glass of wine."

Amy learned long ago to hide her face when it revealed too much. She recalled one instance in particular. She'd been teased at school. By the time she got home, she was weeping, and feeling like she didn't belong to anyone, anywhere. She started for her room, but her mother saw her come through the front door and she called for her to come into the kitchen. By this time she'd learned to obey her mother's requests promptly.

She walked into the kitchen and her mother slapped her suddenly and unexpectedly. She was so taken by surprise that the slap, which normally would have twisted only her head, sent her entire body backward and onto the kitchen floor. She sat up quickly and pushed herself across the cold floor, away form her mother and against the wall.

"Why did you do that?" she screamed as she rubbed her sore check.

Her mother slung the dishtowel she'd been using to dry dishes over her shoulder and walked over to her. As she approached, Amy flinched and held her hand up over her vulnerable head.

"You came in that door crying like a little baby," her mother said. "What's the matter with you? Have you no pride?"

"But, mom …"

"Don't talk back to me," her mother said as she hit her again, a slap across the top of her head followed instantly by a kick that would surly leave a bruise on the back of her leg.

She folded her arms over her head to shield it from the blows that followed but to no avail. Her mother continued to strike her.

"Stop that crying, do you hear me?"

She beat her until her head bounced against the wall leaving her dizzy, and with a slight ringing in her ears.

"Stop it!" her mother demanded.

Amy lowered her arms.

The tears were gone and she wanted to show her mother that she could stop the crying if she wished. Then she put anger in her eyes and her mother responded with a final blow that drove her head back into the wall behind her twice as hard as before. She nearly lost consciousness. But, she feared if she did, her mother might kick her all the more so she struggled to keep her head clear.

She looked up at her mother. This time her eyes pleaded for mercy though her mouth would not utter the words. Agony was welling up inside of her chest and she held her breath to suppress the emotional rupture which would surly have invited more punishment. Her hands were groping at the air, still searching to block blows that were no longer falling. She didn't consciously put them there. She had wanted them at her side. It was as if her arms were detached or as if they belonged to someone else. But she feared any attempt to block would invite more hitting. So she willed her arms down as if fighting against a current, and when her hands were tucked beneath she curled her shoulder around to shield her face.

"Good," her mother had said. "Don't you ever give anyone the satisfaction of watching you cry."

* * * *

She took a sip of the Chardonnay. It was sweet and fruity and the sensation brought her mind back to Brendon and her new home but the emotions remained. They seemed to concentrate in the pit of her stomach and the more she tried to contain them the more they tried to escape. She slouched and wrapped her right arm around her stomach as if her arm could contain emotions so intense they were almost choking her.

Brendon's chair slid over the hardwood floor. She sensed he was moving toward her and she wanted to stop him but she couldn't speak. If she opened her mouth her feelings might escape. She moaned. It was a terrible sound, one unlike any other she had ever heard. It was almost like the sound of coyote howling at the moon, but softer, gentle and meek. It was as much a surprise to her as her hands groping in the air so many years ago.

"I worked with children in an orphanage once while I was still a teen," he said and he was near but not near enough to hold her.

She didn't want to be held. She didn't want to be touched. She feared his touch might connect him to her memories and the feelings she wished never to reveal. Perhaps he knew this.

"The kids," he continued, "all of them, had been taken from their families by the State. A social worker had decided that it was too dangerous to let them remain in their parent's custody.

"It was a part-time summer job that, despite my duties on the farm, I very much wanted to take. They often came to the vineyard for tours and games when we had family days. We never charged them. I became a good friend to one child in particular.

"He had horrendous scars over most of his body—burns actually. His face was marred beyond restoration. His father had done that to him.

"One Christmas morning, he had been making too much noise with his new toy. His dad was trying to sleep it off. He told the boy to be quiet; he told him so often and so emphatically that the boy began to cry. And then his father took the toy from him. He walked out back in the cold, put the toy in a metal garbage can, and poured lighter fluid on it. The boy screamed but his father refused to listen, as the father lit a match, the boy grabbed his arm. The match burned the father's hand. In a rage he picked his son up and tossed him into the garbage can with the toy. And then he set both his son and his son's new toy ablaze."

"Please don't," she said, her back was still to him. "I don't want to listen to this right now."

"When I met the boy two years had passed since the incident," he continued despite her plea. "One night, as I was putting him to bed, I noticed that he was crying and I asked him why. He told me that he missed his father. I looked at the scars and told him that I'd like to be his father.

"I hated that boy's father, a man I had never met but I hated him. I assumed the boy would too. I assumed he needed a new dad, one that would love him.

"But the child became angry. He told me that he had a father, that he loved his father, and that I could never replace his father. I looked into that little eight-year-oldie's eyes and I saw love. The boy had every right to be angry, to never speak to his father again, but he still loved him despite all his dad had done."

"And I'm supposed to feel guilty now?"

"No," he said. "I didn't tell you that story to make you feel guilty."

"Then why did you tell it?"

"I've seen deeper scars than yours. At least, the ones I could see were deeper. Maybe it's not about the scars on your skin. Love dies hard. Look at you. You can't face me. You want to leave the room, don't you?"

"Yes."

"Then why not go?"

"I can't."

"You could, but maybe you want something more. I might be wrong. God forgive me if I am. I surely don't want to hurt you but I think there is a place somewhere inside of your soul that yearns to hear what I'm saying, that wants to do what I'm asking. My guess is that you still love your mom the way that little boy loved his dad. My hope is that you'll reach out and in so doing find reconciliation and peace."

"I'd like that."

"I know you would, and you know I can help. I'm not going to leave you. I'll be your defense and your shield. I'll hold you if something goes wrong and share your joy if it goes right."

The floorboards creaked beneath his feet as he came closer. She tensed. Her body became rigid as if she feared his touch would be abrasive like her mother's. But when he touched her it was soft and gentle. He rested his hands on her shoulders until she relaxed and then he wrapped her in his arms and kissed the back of her head.

"What if she doesn't come?" she asked.

CHAPTER 51

Amy's mother Millie and her brother Chris looked bewildered and lost as they walked through the gate at the airport. Amy wondered if they had ever been out of Philadelphia. Her brother, Chris, had grown and the years had been kind to him.

Brendon accompanied Amy to the airport to greet her family. Amy was squeezing his hand and hoping that her pressure wasn't too hard or her anxiety too obvious. She didn't rush to greet them, and Brendon offered no suggestions or encouragement. He simply stood at her side. He was there if she needed him and his presence made her feel safe.

Millie saw Amy before Chris did, and Millie reached out her hand to Chris. At Millie's touch, Chris looked up and into his sister's eyes. A smile crossed his face, broad and wide. He dropped his bag, and walked as quickly as his dignity would allow toward Amy.

Amy wanted to run to him. She wanted to cry, but she didn't move.

It didn't take her brother long to reach her. He picked her up and when he did she let go of Brendon's hand. Chris spun Amy in a circle and let her fall into a hug the likes of which she'd rarely experienced. With one arm around her waist he held her, and with the other he held her head against his broad chest. He'd grown so tall that, in his arms, her feet didn't touch the ground.

"Amy," his shout rang in her ear as he squeezed.

She grunted. His grip was suffocating.

"My big sister," he said though he towered above her.

His body was warm like a pillow on a cold winter morning. He smelled like home. He was holding her so tight she thought she might merge into his body. She wiggled her hands free and slowly wrapped them around his waist.

"Careful there partner," Brendon admonished. "Let the poor lady breathe."

"No," she whispered so that only her brother could hear. "Don't let go, not yet."

"It's so good to see you," he said. "I've missed you so much." And then he whispered in her ear, "I love you."

Chris put her down and she turned from him and rubbed her eyes, using his body to shield her from her mother and fiancée. Chris kept his arms up strategically blocking her face from view until her eyes were dry. She smiled to let him know she was okay.

"You look like daddy," she said as she stood on her toes to kiss his cheek.

"Look at you," he said as he held her at arms length. "My sisters a babe," he said to Brendon with a sly smile.

"That she is," Brendon agreed.

Over her brother's right arm, Amy caught a glimpse of her mother's eyes. She found no anger in them. She found nothing of the contempt that she so vividly remembered. The woman's lines were deeper, her hair grayer, and she looked somehow smaller.

She'd aged. She expected her mother to be older but she looked so much older, it frightened her.

Her mother took a step forward. She put her arms out and gestured with her hands for Amy to enter their embrace.

Chris released her and stepped to the side yielding to his mother's advance. But Amy took a step back reflexively.

"Amy, dear?" Her mother stopped.

The older woman was familiar yet strange. Could she be the same person that spewed so much anger so many years before? She looked weaker maybe even frail. And yet, Amy was afraid. She'd been nervous about her arrival. Her heart was aflutter with Chris, but for her mother, she wasn't ready. She had no wish to be rude but her body was not operating in sync with her mind. However much she may have wanted to make an effort or at least appear to do so, she could not coax her body any closer to her mother than she already was.

Brendon was watching. He had told her on the way to the airport that he expected her to be overcome with joy. She told him he was expecting too much and that it wouldn't be a happy reunion. She could act but she couldn't dispel the hurt that kept her from her mother's embrace and she couldn't erase the years that put it there. She warned him that her mother's visit might be uncomfortable, even ugly. But he had his hopes and Amy didn't want to let him down.

Then there was Chris. He was watching her too and when she looked to him she saw the hope in his eyes, hope for peace, for the reuniting of a severed and damaged family, hope for what had never been.

Their eyes were on her, urging her so she resisted her desire to run and took a timid step toward her mother. Millie put her arms out as her daughter approached but Amy hesitated inches from her mother's hands.

She looked at Chris. His smile faded and he looked down to the floor but he stepped to her side and rubbed her back with his hand. It was mostly a rub; a gesture of comfort, but it was also a gentle nudge. Her mother's outstretched arms caved in awkwardly like the tiny arms of a praying mantis.

Chris stretched his left hand out to his mother as he pulled Amy under his right arm.

Millie's face turned hot and red and her eyes fell. She didn't move; she didn't take the one necessary step to reach her son's hand. Instead she stood looking at the floor.

"Chris, is it?" Brendon extended his hand to her brother forcing him to release his hold on Amy. Brendon pulled him in front of and then away from her leaving an unobstructed space between Amy and her mom.

"You must be Brendon," the young man said as he pumped Brendon's hand up and down as if milking a cow.

"Yes," Brendon said. "Yes, I am, and I'm so glad the two of you could make it."

"Brendon, you can't imagine how glad we are to be standing here with you and your bride-to-be," Millie said but her gaze was to her daughter's eyes.

Then they were silent. They stared at each. Millie might have been looking for permission and Amy wanted to grant it but couldn't. She wanted to walk forward into her mother's arms but she couldn't. She wanted to move even one step, she wanted even to blink or turn her head but she couldn't. So she stood silently, looking into her mother's face, a face that expressed more tenderness than she'd ever seen in it before. How could she have thought that her mother wouldn't change? Hadn't she herself changed? Doesn't everybody change?

"Amy," Brendon said, "aren't you going to introduce me to your mother?"

She looked at him. It was reassuring to realize that her head really did turn. For a moment she thought she was frozen, incapable of either movement or speech. He recoiled from her glance. She must have had a look in her eye that she really had not intended. She hoped her mother didn't sense anger or hatred from her. She really wasn't angry or resentful. She was confused. Yes, that's it. She was confused and feeling a little lost like on a back road with no map, no direction home. Perhaps Brendon was trying to point the way.

"Oh, yes, of course," she said. "Brendon," she held her right hand out for his and he placed his hand into hers, "I'd like you to meet my mother, Millie." She looked to her mother and tried to smile but she found it impossible to smile at her and look her in the eye at the same time so she dropped her gaze to the floor. "Mom, this is my fiancé, Brendon."

As Millie extended her hand, Amy let go of Brendon and took a small step back. Her body wanted a distance from her mom that her mind had not consciously acknowledged.

"It's nice to meet you, Millie," he said.

"Thank you. Thank you so much."

"I'll get that," Brendon said releasing Millie's hand so he could beat Chris to the bag he had dropped on the floor when he'd first seen his sister.

With his hands free, Chris walked to Amy and put his arm back around her shoulder where it had been before Brendon pulled him away.

"I'm glad you came, mother," she said. She seemed to be deriving strength from her brother's embrace, strength that gave her courage and confidence. She was sheltered under his arm as well and so from that vantage point she could reach out and she did.

"Thank you," Millie smiled and it wasn't merely a friendly social smile. It expressed what appeared to be genuine pleasure, another emotion Amy hadn't expected to see on her mother's face.

She'd expected her to be furious. "Why haven't you called?" she'd imagined her mother would ask. But the vision she'd concocted in her mind, a vision she'd honed over weeks of mental rehearsal, hadn't played out. In fact the reality of the day was nothing at all like what she'd imagined it would be and she was relieved but also perplexed.

"We'd better get down to the baggage claim," she said as she removed her brother's arm from her shoulder and began to pull him in the direction of the claim area.

She looked back to her mother. She hadn't moved.

Brendon approached her and offered her his arm.

"Mrs. Alexander," he said as he extended his elbow.

The dignified and silent woman took in a deep breath that did not enter smoothly. Then she placed her hand gently inside of his arm and allowed him to lead her after her children.

"Please," she said as they walked, "call me Millie."
"Alright, Millie," he said.

CHAPTER 52

The rest of the day and the next, passed with strained but cordial small talk, and stiff, deliberate movements. Amy's sense of personal space became significantly greater than normal, and everyone respected it with unspoken grace. Even at dinner, she sat with more elbowroom than anyone else at the table.

On the third day, as Brendon was helping Ramona clear the diner dishes, he asked Chris to help him.

"Oh let me do that," Millie said.

"Millie," Brendon said. "I want this to be a vacation for you."

"Besides," Ramona said directing her comment more at Brendon than at Millie, "there are already too many hands in my kitchen."

Chris dutifully picked up a pile of dirty dishes and followed Brendon into the kitchen. Once inside they started whispering about something. Amy was left alone at the table with her mother so she began to look for something to clean or tidy but Ramona, Brendon and Chris had all the cleaning taken care of. When the two men emerged from the kitchen Brendon announced that Chris would be accompanying him as he tended to errands around the vineyard.

"Well," Amy said, "I'm glad the two of you are hitting it off."

"Thank you," Brendon said.

"How long will you be gone?" she asked.

"Oh," he looked at this wrist watch, "maybe an hour or two."

"Maybe three," Chris added.

"Are you both insane?" she said.

"Loads of work to do, Amy," Brendon said. "Loads."

"Well," she said, "if there's that much work to do maybe I should come along."

"And leave your mother here by herself?"

"Ramona's here."

"I'm going to visit with Tino tonight," she called from the kitchen.

"When tonight?" Amy asked.

"Right now," she answered as she emerged from the kitchen wiping her hands on a hand towel.

Amy shot Brendon a look that she hoped might convey her displeasure if not her complete horror at the thought of spending the evening alone with her mother.

"Well," he said avoiding her stare, "gotta go." And Chris followed him down the hall and out the front door behind Ramona. The house was frightfully silent after they'd suddenly gone.

"He seems like a fine man," her mother said. She hadn't moved and didn't seem the least bit uncomfortable. She sat with a cup of tea in front of her like she was at a Mother's Day church-sponsored Victorian tea party. Her back was straight and when she wasn't holding her tiny cup both of her hands rested on her lap.

Millie had dressed rather formally each night for dinner. Amy couldn't remember her mother ever doing that at home except for company. No one else dressed for dinner but Brendon was impressed. He told Amy that he thought her mother knew how to dress attractively. "It's clear," he had said, "where you get your fashion sense."

"He is a fine man, mother," she said.

"And this is such a lovely property. I'd really enjoy a stroll through the vineyard. I so love the aroma of the land here."

"I'll get Tino," she said as she moved toward the phone. "Ramona probably wants to visit with Carmen anyway."

"I don't want to walk with a man I barely know. And besides that, it will give us an opportunity to catch up."

"Tino gets upset if someone treads where they don't belong," she explained hoping her mother would be discouraged.

"Okay, then maybe some other time," her mother said as she took another sip of her tea. "Is your dress ready? Perhaps you could show me your dress. I'd love to see it."

Her dress was ready but it wasn't something she wanted her mom to see before the wedding. She was happy with it, and she didn't want to risk deflating that happiness by allowing any potential criticism, at least not the kind her mother was capable of.

"Would you like to see the vineyard, Mom?" She asked with a sudden sense of claustrophobia. Walking through the vineyard at dusk was certainly preferable to sitting around the dinner table trying to pretend she wanted to be there.

"Well, yes, I would. Very much, if you don't think Tino will mind. The vineyard, your dress, it doesn't much matter as long as we have the opportunity to finally speak in private."

'Private,' she didn't like the sound of that. Why would her mother want to speak to her in private and if she wanted it so bad why had she waited three days for the opportunity?

"I've been here for three days now," Millie explained, "and I've enjoyed every moment, but I've had precious little time with my daughter, a daughter I haven't seen or heard from in years. And then one day, I get a wedding invitation. I didn't know you were dating. I didn't know if you were alive or dead."

"You knew where to reach me."

"How could I have known? You never phoned, you never wrote."

"I don't want to fight about it mother," her tone surprised her. She wasn't used to raising her voice or losing her temper. Why did she seem to have such a short fuse now?

"I don't wish to fight either dear," her mother said as she stood and carried her empty teacup and saucer into the kitchen.

Amy stood up and slid her chair in under the table. Then she circled the table sliding each chair under, and making sure they were all equally spaced one from the other around the entire oversized table. If a chore was poorly done her mother's wrath could be quite harsh, she remembered.

"Do you want to walk the vineyard or not?" she asked when her mother emerged from the kitchen.

"I want to talk to you," Millie said. "I want to catch up. I want to hear about Brendon and your career and the wedding. Brendon told me you gave up a contract to perform in a Las Vegas showroom."

"And you disapprove?"

"Not at all, dear," she said. "I think you should do whatever makes you happy."

"Really?"

"Yes," she said. "Really."

Amy folded her arms and taped her toe on the hardwood floor. If she'd been standing a few inches back she'd have been on a Persian rug and the tap, tap, tap of her toe wouldn't have been quite as noticeable.

Millie looked down and Amy stopped her tapping.

"Well," she asked, "which is it?"

"Which is what, honey?"

"Do you want to talk or walk?"

"Why can't we do both?" Millie suggested.

"Yes. Well, okay then," she threw her arms out in exasperation. After her hands hit her thighs with a slap she headed for the front door as quickly as her legs would carry her. She expected her mother to follow. When she reached the door she opened it, and gestured with her arm for her mother to exit, like some carnival employee showing people the way to exit a ride.

"Let's go," she said wishing she had those last few moments to live over. Why was she acting this way? If she were Millie she'd slap her. Did she want to provoke her mother to anger? *Calm down*, she told herself.

Millie picked a sweater off of the coat rack in the foyer. The coat rack was a large Victorian piece. It towered over even the tallest head. It had a marble tabletop over which, inlaid in carved dark wood was a mirror. Brass coat hangers ran up either side of the mirror. She wrapped the sweater around her shoulders and fastened the top button but she didn't slip her arms through. Then she smiled at Amy and walked out onto the porch.

The moment her mom left the house, Amy experienced a sudden urge to slam the door and lock her mother out. For a moment she fantasized about how Millie would look pounding on the door like Fred Flintstone trying to get Wilma to let him in. That moment gave her a smile and the courage to step out onto the porch with her mom.

"In which direction shall we go?"

"This way," Amy led on.

They walked to the fields in silence. Millie trailed a few steps behind but not as far behind as Amy had initially thought for suddenly Millie's hand had taken hold of her own. She was startled by the touch and jumped away.

"I'm sorry, dear. I didn't mean to frighten you."

"You didn't frighten me," she lied.

"Then why did you jump?"

"You touched my hand," she said.

"I only wanted to hold it," Millie explained.

"I'd prefer that you didn't."

"But I haven't touched you yet. At the airport you clearly didn't want to be embraced. I offered but you didn't want to hug me. I've passed near enough over the last few days but you never touch me not even by accident. Can't I touch you?"

"You've touched me enough to last a lifetime, Mom," she said.

"Okay," Millie said casting her eyes to the ground again like she did at the airport, like some poor dejected child. It was a ploy. Her mom was so good at guilt but it wasn't going to work, not this time.

They continued to walk in awkward silence and then Amy asked, "Why do you want to hold my hand?"

"I only wanted to slow you down," she said. "You were walking so fast. I was beginning to get winded."

Amy stopped abruptly.

"Is this better?" she asked.

"One extreme to the other, that's my little girl."

"I'm not your little girl."

"What do you mean 'you're not my little girl'?"

"I've got my own life now," she said. "I like it. And, I don't want you assuming privileges that no longer belong to you."

"Privileges?"

"Yes, privileges. If we're to have any kind of a relationship at this point it will need to begin with an acknowledgement of my independence. I'm a woman. I'm a self-sufficient hard-working woman and I'm no one's little girl, not yours or anyone else's. I fought for jobs in New York and I survived. I beat my way to the top of my profession. I was respected by my peers and by my employers and I'm in love with a man that respects me too. If you want to touch me, if you want to reestablish some semblance of a mother-daughter relationship, then I need you to begin with respect for my boundaries and limits."

"I see," Millie said. "I meant no offense. I know you're a woman now and I share your pride in what you've done and accomplished. But you'll always be my daughter. Even when I cease to be, you'll have been someone's little girl, and that someone will always be me."

"I always felt that I was my father's little girl. But I'm not sure I ever felt that way toward you. I'm not trying to hurt you. But that is what I felt."

"It's true. You were always Daddy's little girl. Fathers do tend to favor their daughters, and daughters tend to lean on their fathers. And he sure favored you. If he could see you now, what you've become, what you've accomplished with your life, he'd be so proud."

"He was always proud of me. I never needed to prove myself to him or become anything for him, or accomplish anything. Dad wasn't about ambition. He loved me."

"Distant memories are nearly always favorable," Millie said. "I can assure you, however, that he did have dreams for you and they didn't involve running away from home to become a vagabond."

"A vagabond," she'd called herself vagabond many times. Rick had called her a vagabond and Jason and Freddie found romance in what they thought was an endearing bohemian term but coming from her mother it felt like a slap in the face. "I was much more than a vagabond." She waved her hands in the air in an exaggerated gesture that she'd intended to suggest she was giving up, and then she stomped off in a huff toward the house.

CHAPTER 53

"Amy please," Millie said as she put her hand to Amy's elbow. She was dragged and nearly fell but Amy stopped before her mother lost her balance. "That was uncalled for. I'm sorry. I want to talk; I need to speak with you. Please."

Amy looked down at the hand that still rested on her elbow. Millie let go and took a small step back.

"And what would you like to talk about, Mom?"

"For starters," Millie said, "is there something you felt you needed to prove to me? You clearly felt your father's acceptance, or at least what you thought was his acceptance. Did you think I held you to a standard too high or to expectations too unrealistic? You said that you knew your father loved you. Did you know I loved you too?"

"Wow, Mom," Amy said. "I suppose I asked for it. Do you really care? Do you really want me to answer, or were you trying to phrase a declaration in the form of a question?"

"I wouldn't have traveled across this country if I didn't want an answer and I wouldn't have tried so hard to get your attention over these past three days if I didn't love you."

"Then, yes. I felt your standards were too high. Yes, I felt your expectations were unrealistic. And, no, Mom, I did not believe that you loved me then and I don't know what it is you're feeling now but I'm not sure it's love."

"But I do, Amy, and I did. The fact is, I've always been proud of you too, like your father."

"Always?"

"Yes, Amy. I may not always have said so but it has always been true."

Amy nodded and started to walk back into the vineyard at a slower pace.

"Why did you come?" she asked.

Her mother stopped walking again and so did Amy.

"Because I'm your mother and you invited me. I thought you wanted me to come. You told me at the airport that you were glad to see me. Was that a lie?"

"I wasn't lying, but you told me that you never wanted to see me again. Don't you remember?"

"That's not exactly what I said," Millie argued.

"You said that I was no longer welcome in my home. Isn't that exactly what you said?"

"You didn't seem to want to be."

"What do you mean, 'I didn't want to be?'"

"You left home. I didn't throw you out."

"I'm not talking about when I left home. I'm talking about the evening of the play—the only play you ever saw me in—the one you judged my whole life by."

"I know what you mean," Millie sighed and looked away.

"Why mom?"

Millie looked carefully at Amy as if she were trying to solve a complex mathematical equation in her head. Amy crossed her arms and waited. There was a little voice inside of her, the voice of a child that wanted to scream, "Why didn't you love me mother." But she was a grown woman now; much too dignified to let those voices find any kind of expression. Still, she hoped her mother couldn't read her mind. She'd always suspected that she might be able to. Wasn't that an ability all mothers possessed?

Millie took a step toward her with her arms open like she wanted to hug her again but Amy put her hands out in protest and Millie stopped.

"Amy, when I said that I was embarrassed, I was angry. I didn't mean it."

"Then why didn't you call me?"

"I wanted to call. But I needed you to come home and I knew the only way that could happen was if it were your decision entirely. I was afraid that if I apologized, you might assume that the apology meant that I approved of your decision to leave home for New York. You were much too young to make a decision like that."

"I think my life has demonstrated otherwise."

"You got lucky," Millie said. "Every child dreams at one time or another of going to New York or LA and becoming a star. Most people outgrow such far-fetched dreams. But you were never one to give up easily on what you wanted. I knew you'd stay and struggle no matter the personal cost. I knew you'd be too stubborn or too proud to ever admit defeat to me, to anyone else, or even to yourself. And, I knew that if you didn't make it, you would kill yourself trying. You made it but do you have any idea of what could have happened? Do you read the papers, watch the news? I worried for you every night."

"You knew all that about me? You worried about me?"

"Does it really surprise you so much that I would know my own daughter's nature?"

"Yes, it does."

"I knew that if you ever came home," Millie said, "it would have to be on your terms and not mine. So, I kept your room waiting. I was going to forgive you, and give you the warmest homecoming imaginable. I'd planned to make it all up to you the day you came back home. Whenever the phone would ring, I thought that it was going to be you on the other end. I'd planned to listen to your story of woe with sympathy. I promised myself I wasn't going to tell you 'I told you so.' Instead, I'd offer comfort. I'd promise to come and get you no matter where you were, or what kind of trouble you were in. I was ready to be needed. I was ready for your call, but it never came."

"My room, are you telling me you left my room as it was?"

"I haven't touched a thing. I've cleaned it, of course, but it is as you left it, and it will always be there if you want or need it."

"If you knew me as well as you say, how could you think I'd ever come home? How could you think I'd ever make that call?"

"I knew the odds. I may not know much about your business but I do know that few survive."

"And what's this 'forgive me' stuff?" Amy asked. "For what did you need to forgive me?"

"I suppose you believe you are the only one that hurt. We needed you, Amy. I needed you. And, instead of fighting for your family, you left."

"You drove me away, Mother."

Millie waved her hands, and then she folded them and turned her back. It was a gesture that Amy recognized as strikingly similar to one she herself had demonstrated only a few moments before. It was then that Amy noticed the mannerism. How was it possible? She'd been away so long. It couldn't be that she'd developed any characteristic reminiscent of her mother. But there it was—hard evidence right before her eyes.

"Did you beat my brother after I left?"

"Yes," Millie answered but she kept her back to Amy. "No. I don't remember."

"Which is it?"

"I think I did. But I never lost my temper with him the way I did with you. He was a good boy. He never worked on my patience. He never challenged me the way you did. He never gave me a reason."

"When did you stop?"

"I don't know when," Millie said. "But I did. And, I'm very sorry that I ever laid a hand on either one of you."

"Is that an apology?" Amy asked.

Millie turned to face her daughter. She looked startled and her eyes were moist.

"Is that what you want?" she asked.

"Not if you don't think you have anything to apologize for."

"You left me, Amy. You ran out on me."

"You beat me 'til I had no other choice."

"I wanted to call," Millie said.

"But you didn't."

"I'm here now."

"What of it?" Amy asked.

"I had hoped that you would be glad to see me."

"I was glad to see Chris."

"You hate me then?"

"No, Mother. I don't hate you, but I don't understand. You should have been a friend to me when Dad died. But you weren't. In fact, you turned into someone I never knew you had the capacity to be. Why, Mother? Why did you do it?"

Millie walked past Amy to a nearby vine and touched it.

Amy waited and then Millie said, "Such a fascinating business your Brendon is in."

"I can't do this," she said as she turned again toward the house.

"Amy," Millie called after her daughter as she followed in a near run.

Like before, Millie's hand caught her by the elbow. But this time, Amy threw her arm out like she was shadow boxing a roundhouse punch. The motion was strong enough to shake Millie's grip but it also caused her to veer from her course enough to come face to face with a vine. Fearing she might stumble into it and damage it, she jumped back and into her mother who was still moving forward. Her mother caught her in both arms and held her much too tightly and much too affectionately for Amy's comfort.

"Let me go."

"Please don't run from me again."

"Let me go."

"Okay," Millie complied and released her.

Amy put her hands to her hips like she had in the dining room before they left. She was tapping her foot too but on dry ground it made no noise.

Millie reached out to hold her.

"What are you doing?"

"Please let me hug you," Millie said. "All I've wanted to do since I got off the plane is wrap my arms around you and give you the love I know I denied you, the love I know you still need."

"I don't want your filthy hands on me," she said as she blocked with her forearms her mother's approach. "Do you understand? Don't touch me."

"Amy, I'm your mother."

"A mother is a caregiver. You gave birth. You did nothing more."

Millie slapped her.

CHAPTER 54

Amy's head twisted to the side. She slowly brought her glance back to her mother's eyes. Millie was covering her nose and mouth with the fingers of both hands. Her moist eyes already carried the sorrow and remorse of her action.

"Is that the best you can do, Mom? Is that the love you wanted to share with me?"

"Amy, I didn't mean it."

"It sure felt like you did."

"I didn't mean it."

"You never mean it. You never intend to hurt but you somehow you manage it."

"Oh, Amy, don't you know what you do to me?"

"What I do to you? That's rich."

"I know you've never struck me the way that I have struck you. I know you've never left the slightest tangible evidence of your resentment and anger but your words cut at my heart. And when I lost you after losing your father, it nearly killed me. I'd much rather have been hit. It would have been more merciful."

"Oh, you are a sly one. You expect me to believe I deserved your abuse. Is that your strategy? Do you think you can appeal to my sympathies after slapping me in the face? A child might have bought that bit—a woman won't. I detest that kind of manipulation so save it for somebody else."

Millie reached a hand out to Amy's face, where she had moments before struck. It was red with the imprint of her hand.

"What are you doing?" Amy leaned and stepped back to get out of range.

"I didn't want to strike you. I was wrong. I'd like to show you I can be gentle. Let me show you. Please let me try. I need to prove it to you."

"You need to prove it to yourself."

"All you will ever remember of me is pain if you don't let me try. I know I don't deserve it, but please let me hold you."

"I'm sorry, Mom," she said as she took another step back. "I can't."

Millie took another step forward with her hand outstretched. Amy ducked and blocked with her arm. She was beginning to shake with fear, something primal and irrational; it was taking hold of her mind and body. She wanted to run but as if in a dream she couldn't get her body to do what her mind asked of it. Her mother was getting closer. She couldn't back into a vine without damaging one.

"Don't you hit me," she screamed and pleaded. "Don't hit me. Don't you hit me again," she shouted as she stomped her feet at the earth and clenched her fists so hard that her nails began to tear at the skin of her palms.

"Honey, please, I don't want to hit you," Millie insisted.

"Let go of me. Let go of me," she screamed though her mother had not touched her. She spun to shake lose a grip that wasn't there, and she stumbled to the ground.

"Amy," Millie said, "are you alright?"

She began to crawl thinking that if her legs wouldn't carry her to safety perhaps her fingers would. She dug them into the earth and pulled her body after them and away from her mother. She pushed herself up high enough to get her feet beneath her then she tried to run but fell again as quickly as she had risen. She curled her body into a fetal position, burying her head beneath her knees and elbows for protection as she'd done so many times, so many years before. She fully expected to be beaten senseless but she hoped against hope that maybe this once she wouldn't be; maybe this once her mom would actually hold instead of hit.

"No," she screamed sheltering her head beneath her arms. "Don't you hit me! Don't you hit me!"

"Amy, oh Amy, I don't want to hurt you, I don't want to fight."

Amy felt naked, struggling with her mother in the land that had been a sanctuary to her, and in the open air where any one of her friends could see. The beatings she endured as a child were always endured in private, behind closed doors. Her relationship with her mother had always been a private affair. She'd never told anyone except Brendon. It had always been a source of embarrassment to her.

Amy waited but no angry words came from her mother's mouth and no furious blows fell upon her head. Still she waited, hoping and wondering, a combination of feelings and emotions she hadn't experienced since she left home and had all but forgotten until this moment.

The impulses of anger and fear were still there, in both of them. Distance and time may have tempered the mind but it was apparent that her body had not forgotten. What it had learned it would never forget, it simply reacted without permission or conscious decision.

"Dear God," Millie said as she sank to her knees inches from her daughters curled up body. "What are you doing? Let me take you home and wash the dirt from these brush burns."

She didn't move. She didn't say a word, she barely even breathed.

"Are you alright?" Millie asked.

She didn't answer.

"Amy, please speak to me."

Though she wasn't looking directly at her mother she noticed the shadow of her hand reaching out to her and then being hesitantly removed. It was obvious that her mother wasn't sure what to do. Amy wasn't sure either. Her mom had started to cry and as she lay in the dirt listening and waiting, she began to feel silly. What had so suddenly possessed her to behave this way was beyond her comprehension, and she was embarrassed now that she had regained a measure of control over her emotions. She was so embarrassed, in fact, that she didn't want to uncover her head to face her mother. She was hoping her mom would simply go away, but that wasn't likely to happen. She was going to have to deal with her past, with the battered child within her, once and for all.

She'd boasted of her maturity and womanhood. She made claims of great independence and accomplishment and here she was all balled up in a fetal position with her mom sobbing over her wanting but not daring to touch her, how ridiculous the whole situation suddenly seemed, how ridiculous, and humbling, and somehow cleansing.

"Amy, I'm so sorry."

Amy peaked through her arm. Her mom was sitting close enough to touch if she so much as took a deep breath. Millie's eyes were shut and mascara streaked her face.

"I promise I will never raise my hand to you again," Millie said. "I will never strike you. I will never hurt you. I will never touch you without your permission."

"Do you mean it?" Amy was surprised to hear her own voice. She thought she had lost the ability to speak in her silly fall.

"Yes dear," her mother opened her eyes. "I mean it. If you want a hug or a pat on the back, or a gentle touch on the top of your head, it'll be my delight to give, but you'll need to initiate. I've learned my lesson. My hands will stay where they belong."

Amy pushed herself out of her protective shell and she sat up to look at her mom. She felt, not only fully sane, but also oddly refreshed.

"I love you, Amy," Millie whispered. "I've missed you so much."

Amy nodded her head. Then she brought her knees up to rest her chin upon and she hugged her legs with her arms. Her knees stung. She worried about how she would explain the brush burn scabs on both of her knees to Brendon on their honeymoon.

"Please try to understand," Millie said. "You're my daughter. You're all that I have; all that I want or need."

Amy's head was clearing. The memory of her behavior was fading and seemed as distant as her childhood memories. It fit so well with that period of her life that she wanted to distance herself from it. She was glad no one else had seen it. It was bad enough that her mother had. It was yet another moment she wished had never happened. It seemed the evening was piling up such moments. It also seemed there was a momentum, an inertial movement like a current in water that wanted to carry her into the next embarrassing moment. But she was determined to break the cycle. What embarrassed her most was that, given the chance, she hadn't stood her ground with her mom. She hadn't even walked out on her. She'd simply crumbled, like a little child full of fear, like the little child she had been and never thought she would be again.

With her newfound sobriety, her thinking was also clear and her insight keen. As she looked at her mother sitting before her in the dirt, she no longer saw a woman she feared. It was as if she were seeing this older woman for the first time, they were strangers but familiar. There was something about her roll in the dirt that killed and at the same time liberated. A part of her died; a memory perhaps, or a fear. But whatever it was it had had a hold on her and it was gone. A new part was alive and this new part didn't fear her mother. Even more, it was able to see Millie objectively with maybe even the smallest amount of compassion.

"Mom," she said, "we've lost a lot of years."

"I've hurt you. I know I have. Tell me what to do."

"You say that you know you have hurt me."

"Yes," Millie said, "I know I did."

"Why didn't you know it when you were doing it?"

Millie was silent.

"I have scars. Did you know that? I'm not referring to the emotional damage; I'm talking about permanent records of your love and devotion in my skin. You beat me, you cut me, and when I most needed you, you rejected me. Your friends were always more important to you than me. Your social image was always your priority. You would have killed me if I had stayed. Maybe not on purpose, but you've got to know you came close more than once. And, I always believed I'd be beaten to the point of death if I ever saw you again. I was afraid."

"Oh no, Amy …"

"And now here we are," she said, "two grown women sitting in the dirt and crying over days long past. What did you expect when you traveled to me? What were your thoughts on the plane? In the airport? Did you think I'd be glad to see you? Did you think I'd have forgotten all that transpired between us? Did you hope for it?

"For my part, I tried not to think about it. Brendon encouraged it, you know. But now that I am thinking about it, I believe I actually hated you. Hate is such a strong word. I think it's rather profane and vulgar. I certainly didn't want to face it, or feel it, or above all deal with it. But, your presence has forced me to. When Brendon first suggested I invite you, I thought he was out of his mind. He told me I had something to deal with. He said I needed to do it for the good of our marriage. And now that I'm face to face with you, I know he was right. I don't know how he knew but he did. Well I'm glad he insisted that I invite you. There is unsettled business between us and if I can't make it right, my marriage to him may never be as good as I want it to be.

"So that's why you're here, Mom. I don't have happy memories of my life with you that I care to reminisce about, but I want to make happy memories with my new husband, and with my new family. Can you do that for me?"

"I'd like to try."

"So what shall we do?" Amy asked. "Where do we begin?"

"After your father died," Millie explained, "I had no idea how I was going to manage. I saw how you were hurting. I wanted to hold you then as I do now, but I was scared.

"You were growing up and your brother was still a child, and I hadn't worked since I married your father. We had no life insurance. I had no employable skills. We had an insurance policy that the bank insisted we maintain as part of our monthly mortgage payment. Had it not been for that, we'd have lost our home.

"We had no money is what I'm trying to say, and I was terrified. I cried myself to sleep every night. And then, somehow, one day, my fear turned into anger. I don't know how it happened or why. I suppose it was like an addiction that you know is wrong but you don't have the strength within you to stop.

"Instead of mourning your father, I became angry with him for leaving me. And, instead of holding you, I became angry that you needed what I felt inadequate to give.

"I was relentlessly angry, and I expressed my anger in inappropriate ways. I gave you every reason to hate me, every reason to leave. But, honey, I never stopped loving you, not then, not when you left, not when you made the choices I hated, and not now.

"You're my daughter. I labored seven hours to bring you into this world, and when I finally held you in my arms, I knew that no matter who you grew to be, or what you decided to do, I'd always love you. I'd die for your happiness. And as I look at you now, I know that every ache was worth it. A mother's labor pains don't end when her baby is born or even after she has grown.

"I know I don't deserve it, but I would so like to be the mother to you now that I should have been then."

"We can't go back, Mom."

"No, we can't relive yesterday. I wish we could. But we can live today. As long as I can breathe I swear to you, it'll never be too late. You'll always be my little girl. You will always have a mother who loves you."

Amy nodded and hugged her knees together under her arms. They still stung from the fall, but the delight that was growing in her heart tempered the pain in her flesh. She looked into her mother's eyes. They were wet and tender and older and maybe wiser.

"Look at you." Millie let her tears fall with no cover or pretense for the first time in her daughter's presence. She'd always told Amy that crying was a shameful thing. But here she was the hardest, cruelest, meanest woman Amy had ever known sobbing like a child. "My little girl, about to become a married woman. I can't erase the years. And I know how weak a word like 'love' is when it's backed up with a history like mine. But I do love you, and I am sorry for what I did to you. I'm sorry for every blow your body suffered under my hands. I'm sorry for every harsh word and for every screaming fit of rage I threw at you. And most of all, I'm so sorry I didn't say this sooner: I made a mistake, please forgive me."

Amy slid her body closer to her mother's and reached out with her hands tentatively, like she was wading into cold water or exploring a flame. She touched her mother's face and she brushed away a strand of graying hair that clung wet with tears. New memories filled her mind. Not of being hit or punished but of being hugged and loved. She remembered the birthday celebrations and the scary nights when her mom would hold her until she felt safe and protected. She remembered her mother, her real mother, the happy confident woman that her father had married. And for a moment, the broken and bitter one vanished.

"Mom …" she said. Before she could say another word, her mother embraced her. Sure she had already broken her promise never to touch, but the hug was liberating for both of them. It broke every chain; it freed every captive, and healed every emotion.

Like a sunken vessel, suddenly filled with air, a feeling swelled within Amy. The memories, heavy with dust, flooded her mind afresh.

She moaned. It was a weak moan but it started to grow. She heard herself cry but she hadn't given herself permission to do so. It was all happening as if she were watching someone else do it.

She sat with her mother's arms around her, crying.

She bowed her head and Millie put both of her hands on top of it and kissed it.

"My whole life's been one big mess," Amy said with her head still bowed. She was looking at the dirt beneath her when a tear fell and made a starburst formation as it hit. She imagined that the water carried within it the freedom and the joy of the moment and that it might find its way into the vine. There it would grow and the land would come to know her as she knew it, it would taste her as she had tasted its wine.

"Everything looks fine on the outside. I could have headlined in Vegas. I have a good man who wants to spend the rest of his life loving me. But inside, there is nothing but decay.

"I thought that if I could become a star, my pain would go away but it hasn't. It was there in Las Vegas and it's here still. Don't look to me for love and forgiveness. I don't know how to give those things. I don't even know what they are."

"You don't have to forgive me," Millie said as she kissed her daughter again and ran her hands over her hair. Then she pulled Amy's head to her chest and held it tight. "You don't have to do anything, but let me love you."

Amy reached up and pulled her mother's hands away from her head. She looked up and into her eyes. Then she turned her hands over in her own and looked down into her open palms and fingers.

"I feared these hands," she said.

"I gave you every reason to."

"Did you hate me, Mom?"

"I never hated you, never."

Amy smiled and kissed her mother's hands. Amy resembled her father, she had the dark hair and olive complexion of Greece, but she had her mother's hands, hands that were capable of anger, and of love. She knew also, in that moment, that she had more in common with her mother than the look of her hands. Her mother was a woman who had experienced pain and suffering like her own, a woman who had passed through the hard times and had emerged better and stronger because of it.

"Mom?" she said.

"Yes, dear?"

"How do I forgive?"

CHAPTER 55

"There's something magical about this day, isn't there?" Carmen asked Amy in a whisper.

They looked from Amy's bedroom window to the vineyard. Mist, like a low-lying cloud, concealed all but the top of the growing vines. The quiet of the night lingered and the morning dew lay untouched by the sun on the grass below. The first light had broken only moments before.

Amy spread her gown on the bed in readiness for the advancing ceremony. Though her first choice had been lost when the tailor closed shop and vanished without warning, she considered herself fortunate. The gown she would wear on this day was the one she believed herself destined for. It was as if fate had arranged the disappearance of her first choice so that she'd find the better choice. In many ways, it was a microcosm of her life. It turned out delightful, more delightful than she could have predicted or expected and in a way that she could not have planned or imagined.

"I've been looking forward to this day for so long," she said. "I dreamt of it long before I met Brendon. And now that it's here it seems in some ways oddly the same and in other ways dramatically different from any day I've ever experienced."

"What's the same?"

"This window," she said, "the bed I slept in last night."

"What's different?"

"Sound and time and my body—I mean my head feels perfectly clear and none of my muscles ache, not one."

"That is rare on a farm or a vineyard."

"I feel great."

"What about sound?"

"It seems quieter, like there's a hush over the entire world."

"As if God did it, a gift for you on your wedding day," Carmen laughed.

"Don't you hear it?"

"I do," she said. "But it's still early. Soon your private little hush will give way to a bustle like shopping on the day after Thanksgiving."

"I suppose you're right," she sighed.

"And time?" Carmen asked.

"I feel exempt today but only for today. On any other day, time flows like sand through my fingers but today is different. I like to think of it as a wedding gift from God."

"Amy, my big sister, you have such an imagination." Carmen giggled again.

"But don't you think so too? It's like there are moments in our lives that freeze with significance, like in those movies where a special moment is accented by a freeze frame or slow motion."

"Si," Carmen said, "that's it! This is a freeze frame moment."

"Thank you," she said as she dropped her arm around the young girl's shoulder. "You're the best Maid of Honor a girl could hope for."

"Do you really think so?"

"My joy is your joy, Carmen. What more could a person ask from a friend?"

Carmen smiled. Then she slid out from under Amy's arm to the bed where the wedding gown lay.

"Wait 'til Brendon sees you in that gown. He's gonna melt."

"I've never actually seen a man melt."

"Well, you will today."

She walked to Carmen and wrapped her arms around her from behind so they could look at the gown together.

"Do you want to get dressed now?" Carmen asked.

"It's still too early," she said, "much too early. I need makeup first and my hair needs fixing, and besides I want to savor. I want this moment to linger." She squeezed Carmen in her arms and kissed the top of her head. "Soon the photographers will arrive, and then the first guests. And then we'll be caught up in a whirlwind. And before we can catch a breath, I'll be waving goodbye to you, and Brendon and I will be off on our honeymoon."

"I know you're looking forward to that," Carmen giggled.

"Carmen," Amy shook her gently and the young girl laughed all the more.

There was a knock at the door and a voice from the other side. "What are you two doing in there?"

"Come on in, Mom," Amy said, and when the door opened both Millie and Brendon's mother, Anita, entered. Millie was tentative, cautious. Things had gone well since their talk in the vineyard but when they were near each other they were polite, almost too polite. It was as if they each feared the peace between them might be too fragile to withstand even a minor infraction of etiquette.

Carmen and Amy were still wrapped in each other's arms giggling like schoolgirls.

"Don't you two look adorable," Millie observed as she snapped a picture with a small camera.

"Mother, what are you doing?"

"I'm recording every moment. You'll thank me someday."

"Someday maybe but not today; I'm still seeing little red dots from the flash."

"Well," Millie said, "let's get you moving. The photographers will be here any minute."

"Christmas is here," Amy whispered in Carmen's ear as she gave the young girl one last squeeze.

There had been many complications preparing for the wedding, many times when she believed disaster would befall their most precious day. But, when the morning had dawned, every detail had worked itself through and she was comfortable, at ease. She couldn't remember a time she'd felt better, healthier, stronger, or more optimistic. But, there was still her mother, still the uncertainty of her intention, a mild distrust. She was determined to leave for her honeymoon with no loses ends.

Amy also had some concerns about Rick. Would he attend? Who would he bring? Would he behave himself? Jason and Freddie said they would come too and she hoped they wouldn't knock over the punch bowl or execute some elaborate, funny, but frightfully embarrassing practical joke. The thought brought the slightest frown to her face but she shrugged it off with a smile.

"Makeup first, Mom," Amy said. Another lump leaped from her stomach to her throat when she looked past her mom and didn't see her makeup artist.

"What's the matter with you," Millie said. "You're beaming one minute and looking like you've seen a ghost the next."

"My makeup artist."

"Relax. She'll be up in a minute. It's not like you couldn't do your own makeup if you had to. How hard can it be to glob on black shadow until you look like you've been dead a week?"

"Mother—"

"I'm only saying—"

"Alexis is the best there is. She's always done my makeup whenever it needed to be perfect."

"And today," Millie said stroking her daughter's hair, "I know it needs to be perfect. And it will be. Relax sweetheart. Think of the man that's been waiting for you. Think about the vows you're about to make and let Anita, Carmen and your old mom take care of the rest."

Amy smiled; she didn't know why she wanted to cry but she did. Even more, she didn't know why she wanted to hug her mother but she didn't. Instead, she hugged Anita who looked like she needed one. She'd been quiet since she'd entered the room. It wasn't like her to be quiet. She wasn't a loud or abrasive person but she was friendly and engaging. This morning she looked like she didn't know what to do with her hands or how to speak with the girl she'd had such lovely talks with before. She looked like a woman about to witness her only son's wedding. It was sweet, and in its own way, it was sad. So Amy hugged and kissed her.

Anita smiled at her but still she did not speak. Amy touched her forehead with her own and gave her hands a squeeze before letting her go. Her own mother was closer than she'd been before. Amy took a half step, really more a lean toward her but she hesitated. It was an awkward hesitation that seemed to send the very message Amy had hoped to avoid. It would've been better if she could have simply ignored her or better still hugged her but it was too late now. Both women rubbed their own arms as if meeting someone intimidating for the first time. They wanted the walls to come down. They were cracked and ready to tumble but they still needed a push.

"Hay, what's going on?" Amy said. "This is the happiest day of my life, right? No tears; no awkward moments; only love and sunshine, okay? No clouds, no rain, not on the inside or the out."

"No rain," Millie said, "only love and sunshine." She hugged her self as if cold. She went to the window, her back to the rest of the room and the people in it. Then Millie said, "Forgiveness is like the dawn. It signals the beginning of a bright new day, don't you think?"

"I do mom. But sometimes the darkest hour is so dark that I lose faith in the dawn."

"But it always arrives," Millie said.

"Perhaps we should leave you two," Anita said. Her voice was soft and mellow, barely above a whisper.

"No," Millie said finally turning from the window. She'd been crying and she was trying to wipe her face dry with her fingers.

"Mother's right," Amy said. "Please stay."

She didn't want to be alone with her mother, not now, not yet. She was too happy to risk it on anything. She wanted to be surrounded by love and though she knew the moment would come, it had to come; she wanted the morning for herself and for her dreams.

She had no show to prepare for and no obligations to fulfill. She was free and she felt free. For the next two weeks, she would spend every moment with her husband on a beach or in a bedroom in France. She giggled. She couldn't stop. She didn't want to stop. She was absolutely giddy. The air was filled with uninhibited joy. She experienced every moment with the freshness of a child.

"I've never seen you so happy," her mother observed.

"I don't think I've ever been this happy. It's weird, you know. I mean, when Brendon first asked me to marry him, I was shocked. I loved him, but I never expected a proposal of marriage. And then, I was scared. I wanted to run."

"But you didn't," Millie said.

"Well, I didn't say yes right away. But when I finally made my decision …"

"You knew it was right," Millie concluded.

"Yes, Mom. I knew it was right."

The joy in her heart was contagious. Carmen couldn't keep herself still. She'd sit for a moment on the bed or a chair and then she'd get up again and spin or twirl or dance like Gene Kelly in the rain. Her mom, though still tentative, was sweeter than she ever thought possible. There was a certain sweetness, a vulnerability, even in her pain. Brendon's mother became tearful but even in her tears there was joy.

As she watched her mother, Amy saw someone new. Millie wasn't the person that beat her, that hated her. She was a new person, a person that emerged from a plane all nervous and frightened like a child on her first field trip, a person who tried so hard and wanted so much for reconciliation. Amy's confidence was building. It had been since their talk. She almost had the courage to say what she felt for her mother and almost the faith to believe it was possible.

Another knock on the door brought Amy's makeup artist into the room. Alexis had been Amy's favorite makeup artist since the time of her first publicity shoot for magic. She was also the wife of the photographer who so often took Amy's publicity shots. But, on this day, he would be responsible for her wedding photographs as well as the production of their video.

Alexis was a lifetime goth like Amy, it defined who she was and always would be.

"Oh boy," Millie said, "another goath."

"Goth." Alexis and Amy both said in unison.

Millie laughed, and Alexis went to work on Amy, which wasn't easy as Amy was squirming and talking.

"Amy," Alexis admonished, "if you don't sit still, we'll be sitting here when the processional starts."

"Heavens!" Amy giggled with a mock look of fright.

"Heavens?" Alexis questioned as she leaned over Amy's face to try again. "Too many old movies, Amy?"

"But isn't this like an old movie?" Amy bit her lip to keep her face from cracking in laughter.

Brendon's mom came to her side and met her future daughter-in-law's eyes in the mirror. Amy's laughter ceased at the sight of her. She put a hand to Amy's shoulder and Amy put her hand atop of it and gently squeezed. They exchanged a smile and then Brendon's mom bent over and kissed her under her ear, one of the few places Alexis had not yet touched with a brush.

CHAPTER 56

Guests began to gather outside. Their laughter and conversations rose like incense to Amy's window. She could not distinguish individual words except for the occasional high pitched 'hello' from old acquaintances reunited.

It had rained earlier in the week. Friday had been overcast but when Saturday, their wedding day, arrived it was picture perfect. As the sun continued its rapid journey across the sky, the temperature warmed with it. The report was that they would enjoy sunny skies and a high of eighty-two degrees. A gentle breeze was also anticipated to refresh the well-dressed guests all morning and kept the sun's warmth pleasant.

As Alexis continued her work, Amy enjoyed the cloudless blue sky reflected through lace curtains in the mirror.

"Has a sky ever been so blue? Could a day be more perfect?" Amy asked Carmen, who had already slipped into her dress.

"Not if you dreamed it," Carmen said.

"I think you're both crazy," Millie insisted.

"No, Mom," Amy argued. "I've never heard sounds so clearly, or smelled flowers as sweet, or seen a sky so blue. It's like I'm experiencing my every sense for the first time."

"You're nervous, dear," Millie said.

"No," Amy said, "I've been nervous before. Nerves make me sick."

"Well, this is the other side of nervous," Millie explained.

"The other side?"

"When I'm nervous about something I don't really want I get sick. But, when I'm nervous about something I do want, I come alive. Every sensation is new to me. I'm thinking we might have something in common there too."

"Yes, that's what this is. I'm alive. I'm really alive. I can remember feeling this way, but it's been so long. I really can't remember the details, only the sensation."

"Welcome home," Millie said.

Amy smiled at her mother's reflection in the mirror. It was a moment of almost perfect reconciliation. But then her mother frowned and looked away. It would require more. A lesser pain might have healed with the demonstration of a friendly disposition but this one was deep. It would never go away with only the pretense of civility, no matter how much time they spent kindly disposed to one another. Wounds as deep and as old as theirs required the balm of words gently and sincerely spoken, ratified eye to eye, soul to soul.

Alexis worked on Amy for nearly an hour. Then Carmen, Millie and Brendon's mother helped Amy into her wedding dress. She stood on a small platform. She could see out the window as the women adjusted her gown, but the guests gathering below could not see in.

Carmen was busy adjusting Amy's train. It buttoned in the back for ease of mobility but when let out it dragged elegantly behind, trailing not from her waist as so many gowns do, but from a few inches above her knee, allowing the dress to hug her hips. The dress hugged her slender form tightly from the sleeveless shoulders, through her midriff, and down her long legs.

Millie ran a hand from under Amy's arm, over her rib cage, waist and hip, and down her leg, partly to smooth any wayward wrinkles and partly it seemed in appreciation for the woman Amy had become.

Only the tip of the toe of her black heels peeked out from under the front of the dress, the bottom of which revealed the outer layer of black lace that covered the entire dress. Though it had no sleeves, she was wearing fingerless black lace gloves that covered her arm. She wanted her fingers bare so she could feel the ring when Brendon slipped it on. Her nails were long, manicured, and polished in her signature black.

The neckline was "V" shaped with a hint of cleavage. Around her neck, she had fastened a satin black choker with a cameo in the middle. A veil did not obstruct Alexis' finest work.

Millie gave a finally tug on the lace that lightly touched the toe of Amy's shoes. Then, the four women stood back to admire their handiwork.

"My little girl," her mom said adoringly and proudly. "I must admit, it's a beautiful gown. I thought it might be morbid. Who wears black for a wedding? But you make it work. I couldn't imagine you in any other color."

"Thank you mom," Amy said. "I mean that. Thank you so much."

Carmen stepped over to her; she was still watching the guests gathering below from the window. Carmen reached up and she took a hold of her hand. She squeezed it tightly and together they stood in silence looking at the guests below.

"It's time," her young maid-of-honor whispered.

"So it is, Carmen," she looked down at her and smiled. "So it is."

Millie was the first to leave the room. She paused at the door and looked back at her daughter. There was a longing in her eyes; a longing Amy knew now how to satisfy. Anita followed closely behind Millie. Alexis gave Amy one final check before nodding her head with approval and leaving. Carmen carried her own bouquet and Amy's and walked behind her to make sure she didn't trip or snag.

As they approached the stairs, Amy caught a glimpse of Dante through the dark wood railings of the banister. Rick and his new young talent, the girl she had met in San Francisco, Celine, were standing next to him as were Jason and Freddie. Celine was giddy, like a schoolgirl, and bounced on her toes. She clapped her hands carefully keeping her fingers apart so her applause would make no sound.

Dante's face warmed and delighted her. He had always been a formal man, always immaculately groomed and dressed. Whenever she had visited him, he wore a tie, dark slacks, polished shoes, and a dinner jacket. He was in a tux today, and for an older man he took her breath away. His hair was gray but for a thin streak of black here and there. It was brushed back and lightly jelled. It was usually dry and a bit long and frizzy. His goatee must have required extra work for there was not a strand out of place. And, his eyes absolutely sparkled.

Her mother hadn't taken her seat in the front row. Instead she was lingering by the door. Her hands were folded in front of her. She looked lost.

As she approached the bottom of the staircase, Rick left Celine's side, reached out for her hand and applied a gentle pressure to assist her down the remaining stairs.

"Wow," he said as he kissed her hand.

"Oh, you like?" she said.

"Bruce is a lucky man," Rick said.

"Brendon," she corrected.

"Okay," Rick laughed. "Have it your way."

"Today Rick," she said, "today I think I finally will."

"You made the right choice, Amy," he said. "It suits you. I'm happy for you. I really am."

She kissed his check.

"You've been good to me, Rick. I'm so glad you came."

"We'll always have the magic years," he said. And, in a whisper intended for her ear only and with a slight glance over his shoulder at Celine, he said, "You'll never be replaced." And then he hugged her and with his embrace, he told her how much he loved her, how much he would miss her, and how happy he hoped she'd be.

"Oh, Rick," she said and in his arms another understanding passed between them. This one was bittersweet. It was love, it was affection, it was a thanksgiving for all they had shared but it was also goodbye.

Rick released her and took a step back. His eyes confirmed what his embrace was intended to communicate and then he gave way to Jason and Freddie. They were both wearing suits that didn't fit. Off the rack, no doubt but that's Jason and Freddie. Their idea of formal was a new pair of flip-flops and a clean shave.

Freddie had a girl under his arm—a rather attractive blond. Jason moved in first and gave Amy a gentle squeeze and a brush stroke of a kiss intended to demonstrate affection without in any way damaging the makeup.

"Why aren't you seated? I'm about to make my entrance. You know how irritated I can get when you guys aren't on your mark at curtain time."

"Um," Jason said.

"It's about that guy," Freddie said.

"What guy?" she asked fearing she already knew the answer.

"You know," Jason said.

"The dude you're marrying," Freddie said.

"Brendon," her voice was louder than she'd intended so she dropped to a whisper. "What did you do to my fiancée?"

"Was he kind of tall?" Jason asked.

"With broad shoulders?" Freddie added.

"Wearing a tux and looking all gnarly scared?"

"Guys come on. Don't do this to me today. Do you realize that as I dressed this morning, while I should have been all goose bumps and bliss, I kept wondering what kind of goofy stunt you'd pull? Now 'fess up. What did you do? Did you dump paint on him? Did you tie him up in the barn? What? Let's have it."

"We congratulated him, Amy," Jason said.

"You what?"

"For winning the hand of the woman we all love," Freddie said.

"Guys," she put out a hand like she wanted to stop traffic. What she really wanted was to stop an onslaught of tears that could potentially ruin an Alexis' masterpiece. The gesture seemed to work as not a tear escaped.

"I've been so worried about the two of you," she said as she hugged Jason this time without reserve or timidity. It didn't matter to her if she crushed her dress; she wanted to hold him.

"We're fine darlin'," Freddie said. "Jason won a surf contest a while back and picked up a sponsor. Now I can't get the man out of the water, and travel—he's all over the globe. I was surprised he showed up today, Mr. Big-time."

"I wouldn't have missed this for a free ride in Fiji," Jason said.

"And what about you Freddie?" she asked.

"My dad put me to work."

"Oh no," she said.

"No," he said. "It's not like that. It's cool. I don't have to wear a suit. I get surf time when the breaks are good and I get a smokin' salary."

"You never cared about a salary before," she said.

"I've never been engaged before," he said.

She cupped her hands over her mouth to hind her astonishment.

"Amy," Freddie said, "I'd like you to meet my fiancé, Casey. Casey this is the angel I've been telling you about."

"I'm so glad to finally meet you," the young girl said as she extended her hand. She looked barely out of high school.

"I'm delighted," she said, "and so glad you came. But I can't believe it."

"What's that?" Jason said.

"So much change," she said, "in such a short time."

"'To everything there is a season,'" Dante quoted. He loved Ecclesiastes.

"I suppose all good things must come to an end," she said.

"So better things can begin," Dante added.

She smiled and extended her hand to his. He bowed and kissed it.

The others took their cue from Dante and made their way out of the house. She stroked the back of her free hand on Dante's face and ran it down into the goatee on his chin. It felt coarse on her fingers.

She tucked in her lower lip to keep it from quivering.

"Now, now, Amy," Dante admonished, "a tear on that lovely face will send Alexis into cardiac arrest."

"It's only that …" she began to explain but couldn't continue.

"… that everything changes," Dante said. "The world spins and we like lost children cling to its apron strings hoping it'll stop long enough to allow us to catch our breath or feel its solid stability beneath our feet. But it keeps on spinning, and we spin with it breathless but for those moments of eternity we share, moments that will last beyond the flicker we call life. Such is the moment we share today, a moment that was meant to be, a moment I'm so very happy to be sharing with you. Don't look back, Amy. Don't ever look back."

She nodded and kissed his hand.

Dante had come to stand in her father's place. His posture was straight and proud. Seeing him again, in his glory, reminded her of when she'd first seen him with her dad so many years before. He represented all that magic could and should be. He represented that which was best in her childhood, in her dreams, and in the career she'd enjoyed for so long.

Their hands interlocked. She squeezed and he also tightened his grip.

"Dante," she whispered.

"Yes, Amy."

"My mentor and my friend, you have shaped my life in so many ways. The gifts you've given me reach beyond the stage, beyond the show, beyond magic itself."

"I was always the better for the time we spent together," he said.

"You've given so much," she said. "Will you give once more?"

"What can I do for you, Amy?" Dante smiled and his eyes sparkled with the flame that had mesmerized audiences for generations.

"Walk with me now," she said, "and give me to the man I love."

Dante smiled, his eyes sparkled with the charisma that had made him a stage sensation but his focus shifted to a point slightly behind her. She turned and looked at her mother who had not moved though everyone else was seated. She was still standing by the door waiting. Dante stepped back. He tried to be discrete and silent but Amy knew he was giving her space and by it, privacy.

Her mother approached. The rhythm of her heart increased and echoed in her ear as her mouth went dry. The isle waited, Brendon waited, and her future waited. Her mother was standing in the way. She would not nor could she pass until she dealt with her.

She wanted to do it. She wanted to speak the words she knew her mother longed to hear. But she thought she could do it later, always later. No matter how ripe the present moment appeared to be there was always the possibility that another moment would be better, more appropriate, and more perfect. But there would be no more future moments. The time had come. The time was now.

Millie grabbed her hands and squeezed the way desperate people do when they are drowning.

"Darling," Millie said, "I love you."

Amy smiled. The two women stood there squeezing each other's hands while the world waited.

Millie bowed her hand and closed her eyes. Her grip loosened. Amy didn't want to let her go so she tightened her fingers around her mother's hands.

"Mother," she said and then she waited for her mother to open her eyes.

When Millie opened her eyes, they were moist, kind and gentle. There was a longing in them, a longing that was familiar. She'd seen it so many times in the reflection of her dressing room mirror and it never went away after the show.

She opened her mouth to speak but the words didn't come. She looked to Dante. He smiled but then he walked past her to the door. His back was to her. Carmen joined him and then they both stepped out and onto the porch. She was alone with her mother, as she had been in the vineyard, as she had been after her father died. She was alone with her but their hands were locked in a fight to save what was nearly dead. Their hands struggled together to salvage the ruins.

"Mom, I want to, I need to …"

"Oh, I'm so sorry." Her mother was sobbing.

"I want to be your daughter. I want to be your friend. I want to share this moment with you and I want you to know that I would never wish it any other way. You're my mother. You're my family. I love you, mom. Know that I do. Please know it's true. I was angry. I didn't want you to come but I'm so glad you did. I couldn't have been more wrong. And for all that I ever held against you, I forgive you. I forgive you, mom."

Her mother smiled but her eyes closed again and she collapsed onto the step behind her. Dante came over and helped her up.

"Oh, do you mean it dear?"

"I do," Amy said. "Mother, I love you and I forgive you, not only for one thing or one time, but for all things and all times. I've thought about it since our talk in the dark. I've thought about what you said and what you must have gone through after dad died. How could I not love you? You're my mother. I decided I wanted to forgive before this moment and when I made that decision something happened inside of me. The moment I decided I wanted to forgive you, I found the power to do it. And now that I'm saying it I feel it even more."

"So many years I've wasted. So many moments we could have shared that I let slip by."

"We have today, mom. And we'll not waste another minute of it on what was or what might have been. I'm getting married. A new life is begging and I hope that in some way, yours is too."

EPILOGUE

Years passed, Amy and Brendon had four children; the youngest was four, the eldest twelve. During those years, Amy took an interest in the vineyard, as Brendon had hoped she would. She could have concentrated her attention on the office, or the winery, or marketing. She could have returned to performing, but she liked to work on the land with Tino and Carmen. She learned to care for the vineyard with the delicacy and ease with which she had taken to motherhood. What the vines taught her, she applied to her children. And, what her children taught her she applied to the vines. Both grew in health and in strength.

Tino had always been protective of the vineyard. Now that she was literally walking in his footprints, her appreciation of him grew to respect and then to admiration.

The summer heat was upon them, and the grapes were beginning to swell with the richness of flavor that this particular season promised. Amy was out early, while the sky was still a dark blue. She had her long hair pulled back tight in a ponytail, but on either side of her face a curly black strand lightly salted with gray escaped.

As she walked among the vines, she gently brushed leaves aside to reveal the grapes beneath to the rising sun. From time to time she would run her finger over her ear, tucking behind it a lose strand of hair from where it would invariably fall again.

On this particular day, as she worked, she remembered the time when her hair was short, and her life filled with anger and tension, anxiety and ambition. Ordinarily she would lose herself in the fields, even the long days of summer would pass like minutes before work that so absorbed and occupied her mind. But last night, before they each turned in for bed, the whole family, including Tino, Carmen, Carmen's husband and their children, gathered around the big screen television to watch the first prime time magic special from Vegas superstar, Celine. Rick's name appeared in the credits as producer and manager.

Two of Amy's children, Alexis her eldest daughter and Dante her only son, both enjoyed the show. During commercial breaks, the kids would argue about how she did this or how she did that.

"Wow, mom," Dante said. "Isn't that lady's picture in your wedding album?

"Yes, Dante," Brendon said. "Your mom taught her all she knows."

"Really." Dante's eyes beamed.

"Don't lie to the boy, Brendon," Amy admonished.

"Well, you did."

"She's been to the house a few times," she explained. "I've given her some advice."

"You've mentored her," Brendon said.

"What's a mentor?" Alexis asked.

"Like a teacher or coach," Brendon said.

"But magic mentors are something more," Amy said.

"Like my tennis instructor?" Alexis asked.

"You love her, don't you?" Amy asked.

"Oh, I do."

"Well," Amy said, "I suppose it's a little bit like that. But a good magic mentor always takes the student beyond the magic. At least that's what mine did for me."

"Is that what you did for Celine, Mom?" Dante asked.

"No, honey," Amy said. "I simply showed her some easier ways of doing things. I really haven't seen her in years, and it's obvious she's doing fine without me."

Alexis came to Amy and hugged her. "We wouldn't be doing fine without you, mom."

"Thank you, dear." Amy laughed and squeezed her daughter tight.

Then the commercial break was over. Alexis returned quickly to her spot on the floor, and the room became silent as Celine performed her final illusions.

After the show, as Brendon walked to the entertainment center to close it down for the evening, he said, "your mother could show you a thing or two about magic."

Their eyes got round, and they looked at her with that same look of awe she'd seen on faces in her audience so many years before, but these weren't nameless faces; they were her children. Magic was a part of her life now long buried. She never regretted walking away from it or walking into her marriage and her family. She had no desire to resurrect the long dead or to see it spawned in her children.

"Could you, Mom?" Alexis pleaded.

"Brendon," she said, "why did you bring that up? That was a lifetime ago."

Alexis ran to her mother and gently pushed her forehead against her mother's so that looking into each other's eyes was both painful and unbearably funny. Alexis had learned long ago how to set her mother to giggling, and once started she would agree to almost anything the young girl asked.

"Please," she said.

"Stop it," Amy demanded already giggling. "Go to your room."

"Not until you show me a magic trick," Alexis said. "And it better be good. None of that coin-from-the-ear stuff like Uncle Chris does when he comes to visit."

"Now," Amy said, "don't be hard on your Uncle Chris. He loves you."

Alexis pulled her head away from Amy, and then she hugged and kissed her.

"Come with me, Alex," Brendon motioned with his hand as he walked toward the stairs. "Let me show you what your mom did before she married your old dad."

"Brendon," Amy warned, but they were off without looking back.

She remained in the den with Tino for a time, after wishing Carmen and her family a good night. When she went to bed, little Dante, Alexis, and Brendon were still in the attic digging through memorabilia. Thankfully her two youngest daughters were already in bed and asleep.

The sun was higher in the morning sky. Her bib overalls and flannel shirt had been comfortable at first light, but now she was warm. She unfastened the top of her overalls and striped off the flannel shirt under which she wore a burgundy golf shirt with the name and logo of the vineyard on the breast pocket. Then she snapped her overalls back into place and tied the sleeves of the flannel shirt around her waist.

She looked down at her feet. They were comfortable in her mud covered and well-worn work boots. She only wore pumps on Sunday or Christmas or when they went to Mass. She preferred her old boots the rest of the time.

"Mom," her daughter yelled in the distance.

She turned from the vines to see her running from the house toward her.

"Stop running, Alex," she warned. "You might stumble into a vine."

The little girl, who resembled herself in so many more ways than physical, slowed her pace but not by much. She was carrying something. Amy couldn't quite make out what it was. Brendon emerged from the house and started walking toward her at a slower pace. She looked across several rows. Tino stopped his work and looked in the direction of her daughter with an expression that seemed to blend anxiety and curiosity. He stood peering over vines to Amy's right, and Carmen was several rows to Amy's left. Both were watching now.

Alexis was breathing heavy from the rapid walk as she approached.

"What's all the fuss, dear?" Amy asked. "And, how many times have I told you not to run through the vineyard."

"I'm sorry, Mom," Alex apologized. "Daddy showed me something, and he told me the story that goes with it."

"What story? What are you talking about?"

"This." Alexis held out a long wooden box.

"Where did you get that?" Now that it was right in front of her, Amy knew instantly what it was.

"Daddy."

"I know 'Daddy,'" she said. "Where did he get that?"

"It was in the attic, Mom," Alex explained. She seemed puzzled perhaps that her mother wasn't delighted to see it again.

Amy looked over her daughter's head to Brendon who was not far off. He shrugged his shoulders and raised his hands in the air.

The innocent routine again, she thought. She narrowed her eyes and frowned at him. He pretended he couldn't see. He even squinted a bit to make it convincing but she was confident he'd received her message. Then she turned her attention to her daughter.

"That belongs to Mommy, honey. You need to put that back where you found it."

"This was your wand, wasn't it, Mom? Didn't Dante give it to you before he died? Daddy said it was his gift, the mentor's gift, he said."

"He gave this to me, yes," she said patiently as she knelt down to converse with her daughter eye to eye. "But he gave me so much more." She took the box from the little girl's hand and opened it. The sun blinded her for a moment when it reflected off of the brass tips of the wand. She tilted the case and the wand rolled out into her dirty hand. She wrapped her fingers around the wood. Her long nails had long ago been cut. They bore no polish, and there was dirt beneath each one.

"What, Mommy?" Alex asked. "What else did he give you?"

Magic is in the details, she remembered Dante telling her. She went back to his study so completely that for that one moment, she forgot she was standing in a field with her oldest daughter.

"Polish your nails," Dante said, "have your makeup professionally done if you can afford it. If you look good, you'll feel good, and the audience can sense your feelings about yourself."

Suddenly, so many memories flooded her mind that she felt overcome by the rush. Her eyes closed as tightly as her fist that held the wooden wand. She could see him again; smell him, Dante her old friend had come to visit. His scent was in the breeze that brushed by her face. She lifted her nose to take her old friend in.

"Amy," his voice whispered her name.

"Dante," she whispered in return.

"Mommy," Alexis asked, "Are you okay?" She put a hand to her mother's shoulder and gently pushed in an effort to rouse her from thought. "Daddy, something's wrong with Mommy."

Her daughter's voice was distant, intrusive, like the voice that doesn't belong in a pleasant dream. She sat down on the ground; her body went limp with the rush of memories. Her grip on the wand tightened but she dropped the case to the muddy earth.

"Mommy, you dropped the case." Alex picked it up as Brendon arrived behind her.

"Alex," he said, "please go on back to the house now."

"But you said mommy would tell me more about the wand than you could. You said she'd—"

"Now," he insisted.

"Yes, sir," Alex said and begrudgingly compiled.

As her little girl walked away she stood up from the ground she'd been sitting in. She turned away from Brendon as he approached, and she walked slowly down the row of vines. As she passed each vine, she remembered the sensations of curtain time. Her heart raced for a moment then as her music began and the curtain came up, the beating all but stopped and her mouth ran dry. It was dry. She was there once more. She held the wand out with her right hand and gave it a twirl. When she was learning that particular wand spin, it flew from her fingers and across the room many times. Now, so many years later, she performed it with the ease of mastery.

"What the body learns, the mind never forgets," she said.

"Did he teach you that?" Brendon wrapped his arms around her from behind, and squeezed.

"Yes," she said. "His lessons and wisdom are still so vividly imprinted on my mind. A moment ago, I thought I smelled him. I closed my eyes, and I thought he was here."

"I'm sorry, sweetie," he whispered in her ear and kissed the back of her head. Carmen and Tino went back to work.

"I loved him so much," she said.

"I know. It was thoughtless of me to resurrect painful memories."

"No, Brendon," she said, "they aren't painful at all."

"I thought you might enjoy the opportunity to tell your daughter about her mom. It's a part of your history, and a part of hers."

"Her mom is a winemaker," she said, "a wife, a lover, a great many things but not a magician, not any more."

"But once upon a time ..."

"Yes," she said. "Once upon a time there was a frightened little girl from Philly. She was a silly girl, but a lucky one. Lucky to have been loved by such as my father, by such as Dante, and by such as you. That's my story. It's not glamorous or exciting in the conventional sense. But it's my story and I'm so happy to have lived it."

He brushed away the long hair that ran down the back of her neck and kissed her slightly below her ear. She turned in his arms and joined her lips to his. Their tongues joined, and their breathing slowed so their senses could savor each other.

His taste was sweet on her lips. Of all the men she'd ever kissed, his taste was the sweetest. When she wanted him most, she'd run her tongue over her lips, think of that taste, and he would appear to satisfy her. He knew when he was needed. He knew how he was needed. He never overstepped or rushed. His patience and kindness lifted her as the steady but slow pace of the vineyard ordered her life.

He picked her up, and she wrapped her legs around his waist and her arms around his neck. She kissed him again and let his unique fragrance fill her like the bouquet of her favorite wine.

"I love you," he whispered into her ear as he began to nibble. "What would I have ever done, what would I have become if you hadn't changed your mind and come back to me so many years ago."

"You were my destiny."

"I always believed so but after that first time I asked you to marry me, I wasn't sure you'd ever believe it."

She smiled and held his chin up with her hand for another kiss. But before she joined her lips to his she looked deep in his eyes. They burned with desire. Though the radiance of her youth had faded, Brendon's face still sparkled every time he saw her. His was a light that never seemed to dim. He'd promised her love, and he had delivered on his promise. His attentiveness and consideration for her never eased through the passing years. If anything, they'd become more intense and mature.

Like the aging of a wine, Brendon had a flavor of affection that grew more intense with each passing day. He continued to find new ways in both word and deed to let her know that she was deeply and wonderfully loved and appreciated. He made her feel like a woman, he made her feel beautiful, and he filled each day they spent together with the wonder and magic of passion.

"Was it difficult to watch Celine last night?" He asked as he rubbed his nose on hers.

"Oh yeah," she said as she rubbed back, and added a little kiss. "I was eaten alive with envy."

"I'm serious, Amy," he said. "I've always been afraid to ask. I have always hoped that you would have no regrets, that you'd be happy with me and with our home."

"You've been afraid to ask?"

"Yes."

"Then ask my dear."

"How are you?" he said. "Really. How are you? Are you happy?"

"I'm never going to be famous."

"Not standing out in the middle of a vineyard in Sonoma County day after day you're not."

"And, I don't want to be," she said. "I am happy here. I was from the first day I ever set foot on this land. Remember? The festival when we met?"

"It was the day that changed my life forever," he said. "I'll never forget it."

"We may never be rich," she said, "and I may never know fame, but I know that I am loved, and I know where I belong. I chased a fantasy once. I believed in its promise to fulfill and satisfy me, and so I chased it the way I've seen our children chase butterflies. Most of the time, the kids never catch them, they flutter beyond the reach of their little arms, but I see the wonder in our children's eyes. 'What would it feel like to hold one in my hand?' I can almost hear them ask. But if they ever actually caught one, the poor little creatures are so fragile, the heavy hand of a child would destroy its beauty and its wonder the instant it was touched. I don't need to touch it anymore, Brendon. All I'll ever need, I already have. I don't want to be or do anything else, ever."

"You don't mind growing old on the land with me?"

She kissed him again, more passionately, and then again. He lowered her to the ground and rested her on her back. With a hand he swept away the curl that had blown into her face.

"My God," he said.

"What?"

"You are so beautiful. I am the luckiest man alive."

As his hands explored her body, a terrain he knew so well, a wind blew, and in its breath was the freshness of the earth and its produce. They both paused for the moment. They closed their eyes and breathed deeply to absorb all the earth was offering.

"I chased the wind once," she said. "The more I chased the more difficult it was to catch. But with you, through the years, in the stillness of this land, I find it so amazing that the wind comes to me."

978-0-595-40798-9
0-595-40798-6